BLOOD BINDS THE PACK

"It has a wonderful weird west vibe and some of the phrasing is simply delicious. Hob is a wonderful character to follow hers is a solid journey and I got a bit choked up when Hob stood up for what she wanted. Alex crafts a host of fascinating characters here the Weathermen, the Bone Collector and I reckon you're going to love their adventures."

E Catherine Tobler, author of the Folley & Mallory Adventures

"Take a dash of *Dune*, a bit of *Fury Road*, and a whole lot of badass female characters and you've got *Hunger Makes the Wolf* a really, really bloody awesome debut from Alex Wells."

Emma Maree Urquhart, author of Dragon Tamers

"It's a science fiction Western thriller, and it is great, and I'm really, intensely, eagerly looking forward to the sequel. This is the sort of thing I really like. UP WITH THIS SORT OF THING."

Tor.com

"Gritty and engrossing, I definitely want Hob on my side when the revolution comes."

Mur Lafferty, John W Campbell Award-winning author of The Shambling Guide to New York City

"This thing drips with tension between characters, within the story itself that makes it impossible to put down. I needed to know what would happen next, what would Hob do. Tanegawa's World may be a desolate and uninviting terrain, but it provides fertile ground for the characters, who truly blossom on the page."

B&N Sci-Fi & Fantasy Blog

"Grab any science fiction book and you'll see they all have the exact same thing in common: the plots and devices of the stories are all predictable and never stray out of bounds. They hardly even push the envelope and, with great joy, I'm glad the author never got that memo. Here's why: Wells adds magic to the mix. It's a stroke of genius I've been waiting for Peter F Hamilton or Alastair Reynolds to pull off to no avail."

The Splattergeist

"It's a well-conceived, smartly plotted, enthusiastically fast-paced sci-fi adventure with some cool ideas and a couple of excellent lead characters who've got plenty growing still to do in future books."

SF Bluestocking

"*Hunger Makes The Wolf* can perhaps best be described in musical terms: imagine the powerful, punchy, awesome death'n'roll of latter-day Satyricon married to the lyrical sensibilities of Billy Bragg in his most pro-trade union and leftist moments. Alex Wells managed to write a 400 page book with that kind of power and political urgency and heart, and I am so very much hoping for a sequel."

Intellectus Speculativus

"Sharp, honed, and brilliant."

Skiffy & Fanty

"Obvious parallels to Frank Herbert's *Dune* will draw readers into this action-packed tale of tyranny and rebellion, but Wells's character developments take the plot in new directions, leaving the possibility of a sequel."

Library Journal

ALEX WELLS

BLOOD
BINDS THE
PACK

ANGRY
ROBOT

ANGRY ROBOT
An imprint of Watkins Media Ltd

20 Fletcher Gate,
Nottingham,
NG1 2FZ
UK

angryrobotbooks.com
twitter.com/angryrobotbooks
Eat me

An Angry Robot paperback original 2018

Cover by Ignacio Lazcano
Set in Meridien and Bourgeois by Argh! Nottingham

Distributed in the United States by Penguin Random House, Inc.,
New York.

ISBN 978 0 85766 647 5
Ebook ISBN 978 0 85766 648 2

Printed in the United States of America

9 8 7 6 5 4 3 2 1

For Gav and Mark,
who were there
when it started.

Is there aught we hold in common with the greedy parasite
Who would lash us into serfdom and would crush us with his might?
Is there anything left to us but to organize and fight?
For the union makes us strong.

RALPH CHAPLIN, "SOLIDARITY FOREVER"

PROLOGUE

Thirsty.

He was so thirsty. Always so thirsty. He'd thought the thirst would go away, when he fell into that cool, bottomless well of stars. Maybe after floating in the bloodwarm water of a foreign ocean, there was nothing that could ever satisfy his thirst again.

Why had he dragged himself out, dripping and panting on an impossible shore? Why had he clawed his way out of the steep walls? Someone. He was missing someone, maybe even himself, but he tried that on for size and it didn't fit. Could not put a name to the faces – the face, *you precious moron* – that kept him crawling.

Sometimes, he almost remembered his name. The shape of it, the sound of it. But no, not that shape and sound. A different one. A newer one. One that fit like the right skin, only he couldn't find the measure of it because his skin clung so tight, dried to leather in the sun.

Mostly, his thoughts were not so coherent as to be sad, or filled with longing. There wasn't room for anything but that overriding thirst. His body now whole, he walked the desert without making a sound, leaving no footprints.

On the wind, he smelled it: water, and salt, and oil. Hot metal thick on his tongue. The scent was a whetstone that sharpened his thirst, drew him in like a ragged rope.

After formless time with only the murmurs of wind and whispers of sand for conversation, the sudden babble of voices, hum of motors, was overwhelming. Disorienting. Color and unnatural shape and things that did not belong. They surrounded him, chattering, poking and prodding. He swiped a hand at one, just wanting some space.

They piled onto him. A sharp jab, and electricity coursed through his nerves, locked his muscles. He whimpered, and they laughed. And then, still laughing and gabbling harshly, they dragged him across the sand and threw him into something metal, a wrong metal that wasn't familiar, and drove away with him.

His muscles would unlock soon. He knew that. He had only to wait. And pain was an impermanent state, unlike thirst. But he smelled the water so close now, hot and sweet and salty and thudding under skin, and it drove him wild.

Somehow, above the high whine of *need* and *thirst* in his ears, the noise sorted itself into voices, as if he had become used to it. Noises that became curious as the metal around him stopped moving, as the… the *men* dragged him through hot light and then into the dim mouth of a canyon. Sand then rock grated his toes as the shade became even darker, yawning into the mouth of a cave that was really a fault spread wide enough for shelter.

"This one's got to be a witch."

"No shit. We should shoot him. Crazy fucker."

"Orders say to capture, not kill."

"We don't have time to run him in."

"Send a message. We'll hold him until they get a squad

out here to pick him up. He went down easy enough with one shock. Good bonus for witches."

Hold him, he thought, hold onto what? You could try to hold sand but it would always slide through your fingers. You could try to bend nature to your will and just discover that it was you, bending around it.

And he was still so thirsty. The thirst pushed the numbness from his muscles, leaving the parched fibers to demand, once more, that he wet them.

The men started binding him with something, scraping at his wrists. A rope, perhaps. He snapped it like twine. They weren't expecting it.

They *really* weren't expecting it when his teeth closed on the throat of one. Water, a hot, salty-sweet water, burst into his mouth. It gave him strength, gave the thirst strength as it roared for more, *more*.

"Shit! Shit! He's—"

His fingers sank into an eye socket, and found it warm and wet. He hooked his fingers away and brought them to his mouth, straining the fluid through his teeth.

Yes. Better already.

CHAPTER ONE • 72 DAYS

"Three… six… I count twelve now," Geri said as he peered through the scope, into the mouth of the canyon, black rocks spreading over pink-orange sand. The white skunk stripe in his hair, souvenir of a head wound, tilted as he scanned the situation. Sweat beaded on his black skin – the sun was punishing hot. "That's a hell of a lot more than Mag said we'd be running up against."

"Said it was an estimate," Hob Ravani remarked around the cigarette clamped between her lips. She lay belly-down on the rocky outcrop, sandwiched between Geri and his twin Freki as they formulated their raid plain. Gravel tried to dig into her skin through the thick leather of her duster, and the undertaker's waistcoat and shirt beneath. She had almost ten centimeters on the twins, but they had to be twice as wide in the shoulders as her, heavy with muscle where she was wiry. They had their tightly curled black hair shaved close – it was more comfortable under helmets that way – and she still kept her pin-straight, mousy brown hair long, braided into two plaits. Thanks to the witch fire in her blood that she'd paid for with her left eye, at least she wasn't sweating or burning from white to a raw crisp. She could just drink in the heat and store it up to use later. Use like setting some damn bandits on fire.

Behind and below them, she heard the rest of Ravani's Ghost Wolves, twenty-eight mercenaries strong now, shifting restlessly. Though not talking. They all knew the hammer would come down on them for that kind of bullshittery.

"Not much of an estimate," Geri growled. "Two more puts us at fourteen. And you know there's gotta be more back in that canyon."

"Question is, is the number this fucking wrong 'cause Mag's people done fucked up, or because they been hiding their numbers?" Of the options, Hob liked the first. Incompetence was a constant that she counted on. But on Tanegawa's World, wholly owned and operated by TransRift, the company having its fingers up to the second knuckle in everyone's asshole was also something to count on.

Geri cussed under his breath and handed the scope off to Freki, who accepted it without comment. "You think this is another fuckin' Mariposa operation?"

As if to say he thought his brother's question was a dumb one, Freki snorted.

"Ain't most of 'em?" Hob asked. Bandit groups tended to either be criminal bands filled out with spies from Mariposa, TransRift's private security company, or they flourished by the company turning a blind eye.

She considered the shitty lay of the land at the canyon mouth and grudgingly admitted to herself that these bandits had picked a good place to put down their tents. "Conall and Davey ever come back with an answer?"

"Found a route could get us up on the north wall, but it's about thirty kilometers," Geri said. "And there might be a problem."

"North wall come with a way to get down?"

"That'd be the problem."

Hob took a long drag of her cigarette, like she'd pull smoke and calm down into her toes to keep her from wringing someone's neck. A quick calculation, remaining supplies versus the stupidity of a frontal assault. The math was simple, even for someone who'd never had formal schooling. "Guess I can tell Conall it's his lucky day and he can finally play with his fuckin' rappel gear," she started. "We'll leave a small group here to play distraction. Geri, get–"

"Hob," Freki said.

The fact that Freki stirred himself to speak was like another man shouting. "What?"

Freki pointed down to the mouth of the canyon. "Somethin's happenin'."

Hob snatched up the scope as he offered it to her. It was difficult to see, between the contrast of light and shadow and the narrowness of the canyon mouth, but she made out men running back and forth. Someone staggered blindly out into the light, their face a mask of blood. "Well, fuck me."

"What?" Geri asked, going for the scope. She let him have it. "Holy shit."

"That's one hell of a distraction." She shoved back from the ledge, confident that no one was looking. Seemed like the bandits had other problems. Below, in the sharp shadow of the rock, twenty-eight faces snapped around to look at her. The Wolves who leaned on their motorcycles straightened right up. "I ain't gonna say no when someone gives me the element of surprise on a silver platter. Mount up!"

The clamor of confused screams and shouts was loud enough for Hob to hear through her helmet, over the near-constant, staticky chatter of the shortwave radios as they angled their motorcycles toward the entrance of the canyon. The electric motor driving the chain mesh wheels beneath her made a constant, familiar hum through her bones.

More bandits spilled out across the sand, many of them bleeding. It had to be a goddamn riot going on in there. A woman, her shirt torn to ribbons, stumbled out of the canyon, turned, and looked directly at Hob. She opened her mouth to scream, but the sound was lost in the rest of the pandemonium. She still had the presence of mind to draw a gun, though, raising an unsteady arm.

Hob shouted, "Break formation!" and turned sharply, drawing her own revolver. A shot ricocheted off the battery stack of her motorcycle, by her knee, leaving an ugly score across the sandblasted metal. Better that than her knee cap. Hob aimed at the bandit woman and pulled the trigger as she flashed past.

One down.

More bandits began to scramble into a loose sort of defense, but with more coming up against their backs from the canyon, they couldn't form any kind of line. The Wolves swept through the stumbling crowd. Hob saw Geri firing his sawed-off shotgun, while Freki reached back into one of the holsters on his motorcycle and pulled out a length of heavy pipe that Hati the garage master had welded into a mace in a moment of bloodthirsty whimsy. There were only four men on the base big enough to wield that thing, and Freki whirled it around his head like it was a damn banner before whipping it across the skull of a bandit who'd been aiming at his brother. The mace won.

Hob shot at another bandit in the quickly shrinking crowd. She saw three break for the dunes, too confused or scared to try to defend their own camp. "We got runners, get on 'em."

Akela and Davey, discernible by the bull horns on

Akela's helmet and the jagged black bolt painted on Davey's, arrowed out in pursuit. Hob didn't need to watch what happened next.

Gunfire cracked through the air, a few bandits finally getting their wits together enough to shoot back. Freki went sideways off his motorcycle. The machine slid across the sand and knocked Lykaios off hers, though she rolled out of the way before either hit her.

"Freki!" Geri shouted. Not caring about the melee still going on around him, he dropped his own motorcycle and hit the ground running.

"Sing out, Freki," Hob said, keeping her voice flat as she tried to watch from the corner of her left eye. She aimed up where the shot must have come from, saw a glint of metal on the canyon wall. Instead of squeezing the trigger, she focused down the barrel, that bright line of metal, and poured all of that worry about her second-in-command into the witchfire that always pounded through her blood. The empty pit of her left eye filled with momentary, searing heat, and then fire surged through the air. Fifteen meters away and halfway up the canyon wall, the sentry burst into flame like they'd been soaked down with oil. Sun-bright, they left a trail of flame across their short fall to death.

When her heartbeat retreated enough for her to hear the crackle of the radio again, the first sound to assault her ears was Freki cursing. For someone who didn't talk much, he had an impressive vocabulary. "Get the fuck off me," he growled, probably at Geri. "Shoot the fuckin' bandits afore they fuckin' put another motherfuckin' hole in me."

"What's your status?" Hob asked. She raised her revolver again, had to take a deep breath and let it out slow when her hand shook at first. She had to practice more. Had to do a lot of things more, and there was never enough time. "Other'n pissed off." Before she could squeeze the trigger, Raff took the bandit's head off with an ax.

"Just got me one in the arm. Pride's more hurt." And to her relief, she saw him get up, and head toward his downed motorcycle. He paused to tackle a bandit to the ground.

The skirmish – it hadn't even been big enough to be called a battle, just another day in the bandit hunting trade – was effectively over. The bandits, for whatever reason, had routed themselves before the Wolves even got there. It was cleanup now, though Hob didn't trust that to be *easy* so much.

But she still had it in her to smile. "That the one, took your pride?"

Freki slammed his right fist solidly into the bandit's face and got back up. "No."

"Better keep lookin', then."

With the toe of her boot, Hob nudged the blackened body of the sentry who'd shot Freki. She did her best to take shallow breaths around the bandana she'd tied over her nose and mouth – no matter what she did, she couldn't escape the stench of cooked meat. When there was no response to a firmer kick, she squatted down to shove the body over. It rolled stiff and crackling. Hob swallowed firmly. Retching in front of her men wouldn't do her any good. Maybe the biggest downside to having blood full of witchy fire wasn't that TransRift wanted her dead or imprisoned in a lab, but that it made for some disturbing corpses that left her unable to enjoy any kind of grilled protein for weeks afterward. It was another thing she wondered if Old Nick Ravani had ever gotten used to. She still cursed him for dying without ever giving her a proper handle on their shared power.

She made a cursory search to see if there was any kind of identification, weapons, or jewelry on the charred corpse. Outlaw mercenaries still needed to eat, and dead people didn't have use for their remaining bits of shine.

And she was looking for someone in particular.

Flesh and clothing had melted into a blackened mass on the corpse. Hob gave the patches – recognizable as having once been a pocket or bit of fabric – a desultory poke with one of her knives, then stood. As soon as she was a few steps away upwind, she pulled her bandana down and sucked in lungfuls of air still full of smoke and blood. She pulled out her silver cigarette case, another piece inherited from Old Nick, along with a large stock of his favored filthy black cigarettes. With relief, she lit one of the cigarettes by snapping a spark of fire off her fingers and focused on the greasy taste across her tongue.

The ones wounded in the fight, only a few of them with Freki the worst, lined up to be seen to by Davey, who had once been training to be a veterinarian. It was the most medical knowledge anyone on base had, so he was their doctor whether he felt competent or not. He hadn't killed anyone yet.

The rest of the Wolves spread out through the camp in a regular pattern that guaranteed nothing would get missed – and no bandit would be left alive. That's what they'd been paid to do, after all, and a bullet in the head now was an act of mercy compared to leaving someone to wander off into the desert and die of thirst, or get picked apart by the genetically modified great eagles that already circled lazily overhead, drawn by the scent of blood.

There were more than a few things she'd changed since taking over from Old Nick – starting with publicly declaring themselves the enemies of TransRift by derailing a company train and killing the Weatherman

.it carried – but the routine, bloody business of cleanup wasn't one of them. Hell, she had a feeling this had been the routine since before Old Nick had been Young Nick and getting kicked around by the previous Ravani.

Hob listened with half an ear as Wolves called back and forth to each other, punctuated by an occasional single round being fired. She turned over another corpse and searched the dead woman's pockets, coming up with a tattered wallet and a wedding ring. She tucked both away in her duster. They weren't in the charity business, so the ring would go to get sold for supplies. But if there was any sort of identification or letter in the wallet, they'd always done their best to pass such things along. Most of them had experience, one way or another, with the hell that was not knowing.

Another corpse, a pocket full of plastic chits and a few slippery bills. And another, this one a woman with a face marred only by a perfect bullet hole in the middle of the forehead – Maheegan's work, probably – but the clothes were a little too high quality. It wasn't the sort of thing that showed on looking, but she felt the heaviness of the fabric, the slightly slick quality that showed it was probably flame and chemical retardant too. Definitely not typical for mine rats or bandit scum.

Hob made a thorough search of the dead woman's pockets, then the lining of her coat. She found what she was looking for hidden in the hem of the left sleeve: a gold lapel pin shaped like a maple leaf. She'd seen a tie tack like that before, what felt like lifetimes ago, on the corpse of another so-called bandit. This time, she knew enough to look in as close as she could and see the subtly raised patterns on the back, which indicated it was a short-range tracker and a secure electronic identifier. This was the spy, then, Mariposa security.

Hob took one last draw of her cigarette and then

flicked the butt away. A moment of thought, a little slap of heat, and the bits of paper and ash dissolved into a shower of sparks. She turned her attention to the pin still held between her fingers and drew more fire from her blood, forcing it into the metal. For a moment, the pin looked normal, then emitted a puff of smoke – all the tiny circuits melting, probably. Hob dropped it on the corpse's chest. The pin sizzled when it hit, and sagged out into a vaguely leaf-shaped golden puddle.

"That one?"

She glanced up to see Freki, his upper arm now wrapped with a clean bandage, though indistinct shadows of blood peeped through. "One of," she said, and pushed back up to her feet. "Gotta see if she had friends. But let Geri know we got one at least."

"He got one, too."

Hob grimaced. "Group this big, guess it makes sense." Her hand went to her pocket, habit having her go for another cigarette. It was the only thing that helped, sometimes, when she felt like her blood was going to boil over – not from anger, but from too much damn fire. "And with the kind of trouble they were making."

As far as Hob knew, the Ghost Wolves were the only group who'd ever successfully – and repeatedly – raided TransRift trains. Before they'd ever even thought to derail the one carrying the Weatherman, they'd made moving snatch-and-grabs, breaking into freight cars and taking the supplies they needed while the trains barreled through the desert. It was a benefit of being a cavalry company of sorts, where even the people who were iffy shots could play circus on a motorcycle before they were ever allowed out. Bandit groups like this one focused on attacking softer targets that moved between towns, normally groups of miners trying to get by under the company radar.

The reason Hob's adopted sister Mag – and the growing group of miners out of Ludlow, Rouse, and Walsen that she seemed to be building whether she admitted it or not – had paid the Ghost Wolves to go after this particular group was that it had been haunting their attempts to have meetings, too often to be coincidence. And Mag was certain that there had been other times when they were being watched. Mag'd had a sense about these things ever since she'd been abducted and held in a TransRift corporate lab for almost a week, and Hob wasn't about to start questioning it when it came attached to a paycheck.

Hob lit the fresh cigarette with a snap of her fingers. "Think Mag ever gets tired of bein' right?"

Freki grunted and turned to head back into the camp.

Freki found Geri easily in the shredded camp. It was instinct for the twins to keep an eye on each other, a subconscious thing – definitely not any kind of witchy nonsense like Hob or Mag. Freki had always been a keen observer, and he'd known Mag almost as long as he'd known Hob, so it was damn obvious she had some kind of spooky shit going, not that it mattered to him one way or another. He and Geri had been pulled out of an orphan work gang by Dambala and handed over to the witchy old bastard Nick Ravani, and of all the people that had tried to kill one or both of them, there'd never been a witch in their number. Good enough for him.

Geri straightened up from the corpse he'd been bent over, scrubbing his palms on his dusty leather pants. "You get your arm seen to?"

"Slow bleeder. Gonna be dead in three days," Freki said. He grinned at his brother as Geri flipped him off. "Hob found another spy."

Geri cussed. "This one makes three."

"Fuck."

"Yeah." Geri looked at the torn-up camp. "And we ain't done yet. Guess we earned our pay."

And shit in TransRift's porridge to boot. Lovely. "I'll get lookin' too."

"Might as well give all the good news to… Hob at once." The hesitation there still said *the girl* to Freki's ear, but Geri had been changing his tune since he saw Hob turn the Weatherman into ash. About damn time, mostly because Freki got tired of watching his brother posture over losing a fight that had never even been a fight to begin with. They both had better things to do.

Freki only waved a hand and headed deeper into the remains of the camp. There wasn't really a section of it that didn't have someone going through wreckage and bodies; everyone had picked their spot while he was still getting his damn arm wrapped by Davey. As if to remind him of that fact, the wound throbbed. Davey had wanted to put his arm in a sling, and he'd said no. Maybe when they got back to base.

But he doubted anyone was focused on what he thought was the much more interesting question – what the hell had started tearing things up before the Wolves ever got there? Unless the bandits were a full Mariposa detachment pretending to be outlaws, they would still be a mix of criminals who'd been cast out by their own folk and the blacklisted. Those kind of mixed groups were bound to have squabbles, power plays, fights. Boredom and despair did that kind of shit to people. Maybe this was more of the same, but he'd never seen bandits running *from* a brawl like that, not all frantic and shitting themselves.

He wandered the camp, quietly going around the other Wolves and noting the torn tents and camo nets, the threadbare personal belongings scattered across the ground and trampled – along with no small amount of food. There was even spilled water, and to emphasize the fact, he heard one of the Wolves fire into the air, to scare off one of the circling eagles.

Some of the damage had probably been caused by the raid. But by the time they'd come in, most of the bandits had been at the mouth of the canyon, scrambling over each other.

He kept following the wreckage and found a smear of blood at the edge of the camp, another spray on one of the canyon walls, dull brown on the shiny black rock. And the sand on the canyon's flat floor here was churned up, then dug into a channel – something heavy getting dragged. Considering the blood, probably a body.

Freki drew his pistol, just to have it at hand, and followed the irregular splashes of blood.

The trail led him up the slope of the shallower of the canyon walls. He looked up and saw a human hand hanging over the edge of a rock above. He had to tuck his pistol back into its holster so he could scramble up the steep, not-regular-enough-to-be-called-switchbacks, mentally calling himself seven kinds of idiot as he did. Well, he always figured he'd go out satisfying his curiosity. It wouldn't surprise Geri one bit.

He pulled himself up onto the rock overhang and found the corpse. He squatted down beside – yes, it had been a man, he was pretty sure – and looked at the red ruin that had once been a throat, the torn out cheek. Animals, maybe, though it didn't look like the work of the circling eagles. He'd seen enough of their leavings to know that. And there weren't any other large predators on this lifeless dustbowl. The eagles weren't even native – they were genetically modified water sniffers that the settlers had brought with them, to the regret of their descendants.

He should go back, he thought. But he also needed

the end to this fucked-up story. So he straightened and looked hard at the canyon wall, saw more smears of blood. Right at the height where someone might rest their hand to help them climb.

He didn't like this one bit, but he kept going to find a cave, and drew his pistol again. Maybe it was just the wind, blowing past the rocks, but he swore he heard ragged breathing.

Freki tried to look into the cave, but the difference between bright and dark was too great. He'd have to tell Hati about this, he thought vaguely, as he fumbled a chemical light out of his belt with his good hand. The man had delusions of being a writer, and this shit was right up his alley. It'd make a damn creepy ghost story.

He shook the light into life and tossed it into the cave. It lit up the narrow interior with a sickly green glow and... that wasn't a rock over there. It was a person, crouched down, thin arms over their head, rocking back and forth.

Freki cocked his pistol, aimed it just short of the person's feet before speaking. He hadn't survived this long by letting his urge for charity overwhelm his good sense. "Hey."

The person sucked in a breath and looked up and—

It was fucking impossible.

Fucking.

Impossible.

Maybe it should have been harder to recognize the man looking at him, when he had a scraggly beard and ragged black hair and dirt ground into every inch of his skin. But Freki'd spent too many days getting his ass knocked over and seeing that same foxy face hanging over him, grinning while Makaya the Knife laughed in the background and said he still wasn't ready to play with the big dogs.

"Coyote?" And it was impossible, because Coyote had disappeared months ago, swallowed by the sands after his scouting mission to the farming town of Harmony had gone wrong. Abandoned, according to Geri with an extra curl of disgust to the words, by his own *brother*, the government spook. For a moment, Freki desperately wished that Dambala had been in on this raid, instead of holding down the base thanks to a badly broken leg. Dambala had always been Coyote's closest friend, and who the hell knew what else, because that wasn't the kind of shit anyone needed to go speculating about.

The ragged man – it couldn't be Coyote, *couldn't* – exhaled a sound that was almost a word, but too dry, and stood. And suddenly, Freki was horribly glad that Dambala wasn't there. Coyote's mouth was dark and wet with what had to be blood, and Freki recalled the ruined throat and face of the corpse just down the path.

"Say somethin'," Freki said.

The ragged man that had Coyote's face launched himself forward, hands with broken fingernails outstretched.

Freki had a split second to make the decision, to shoot or not shoot, and he couldn't. There was too much horror, either way. But he was also too well trained to be frozen by it – too well trained by Coyote himself, who'd always loved the asshole sneak attack method of doing things. Freki reversed his grip on his pistol in an instant and whipped the butt into Coyote's face.

It didn't seem to make a difference. Coyote's hands, impossibly strong, gripped his wounded arm. Squeezed. Freki's vision went red, and he screamed. He hit Coyote three more times with all his strength, just trying to dislodge him. At the third strike, Coyote staggered back, his cheek opened in a long split.

Panting, Freki moved back out of the cave doorway.

"Don't make me shoot you." What kind of hell would it be, to find a lost friend and then have to put them down? His own damn fault for wandering, maybe. He felt something wet and hot trail down his arm – his own blood again, thanks to the bandage being ripped aside. Davey was going to be pissed.

The animal that wore Coyote's face didn't seem to hear. He raised his fingers, newly wet and dark, and stuck them into his mouth.

"What the fuck..." Freki breathed.

And then Coyote's eyes went wide and a different sort of wild. He looked at Freki, really *looked* at him. His voice was a cracked, barely there whisper: "Freki?" Then his eyes rolled back in his head and he crumpled down to the floor of that narrow cave, his head scraping rock as he did.

CHAPTER TWO • 71 DAYS

Full rotation of the arm, vertical axis please. The words floated into Shige's awareness as impression rather than sound, and he wordlessly complied, slowly swinging his arm in a circle. Two months after having his network implants reactivated upon return from Tanegawa's World, he was finally used to the flow of information. At first he'd felt like he was seeing ghosts flickering across his vision, odd considering he'd grown up with the network always a thought away. Tanegawa's World and its necessary backwards technologies had a way of lulling one out of their accustomed life.

A few lights flickered along the pale green wall of the booth, visual alerts that another round of scans were being done. His attention turned inward, searching for the slightest hint of stiffness, of tendon creaking or bone grinding that would indicate the healing of his shoulder had been imperfect. All felt good, though he'd do his own sort of confirmation later, in the privacy of a scan-locked apartment as he ran through well-learned assassination routines.

Acromioclavicular and glenohumeral joint function confirmed at 99.999%. A note has been made in your file. Have a nice day, Mr Rolland, the medical computer informed him.

"Thank you," Shigehiko Rollins said, very accustomed to the use of his assumed name. The *thank you* was another strange habit he'd picked up from Tanegawa's World and hadn't bothered to break himself of, talking back to various programs as if they cared. He'd be back on that planet soon enough, and being inoffensively polite had served him well.

Being on time to his next appointment would also serve him well, which meant he needed to be quick about it.

The door to the booth slid open and he exited, pulling his jacket, the particular dark shade recognized universally as "TransRift Corporate blue" back on. He blended effortlessly into the throng of other personnel wearing the same suit in the same color as he exited the medical suite.

Shige was an innocuous figure, literally by design. He was well aware that his parents had put a lot of illegal genetic tinkering into his conception after the utter disappointment that had been his older brother. He was of precisely average height, skin a light brown that would blend in with nearly any crowd, black hair straightened from its natural waviness and shaped in the haircut most popular with male-identified TransRift employees. His blended northwest-African and Japanese facial structure had been surgically altered to smooth out the few family-specific features he'd ever carried. No one noticed him, and he preferred it that way.

An anonymous one among many, he dropped into the main grav slip that made up the Corporate tower's central shaft. It was wide as a swimming pool, human traffic lanes marked with network-transmitted light overlays. He narrowly avoided a collision with someone drifting up the slip and kicked downward like he was swimming through thick water. The slips in the TransRift building were larger and more comfortable than any he'd encountered elsewhere, state of the art. It was more technology enabled by the strange materials of Tanegawa's World. And while it rankled with him, that the Federal Union of Systems offices in New Mumbai were practically stone age in comparison – well, that was the whole point of him being here, wasn't it?

He spun adroitly to miss another blue suit-clad Corporate peon. If he survived to the end of this assignment, maybe he'd just have to start calling himself "Slayer of Monopolies." It sounded so much grander than "spy."

The New Hazlett Theater had been renovated so often that it was a new building several times over, but the various designers had always been careful to preserve its feeling of age. Most recently, the director of the theater had ordered a cut-off installed that blocked all non-emergency network transmissions, so that patrons would be able to experience theater as it had been centuries before.

It hadn't been a popular move for any but the hardcore theater buffs. But that made it ideal to Shige for two reasons: it was much harder for someone to eavesdrop on him there, and the matinee performances tended to be almost deserted. The network silence, so reminiscent of Tanegawa's World now, was both comforting and slightly eerie.

He sat in a corner box seat, disadvantaged because it was partially blocked by a column, and waited. The internal silence was almost deafening, with only desultory murmurs and the attendant sounds of the few people shifting around in the not-quite-comfortable seats to keep him company. He was keenly aware of the muffled footfalls that approached him, though he did not look up until their source had slid into the seat next to his.

The woman, Ayana Tsukui, was not noticeably old, but thanks to modern medical and cosmetic technology, at least on Earth and its near colonies, no one ever did look old until they were so positively ancient that they already had one foot in the grave. Her light brown skin was as smooth as his, her straight black hair hanging loose and without a single trace of white, and her dark brown eyes in her foxy face were utterly piercing. She drew a small sound scrubber from her pocket and set it on the arm of the chair between them.

"Corey was at the cabinet meeting today as a witness," she said without preamble. "Making noises about a new technological surge being imminent. I don't like surprises."

Grace Corey was the CEO of TransRift, the person to whom Shige's nominal boss in his secretarial cover job, Jennifer Meetchim, reported. Well, that answered his question of whether the company would be silent about their potential new discovery, or try to leverage it. "I have been waiting for you to contact me," he said, keeping his tone even. "I don't have any other way of safely reporting."

She waved a hand as if flicking away his complaint. "We're certain this is a preamble to Corey or Sadine–" Hara Sadine was the president of TransRift "–getting put forward as the next minister of Trade."

He shouldn't have been surprised, but still felt the shock of that. It had been a bad practice in some governments a few centuries ago to take people directly out of the corporate hierarchies and place them in high civil posts. They were supposedly long past doing that. And worse, the previous minister of Trade had been one of their ever-shrinking faction's staunchest allies. He'd heard enough in the executive halls of the TransRift tower to be certain that her downfall had been Corey's idea. "And no one sees a problem with this?"

Ayana snorted. "TransRift is still the savior of humanity, the foundation upon which interstellar government is based. They placed Earth back at the center of civilization, where it belongs. We're very grateful to them, and certain they can do no wrong. Who better to understand the trials and travails of moving people and goods between the worlds?" Her tone was so dry, he could almost taste the air of Tanegawa's World in it. "The wedding between Devra Sadine and Laura Montejo was lovely, by the way."

Shige grimaced. That was another thing that had been on the horizon as he departed for Tanegawa's World, and he'd almost forgotten – the president of TransRift's daughter marrying the prime minister's granddaughter. Nothing at all troubling there, just two young people in love. He pulled a bio-locked memory thread from his sleeve and laid it over Ayana's hand. "That's all of my notes, and everything I was able to fish out of the on-planet servers. They deal mostly in flimsies there – the claims about technology not working properly actually are true."

"Startling. So they really do need to keep importing all of those unskilled laborers."

"Yes and no." He sketched out what he'd heard and seen, about the so-called witches, the strange alterations that seemed to happen to people, the Weathermen. Ayana's poker face was second to none, but he could read the disbelief in the angle of her chin.

"I think you've been inside too long," she said.

"I assure you, no. If you don't believe me, feel free to send another agent – so long as they don't disturb my cover." Of course, they both knew that was an empty taunt. The Bureau of Citizens' Rights Enforcement was understaffed and shrinking, thanks to concerted efforts by TransRift and a few other large corporations. Ayana didn't really have anyone but him.

The smile she gave him made him question that assumption. "I've managed to stir up just enough trouble to force Montejo's agreement that we should send an inspector to the last uncharted frontier. She even thinks it's her idea, to prove there's no malfeasance and therefore no problem with TransRift basically taking over Trade."

Shige considered this. "Which inspector are you putting on it?"

"Liu."

Not a bad play, since Liu Fei Xing was one of the strictest inspectors the BCRE had, but everyone in the government seemed to forget that because she hid her fire under soft words. "They're going to just wine and dine her in Newcastle, though. The nearest mining town is hours away by train, and it will be easy to polish up as a model." Primero wasn't quite miniature Newcastle – it was still off the limited grid that allowed the use of basic technology – but it was very conscious of its position as the main rail depot and recipient of all the newest supplies.

"It's your job to counter that, then," Ayana said. "Make certain that there's enough smoke and fire by the time Liu arrives that they can't possibly hide it all."

Shige sat back, exhaling like he might deflate. The look Ayana shot him wasn't complimentary, but he didn't particularly care right now. "This could compromise my cover."

"If Liu sees enough, you won't need the cover anymore. I'm not above leaking information to the press. Give them a few bodies in the street and they'll eat it up. There are plenty of reporters angry that none of them can get onto TransRift's pet planet."

"Can you provide me with a resupply?" While his most valuable asset was always his mind, the little gadgets that came out of the top clearance laboratories, wedding high biotech and simple mechanical tech, did help.

"Expect a secure package soon."

That was a relief. "How much time do I have?"

"Ten weeks. I let them think they were scoring a victory by having her come in with the next supply ship."

"How magnanimous of you." That didn't give him much time to act, and he was still going to be on Earth for a while longer, waiting for the laboratory to release the replacement Weatherman for transport.

Ayana stood. "I have confidence in your training."

And so that meant the method was up to him. Shige felt a bit weak in the knees, but he hastened to stand as well. There was one more piece of information he hadn't wanted to include in his official report. "Mother."

She turned to look at him, one eyebrow arching up slightly. Ayana hadn't been *mother* to him except on a handful of occasions after he'd begun his training in earnest at the tender age of eight.

He licked his lips. "I saw Kazuhiro. On Tanegawa's World."

Ayana's face might have been made of marble, for all her expression changed. "Has he finally seen the error of his ways?"

Shige thought of Kazu – he couldn't think of him as Coyote no matter how he tried – as he'd last seen him, feverish and oozing pus from a wound in his shoulder in a root cellar in Harmony, but still grinning and defiant. The part of him that had never forgiven his older brother for running away wanted to trumpet that sign of abject failure to their mother, as if to confirm that she'd been right to make herself a better son. And yet the memories of Kazu sneaking him from the house to go to the nearby park and play in the fountain at midnight were still keen. That thrill of the forbidden and the terror at the inevitability of being punished were like the tart-sweet of pomegranate. Because of course Shige told their minder what they'd done the next morning; Kazu must have known he would have after the first time. He'd kept doing it anyway, laughing with his teeth white in the street lights until he got Shige to laugh as well.

Just as Kazu had known Shige would abandon him, he supposed. Yet why did he keep coming back to that moment, that pained smile, that flash of teeth in the dark of a stinking cellar? They'd both been inculcated with duty along with their mother's milk. It had gone into Shige's bones, while Kazu had spit it out and endlessly fussed.

"I was told he died shortly after I saw him. Lost in the desert." He still refused to lie a heroic death into reality for Kazu, and didn't want to make his assumed name a point of argument.

"I'll pass the news on to your father. I think he'll be... relieved. It is the not knowing that is difficult, after all. Thank you." She turned to go. "*You* have our full confidence."

Shige bowed his head, feeling the weight of those words. "I won't disappoint you."

CHAPTER THREE • 71 DAYS

They felt the blast a bare second before they heard it: first the roll and boom like too-near thunder, then the rumble that came up through their bellies, pressed flat against the sandy top of the bluff.

Anabi clutched at Mag's shoulder. Mag didn't look away from the small billows of orange sand and dust in the distance, but she still felt that warm pressure down to her toes. She rested her hand over Anabi's, but she didn't think the other woman was looking for comfort. Anabi was so much stronger than she seemed, a quiet and deep sort of strength. "Must not've found what they were looking for at the last one," she commented. This was the fourth blasting survey that they'd tracked out into the desert in so many weeks. Explosives and basic seismographs were simple enough technology to still be used out in the wilds of Tanegawa's World.

No verbal answer from Anabi, just a brief squeeze of her fingers, but the woman was mute. She communicated via scribbled messages or an organically developed sort of sign language. Mag also knew from what Anabi had told her in written conversation before that it wasn't a condition she'd been born with. She didn't ever want to tell the story, and Mag wasn't one to press her on it. The topic smelled of witchiness, and that was a very personal thing.

"Still don't know what they're lookin' for so hard." All of the mine shafts at Ludlow were operating at full capacity, though the crew leaders Odalia and Clarence Vigil – no relation despite having the same last name – had been doing their best to put the brakes on the work speed before another major accident could happen. The ore veins showed no sign of thinning out, and two of the three in operation were fairly new discoveries. It didn't make sense for the company to be doing exploration here.

"And it ain't been that long since the last worker ship, has it?" Mag asked. She rolled to her side and looked at Anabi, who shook her head. Anabi had red-brown skin, and her wavy black hair had finally grown out from the depredations of escaping her home town and then almost being executed as a witch in the next she got to. Her skittishness had calmed over the months until, at least around Mag, she was willing to hold her head high and let the light fall on her face, showing full lips, broad cheekbones, and wide brown eyes. She was a beautiful woman, something Mag found herself thinking about with increasing frequency. Mag didn't think of her own looks overmuch; she was plain, and she'd looked too like her adopted sort-of-sister Hob for anyone's comfort when they were growing up, except she mercifully had a smaller nose. Though where Hob was long and lean Mag had stayed compact, big-boned, and was as plump as anyone could get on the amount of food they had. She'd kind of liked the resemblance, but she'd had to cut her own braids off and dye her hair black when she started hiding from TransRift.

Anabi took a small bit of slate from the pocket of her skirt and scribbled: *Eight months?*

"Sounds about right," Mag agreed. While supply ships came in regularly every few months – they had to, Anabi had told her, since more and more of what the farmers grew were medicinal plants that got shipped off, and they got their food in cans, boxes, and ration packs the same as the miners – the massive ships that brought in workers were a much rarer occurrence. "So at the least, it's gonna be another six, maybe ten months before they have anyone that could work it if they open up some new shafts."

Anabi indicated her doubt of that with a movement of her hand. They were short enough on workers for what they already had, thanks to the attrition of accidents, injuries, and people pissing off the company so bad they got disappeared off into the desert.

"Vendra from Walsen said they been getting surveys like this too." She worried at her lower lip with her teeth as she thought. At the last meeting of shift leaders from the various towns, all secret-like in the back corner of a warehouse, they'd all wondered over and over what in the hell TransRift was looking for. Two ideas had taken root in the back of Mag's brain, then. Least likely: maybe they were looking for Hob's strange friend the Bone Collector, whom she'd left buried out in the sand months ago and still seemed tore up about. The man could turn himself into stone at will, so maybe that was the sort of thing a seismic survey could find – and considering that the Bone Collector had been instrumental in killing the last Weatherman, TransRift had a mighty hate-on for him.

The other possibility seemed far more likely. Mag remembered, right before she and her papa had departed for Newcastle and their lives had changed irreparably, he'd brought something odd up out of the mine in Rouse. A shaft had collapsed, and a dying company man buried under the debris in it had given Papa a sample bag, with some kind of mineral in it that he'd never seen before. Mag still couldn't be certain of anything to do with it, but there'd been *some* reason TransRift had detained her, had let the Weatherman have her. She still had nightmares about him, his voice, his black eyes that had swallowed her up.

There were plenty of things on the planet that no one knew about yet, and plenty more that some people knew about and were keeping tight behind their teeth. Mag had thought about mentioning that during the meeting and discarded the idea just as quick. She wasn't interested in telling anyone here about being stuck in that laboratory. She'd talked the coalition of miners into not turning their backs on the witchy ones during TransRift's witch hunt, but that had been without any of them knowing she was something past witchy herself.

"Anyone knows the answer, it'll be the pit boss," she said. Anabi shrugged in response. It wasn't like they could just ask Bill Weld out straight. He was an OK sort for a company man, in that he wasn't cruel for the sake of making himself feel like a big man, but Mag was under no illusions that he was a friend to the workers. Just a softer boot heel than most.

But they also didn't have to ask Bill. TransRift liked its paperwork, and the papers *were* papers, since nothing electronic survived long on the surface of Tanegawa's World. There had to be documents, just waiting to be read. "Bet he's got it stowed in his office."

Anabi gave her a look of concern, then shook her head. *I'll look out for you.*

Mag smiled, pretending she felt more certain about it than she did. This had always been Hob's kind of trouble, but Hob wasn't here, and Mag needed to get used to doing her own work, her own way. Mag had always been a lot better at quiet anyway. "And I got my own tricks, too. We find something, we'll take it to Clarence." She pretended to be Clarence's niece, which made a decent cover story. A few people did know that she was the daughter of murdered, well-respected crew leader Phil Kushtrim. It gave her a certain power as a symbol, something that made her deeply uncomfortable at times, for all she was willing to use it.

They wormed their way back from the edge of the bluff, then took turns helping each other straighten skirts and brush off the worst of the dust. "There, don't look any more dirty than normal," Mag remarked.

Anabi smiled and poked her lightly on the end of the nose.

Mag thought, then, about kissing that smile. But she'd never been an impulsive person – that had always been Hob's lookout. She smiled the warmth she felt instead. "Come on, we got some crime to do."

They'd "borrowed" a small, solar-powered cargo from one of the warehouses to get out here. Not as fast or stylish as Hob's beloved motorcycles, but also guaranteed to not scare Mag half to death. The hauler was technically also a one-seater, so they had to squeeze in together tight to both fit inside. Anabi was the one who drove the thing, since she'd claimed it was similar to the farming equipment she'd once known. Mag kept a firm hold around Anabi's waist, the fabric beneath her arm going damp with sweat that couldn't be dried away in the hot wind that flowed over them.

When she leaned forward a little, she saw Anabi smiling, so that seemed all right too. Mag let the wind carry her worries away until they got back to town.

Once upon a time, Mag reflected sourly, the security men in Ludlow had been too damn lazy to want to spend their time watching the on-site company office. They'd always been drunk on duty, or off gambling, or sleeping in a corner of the food warehouse, the only one that had any kind of cooling system. Or hell, wandering through the town and looking to pick fights with whatever miner crossed their path, because they were all damn bullies. Even that option was at this point preferable to two of them lounging around in the shade of an awning, rifles across their laps and not an ounce of sleepiness to them.

This was the sort of thing that happened when a special company train got derailed and all but one man aboard killed. And Mag couldn't even complain too much about *that*, since she was the one who'd paid Hob to do it. But damn, it was an inconvenience now.

She and Anabi had tried every hour of the day, hoping to find one when the Mariposa men would be inattentive enough to let her slide by. She was fresh out of hours, and fresh out of patience now, and she hadn't tried *everything*.

There was the power sitting in the back of her head that had been growing since her capture by TransRift. The power itself felt tentative and nebulous because she was more than a little afraid of it. She *felt* other people out there like pressure on her skin, like their thoughts were within her grasp if she was bold enough to reach for them. Murmurs just under the range of her hearing, maybe, if hearing was a sensation of physical pressure instead of sound. She hadn't trusted herself to learn the power's boundaries, because she couldn't think of a way to do it without the risk of hurting someone.

During the witch hunt, she'd used it because she hadn't had any other choice. A security guard had come into Clarence's house, intent on dragging Mag and Anabi off to the platform to stand in front of the Weatherman. Mag had vowed to never let that happen again, and

Anabi said she'd rather die than be captured. So Mag had used her power to lean onto the man like she was leaning on a stone wall, like she was a giant with the weight to crack mortar. She'd felt him give under her, and had told him that he'd seen nothing and should leave – and he'd obeyed.

Was it evil to bend other people like that? It didn't feel right, after what the Weatherman had done to her. But on the other hand, she doubted any of the Mariposa men would concern themselves a hair over mercy for her. It was a calculation, and she'd always been a lot better with figures and sums than Hob. The difference was, mathematics had never made her skin crawl. Being able to do a square root in her head had never forced her to lie to Clarence out of fear of what he or the other miners might think. But something needed to be done, and she had to weigh her own worries against what they didn't know. Knowledge was power, and the miners needed all the power they could get.

Besides, she thought grimly as she stepped out from behind the boxes she'd been using for cover, TransRift had never hesitated an instant in using the Weatherman against one of them. And she wasn't like that monster. She just *wasn't*. She waved at Anabi to stay and keep watch.

"Where do you think you're going?" one of the guards called in a bored tone as she walked up.

"Appointment," Mag said, on the offchance a direct lie would work.

"You must have the wrong time," the other guard said. She sounded more alert than her friend. "Your boss isn't in."

"I could wait for him," Mag offered.

The female guard laughed. "Nice try. Move along." She waved a hand like Mag was a sand flea that needed to be brushed off.

It would have been easier to muster the power if they'd been nasty to her, or threatened her. But both of them plainly didn't care. She considered trying again later, because maybe then the guards would be nastier and she could feel better about what she was going to do. But then these ones still would have seen her, and they'd remember.

Mag closed her eyes briefly, tuning out the sound of the words as the male guard started to speak again. She felt the pressure of their thoughts against her like a gentle press of fingers through fabric, closest out of everyone. She remembered how she'd leaned back into the guard months ago, a mental rather than physical movement. This wasn't any different, just because it was two of them. She opened her eyes, still aware of them, and leaned her will against theirs with all her might.

It was like pushing against two walls at slightly different angles. She had to find her balance, even harder when the walls were pushing back. But she was stronger than them, she already felt it. Something sang in her blood, turned it to hard diamond in her veins, but the kind of diamond that lived at the heart of a super massive star. She was greater than them. She–

For an instant, she almost lost her mental grasp on them because she felt something far bigger, like singing on the horizon, like lightning dancing across her skin. She felt like she might tip into it and fall forever. Mag kept her eyes open and focused with all her might on the guards. It was just them and her in this dusty street, and the seconds ticking away meant slices of danger falling onto her. All that greatness that threatened to drown her needed to *wait*.

Mercifully, whatever it was retreated, and it was just the three of them again, the guards gasping and wide-eyed. She felt a tickle start up in her nose, probably a bleed from the continual strain of pushing and pushing. Mag licked her lips, tasted salt and copper, and spoke evenly, "No one's bothered you all afternoon." She pressed the words deep in on them. "You ain't never seen me. And you ain't gonna see me when I leave, neither. You're both gonna take a nap for the next twenty minutes."

Both guards slumped back in their chairs. She pressed their eyes closed with the weight of her words and shoved them under the surface of sleep. Only then did she let up. A wave of dizziness washed over her and left in its wake a pounding headache, but she did her best to shake it off. A few uneven steps took her past the deeply breathing guards and into the office. Thank all that was holy and un- that the door was unlocked. She hadn't even thought to check. For a moment, she visualized shaking one of the guards awake and demanding the key.

She swallowed an unhealthy little giggle as she shut the door behind her. It had worked. Now she needed to be fast.

Her stomach sank, though, when she looked across the office. It was like a dune sea made of nothing but flimsies and scattered sample bags. She would need days to sort through it all, but who knew how quickly the pit boss would be back. And she didn't dare disturb any of the piles overmuch, in case there was a method to the madness.

As quick as she could, she scanned the top layers around the room. Her papa had taught her plenty about mining when he was alive, enough that she could make some sense of the mess. It was daily reports, and supply sheets, and ore tallies mostly. Maybe if she dug deep enough into those, she'd be able to find patterns in the minutiae that would be useful to the miners. But what she wanted was any kind of information about the surveys.

She focused on words that might be useful: *survey, seismic, results*, and things of that nature. She felt the seconds slipping away like grains of sand as she kept reading and reading until she thought she'd be swept away on a torrent of useless words.

Under a pile of fresh mine tallies, she found what she was looking for. Sheet after sheet of flimsies showed closely stacked rows of wavy lines. She didn't know what any of it meant, but the labeling was clear. She stared in dismay at the thick sheaf of seismic survey lines. Why had she thought this would be something she could just read and understand? What did any of it even mean? She considered taking the whole bunch with her and showing them to Clarence, but that many sheets would surely be missed. She did extract one from the middle of the pile and stuffed it into her pocket. One sheet could be excused as something that got lost in the shuffle.

Then she kept looking. There had to be more than that, some kind of report to go with it, right?

She was so caught up in her frantic search that she didn't realize just how much time she'd wasted until she heard voices outside the office door. Even muffled, she recognized the voice of Bill Weld, the pit boss. And from his tone, she could tell he was yelling at the guards. The door cracked open, and Mag's heart almost stopped. Then she heard Bill say, "Well, what do you want? Speak up. What do you – oh for goodness sake, why are you waving that slate at me?"

That had to be Anabi, buying her a few more seconds. Frantically, Mag glanced around for somewhere to hide. The only way out was the front door, and she didn't want to have to try to lean on Bill if she didn't have to. The very thought made the ache in her head worse.

She spotted a narrow supply cupboard and jammed herself into it as Bill dismissed Anabi with an annoyed, "Take it to your crew leader. That's not my concern," and swung the door fully open. It was a plain miracle that she didn't make noise knocking things over; the closet was filled to bursting with pens, boxes of blank flimsies, and all sorts of office supplies. Something poked her bruisingly in the back. She held her breath in the darkness and listened to Bill's footsteps move back and forth across the floor. Then he moved further away and she heard another door open and shut.

With any luck, it meant he'd gone to the bathroom, or into one of the other rooms of the office. Mag cautiously eased the closet door open a crack and listened. No, she couldn't hear anyone in the room now. And when she tried to reach out, to feel if other people were there, like stretching out an invisible hand, none of them were too close. She stepped out of the closet.

As she was about to close the door, she noticed what had been poking her in the back – it had been the corner of a bin marked "destroy."

It was a risk, but she pushed the bin open and scrabbled through the flimsies at the top. She found more survey sheets among the disorganized mess and... a sheaf of flimsies marked "report." A quick glance showed multiple corrections scrawled across them in red grease pencil.

She heard the whir of the compost toilet crank. Mag stuffed the report in her shirt and shut the bin, then the closet. She sprinted out the office door. As her foot crossed the threshold, she felt a thrill of fear, waiting to hear the guards shout after her.

Silence. She risked a glance over her shoulder and saw them both standing, alert now, and staring right past her like she wasn't even there.

With an act of will, Mag made herself slow to a quick, purposeful walk. The flimsies crackled in her shirt as she moved. She just had to hope there'd be something worth reading in them when she got back to Clarence's house.

CHAPTER FOUR • 71 DAYS

"He's singin'," Dambala said, his low voice filtered to a hoarse growl with emotion. Sweat stood out on the dark brown of his shaved head, running down his square jaw and the tattoos that wreathed his thick neck. "And he ain't even awake. Why the fuck's he singin'? Coyote never sang a day in his life, no matter how fuckin' drunk he got."

"Sit your ass down, Bala," Hob said. Not gentle; she never did gentle. But not unkind, either. She still felt like she'd taken a step off solid rock and found nothing beneath her. She'd kept herself moving when Freki had dragged in the ragged, bloody mess of bones barely contained by skin that used to be Coyote by sheer force of will. There were things that still had to be done at the bandit camp, no matter what other fuckery had fallen into their laps. They had to finish going over the bodies, collect all the salvage, and leave their calling card where it could be seen – in this case, Davey had painted the wolf's head on one of the canyon walls. He was getting good at that sort of art.

But now, back at their base, with Coyote stowed in the infirmary, she'd made the mistake of sitting down. Of breathing. And the harder she tried to breathe, the less she felt she could. The night outside, moons waxing oval, pressed in against her office window.

To her relief, Dambala sat – collapsed, more like – into a chair, which creaked dangerously under the bulk of his muscle. Then she took out a cigarette and lit it with a snap of her fingers, which were somehow still steady. It was an automatic twitch and a calming ritual that could have passed for prayer in anyone but her. After a moment's thought, she offered the cigarette case to Dambala. He took one with shaking fingers – Dambala had never smoked a day in his life, as far as she knew, but this didn't feel like a day that belonged in anyone's life – and she lit it for him with the same little snap of the fire from her blood.

He sucked a drag of the cigarette like it'd save him from drowning, went into a coughing fit, and then did it again.

Hob waited for the next jag of coughing to pass. "Now what's this about him singin'?"

"Just that. Singin'... no. More hummin' in his sleep. If asleep is what he is." Dambala scrubbed his face in his hands. "But there's music to it. No music I ever heard, but music."

"Davey takin' good care of him?" She'd made her own attempt to hover once they were back at the base, but the infirmary was barely big enough for the wounded, and Davey had told her to fuck off the third time she stepped in his way. Coming from someone normally so mild-mannered, she'd taken the hint and stopped fighting Geri when he dragged her out of there and told her she needed to update the bandit maps.

But Dambala wasn't the sort to get dragged away by anyone, unless they had a tractor and a tow chain. "Yeah, seems so. Got two IVs runnin' into him. Gave him antibiotics, sewed up his wounds. Let me..." Dambala rubbed his eyes again, "...clean him up a mite. He had blood all over his hands, Hob. His mouth. His *teeth*."

"I know. I... know." She'd never be able to forget as long as she drew breath.

"They swore up and down in Harmony that all they done was shoot him in the shoulder and stick him in a cellar," Dambala growled. "Swore he was doin' just fine up until he escaped and got lost in the desert on their fuckin' tractor. I'm gonna go back there and fuckin' *kill them*–"

"Bala." Hob held up a hand. She understood his urge. She was half ready to punch the next person who came in her office door, just because it felt like that or screaming. "There's... a lot of shit that can happen to someone in the desert when it don't kill you."

She knew from personal experience, and when the words came out of her mouth, she suddenly wondered if Coyote had seen the phoenix like she had. If it had worked some change on him at a price he hadn't fully understood, for the chance at surviving. She shuddered.

Dambala put his face in his hands. "I thought I was all right," he said, and she'd never heard such a big man sound so small. Dambala had always been a mountain, first literally when she'd been a scrap of a child, picked up fresh off the rift ship by Old Nick, and then figuratively when he'd always stood steady at her back as she'd grown, fought, and taken charge in the wake of Old Nick's passing. "I thought I was all right with him bein' gone. No, not *right* with it, but used to it, like you get used to a bad ankle always hurtin'. But now..."

This was territory no one in the Wolves was any good at, least of all Hob. They all hid their pain under bravado, pretended to be untouchable. That was a really stupid idea, Hob realized suddenly. Because it meant none of them had a fucking clue how to deal with anything more complex than getting angry and shooting shit. But that revelation didn't help her do anything but wish Mag was here. Mag had always been so good with people, always knew what to say and how to listen so that when you poured your troubles out to her, they felt like they really had drained away.

"Bala..." She cleared her throat, trying to get out the words stuck there. They wouldn't move. Finally, she rasped, "Let's have a look at him. I wanna hear this singin'."

She followed Dambala to lean in the doorway of the tiny infirmary room that had housed Old Nick in his final days. The infirmary was probably the most comfortable place in the base, where the fans mostly worked and they had some cooling lines set up. That had been Diablo's pet project, between people getting their bones broken and asses beat; he said people healed better when they were comfortable.

A solar-powered fan in the window sullenly stirred the air. Coyote looked like a brown skeleton surrounded by sheets that had once been white but were now soft gray-brown from washing by disinterested recruits. And he looked even tinier and more scraggly when Dambala sat unsteadily in the chair next to his bed, his splinted leg stretched out at an awkward angle.

In the heavy quiet cut only by the metal fan blades, she heard what Dambala had called singing or humming, and it wasn't really either of those. Like every time Coyote breathed, there was a note of music he exhaled. The sound of it crawled across her skin and set every hair of her body about on end, because within a few notes, she recognized it. She'd heard it before, louder and sweeter and clearer, with a voice she was losing hope she'd ever hear again.

Hob tucked a cigarette between her lips, barely

remembered at the last moment that she shouldn't light it. Not in a sick room.

"You look like you been gutpunched," Dambala said.

"Ain't far from the truth." Hob made herself breathe. "Let Freki know he's gonna be in charge for a couple days." She pushed away from the doorframe.

"Where you goin'?"

"Out." She didn't want to say more than that, didn't want to give Dambala false hope. Hell, she didn't want to give *herself* false hope.

But if the Bone Collector hadn't come when she called, maybe she just needed to go to him. And for once, she knew where he was supposed to be.

"Hob!" Mag said, her hazel eyes wide with surprise. Even after so many months, her short hair, dyed black, still didn't look right to Hob. Not even with the sunset softening the harsh contrast between that and her miner-pale skin. "What brings you here?"

The little splash of wariness in Mag's eyes hurt a bit, but Hob couldn't blame her for it. Most times she stopped off in Ludlow, it was to bring bad news. Having a price on her head had really put a damper on casual visits. "Nothin' bad. Was in the neighborhood and thought you'd want to hear how your job came out."

"Job… right! Yes. I would." Mag waved her inside.

Hob paused at the threshold long enough to pull her half-finished cigarette from her lips. She regarded it, sighed, and the rest vanished in a shower of sparks between her fingers. Mag had never liked her uncle smoking, and that dislike had extended to Hob's copying his filthy habit. Hell, Mag still seemed to want to blame Old Nick's lung troubles and eventual death on the cigarettes, no matter how often Hob told her it had to be something else. Smoke and fire couldn't kill you when you were damn well made of smoke and fire. "Thought you'd be more excited about it," Hob commented as she followed along to the kitchen.

"So you found them?" Mag asked, as she poured her a glass of lemonade.

"Yeah. Hell of a lot more than you said there'd be, by the way."

"Was that a problem?"

"'Course not," Hob snorted. "Mostly 'cause our timing was lucky. I got a passin' strange story to tell ya after the business is out of the way." She took her accustomed seat at the kitchen table – it almost felt natural now, to be in Clarence Vigil's kitchen in Ludlow instead of the one belonging to Mag's mother, Irina, back in Rouse. It still didn't smell quite right, burnt coffee and garbage that needed to go out rather than sugar dough or sausage klobasnek. In the grand scheme of things, it hadn't been that long since Mag's papa Phil had been murdered, and then Irina burned alive in the house they'd shared together. But it felt like another lifetime, and she wished it didn't. Was wrong, for someone so kind as Irina to be fading away with such ease.

Hob sipped her lemonade and detailed the job to Mag, the number of company spies they'd found, and then the presence of Coyote. Mag started that part of the conversation with her hand over her mouth in plain shock, but finished it leaned forward, elbows on table, intent.

"So you're goin' for the Bone Collector." Statement, not a question. Mag had picked that up quick. Ludlow was the closest town to where he'd buried himself, after all.

"Gonna try, at least."

"Surprised you stopped here first, then."

"Like I said, was passin' through." And maybe she

was playing the delay game, because she didn't want to break that last sliver of faith she had. Hob regarded Mag over the top of her lemonade glass. "You wanna come along?" The words echoed sour in the pit of her belly the moment she said them. Part of her wanted the Bone Collector all to herself, in a way. Like he was somehow hers. The other part of her didn't trust that one damn bit.

Mag nibbled on her fingernail. "You know? I think I might. There's... somethin' I think I better ask him about." Mag stood abruptly. "Let me show you."

Hob made no move to stand as Mag opened one of the kitchen cabinets and wormed half into it. Probably a hidden panel in the back, she figured. A moment later, Mag emerged with a roll of flimsies tied with a scrap of twine. She spread them out in front of Hob.

"What do you think?" Mag asked.

Hob looked at the one on top, a collection of wavy lines. "Think your art could use some work," she said dryly.

Mag laughed and slapped her on the arm. "That's a survey line. One piece of it. I only took one page."

"Don't know about no wavy line survey."

Mag traced the line. "Don't rightly understand it myself, but they stick these hearin' devices in the ground, and then set off explosives nearby. That sound from the explosives goes through the ground and them hearin' devices pick it up and different kinds of rock pass the sound different and... somehow you can read it all off here."

Hob raised her eyebrows. "Any of y'all know how to do that?"

"Clarence does, a bit. 'Cause he's old as dirt." Mag shook her head. "But the point is that they been doin' a damn lot of surveys. And there's this." She slid the top sheet aside to reveal a report, covered with corrections made in grease pencil.

Hob squinted at it, doing her best to read over it quick. She'd never been as strong at reading as Mag – she'd learned late and not well – and bless her adopted sister for forgetting that all the time. She did catch one phrase repeated over and over again: *unknown ore type A*. She tapped the words with her finger. "This what they're lookin' for?"

Mag nodded. "Must be. And there ain't been a new ore type found in decades. So they're lookin' for it hard. In all the towns. And the company men pushing hard, too. Been accidents. The kind with explosives."

"Always accidents, aren't there," Hob said, trying to puzzle out a bit more of the report.

"More'n there should be. But you know what I think that unknown ore type they're looking for is?"

Hob glanced up at Mag, then sat back. It wasn't something they'd talked about much, but she remembered the little sample bag that had been in Phil's pocket when she'd found his body, and she remembered what the blue crystals inside had done when she touched them. She remembered also what the Bone Collector had said about it when she'd shown it to him: *...that moment, when the claws of the phoenix sank into your eye? Like that.* It still didn't make sense to her, but her eye throbbed with the memory of it all the same. There was some kind of power in those crystals, and of course TransRift wanted more power if they knew about it. "Shit," she said.

Mag nodded, like she could hear what Hob had been thinking. Maybe she could. That was another thing Hob had never quite had the guts to ask about. "Finish your lemonade."

CHAPTER FIVE • 70 DAYS

"Welcome, Mr Rolland. I assume you're here to check on the progress of the newly assigned Weatherman?" The woman, whose ID proclaimed her to be Dr Ekwensi, had deep black skin, was of medium height and heavyset, with hooded eyes not quite perfect enough to be the result of body modification. She also had her salt-and-pepper curls cut so close to her head that in the harsh light her scalp shone through. Not someone who cared about fashion, either, and her self-assurance rendered it unnecessary.

"Yes. I've been tasked with arranging our travel back to the outpost–" the office slang for Tanegawa's World, which still didn't do justice to what a backwater it truly was "–and would like to get started. We have to arrange for a courier rift ship, and I'd rather cause as little disruption as possible to the regular routes."

"Laudable, I'm sure," Dr Ekwensi said in a tone of utter dryness. "Yet you have no issue disrupting my day for this visit."

Shige bowed apologetically. He already knew she was the chief doctor on the team assigned to the new Weatherman – not that her network file specifically said "Weatherman," but rather "Fast-Tracked Experimental Projects."

"My requests for transmitted status reports were denied, I'm afraid. Thus, I've had to come bother you personally."

She blew out an annoyed sigh, but the emotion no longer seemed to be directed at Shige. "Mariposa is still keeping all internal mentions suppressed, then?"

"So it would seem."

"Paranoid fools. Even if someone could slice through the network, any research they recovered would do them no good." Dr Ekwensi clapped her hands as if to end a treasured rant before it could begin. "He isn't ready. He won't be for several more weeks."

Shige quietly disagreed with her first statement in his capacity as an agent for the Federal Union of Systems. Even if the proprietary research was quite literally of no practical use for anyone who didn't have access to the unique materials that came from Tanegawa's World, those sorts of files would be immensely helpful for putting the entire R&D department and most of the upper management of TransRift into prison on various illegal human engineering charges.

Later, he promised himself. When the BCRE regained the teeth that TransRift had pulled. He smiled politely. "I'm sorry, but can you be more specific?" He had only a limited time to return to the planet and foment a rebellion that would go into full force at precisely the right time.

"No," she said shortly. "Come with me."

She led him down a series of hallways, interrupted by three separate security doors that required biometric scans. Past the last, the floor went from slightly springy carpeting to smooth plating covered with the same nonporous paint as the walls and ceiling. It was slightly disorienting, walking down a squared-off, pale eggshell tube, with only the steady pull of gravity as an indication as to which way might be up or down.

Dr Ekwensi stopped at a section of wall that looked no different from any other. As Shige halted next to her, the smooth expanse shrank back to a lattice, then became invisible, revealing a floor-to-ceiling viewing window. Through the window was a blank-walled room, the same color as the hallway. The room's single occupant was almost shocking as a source of color: the black stubble of shaved hair, pale blue veins threading a naked body contained in thin, sallow skin, and, most out of place and shocking, the red drops of blood where needle-fine wires were laced along the spine and hairline-like mesh.

It took Shige a moment to resolve the body into something truly person-shaped, tall and lean and curled up with its limbs tangled, shuddering faintly. This could only be the new Weatherman he was expected to collect and return with. "Is there something wrong with… him?"

Almost, he said *it*, because it was difficult to encompass the Weathermen as people at times, and his mind rebelled at the thought of coolly watching a *person* undergo something that looked so like torture. In his nightmares that might be him, after all. He was all too conscious of his own existence as a being created in a lab, just one designed for a job that required more human functions. There were many in the Federal Union of Systems who would consider him an *it* as well, though there was an unsubtle difference between Shige's life as an independent agent and that of the Weathermen.

"All Weathermen are nominally male. It's easier to source all of the modifications to the Y chromosome." Dr Ekwensi looked at him, and seemed to realize she'd answered a question he wasn't asking. "He's perfectly functional. But we're integrating some new components into his neural net – components utilizing that sample you brought us. The potential is... enormous. We're going to need new technology to fully utilize it, rather than just incorporating those crystals into our current circuits."

This was the first he'd heard of that development, though he would have found out eventually. One of the major uses of playing executive secretary was being able to read nearly all of the documents given to his superior. "I... see."

"I don't think you do. I don't let experimental modifications run around unmonitored. But this has come down from the highest level."

"Ah. I understand."

"Good, because I don't." She frowned. "What is going on at the outpost, that you *need* unproven resources so badly?"

He gave her a bland look. "If it's above your pay grade, Dr Ekwensi, then surely it is above that of a secretary."

She didn't buy it, he could see that much. "I'm given to understand you'll be assigned to him as his handler."

"It is my honor to serve in that role again." He'd been similarly assigned to the previous Weatherman, though not by his own design. Mr Green had taken a liking to Shige that he'd never understood or wanted. He'd crafted that into his current opportunity, which he'd now need to parlay into access to the research he had no other way of attaining. "Would my presence be of comfort to him?"

She looked as if such a question had never even occurred to her. He wondered if she, who built the Weathermen from the ground up like engines or network displays, also had a difficult time thinking of them as people. Or if she'd argue that they weren't people at all, merely... people-shaped. "It certainly will do no harm. Just remember–"

"–don't look him in the eye," Shige finished. That was

the first rule anyone learned when about to be in close proximity to a Weatherman.

"His designation is Mr Yellow. I'd appreciate you reinforcing that to him." Dr Ekwensi must have sent a silent, local network command. The viewing window reshaped itself into a two-doored airlock of sorts for him.

Shige stepped through. The little sounds of Dr Ekwensi shifting her weight, breathing, and the subliminal hum of the air exchange system cut off. When the door into the featureless room opened, there was another sort of sound – ragged breathing, the sort that caused an instinctive adrenal response just hearing it. And also a rapid clicking that it took Shige far too long to recognize as the Weatherman's teeth chattering. There was also a smell, a strange, dry thing with a flavor of blood to it, far stronger than he'd noticed around Mr Green. It made the hair on the back of his neck stand on end, whispering directly to his most irrational mind.

He'd never encountered a Weatherman in a state like this. Mr Green had moments of incoherency and strange fugue states, but there'd always been a cause to those that Shige had witnessed. And even at the worst moments, Mr Green had been fully clothed, dressed in the same sort of suit as Shige. Always more obviously *subject* than *object*.

This was a test, Shige realized. Perhaps Dr Ekwensi was testing him, to see how he reacted. But beyond that, it was an internal test, of his own humanity. He'd been instrumental in the death of Mr Green, and had little doubt that his presence would ultimately be deadly to Mr Yellow as well. The power of a Weatherman was antithetical to the goals Shige had to achieve. But that did not require that in the meantime, he must be cruel.

He squatted down by Mr Yellow, though still a healthy distance away. He'd seen how fast Weathermen could move when they wanted. Mr Yellow had his long-fingered hands clutched over his face, twitching as little muscle spasms ran through him. "Hello, Mr Yellow," he said, slowly and carefully. "My name is James Rolland. Some day soon, I'm going to take you to a remarkable place called Tanegawa's World. I hope that we can be friends."

At first, Mr Yellow gave no indication that he had heard anything. Then he uncoiled in a sudden spasm – human bodies did not move like that – and crawled forward. Shige held himself still through sheer will, and kept his eyes focused on the blue line of a vein in Mr Yellow's shoulder. In the periphery of his vision, Mr Yellow's eyes were wide, irises and pupils alike black.

He forced himself to remain passive as Mr Yellow reached out to grab his hand. The Weatherman's skin was soft, smooth, and very cold. Mr Yellow sniffed his hand, like Shige had seen dogs do before – not that he'd ever had a dog, his parents hadn't had time for pets – and then cradled it against his cheek.

He had no way of knowing what the Weatherman was thinking, but he noticed that Mr Yellow had stopped shaking. He stayed where he was, wondering how long Dr Ekwensi would observe. To fill the heavy silence, he began to talk. "Would you like to hear of your new home? The Corporate tower is very nice. You shall have your own rooms with whatever furniture you like..." He continued on with glowing descriptions of the amenities on the planet. If Mr Yellow understood his words, he gave no sign.

"That is enough for now." Dr Ekwensi's voice came clearly through the observation window. "Return to the door."

"That is all the time we have for now," Shige said to Mr Yellow, since he couldn't quite bring himself to yank his hand away with no preamble. He had to tug against the Weatherman's grip, which to his relief at least didn't tighten as he slid his fingers away.

"He will be visiting you regularly," Dr Ekwensi agreed through the window.

A useful victory, then – he had his excuse to return. "As often as I can," he said, and turned to leave.

Mr Yellow curled up again, his hands returning to hide his face. And then, so quiet that Shige almost didn't hear it over the fall of his own footsteps, he began to hum. Shige stopped, gooseflesh prickling over his arms, mercifully hidden by his jacket and shirt. He'd heard that sound before, on Tanegawa's World, a strange song that Mr Green had croaked to himself with a voice ruined by being shot through the throat by Hob Ravani. How the hell could Mr Yellow know it?

"Mr Rolland?" Dr Ekwensi's voice called him back into motion, and he quickly left the room. It was a relief when the door cut the sound off. He came to stand next to her; she had her lips pursed in a frown of curious contemplation. "You were assessed for contamination before being allowed off world, correct?"

"Of course," he said, letting his alarm at the thought show. It was a natural enough reaction. "Is that a concern?"

She hummed to herself. "I trust our methods. I helped develop the latest generation, after all. Is there room in your schedule for daily visits?"

Better and better. "I shall see to it, if you wish."

"I do." She gave him a piercing look, like her dark eyes could carefully dissect him where he stood. He held on to his bland expression. "I've never seen a Weatherman react quite like that before. You might be a remarkable man, Mr Rolland."

He bowed his head, keeping the role of Rolland, who

was exceedingly ordinary, fixed in his mind. "I should like to believe so. I have... hopes for the future."

She snorted. "Remarkable and ambitious are a combination that calls for caution. Without it, you may end up in an... untoward permanent assignment."

Personal ambition was not a problem for the man beneath the role; he'd been created to fulfill the thwarted ambition of his parents. Shige sometimes wondered what he would want for himself otherwise, and the question felt like it came in a foreign language. Nurture or un-nature? No knowing. He smiled. "Thank you, Dr Ekwensi. Until tomorrow."

CHAPTER SIX • *70 DAYS*

The desert was a restless, ever-changing sea that erased all impressions almost as soon as they'd been made. Hob had learned this lesson the hard way when it had almost killed her, a bare two days after she'd set foot on Tanegawa's World. Now it made her vivid memories of blood and fire and the wreckage of a train seem distant, like a story she'd heard rather than lived.

As she drove out of the canyon mouth where the Bone Collector had derailed the Weatherman's train, she had to jump her motorcycle down a five-foot drop from the canyon to the ground below, something that made Mag grip her waist tightly and choke back a scream. In the light of the two moons, the walls of the canyon were still visibly blackened from the fireball of the engine exploding. There was no wreckage now, though. TransRift had no doubt cleaned most of it up, and anything that remained was buried in the sand dunes that had shifted and flowed, driven by slightly new wind patterns.

If she hadn't been in that battle, she wouldn't have recognized even the burn marks. The rocks jutting up from the sands remained the same, but everything around them had shifted. What had once been a long flat of salt hardpan punctuated with the silver lines of tracks was a sea of undulating, orange-red sand.

And of course, to complicate matters, Hob hadn't taken the Bone Collector to bury himself at the mouth of that canyon. He'd needed the sands, and they'd been a healthy few kilometers out back then. Thankfully, she'd had the brains that day to mark the location on the map stored in her motorcycle's dumb, simple computer. The maps ran off solar, lunar, and stellar bearings, perfectly tracked on date and time, with the unmoving rocks as the necessary landmarks, and the computers had barely enough processing power to do all of the angles and calculations on the fly. It was the best system anyone could manage on a planet where satellites tended to drop inexplicably from orbit or stop functioning, and where the ever-shifting magnetic fields prevented the use of something so simple as a compass or as complicated as a computer that wasn't mostly mechanical relays.

Easy with long practice, she guided the motorcycle around and over dunes, mindful of what Mag's weight on the back would do to the handling. That ease gave her a little too much time to think about what might be coming. Dread it, almost. She'd tried again and again to summon the Bone Collector to her, the way he'd sworn would always work: her blood on the sand. One of the more stupid times, she'd opened a big vein and had to fight off an eager young great eagle while on the verge of passing out. She'd been angry as hell at herself after that, almost getting killed over a man – because whatever else the Bone Collector might be, he was still just a man, and didn't deserve that kind of power over her. But Hob had never given up on anything in her life, just regrouped for a new angle of attack.

And now she wasn't sure what would be worse in this excursion: not finding him at all, or finding him as lifeless stone that couldn't be woken. Not finding him left room for hope, which would plague her in a thousand ways she didn't need. Finding him completely inert meant having lost one more of the few people who knew her as anything but "the Ravani." He'd reminded her not so many months ago that neither of them had a lot of friends, and he'd been damnably right.

The map display showed that they'd reached the waypoint she'd set, what felt like so long ago. Hob braked them to an easy halt and nudged her kickstand down with the toe of one boot. A wide pad fanned around it as it moved, to keep the motorcycle from sinking into the sand as it leaned. She held the bike steady while Mag climbed off the back, a little clumsily, then gave the battery stack a fond pat with her hand. The sandblasted paint of the motorcycle, a mottled red, orange, and gray that acted as decent camouflage out on the dunes, wasn't much to look at, but the machine had served her well.

"I think my ass is gonna be one big bruise," Mag said, walking in stiff circles around the small low spot where Hob had parked.

"We don't normally carry passengers," Hob said. She'd taken a bunch of the holsters and the two big saddlebags off the back to give Mag somewhere to sit, so it could have been worse.

"This the spot?"

Hob checked her map again and frowned, turning to orient herself. "About halfway up that dune." She pulled two collapsible shovels off where they'd been strapped on the back.

"That's a lot of sand to move."

"Could be worse." Hob tossed Mag one of the shovels and walked up the side of the dune. Her boots sank deep into the fine orange sand.

Mag snorted. "Now I know why you invited me

along." But she started digging readily.

Comfortable silence sat between them as they both dug, just the sharp sounds of shovels spearing into sand, the hiss of the orange grains being poured away. Sweat rolled down the end of Hob's overly long nose. She was glad they'd come here close to the middle of the night, when it was cold out in the desert. Mag would have cooked in the middle of the day before they even got half a meter down.

Without anything to shore up the sides of the hole they dug, it became a wide pit by necessity. That was the only way to keep the loose sand sides from collapsing in on themselves. By unspoken agreement, Mag kept digging down, and Hob worked to shape the sides and keep moving sand.

Two meters down, Hob was about ready to give up, though Mag's jaw was set, her movements focused. It looked like not finding anything, and that damnable breath of hope – for what, she carefully did not think on – would remain. Then she heard Mag's shovel clang and scrape, like she'd hit a rock.

"Hob?"

Hob scrambled down the slope she'd made. "Might just be…" Maybe just a rock. They still existed out here, far from the outcrops, moved by some unknown geological force. But by another unspoken agreement, they both dropped to their knees, digging with their hands like dogs. Hob didn't know what could happen to the Bone Collector if he got damaged while he was made of stone, but she didn't want to find out.

Hob's hand found solid stone first, and she knew instinctively the smooth lines of the Bone Collector's low, flat cheekbones and the gentle slope of his nose. "Fuck. It's him."

"Better than the alternative, ain't it?" Mag asked,

moving to help clear more sand away where Hob was.

Hob held her tongue until they'd exposed half of him, a statue of pale limestone dusted with orange sand. In the moonlight, he almost looked like he could have been asleep, if she hadn't felt how cold and unyielding he was. He'd always looked strangely washed out, a little like someone had sucked all the color out of a regular person so he had blue eyes instead of brown. Maybe that happened when you spent part of your life as a rock. They gripped his elbows, which stuck out a little as he'd crossed his arms over his chest, and pulled.

He didn't move an inch, but Hob felt like her arms were going to yank out of their sockets. "Stop."

Mag let go and dropped back on the sand. "You bring a chain on your motorcycle?"

"Yeah." Though she wasn't sure how much dead weight the machine would really be able to haul on a sand slope. And what would be the point if he was just so much stone? Was she going to drag him all the way back to Ludlow? The mental image that conjured up made her hastily swallow a laugh just this side of hysterical.

She squatted down next to the Bone Collector, looking at that still, pale face. She'd thought it was peaceful at first, but now she could make out the expression of fatigue, the little twist of pain on his narrow lips. He'd been badly hurt when she'd brought him out here.

Summoning him with blood hadn't worked before, but she hadn't been right next to him before. She pushed her left coat sleeve up, then slipped a throwing knife out of her boot.

"Hob?"

"Hush," Hob said. "Get a bandage out the kit on my motorcycle." The knife point, razor sharp, slid so easily through the skin of her forearm that she didn't feel it as more than a thin sting of sensation. Dark blood welled up around the silver blade. She let the blood run down to her slightly cupped palm and pool there. Then she tilted two fingers to lightly touch the Bone Collector's stone lips, making a path for that blood.

For a moment, nothing, other than a dark line of liquid running down from the Bone Collector's lips to his cheek, obscenely like when he'd been wounded.

Then she felt him shudder, a movement against her fingers that echoed in the ground. She felt him suck in a breath, and saw faint color flow across his face and even his clothing. His eyes – she'd forgotten how goddamn blue his eyes were – opened wide, then turned to find hers. And then his lips parted, tongue curling to lick the blood away.

She should be happy she'd found him, happy he was alive, and now happy he was awake. And she was, so much it hurt, so much it made her angry. She'd learned long ago in the ugliest way possible that it wasn't safe to care about anyone so much she couldn't breathe. Drowning was a foreign concept to Hob. She could imagine drowning in sand, maybe, buried alive and sinking fast. But looking the Bone Collector in the eyes right now was the closest thing she could imagine to drowning in water. She froze.

The Bone Collector laid one hand over the back of hers, his cool fingers sliding up to grip her wrist. He pulled her down so he could press his lips against the cut she'd made on her forearm. She felt the press of his tongue, a sharp throb of pain, and tried to jerk away. He kept hold of her, and in a panicked moment she thought about drawing one of her pistols. She'd threatened him before, when it felt like he was pushing across a line. But he smoothed his hand over hers again, and it felt damnably good, and her wrist didn't hurt any more.

"Won't you lay down with me?" he whispered.

And she almost said yes, fuck him anyway, unable to avoid wondering what it might feel like to have his arms around her, if that's even what he meant. Might have, if Mag hadn't cleared her throat. "You still need that bandage, Hob?"

Hob tugged her hand back. She felt reluctance in the Bone Collector letting her go, but he didn't fight her. She glanced down at her wrist, mindful of the question she'd been asked: there was blood on her skin, but the wound was gone like it had never been, not even a scar. "Seems it wasn't as bad as it looked."

The Bone Collector slowly pushed himself up on one elbow, twisting to look at Mag. Blood still trailed down his cheek, too far for his tongue to reach. He idly wiped it away with his other hand and licked the red from his fingers. "You seem to have come a long way," he remarked.

Not so long as that, from Ludlow to this point. But Hob knew physical distance wasn't what he meant, felt it in the tone he'd used, before she even saw the set expression on Mag's face. She just wasn't sure what he *did* mean. "Got a question to ask you," Mag said tightly.

The Bone Collector glanced back at Hob, his lips curved in amusement. "And here I thought you'd dug me up because I'd been missed."

"Shut the fuck up," Hob growled. She rose, brushing the sand from her leather trousers. "I got a question or two myself, but Mag should go first."

"So nice to feel wanted," he said dryly, and sat fully up.

Mag came down the slope to squat next to him. She showed him the survey line and the reports like she'd shown Hob, which he didn't seem to comprehend any more than she did. Hob didn't know why they'd expected him to have any better ideas. But when Mag laid out their thoughts about the blue mineral, the Bone Collector grimaced. He rubbed his left forearm, where Hob knew one of his veins was hard and blue with those crystals. "It's something new. Of course they want it." His lip curled in disgust. "And there's more of it than you imagine, though not close to the surface as that. Not out here."

"Deeper," Mag murmured. "That's gonna be a lot more dangerous for all of us."

"More than you know," the Bone Collector said coolly. "It will damage this place fundamentally. It might kill it."

The implication that the planet itself was somehow alive stuck in Hob's craw, but Mag didn't bat an eyelash. "Then I guess you might want to help us."

"You won't be able to reach it."

"What the fuck is it?" Hob asked, hoping for a better answer this time.

The Bone Collector glanced at Mag. "She knows."

"No, I don't."

His lips curled in a smile. "Yes, you do. It's what whispers in your blood." His eyes found Hob's, gaze sharp as a knife. "What makes your fire."

Well, that was a hell of a lot clearer, and Hob found herself wishing it hadn't been. The fire was a thing in her blood, which meant this... crystal was somehow a thing in her blood too, somehow powering her witchiness. "I ain't ever seen that stuff before..." she couldn't help but glance at Mag, "before Phil got murdered."

"You saw it in the sky."

"Sure, I seen a damn rock in the sky." But it was the phoenix again, Hob was sure that was what he meant, the vision she'd had on the verge of death. She wanted to assure herself that those things weren't solidly real, but her missing eye said otherwise. Hob rubbed at her arm with one thumb, half expecting her veins to have gone hard and blue like his had. This seemed to amuse him, which just pissed her off all over again. "Had a good long time to think about it, huh," she snapped.

He laughed. "Is that what you wanted to ask about?"

"No." Without Mag's eloquence, Hob laid out the discovery of Coyote.

"I must see him," the Bone Collector said.

Hob glanced at Mag. "Gotta take Mag home first. You wanna do that... tunneling through rock thing and meet me back at the base?"

"I'd rather do that than ride on your blasted machine."

Hob snorted, thinking about what being yanked through the ground like it wasn't solid had done to her brain and stomach. Mag looked green around the edges just considering it. "Feelin's mutual, cupcake. I'll be back at base tomorrow evening."

She turned and headed back to her motorcycle. The shuffle of Mag's feet through the sand behind her didn't quite cover the Bone Collector's half-bewildered, half-exasperated, "...cupcake?"

Hob grinned as she shoved her helmet on.

CHAPTER SEVEN • 70 DAYS

Mag chewed over her brief conversation with the Bone Collector as she rode behind Hob, back to Ludlow. The only really new piece of information he'd told her was that mining the unknown mineral wouldn't just get a bunch of miners killed as TransRift drove them hard, it would somehow harm the planet itself. The more she thought about it, the more important she realized that was. Not out of concern for the planet – she mentally set that aside as a separate issue she'd really need to think about – but because of what it meant to hear that from the Bone Collector. He might not like the miners much at times, but he hated TransRift and their Weathermen a hell of a lot more, and TransRift would be the one pushing the miners. That meant she might have him as an ally against TransRift again.

She was so caught up in these thoughts that she barely noticed when Hob coasted to a stop. She looked up and saw the town walls – they were still outside. Hob hadn't been shy about coming in before, price on her head or no. "Hob, what's–"

"Take your helmet off and listen," Hob said.

Mag did so, frowning. "The mine works." The cold, *silent* night air bit at her unprotected ears and cheeks:

the mine works had gone still. Normally the endless metallic scrapings and clangings of the drive chain filled the air, driven by electric motor and the muscle power of engineered oxen, until they were background noise that you learned to ignore in order to sleep. Their absence made the hair on the back of her neck stand up. The drive chain only ever stopped for blasting and accidents.

"Something scheduled?" Hob asked.

"No. The gates closed?"

"Looks like."

Had an organized group of bandits attacked? But there was no sign of anything like that. Mag's frown deepened. "Fine. We'll go in a different way. Head to the north side."

"There a gate I don't know about?"

Despite her worry, Mag smiled. "Remember telling me about those escape tunnels Uncle Nick had all around the base? Thought it sounded like a fine idea."

As soon as they were in the walls, Mag heard a far-off murmur of voices that was more damning than the silence of the drive chain could ever be. It wasn't often that many people in the town got all in a group. It made the greenbellies nervous, wasn't worth the risk unless someone was getting married or buried – or they were looking to make a statement. Even at this distance she could tell that the people were angry.

Mag dropped her helmet near the trapdoor they'd come through, with Hob still climbing out behind her. This particular tunnel led into the warehouse furthest from the mine works, which only got used when there'd been unusual train delays for several days running. It had never happened in the entire time Mag had lived in Ludlow.

"Mag?"

She made a vague gesture at Hob – *stay here* – and kept going at not quite a run. The streets were deserted, strange in a town that ran all hours of the day.

Ludlow had been spared the witch hunt of the previous year thanks to the Wolves killing the Weatherman before he got there. And Mag had thought she'd done enough cajoling and reasoning and shouting to get it through all the thick skulls in the town that the witchy ones weren't the problem, that the company was just trying to keep them all divided.

But as she made her way toward the sound – by the mine, it had to be by the mine, but that didn't make her feel that much better since the train depot was over there too – her mind produced image after horrified image of witchy people hanged, witchy people about to be burned, and Anabi–

Anabi's beautiful, dark face gone black with strangled death. Anabi struggling to free herself as she was doused with cooking oil. Aside from Mag, Anabi was the witchiest one in town, and she'd only just started to relax and unfold in perceived safety.

A hand clamped on her arm and Mag bit back a yelp. She turned to see Anabi, reaching out from the doorway of the company store. Anabi shook her head when Mag tried to speak. Her face was pinched with worry and fear. She held out a bit of flimsy, an old report, that she'd written over in grease pencil: *Accident at the mine earlier. Walkout. Clarence said stay back.*

Mag read the words again, just to make sure she had them. The third sentence, she had a problem with. When she'd first come to Ludlow, hanging back had been important, because she was a wanted woman. But she'd established her new identity over these last months. Now it was just Clarence being a soft, overprotective fool like he really was her uncle, and it served only to tell her that he thought things were going to get ugly.

She gave the flimsy back to Anabi. "Stay here. I ain't gonna let this alone." When Anabi opened her mouth in mute protest, Mag found one of her hands and squeezed it. "These are my people too. Clarence should've damn well figured that out by now."

Anabi gripped her hand tightly for a moment, but stayed in the doorway when Mag turned and walked toward the train depot, her shoulders set.

There was blood on the smooth, light gray surface of the plascrete pad they'd built in front of the train station in anticipation of the Weatherman's arrival months ago. Smears and clouds of it, a crumpled form in mining coveralls that Mag hoped wasn't dead. The miners, all of the night shift and a large part of the day shift that Clarence must have roused out of their beds, flooded the square and the streets around. They shoved and shouted, surging against a line of men in dark green and blue suits. The company men, Mag realized dizzily, were badly outnumbered. But they also had guns, and she needed to not forget that. The roar of shouting, men and women from both sides, was deafening.

One of the Mariposa men raised his rifle. The miners surged unevenly, some trying to struggle forward, some trying to flee. Mag stumbled, shoved in first one direction, then the other. She couldn't make out what the guard shouted as he pointed his rifle at the crowd, and it didn't matter.

A shoulder slammed against hers and she ignored it. She focused on the guard, staring until he was the only thing in the world. Somehow through the surge and press of so many people, so many minds, she found him all hot with anger and fear and hate for the damned lazy rats, looking for an excuse to riot – she grasped him hard with her mind and whispered: "*No.*"

He froze, then lowered his rifle. A miner broke through the line and lunged at him, but got snatched up before they could make contact by another greenbelly. Then she saw Clarence, coming in that break, trying to separate them, his mouth open to roar.

Mag focused on the miner and security guard. She found them too, pressed against them, and said: "*Stop.*"

It made sense, that a single, focused, simple command was easier to grind into someone than a complex creation, like telling them to forget some things and remember others. Her head throbbed sharply and she ignored it. Clarence had the small fight under control and was shouting again. Another guard raised his rifle, and she quelled him. Blood tickled in her nose and on her chin and tasted thickly metallic on her tongue. Someone shoved her from behind, and another person caught her.

Another miner to quell. Another security man. A hand gripped her arm, supporting her. She didn't bother to look and see who, because it felt familiar, not hostile. The crack of fist against flesh as she was jostled again, but it wasn't her fist or her flesh, so she ignored it.

And then somehow, by some grace she didn't believe in, she heard Clarence's shout over the crowd. "Stop! Stop!"

The miners quieted to a dull roar, glaring at the security men, who glared right back at them. Mag sagged a little bit against the person next to her. She had a dim perception of tall and lanky, brown hair in plaits – of course it was Hob.

She watched the pit boss, Bill Weld, finally let himself out of the train depot. He was a big man with a pronounced bald spot. At the sight of him, the assembled miners howled out a chorus of boos and jeers. Clarence waved them to something close to silence again.

"Well, Bill?" Clarence asked, loud enough for everyone to hear. "We're waitin' for your answer."

Bill looked nervously around the crowd as there was another roar of sound, more ferocious than jeering. "After reviewing the incident report and Corporate guidelines…" he paused for more shouting "…I have concluded that your request to have the mine down for a complete safety inspection is not…" a swelling roar of triumph that he gave up trying to shout over, "…is *not* out of line. Work resumes tomorrow at 18:30 hours. We will take *volunteers*–" the crowd erupted into loud booing "–for the inspection."

Clarence waited patiently for the miners to quiet down. "We thank you kindly for reconsidering your first decision," he said, ignoring the few jeers that erupted from the crowd at that. "I look forward to meetin' with you tomorrow to take a look at the inspection results." He turned back toward the crowd. "Everyone not on a safety crew, go ahead and get home."

The miners roared at the line of Mariposa men still standing at Bill Weld's back. One of the greenbellies – Captain Longbridge with his square shoulders and shaved-off hair, the security chief – started raising a hand, a rifle toward Clarence. Mag had only to feel that intent. She smashed Longbridge flat with the weight of her will, ruthless. He staggered and strained, fighting her, but she held him long enough for Clarence to move out of his line of sight.

And slowly, the crowd began to peel away, people from both shifts filtering back to their homes.

Next to her, Hob shoved a handkerchief into her hand. Mag used it to plug her nose. Only then did the enormity of what she'd done hit her. She'd used this power she still didn't really understand to stop a riot. To stop the Mariposa men from hurting her people. Part of her was horrified, but it had been necessary. It had saved a lot of blood, at least for tonight.

"I think you should come back to base with me," Hob said, bending to speak in her ear.

Mag shook her head. She thought about Anabi. She needed to find a way to soothe the fear out of her face. She needed to talk to Clarence. She had a million other *need to*s crowding around her, and the sudden exhaustion that flowed out of her bones and threatened to drag her flat didn't matter. "No," she said thickly. "Got too much work to do."

Mag found Anabi where she'd been hiding by the company store, though she had to practically swim through the crowd of miners heading back to their homes to do it. She still had Hob's handkerchief pinching her nose, but with her other hand, she found Anabi's and gripped it tight. "It's OK," she mumbled around the handkerchief. "Clarence got 'em all calmed down for now."

Anabi's grip near crushed Mag's fingers, her palm fear-damp. She stuck close to Mag as they headed back to Clarence's house. Mag got her seated at the kitchen table and made a cup of tea for her one-handed. She wasn't sure if it was to make Anabi or herself feel better that she stood next to her and kept her hand on the woman's broad shoulder.

"Hope you weren't waitin' on me too long," she said, after she felt some of the tension go out of Anabi. The woman shook her head, and reached up to pat her hand, then carefully leaned back against her. That was just fine with Mag, feeling Anabi breathe against her.

They still stood like that when Clarence came in. He looked exhausted; he was supposed to have long since been asleep. "Was wonderin' when you'd get back," he said.

Anabi finally slid away from Mag, so she could go about getting Clarence something to drink. He offered her a grateful nod.

"Might've got some information," Mag offered. She took Anabi's seat. "That new ore the company's lookin' for, they ain't gonna find it here or in any of the towns. And it's deep. Real deep."

Clarence blew out a breath. "Somewhere else and real deep. That don't sound good."

"What happened?" Mag asked. "Shaft collapse?"

"Yeah," he nodded. "They ain't takin' the proper time, and they ain't been lettin' us give the timbers time to settle. Was bound to happen."

"How many?"

"Six, this time."

It could have been worse, she knew. But six down was six too many, and it didn't need to be that way. "So we walked out?"

"We walked out," Clarence agreed. "And they ain't takin' kindly to it. But Bill listened."

"Halfway." She hadn't missed the part about the safety "volunteers." And it could have been a riot, with a lot more than six dead. She could feel it coming, on the horizon.

"Can't count on him," Clarence agreed. "He's a company man, for all he likes to play merciful god."

Mag laughed softly, without humor. Most other towns weren't as lucky as Ludlow, and luck never held. "You find that merciful god, you tell the rest of us, hear?"

Clarence raised his glass to her.

CHAPTER EIGHT • *69 DAYS*

"Good morning, Mr Rolland."

"Good morning, Dr Ekwensi." Shige smiled politely at her. They'd established a routine of sorts over the successive days of visits, which had the desired effect of attenuating the doctor's undercurrent of suspicion. Today, Dr Ekwensi offered him a slightly distracted smile in return as she looked off into the middle distance. It was a look he recognized as meaning she was going over some sort of data on the local network. "Is Mr Yellow feeling more himself today?"

"He seems to recover more quickly from the calibrations after your visits," she said, after a long pause. "Some of that might be that gross adjustments have given way to fine tuning, but the size of the calibration has never had a linear relationship to how the Weathermen react to it." She blinked, seeming to finally recall to whom she spoke. "Feel free to proceed at your leisure."

Shige had long known how to ingratiate himself within the TransRift Corporate system; it was gratifying to know that the culture changed little in the labs. Show up, be consistently quiet and efficient, be pleased with work but not too loudly cheerful, and silently resist all attempts to be sent away. It wasn't a recipe for getting noticed, but rather for becoming part of the office equipment, accepted and ignored. It was a work role that suited his purposes.

He faced the door into the Weatherman's room, which had formed in the wall during his short conversation with Dr Ekwensi. He no longer had to steel himself to enter it; familiarity bred ease in him too, which he needed to be more cautious about.

The dry, bloody smell of the room still made his skin go tight with the anticipation of flight, though he was prepared for that now. As he entered the room, Mr Yellow moved immediately. This was new. Before, he'd only ever reacted after being directly addressed. Shige halted, keeping the motion soft.

Slowly, Mr Yellow pushed himself up onto his hands, leaning one bare hip on the floor. His head, freshly shaved so that it was pale as an egg, hung down as if too heavy for his neck.

"Hello, Mr Yellow," Shige said, after waiting to see if the Weatherman would move more. "Or rather, good morning. It is morning, you know. Would you like to hear what the mornings on Tanegawa's World shall be like?"

"The wind blows," Mr Yellow whispered. This was the first Shige had heard him speak, and he'd half-expected his voice to be the same ragged croak he'd always heard from Mr Green. But Mr Yellow's voice was very pleasant and surprisingly deep, the kind of voice he would have expected to hear in theater or music. There was no block of scar tissue to interfere with his throat. "And it is always dry. Are you thirsty, brother?"

Hearing the word *brother* washed coldly through Shige's stomach, but he kept his expression smooth, slightly curious. James Rolland was an only child. Shigehiko Rollins and all the complicated tangles that came from the word brother – *you know they had you made in a lab like one of mom's custom roses* – did not exist in this place. "I'm afraid I don't have any brothers. Do you?"

"Many," Mr Yellow agreed. "None. All the same. We sing together at night. We will eat each other."

He used every trick he knew to commit the words to memory as Mr Yellow spoke them. He'd learned to not ignore what Mr Green said, even if it had made little sense at the time. The problem was that he did not know how the Weathermen thought, and no one in TransRift seemed to care. They were living black boxes that performed miracles. "Are you hungry?" Shige asked. An innocuous answer seemed best, since he had little doubt Dr Ekwensi was watching keenly by now. "Thirsty?"

"Always hungry. Always thirsty. Always drowning," Mr Yellow said, though by his tone he wasn't particularly bothered. "Does the wind blow?"

"I don't know. I haven't been outside in days." The atmosphere wasn't particularly pleasant on Earth anymore; nearly as hot as Tanegawa's World, but heavy with humidity and filled with pollutants and particulates. "Would you like me to check?"

"We will grasp it," Mr Yellow said. And he began to hum to himself again, that same eerie music as before.

Shige listened for a few minutes, then tried, "Would you like me to tell you about the winds on your new home?" Mr Yellow didn't seem to hear him this time, still humming. After Shige judged he'd been at it long enough, he exited the room.

"I didn't realize he'd started talking," he said to Dr Ekwensi.

"He hadn't. That was the first he's spoken since we upgraded his neural net." She wasn't even bothering to look at Shige. "It's remarkable. He's… yes. He's trying to interfere with Earth's atmosphere. That pattern is for the magnetic field–"

"Can he?"

"Don't be stupid. We have them governed when they're on regulated worlds."

"Of course, my mistake." Shige filed that little fact and all its attendant implications away for later. Since she seemed so distracted, he offered: "I never noticed Mr Green speaking of himself as *we*."

"They often do that when first decanted. We take care to train that out of them, since they need to understand themselves as individual actors. Mr Yellow seems to have... reverted." She didn't sound like she was talking to him any more, but rather to herself. She began patting down the pockets of her lab coat.

"Is something the matter, doctor?"

"I want to run him through the basic repatterning game again, but I left the module in my office. I didn't think he'd progress this far already..." She trailed off as Mr Yellow pushed himself unsteadily to his feet.

"Would you like me to fetch it for you?" Shige offered gently.

Eyes still fixed on Mr Yellow, she pulled a lanyard with a code tag on it over her neck. "Office 171. There's a green carry box on the cabinet next to the door. Bring the entire thing."

"Of course," Shige said, taking the lanyard. This was the opportunity he'd been waiting for, the entire purpose of the daily visits and his quest to make himself at least temporarily indispensable. "I'll be back in just a moment."

Shige shut the door of Dr Ekwensi's office. With the proper code tag confirmed by entry, he slipped it into a thin memory film sleeve that served as a tag copier, one of the bits of helpful technology that had been in

Ayana's promised resupply. As soon as he removed the tag, the sleeve would bond up into a code-perfect copy, suitable for later use. He now had access to everything that Dr Ekwensi did, so long as he was cautious about it and didn't do anything that would alert the security algorithms to suspicion. And considering Dr Ekwensi was the head of the program, there should be little barred to him now.

That was the only delay he allowed in his task, that and a quick glance around the office so he could confirm where the doctor kept her dumb terminal – tasks that required multiple displays were still best completed on larger canvases than one's optic nerves – and where the security monitors discreetly hovered. That was another bit of training he'd have to do; no doubt his presence would be remarked upon today, and Dr Ekwensi could confirm he had her permission to be in her office. After that, he'd be able to do nearly anything he liked without security being alerted. Scientists were like management, in that they didn't like being bothered with the details of their underlings' coming and going.

He stopped his circuit of the room at the cabinet Dr Ekwensi had mentioned, for all the world like he'd merely been looking for that. Then he picked up the green toolbox and hurried back down the hall.

With luck, the doctor would make his life easier by sending him back to her office at least twice more before he and Mr Yellow departed for Tanegawa's World: once to use the code tag to plant a data acquisition leech into the terminal and thus the private network of the labs, and a second time to retrieve it, with all of the files for his queries invisibly copied over. Otherwise, he'd manufacture his own reasons to be there.

He stopped next to Dr Ekwensi. Inside his room, Mr Yellow walked slowly past the walls, one hand sliding along them, his head still hanging. "Doctor? Is this the right toolbox?"

"Oh!" She started and looked at him. "What? Yes. Thank you, Mr Rolland. You've been very helpful."

Shige smiled as he handed the toolbox to her. "I am always glad to be of service."

CHAPTER NINE • *69 DAYS*

"Shoulda tied her ass to the back of my bike," Hob muttered to herself as her motorcycle rolled to a stop in the entrance of the base's garage. It was dark, close, hot, and stank of grease. Motorcycles, each lovingly modified to suit the preferred weapons of its rider but alike in sandblasted paint jobs and lack of identifying marks, lined each wall.

"What was that?" Hati, the garage master, asked. His deep red-brown skin sported smudges of grime, one of them right over the crooked bridge of a big nose that had its already low profile repeatedly flattened in fights. His long black hair was tied back in two tight braids.

"Nothin' for you to worry about." Hob tossed him her helmet.

"You're in later than you said you'd be."

Hob toed her kickstand down and stepped off. One advantage of being in charge was that she didn't have to do the maintenance on her own bike any more. Hati had always done better than she could anyway. "Some excitement in Ludlow."

"Shootin' kind?"

Hob sucked at her teeth. "Near thing."

Hati let out a low whistle. "Gonna be a fat contract

rollin' in from there afore long."

"Hope you're wrong on that, but I don't think ya are." Another damn reason she should have just knocked Mag over the head and dragged her off. Hob pulled her saddlebag off her motorcycle and looped it over her shoulder.

"Oh," Hati said. "That pale friend of yours blew in about six hours ago. Last I seen, he's been talkin' with the sand out in Lobo's garden."

Hob froze for just a second. Well, she'd told him to meet her here. She should probably count herself lucky that he hadn't gotten bored waiting and fucked off. If bored was even a thing someone who spent part of his life being a rock did. "Anythin' else interesting happen while I was away?"

Hati shrugged. "Only know about him 'cause he came through to collect his fuckin' dust catcher." The Bone Collector's staff had been living in a corner of the garage since they killed the Weatherman, the wildcat skull on top glaring at everyone who passed it on their way to mount up. "Nobody tells me nothin'."

Hati wasn't so isolated as that. He just preferred to sit in the corner of the garage and scribble long stories out in the margins of recycled flimsies. Everyone on base had been subjected to reading at least one of his efforts; it was another hazing ritual for the newcomers. The real hell of it was, not that anyone would ever admit it to Hati, he wasn't half bad. Hob waved in acknowledgment of his well-worn complaint and headed into the yard.

The entire base, a square with the yard a hole in its center, was brown and orange, hung with tarps and camouflage nets to keep it safe from the extremely rare security flight or drone that dared the unpredictable weather and magnetic fields. The Bone Collector was a pale shape against the camouflage netting that hid the dark green shoots of Lobo's garden, which the cook had recently re-planted after confirming they had enough extra water for it. His staff, the wildcat skull turned unerringly toward her, stood straight up from the ground next to him.

He turned as soon as she emerged from the garage and walked toward her. There was something different about the motion, Hob could tell immediately. He had never been the kind to bound around or make a show of being athletic, but there'd always been a kind of lightness to his step before, like he floated bare millimeters above the ground instead of touching. Now, he seemed heavy, or at least in the same class as the rest of them mere mortals. As he came closer, she noted the lines of his face, harsh in the morning sun. She hadn't noticed them before – the man looked *tired*.

"Sorry to keep ya waitin'," Hob said.

"I suppose it's only fair." He offered her a small, tilted smile, one she realized she'd missed, somehow. Like hell she wanted to miss someone who only showed up when it was convenient to his mysterious act. But he reached out to touch her hand with just the tips of his fingers, and she didn't know what to make of that either.

Before she had a chance to say or do something stupid in either direction, the door that led up into the offices and supply rooms popped open. It was a hell of a relief to see Freki, the close-cropped black hair on his head showing no sign of the white lock that marked out his brother. He must have been watching for her from her office window; it had the best view of the yard.

"Ravani." He spared a quick look at the Bone Collector, a quirk of one brow that let her know she'd better spill the story to him later. "*He* woke up. Ain't pretty."

There was no doubt from his tone just which *he* Freki meant. Hob looked at the Bone Collector. "All yours."

They'd been ready for Coyote to wake up and go wrong, Hob saw. Someone had thought to rig a ring in one of the hallway walls so they could secure his door shut with rope. Benefits of them all being paranoid desert rats keen on not being murdered in their beds.

"Bala's asleep. Went off before… before *he* woke up, and I thought it best he keep sleepin'," Geri said, in answer to Hob's questioning look. He'd stationed himself outside the door in a chair, a tattered sheaf of recycled flimsies on his knee – and yes, there was the title of one of Hati's efforts, *The Ghost Rider Along Red Ridge*.

She ignored the question he silently asked her in return, the mirror of his twin brother's – same eyebrow twitch and everything – as the Bone Collector slid past her and laid his hands on the door. "You think you can handle this?" she asked.

The Bone Collector tilted his head slightly, eyes half-closed, like he was listening. Under his hands, the door shook, like Coyote slammed his body against it from the other side. There was no sound but a *thump* and muffled, ragged breathing. "Yes. Open the door."

Well, what the hell else could they do? This was what she'd brought the Bone Collector here for.

She heard a soft splatter of pages on her blind side, and turned to see that Geri had dropped his novel on the floor and drawn his pistol. Hob slid one of the knives from her sleeve and held it poised over the rope as the doorknob rattled again. "In three… two…" The Bone Collector smiled like he thought it was funny, the bastard. But she kept going, because he might be able to turn into stone, but she and Geri were both very vulnerable to having their soft parts eaten. "One."

Her knife was sharp and the rope holding the door shut was under a lot of tension. The blade sliced through cleanly. The Bone Collector put his shoulder against the door – somehow, she'd never envisioned him doing something like that, it seemed too physical – and shoved it.

There was a thump, a crash, and the door sprang open. Hob caught a glimpse inside, of Coyote's compact, emaciated form sprawled out on the floor. He started scrabbling to his feet. Someone had shaved his hair, once one of his points of vanity, off while she'd been gone, probably because it was the only way to get rid of the knots. There was nothing hiding his face with its wild and inhuman expression.

An instant later, the Bone Collector was on him, pinning him to the floor with both hands and one knee. Coyote screamed, struggling. The Bone Collector might as well have been made of stone again, for all it moved him. His eyes were fixed on Coyote, lips moving. And slowly, Coyote began to quiet down, struggles ceasing and screams turning to whimpers. Hob could hear then that the Bone Collector wasn't speaking, but singing, the song Hob knew – the song Coyote had been singing in his sleep.

The Bone Collector leaned closer and closer to him, until their cheeks were almost touching. Coyote closed his eyes tightly, and his lips moved, though she couldn't tell what he said.

"Give me the knife," the Bone Collector said quietly.

Hob didn't move until he looked back at her; she'd almost missed the words because he'd gone back to singing seamlessly, like that was just another part of the song. She flipped the blade in her hand and offered him the hilt, leaning in enough so he could take it.

Still softly singing, the Bone Collector straightened enough to cut a line down his arm with the knife. He offered the freely bleeding wound to Coyote.

"Are you fuckin' serious?" Geri whispered behind her.

Coyote latched on to the Bone Collector's arm, lips closing around that flowing blood, hands clutching like it was a lifeline. Hob looked back at Geri, her stomach turning. "You ain't seen nothin'," she said.

"Sure as fuck don't want to be seein' this," Geri agreed.

Hob kept looking at Geri, for once not out of hostility, but because she didn't want to see what was going on with the off-kilter breathing and soft swallowing sounds behind her. Geri kept his eyes fixed on her, she would have bet for the same reasons. Some things, a body just didn't need to witness.

Slowly, she became aware that the sounds stopped, difficult to notice after trying so hard to ignore them.

"You gonna look?" Geri asked.

"*You* gonna?" she asked.

"Wouldn't want to steal your thunder."

Hob snorted and turned. The two men had shifted, Coyote prone on the floor, the Bone Collector leaned over him so that their foreheads lightly touched, his hands planted firm on the floor on either side of Coyote's head. A vivid smear of blood dragged out the corner of Coyote's mouth. There was something about looking at that which felt so intimate, it made her feel even more uncomfortable than the whole blood-drinking thing. Seemed she was discovering some standards she'd never known she had.

The Bone Collector pushed himself up slowly to sit back on his haunches. Coyote opened his eyes and looked around, his gaze fixing on Hob. He was there again, at home in his own eyes, that quick intelligence burning brightly as he scooted back to lean against the bed frame.

The Bone Collector wiped Hob's knife off with his handkerchief and offered it back to her. "He's seen it."

"Seen what?" Hob asked, stepping into the room. It was a wreck, every piece of furniture but the bed overturned.

The Bone Collector's eyes were fixed on hers. "The deepest part of the world. The place that is not a place, from which all life and change comes." He turned his arm over, the one he'd cut, and there was no wound there now. Not even a scar. But Hob saw the hard blue vein under his skin, a thing that had showed up after he'd once vanished for weeks and come back half-spooky. "I've been there in my own way. I didn't think anyone else ever had. Or ever would."

Hob looked over at Coyote, who was trying to wipe the worst of the blood from his mouth with his sleeve, like he was embarrassed. He offered her a crooked, uncertain grin. "What happened to you?" she asked. She really wanted to ask: *was it the same thing that happened to me?* Maybe that was why she suddenly didn't want anyone else listening in.

"I don't know. I don't... I don't remember so many things."

Hob righted the room's single chair and sat down on it, on the very edge. It wobbled alarmingly under her. Coyote was near twenty centimeters shorter than her on a good day, and she didn't feel right looming over him while he was looking so small. "Begin at the beginning. You were in Harmony town. I know that much. They had you locked up. Your brother let you out."

Coyote sat back, startled. "How do you... no, never mind. He told you, obviously."

"I think he's an asshole, if that makes ya feel any better," Hob said dryly.

Coyote relaxed a few centimeters with a sheepish laugh. "It does, actually. What did he tell you about me?"

"Personally? Nothin', and I didn't ask. Give me some

credit. Harmony. You were in Harmony town."

"Right." Coyote sketched out the details, confirming what Dambala had found out months ago about his capture and escape. Mentally putting together some kind of report seemed to steady him as well. "And then I kept walking, until I couldn't walk any more. I thought I heard... Do you know what a real coyote sounds like? That yipping. I hallucinated one speaking to me, and I made a deal with him." He huffed an odd little laugh. "I said I'd teach him to run with a pack, if he'd just show me water."

Hob examined her own hands for a moment, and called up sparks to dance across her fingertips. "There are worse deals to make for survival."

"I imagine so," Coyote said.

"What happened after that?"

"That's when it gets... blurry. From hallucination to incoherent. I remember walking... so long. Forever. I remember..." A shudder ran through his body. "I remember drinking. Water. But it wasn't water. Not blood, either. But... like it, somehow. Rich. Deep down. Like a well," Coyote finished hollowly.

"A well from which all things drink." The Bone Collector traced the hard blue line under his skin. "From which all power flows."

Hob could put two and two together easy enough. A "well" of some kind that was the source of the blue mineral, and therefore the source of all that witchiness. And now they knew TransRift was looking for that mineral for their own reasons, which meant they damn well better not get it. Hob took a mental step back from all the implications and the spooky half meanings and focused on the practical. That was what she was good for, point and shoot. "Where?"

"I can't remember," Coyote said.

The Bone Collector shook his head, voice becoming slow and thoughtful. "I don't know."

"Well, that's fuckin' helpful." Hob sucked at her teeth.

The Bone Collector rubbed his face with one hand, covering his eyes. "I almost lost myself in that well before, Hob. It's... too massive. Not a place like you understand it."

Coyote managed a dry laugh. "I did lose myself and haven't gotten all the bits back yet."

"You're stable for now," the Bone Collector said, barely more than a whisper.

"D'ya think..." She realized that the Bone Collector's head had drooped down even more. "Did he... Is he *asleep*?"

Coyote leaned forward and chuckled, a little strained. "It would seem so. I don't think I drank that much."

Hob huffed a laugh. Laughing was better than sorting through the million things that made her want to scream just now. "Ya mind if we stick him in your bed?"

"Then where will I go?"

"We ain't sold your old bed yet," Hob said. There was a flash of shame on his face, fleeting, and Hob hated that she'd landed in a world where shit could happen that could make Coyote of all people feel ashamed. "Ya feel up to dealin' with the others now?"

"Do I have a choice?"

"You know you don't. Ain't that much room around here." But she knew that feeling so intimately herself. She'd spent years re-earning her place in the Wolves after she'd fucked up titanically. Though in her case, she supposed with grim amusement, it hadn't involved cannibalism. Old Nick might have been more forgiving of that. "And you're gonna have to talk to Dambala eventually."

"I don't know what to say."

Hob raised an eyebrow. "That'll be the fuckin' day. You could talk the feathers off an eagle."

"Yes, but I don't care in the slightest what the eagle thinks of me later." He laughed again, a more despairing sound. "Don't tell anyone about the blood?"

"It don't get better, exactly. But you get used to it," she offered.

"Is it more of that witchiness, like you and Nick always pretended carefully not to have?"

"Might be," Hob said. "But I ain't the expert. Scat. Go get some food and bring Bala his breakfast in bed. Ought to get you on his good side."

Geri cleared his throat from the hall. She'd almost forgotten he was there. "You think that's a good idea?"

Hob raised an eyebrow toward Coyote. "Think you can get your ass back here, you start feelin'... thirsty again?"

"I can balance my machismo against not wanting to come back to my senses and find I've chewed up the face of someone I like," Coyote said dryly, like it didn't matter. But she saw in the dark brown of his eyes that it mattered to him, a hell of a lot.

"Go on, then."

"Hob..." Geri said as Coyote brushed by him.

"We ain't in a position here to be havin' prisoners," Hob said. She gave the Bone Collector an experimental prod, and his eyes half opened. She nudged him toward the bed, and he slowly unfolded to standing. "Coyote knows that. We gotta find out if he can keep his shit together."

"And if he can't?" Geri asked.

She kept a firm grip on the Bone Collector's arm to guide him the few steps and help him sit. This was an ugly thing to be talking about, but there wasn't much of being in charge that she'd found to be pretty yet. "Either the Bone Collector takes him, or Coyote'll do what he's gotta."

"Fuck," Geri muttered. "Don't seem right, dyin' twice."

Hob snorted. "It's what happens when it don't take right the first time." But she didn't want it to be that way either. She'd killed Coyote once, sending him off on his own. She didn't want to do it again. Hob glanced over her shoulder at Geri. "Go get yourself a cup of coffee."

Geri's lip curled. "Need a minute?"

Well, it had been days since Geri had been a prick to her. It was nice to know some things were still right in the world. "Yeah, I'm gonna fuck him and don't want an audience. The fuck do you think? Get out of here."

She wasn't sure if he got the sarcasm or if he'd be whispering nastiness around the base in the next five minutes. And she realized, as he shut the door, that she didn't have to give a shit either way. She wasn't the fuckup trainee any more, and this was her goddamn base.

Hob sank down onto the edge of the narrow bed. The Bone Collector had already stretched out, his eyes closed. Fine, because he didn't have to be awake. She pulled off her gloves and felt his forehead – seemed cool enough – then unbuttoned his waistcoat, then his shirt. Halfway done with the small, yellowed bone buttons, his hands moved to clasp over hers.

"Undressing me?" he asked, eyes opened to bare slits.

"Last time I saw, you got shot." She continued unbuttoning his shirt, and he didn't stop her. But it did feel powerful strange, for his hands to be over hers. She did her best to pretend that her stomach wasn't doing a weird, slow flip, filled with emotion she did not want to acknowledge.

Under the shirt, he was pale as ever and thin, which

was what she'd expected. He wasn't the muscular sort. What strength he had flowed out of his brand of witchiness, and maybe it ate him from the inside. The bullet wound that had taken him down was still visible in his side, angry and red. It didn't look much healed, like it really should have opened back up with all the moving around. "You shoulda been healed up by now," she said. "If I'd been shot like that, I woulda been."

"Time doesn't pass the same way for me, when I'm in the ground," he said, almost sighing out the words.

"Would you have died?"

He was silent so long, she thought he'd fallen asleep again. But then carefully, he slipped his fingers between hers. "Yes."

"Need me to take you back?"

"No. I just need… time." His fingers tightened slightly against hers, and she let him pull her hand away, up to rest on his chest. "Now that I'm here, I'd miss you too much."

She swallowed thickly. "Keep talkin' like that and I might think you like me." She didn't want to walk down that path again, even if there were certain parts of her that begged to differ just now. Those same parts being what made her move her fingers lightly against his, and brush her fingertips against the smooth skin of his chest.

A tired smile curved his lips. "I shouldn't want to give you any other impression." He tugged at her hand lightly. "Won't you lay down with me?"

She wasn't strong enough to say *no* a second time, with no one watching. Feeling a hundred kinds of foolish, she stretched out along the edge of the bed on her side. She felt the rise and fall of him breathing, even the faint beat of his heart. Both served as steady reminders that he was here, and alive, even if they couldn't answer her anger at herself for caring about either of those things.

The Bone Collector turned his head to rest against hers. His lips were so close to hers she could almost... "No. Don't." She wasn't even sure if she was saying that to him or herself.

"Don't what?" When she didn't answer, he squeezed her hand, his eyes slipping shut. "It feels good to have you here, is that so strange?"

Hob took a deep breath and closed her own eye for a moment, trying to sort out her thoughts. Because it wasn't strange at all, other than maybe what would feel good would be more than just cramming onto a tiny bed with him. She could imagine all too easily kissing him, unbuttoning him down to the skin, riding him as he arched into her. She hadn't had anything between her legs but her own goddamn hand for so long, she ached with it. But it would be one thing, if he was a way to get herself off and she wouldn't have to worry about him again. She liked him too much in all his infuriating strangeness. Even assuming he fucked like regular men did, since he sure as hell didn't do anything else half normal. She licked her lips. "The hell do you want from me?"

No answer. She opened her eye to find he'd fallen asleep again, a soft smile on his face. All that saved him from a punch in the throat was how damn relieved she was that she wouldn't have to hear his answer.

CHAPTER TEN • 69 DAYS

"It was an accident," Bill Weld said. "Accidents happen. You know that, Clarence." Behind him, the town's security chief, Captain Longbridge, glowered over his crossed arms. The high neck of his Mariposa green uniform almost swallowed his chin. It would've looked funny, if the man wasn't a chunk of solid meanness denser than any rock.

Clarence leaned forward, the table creaking beneath his elbows. Even outside, huddled up against the window so she could eavesdrop, Mag felt drawn by his intensity. Clarence kept his tone reasonable somehow. "Don't try to bury me in shit and call it rock dust, Bill. It stops bein' an accident when the safety crew pay dries up, and we're goin' too deep, and you're drivin' us too hard with quotas." Bill tried to interrupt, but Clarence raised his voice and just kept talking. "I'm not gonna ask my people to risk their lives for this."

"They aren't your people. They're my employees. Just like you." Bill sat back, crossing his arms over his chest. He was normally a good sort, as pit bosses went. Normally willing to listen to Clarence and Odalia. "We all have quotas, and I hear you folk like to eat."

"You ain't gonna be makin' too many quotas without

us," Odalia said, from where she stood just behind Clarence.

"The both of you are getting a bit high and mighty," Longbridge growled behind Bill. Something about it, the tone maybe, ran a shiver down Mag's back. The pit boss nodded.

"If we're not that important, you won't mind if we take a few days off then," Clarence said laconically. "See if you can find other people, can run the crews so smooth."

Bill's expression darkened. "You don't want to go down this road, Clarence. If we miss our quotas, Corporate will want to know why. And they'll decide they should fix the problem instead of leaving it in my hands. Do you want that?"

"What we want," Odalia cut in, "is regular safety inspection of the mines. Like we used to have. And for safety work to be *paid*. I'm pretty damn sure you don't want Corporate stickin' their noses up your ass any more than we do."

"What you have to worry about isn't the noses," Bill said. He stood. "You think about it, both of you, before you make this trouble any worse. Think about how good you have it here."

"Is good the part where we lose another work crew in an accident?" Clarence asked.

Bill didn't answer that, just raised his eyebrows and walked out the door. Longbridge stayed and stared at Clarence fit to shoot him.

Clarence and Odalia both ignored Longbridge as they moved toward the door. Mag slid off the windowsill, ready to scuttle away from the building. Neither of them knew she was there. But as she headed down the side street, she heard a sickeningly familiar crack, the sound of something unyielding hitting flesh, and a shout from Odalia.

She turned and ran back.

Longbridge blocked off the doorway of the office, a squad of his men packing in behind him. Mag gasped and pulled back around the corner before they could spot her. But she could hear muffled yelling, the crack of rifle butts meeting muscle and bone, from out here. Clarence had thrown himself over Odalia, taking blows meant for her.

Mag leaned around the corner, driven by urgency, and reached to try to grasp at the greenbellies. There were twelve total, between those blocking the door and those inside. She pulled at a couple of them, and saw their backs stiffen in response. *Stop*, she forced on them. But that was only two, and she felt her control slip away even as she reached for more. She was rushing too much, trying to do too many things at a time. She hauled back Longbridge's fist as he raised it, made him hesitate, then he snarled, "You're behind all the trouble in this goddamn town," and swung at Clarence. She felt fist crack on cheekbone from both sides.

More. She needed all of them. Her hands moved involuntarily as she tried to grasp the whole group of them, swaying with their violence. It had seemed easier, somehow, in the crowd before, but she didn't have the attention to consider why. Her head throbbed and her nose tickled, and she felt like her eyes were going to pop out of her head from the pressure.

Too many. She couldn't grab them all at once, and as she slowed one greenbelly, another would shove them aside, lip curled, and take their place. Mag sank to her knees, still trying to find a way to control them all, her vision starting to black out.

And then they stopped. Not because she told them, but because they were done. They dragged Clarence and Odalia – still alive, they were both still alive, she dimly felt that over the echo of blood pounding in her ears – out in front of the office and dropped them both. Then walked away like they were trash. They passed right by Mag, huddled against the corner of the schoolhouse, and didn't even notice her.

Dizzy, Mag dragged herself to her feet and staggered to the two crew leaders. She fell to her knees by Clarence, fumbling for her handkerchief to press against the bleeding gash on his head. He groaned and opened his eyes into swollen slits. "Hold this," Mag told him. Nothing in his arm *looked* broken, so she dragged his hand up and pressed it against the handkerchief. "I'm gonna get help."

There wasn't anything else she could do. She'd tried, and failed. She staggered to her feet and ran down the street, heading for the nearest house.

"We don't want no one startin' fights right now," Clarence said, enunciating each word carefully through his bloody lips. His face barely looked like a face any more.

"Do you really expect us to do nothing?" Ira Chadha said, crossing her arms over her chest. She was a dayshift miner, one of Clarence's. Hers was the house Mag had come to first, and her entire family had rushed out to help her bring Clarence and Odalia into their living room. Her husband, Arjun, was doing his best to doctor them both with help from his oldest son, Sai. Arjun had been on the night shift when Mag first arrived, but he'd lost most of his right leg in an accident with the drive chain not long after.

"We're ready to fight," Arjun added. "This is enough. Too much. Our oldest–"

"I'm right here," Sai said. "And I want to fight, too!"

Arjun shot him a nasty look and he quieted, "–is about to leave the breakers to join Ira in the mine. We want better for him!"

"I want to fight too, but not yet. They either want us scared, or not thinkin'. Not organized. They want an excuse to make an example of more of us," Clarence said.

"They got guns and we don't," Odalia added. A growing bruise stood out red on her cheek and her lip was split, but she seemed all right otherwise.

Arjun subsided, though Ira still seemed fit to steam. "The whole town will know of this by shift change anyway."

There was no stopping that kind of gossip. Mag wished she could think a little better over her headache. She had another handkerchief holding in bleeding of her nose, and she'd let Arjun and Ira think that she'd gotten punched. She felt bad about that. "It ain't bad for people to be mad. We need that. All that's gonna take us through it is blood and rage. But we gotta be smart-angry, not dumb fightin' angry." Not like Uncle Nick, flying off the handle and almost getting his people killed. "We pushed them and they gone and pushed us back. If we stay quiet, they're gonna swagger around and think they won, and is that so bad right now?"

Ira made a dismissive growl, but she saw Arjun paying attention – and so were Odalia and Clarence. Mag continued: "Let 'em think they got us cowed. We play it sweet and let the fire burn and keep organizin' and gettin' ready under their damn noses. They think we're down, they ain't gonna be lookin' for us when we come at their necks."

Clarence made a sound like a laugh. Ira blew out a long sigh, then shook her head. "I hope you never have cause to be angry at me, Mag."

It was sort of a compliment, and Mag was willing to take it. "You tell everyone that. We ain't gonna let 'em pull us by the nose."

Ira nodded. "We'd better start telling that, then, before rumor has all three of you dead and buried."

"I can watch 'em while y'all go talk," Mag said.

Arjun gave her a doubtful glance. "You look in the grave, yourself."

"Only halfway there."

He laughed, to Mag's relief. The family filtered out of their own house, heading in different directions as they left to make sure the right sort of news spread. Mag sagged against the wall. She had so much she needed to say, but now wasn't sure where to start.

"My boy's Sai's age. Damn glad he's not here, or he'd have rushed off already," Odalia said. Mag knew that most of her family was in Segundo; Odalia had transferred to Ludlow to get a better paying job and left them behind. She'd said a time or two that the school in Segundo was better too, since it was closer to Newcastle.

"Makin' me glad I never had any," Clarence remarked. "Got enough worries with everyone else's."

"Easier life when you only got yourself to worry about." Odalia lifted the damp cloth from her face to peer at Mag. "How'd they get you?"

"They didn't. Not like that." Mag cleared her throat uncomfortably. She hadn't ever told either of the crew leaders about the witchiness growing in her. They needed every weapon they had, and she'd come to trust both Clarence and Odalia as good people. Still, every instinct she had screamed at her not to speak, because it would surely get her killed. Her throat had gone so dry that the first few words sounded more like croaks as she said: "There's somethin' I can do. A witchy thing. Been able to do it for a while. I can… lean on people, like. Tell them to not do something, tell them to stop, and they stop. That's how I kept me and Anabi from bein' taken to the train station, the day the Weatherman was supposed to come." She looked Clarence in the eye. He seemed strangely serene under the bruises. "An' when people were tryin' to fight yesterday... that's how I stopped 'em. And I tried to do that again today, tried to help you two, but it didn't work. Too many of 'em this time."

Odalia sucked in a breath. "You're a fuckin' *witch*."

"Weren't a choice on my part."

"You ever do that to one of us?" Clarence asked quietly, the kind of quiet that said he was very, very angry.

"No." Mag shook her head. "Never."

"You ever try?" Odalia demanded.

"Never!" This had been a mistake, but she couldn't take it back.

"Why the fuck should we trust anythin' you say? You didn't tell us till now, with us half dead 'cause you let 'em–" Odalia said.

It felt so unfair. She'd *tried*. "Because if I was... was *doin'* somethin' to you, do you think I'd be telling you this at all?" Mag demanded, annoyance somehow cutting through her fear. "Do you think I'm an idiot?"

"I think it's disgusting," Odalia said.

Clarence gently probed at his cheek with his fingertips, winced, and stopped. "All's fair in love and war, they say. Don't know 'bout love, but we sure got a war coming." When Odalia started to protest, he gave her a quelling look. "I gotta think about this. Don't go tellin' anyone else, Mag. Nor you, Odalia. And... don't go about using it. Not if you don't have to."

She licked her lips. "You're trustin' me?"

"You're the one who said we had to stick together." His lips twitched in a frown. "Guess I know why now."

"That wasn't the reason, then." But she didn't entirely believe herself, even, and she could tell Clarence didn't either.

He continued to just look at her through that swollen, bruised mask of a face, like he'd read an answer he liked better on the inside of her skull. "You were right then and still right now. 'Bout plenty of things. If we're gonna take action…"

"Then we still got to lay supplies," Mag finished. "Can't hold the mines hostage if they can dry us out in a few days."

Clarence nodded. "We're gonna get more volunteers off this. People mad as hell and wantin' to do somethin'. Collect 'em up, and keep gettin' us ready."

Odalia frowned and cut in: "If you think you can do it without messin' about with their heads."

That felt like a slap to the face, and damn unfair after working with them for months. But she reminded herself that Odalia was still hurting bad, and no one was ever reasonable in that state. "I never have and I never will. You know that."

Odalia just glared at her, one eye swollen shut. "Not sure I do."

The sick feeling of it was still foremost in her mind when she told Anabi what had happened, later that night. "Maybe I shouldn't have said anything. And I don't even feel right using it."

Anabi pulled out her slate and wrote: *Because it's wrong, or because you're scared?*

"Both, I guess." She hated to admit that, but it did scare her. It felt too easy, to stand on someone else's mind and just push them this way and that. She couldn't do it with a group yet, but one person seemed trivial now.

Scared doesn't matter. Do it anyway.

That felt unfair. How much had Mag been through, terrified out of her wits, and still kept going? She'd made it out of that goddamn laboratory and hadn't hidden away. She'd kept fighting, even when she'd lost everything. "You're scared all the time," she snapped. "And I ain't seen you do anythin' with your witchiness."

Anabi sat back like she'd been slapped. She shook her head and wrote: *What I've got is different.*

"What I got is different too." She'd always known Uncle Nick and Hob with their sparks of fire, and now seen people who could call the wind or walk on sand without leaving tracks. She'd never heard of anyone being able to do what she could. Maybe that was just because they'd all been killed for it already.

Not different like yours.

"Then explain it to me," Mag said. She'd never demanded this story from Anabi before, but she was tired of feeling judgment from all directions, from Odalia because she even had her power whether she used it or not, and now from Anabi for not using it. No one knew a damn thing about how it felt.

Anabi stood abruptly. Mag's heart felt like it'd sunk down to the floorboards – had she made her so mad that she was leaving? Even angry, she never wanted to do that. She stood as well, tongue tangled with apologies and frustration. But instead, Anabi simply went over to the stove and set some water boiling. She gave Mag a glance over her shoulder and pointed imperiously at the chair, so Mag sat again and waited. Silently, Anabi made them each a cup of coffee and then returned to the table. She wasn't smiling when she set the cup in front of Mag, but her frown wasn't angry either. More like she was thinking really hard.

Mag waited silently as Anabi fortified herself with a sip of coffee. Then she picked up her slate, and bit by bit wrote out: *I didn't get thrown out of Harmony because I was witchy. I got thrown out* – she looked at Mag for a long moment, then continued firmly – *because they wanted me to be a man, and then my brother caught me kissing a minstrel girl.*

Her shoulders hitched as she looked at Mag again, this time from under her lashes, like a little girl peeping scared out of a blanket.

Why did any of that matter? Well, it mattered to Anabi because it meant she'd broken with her kin, in that far-off, strange town of hers. But she seemed to expect some kind of break from Mag too, some kind of reaction. She was tight as a spring with that tension. Perhaps it explained a thing or two: some of Anabi's shyness, how she kept her back to Mag when she bathed. But Mag hadn't ever pried because it wasn't something to be questioned, and that hadn't changed. Anabi still felt just like Anabi always felt to her, like the strange, beautiful damp wind blowing off a green field near a farm village. The only thing Mag felt was angry that someone had made Anabi that scared, when your kin were the ones who were supposed to protect and love you. "Fuck 'em, then," Mag said.

Anabi stared at her for a moment, and then burst into silent laughter. She was beautiful like that, unfairly so, Mag thought.

And then thought again, of the other thing Anabi had said. About kissing a minstrel girl. It made her want to ask if Anabi would mind kissing her, too. It seemed an awful thing to say, when they were in the midst of some story that had shaken Anabi so much. Instead, she reached out to touch her hand and give it a gentle squeeze.

Anabi squeezed her hand in return and went back to writing: *I ran away before they could come after me. As I left the valley, I met a man. He had eyes like a cat's, and he told me that he was a witch. The valley near Harmony* – Anabi paused, seeming to gather her thoughts – *there's this wind that tears down it, regular. It sounds like a wildcat screaming, and it'll rip living things to shreds. He said he was the wind. Then he* – a longer pause – *attacked me.*

Mag squeezed her hand again as Anabi wiped the slate clean, her movements slow.

He was going to let loose that scream on me because I was fighting him. So I kissed him. And I ate the scream. It lives in my chest now. I feel it, like spikes. Every time I breathe.

"Shit," Mag whispered.

That's why I don't talk. I think I still can. But if I make a sound, the scream could escape. Like I said. What I have is different.

"Thank you," Mag said. "But you didn't have to tell me all that. I'm sorry. I shouldn't have made ya."

Anabi smiled crookedly, wiping the chalk away to write just a bit more: *I didn't, but now I'm glad that I did.* She reached out with one dusty hand and touched Mag's cheek.

Mag couldn't help it. She covered Anabi's hand with her own, turning her face into that touch as her stomach gave a warm little flutter. "Witchy ones gotta stick together," she said, her voice thick. She smiled. "Even if you're strange for a witchy one."

Anabi's thumb brushed over her cheek, slowly, and her smile shifted to become something warm rather than ironic.

Mag swallowed hard. She felt grubby and small-minded even still, but she couldn't help but ask, "Do ya ever like girls that aren't minstrels? I ain't got much of a singin' voice, even if I'm not as bad as Hob. And–"

Anabi's lips parted in a silent laugh again, and she stopped Mag's nervous chatter with a light touch of one finger. Then she wrote on her slate: *I like hellraisers and troublemakers.*

Mag laughed. "Then you'll be wantin' Hob, won't ya?"

Too skinny. And she smells like cigarettes. Anabi leaned forward to lightly poke the end of Mag's nose. *You're the biggest troublemaker around, and best at it because no one notices.*

"I think that's a compliment."

It is. Anabi dotted the simple sentence with an emphatic period, then rose and took Mag's hand. She tugged her to her feet and mouthed "bed time" before kissing her on the cheek. Mag followed her upstairs, happy to have the slow sway of Anabi's walk rather than rebellions and numbers and witchiness on her mind for the rest of the night.

After two weeks of waiting for Mr Yellow to be released into his care, Shige was on edge. Every day of delay would make it more difficult to execute his orders once he landed; the likelihood that it would be impossible to achieve enough chaos at this point was frighteningly high. He'd begun to look for ways he could push in the Corporate hierarchy without it being obvious when he received a special afternoon summons to Dr Ekwensi's office. The instructions attached were precise, and an immense relief.

"Ah, Dr Ekwensi. I hope that I haven't kept you waiting too long," Shige said, finding her at Mr Yellow's room as usual.

"You're well in time. Mr Yellow is completing his final checks. Are you ready for departure?" She favored Shige with a distracted nod. Mr Yellow stood, head slightly bowed, at the center of the room; someone had given him a blue suit like Shige's, and he'd dressed himself competently.

"Yes, fully packed, and I saw to it that the ship is ready as well. Your instructions said that I will need to take Mr Yellow directly to the departure port."

"Regulatory requirement. We don't want to risk

contamination due to delay." She blinked and focused on him. Shige gave her his best "helpful underling" smile. "Follow me. I have a set of care instructions for you to carry to the field lab."

Useful, that. Shige wouldn't have to manufacture a reason to visit her office, just a moment of distraction for her. "It would be my pleasure to help."

He followed her to her office and kept up a patter of polite and insubstantial small talk that Dr Ekwensi simply ignored. He'd learned that she seemed to treat such things as white noise, and it helped him to fade into the background of her attention even when he stood right next to her.

In her office, she pulled a blank data card from her desk. The cards were vehicles for minuscule storage synapses that would be far too easy to lose or forget if they didn't travel in a much larger container. These particular ones were size optimized to be difficult to misplace, but easy to store. Dr Ekwensi made a face as she tucked the card into the terminal, the screen coming to life with a scroll of commands she transmitted to it. "Ridiculous that we have to rely on such archaic things."

"I promise I shan't lose it." Shige thumbed a small shock sphere out of his cuff and into his palm.

She snorted. "You'd best not even joke about it." She reached to pop the card from her terminal.

Shige flicked the little sphere at the tool box he'd once fetched for her. His aim was precise. The shock sphere struck the box square on and popped into dust, a harmless and nearly soundless concussion that was enough to knock the toolbox off the precarious perch he'd left it on during his last visit to her office. It plummeted off the cabinet and smashed loudly onto the floor.

Dr Ekwensi jerked around as Shige moved to investigate, the picture of surprise. "Oh no, I think it might have broken..." he said, and bent as if to pick the contents up.

"Let me see," Dr Ekwensi said, brushing past him. Shige backed up out of her way, to stand by her terminal. After that, it was a trivial matter to replace the data card with his own, which pulled in all of the leached queries. He switched them back with a second and a half to spare as Dr Ekwensi straightened.

"Is it all right?" he asked.

"Nothing broken," Dr Ekwensi said. "I would have been surprised, really. This equipment all has to survive close contact with fresh subjects. They tend to be hard on things." She walked back over to the terminal and removed the data card so she could offer it to him. "A word of advice, Mr Rollins."

"Yes?" His fingers closed on the card, but she didn't let it go.

"You seem like a kind sort. I'm surprised you've gotten this far in the business side without having killer instinct." She waved off his dissembling. "You're going to be spending a great deal of time with Mr Yellow. Don't make the mistake of thinking he likes you."

"Does he dislike me?" Shige asked.

"Do you think a scalpel likes or dislikes you?" She let the card go, and he tucked it into his pocket. "All that matters is that you handle it with care."

He bowed to her. "Your concern is appreciated, Dr Ekwensi."

"If you make it back from the outpost, consider applying for a transfer to the lab. I hate to see reliable resources wasted." She headed for the door, waving for him to follow. "Now, I believe you have a ship to catch."

The *Kirin* made a streamlined shape on the landing field, its skin reflecting the pink, purple, and deep blue of the final moments of sunset. The ship's solar sails, there to bolster the more conventional engines with every bit of spare velocity possible, were stowed while it was on the surface.

It was one of only three courier rift ships, and the newest of them. Most rift ships were ugly, massive drifters that moved slowly from rift point to rift point, and temporarily disassembled into still-enormous cargo landers. Shige doubted that the cargo landers were able to land and take off through normal means; the propulsion system designs were something he'd never been authorized to look at, but he assumed there was a healthy dose of proprietary, Tanegawa's World-driven technology built into them. Ships like the *Kirin* and its sister, the *Raiju*, which had originally brought Shige to the planet, were built to be super-light and had conventional, if sophisticated engines. It meant no cargo carrying capacity, but they were intended purely to move personnel and messages as quickly as possible.

Mr Yellow had been quiet during the entire drive out to the landing field, staring into a distant point of space that Shige couldn't see. He found himself almost missing the odd, croaked mutterings of Mr Green; a silent Weatherman was a strange, ghostly creature.

Once they set foot on the smooth surface of the landing field, Mr Yellow came alive. He stood straighter, his face turned toward the rift ship. His expression was the smile of someone who had never actually seen such an expression, instinctive rather than learned.

"Are you ready to go to your new home?" Shige asked. The silence had started crawling along his spine, something he didn't want to admit to himself.

"We are ready," Mr Yellow said.

They made the short walk to the boarding ramp and up into the ship. The rift ship's captain, Jiang, identifiable by the star-patterned tie tack she wore, waited for them at the top of the ramp. She offered Shige a polite smile and they shook hands before she ushered him and Mr Yellow – though she didn't directly acknowledge his presence – into the ship.

"Earth's in a good position right now. We've been able to cut the in-system journeys to three weeks."

"Excellent." Shige could appreciate that as an achievement, while simultaneously wincing at the length of even this fast transit. It would be another three weeks once they reached their destination, and that would give him only two weeks left to see that things were prepared for the inspector.

"We've received orders that Mr Yellow is to pilot us through the rifts," she continued.

"I wasn't aware of that," Shige said. He would have thought that Dr Ekwensi would at least tell him.

"It's often good for them to have a shakedown flight. Very common. Our Weatherman, Mr Red, will be keeping a hand on the controls as well, so you needn't worry. Mr Red has taken us successfully through fifty-seven rifts."

Shige raised an eyebrow. "Any unsuccessful?"

Captain Jiang laughed, a rather hollow sound. "Unsuccessful rift transits don't come back, sir."

Space and mass were both at a premium; as much as possible had been removed from the ship design, so corridors became open at odd intervals where only support struts were needed. Small cargo crates were lashed around the support struts, making partial walls, standing starkly against the ship's otherwise soothing interior paint job of cool greens and pale creams. Captain Jiang led them to the engine room, where another Weatherman waited. He looked appreciably older than Mr Yellow; there were crow's feet at the corners of his black-in-black eyes. In uneven patches, his dark brown skin had gone white, along with shocks of his tightly curled black hair, which had been shaved close to his skull. It took Shige a moment to remember the name of that condition as vitiligo, a disease that had been all but eliminated on Earth and its closest colonies.

Captain Jiang caught his curious look and remarked, "I've been assured that's a harmless effect of aging on the older Weatherman models. Some sort of unintended side effect. Newer models like your Mr Yellow ought not be affected."

"I don't think I've ever seen an old Weatherman," he said.

"From my viewpoint, age is a sign of reliability," Captain Jiang remarked. "That is why Mr Red has been entrusted with this ship."

Shige watched as the two Weathermen moved to stand together in front of the rift control nexus. It was just the tip of what made the heart of the ship, a crystalline core that glowed faintly green from within and looked like it had sprouted a multitude of glass fibers – the direct neural connections. Not quite touching these fibers, the two Weathermen leaned toward each other so their foreheads almost touched. They were utterly silent; he wasn't certain if that was normal, since he'd never seen more than one Weatherman in the same place at the same time. Captain Jiang ignored them both.

"We've a seat for you on the bridge. The view during take-off is excellent." When Shige glanced at the Weathermen again, she said, "We no longer exist for them."

"Then I would be happy to appreciate the view," Shige said.

After they'd successfully exited Earth's gravity well,

Shige excused himself to his cramped cabin, a remarkable space on a ship where the only other person afforded true privacy was the captain herself. Two small cases that had seemed so modest in size when he packed them took up almost the entire free floor space. He opened the one with a security seal to reveal the thick packet of flimsies he was to take to Ms Meetchim, as well as the data card – and his own well-hidden equipment. The flimsies were an unheard-of thing for any other planet, but without reliable computers anywhere but the secure basement laboratories on Tanegawa's World, the switch to old technology had been necessary.

With painstaking attention to detail, he read through the sheaf, sheet by sheet. First, he wanted to be familiar with every order and bit of information. Most of it concerned the mineral sample that had been sent back to the labs with him – now dubbed "amritite" by Corporate – and its possible applications. Ms Meetchim was ordered to immediately cease all other mining operations and focus on tracing the origin of the amritite vein and finding more deposits. More personnel would be sent on the next worker rift ship to take over the regular mining and farming operations, but this effort was the top priority. Shige saw opportunity in that; the miners and famers wouldn't like the disruption to their routine, and he was in prime position to make things as rocky as possible.

More importantly, there was a very specific piece of information he sought out. He found the first occurrence on the third page of the orders: *BCRE labor inspector Liu Fei Xing will be arriving for a "surprise" inspection between one and four weeks after your receipt of this message.*

So much for Liu's arrival being a surprise. Shige marked the place and kept reading. He noted every mention of the incoming inspector. His next task was to remove each one and seamlessly restructure the documents. That wouldn't be challenging, just time-consuming. Unfortunately, there was nothing about the source of the information, though that was really Ayana's problem and not his.

Shige pulled a padded roll from the case, which contained a portable scanner and flimsy printer. It would be reduced to a mass of metallic polymers and fused circuits as soon as he landed on Tanegawa's World, but it didn't need to last beyond this project. A little more digging through the case and he found the roll of security fibers he'd liberated from TransRift Corporate storage before leaving. Humming quietly to himself, he rolled the scanner over the first page. He'd always been good at this sort of detail work; it fell in the same array of enhanced cognitive skills that had let him score perfectly on test after test all through his childhood. He recalled his results being laid side-by-side with Kazu's older scores in their father's office for consideration by the whole family. Ayana had always looked so triumphant, and as Shige had grown older, the fact had tainted his pride with severe discomfort, made worse by Kazu's studied lack of any interest in the proceedings. It had been so easy to get praise from their parents; all he had to do was precisely what they asked, and Kazu had already lowered the bar precipitously.

And, once again, Shige had succeeded where Kazu had failed, in that he still lived. He didn't feel at all proud of himself now. However, he also didn't need to feel at all good to get the job done. He'd learned that a long time ago.

Shige had just begun his side-by-side comparison of the old documents and the fresh, altered copies when an urgent message came over the ship's network from

Captain Jiang.

You aren't disturbing me at all, Captain, Shige returned. *How may I be of service?* He hadn't expected to hear anything at all from her until it was time to fully deploy the solar sails, another pretty sight that ship captains liked their passengers to exclaim over.

Your Weatherman wishes to open the rift now.

He wasn't certain how he felt about Mr Yellow being listed among his possessions, but that was a very distant, secondary thought. *We're too near the gravity well, are we not?*

By hundreds of thousands of kilometers, Captain Jiang said. *But he insists. And Mr Red agrees with him.*

It is your *ship, Captain Jiang.* She could tell the Weathermen "no" just as effectively as he could, if not more so because she had actual control of the engines.

My orders from Corporate say that I'm to let Mr Yellow open the rift as soon as he feels ready. He's your *Weatherman. Perhaps you ought to point out to him what a foolish idea it would be.*

Shige considered all of his interactions with Mr Green. He'd done a little cajoling, but never truly convinced him of anything. He also didn't particularly want to die in some sort of experimental rift accident; he had too much still to do. *I'll make the attempt.*

He set his work aside and hurried down to the engine room, where the Weathermen still stood together. An engineer had been added to the mix, attending to the in-system engines. It made for a tightly packed room.

Shige addressed the Weathermen: "Mr Yellow. You've caused the captain no small amount of concern. We're too close to Earth still."

"We see it," Mr Yellow said. "We feel it. It is close enough for us to touch."

That wasn't a terribly comforting statement. "Yes,

Earth is still very close," Shige tried again.

Mr Yellow shook his head. "We speak of home." He stepped back from Mr Red and approached Shige, who fixed his eyes on Mr Yellow's left earlobe. From the corner of his eye, he saw Mr Yellow's thin fingers, then felt them on his face, dry as spiders.

Shige swallowed, his throat suddenly very thick. He maintained a calm tone through sheer force of will. Nothing good had ever come of a Weatherman being this close to him. "Yes, Mr Yellow?"

"You know us," Mr Yellow whispered, and there was that music in his voice, somehow. Not quite singsong, but it echoed in Shige's body and he swayed slightly, toward the Weatherman, before he caught himself. "And through you, we hear our home. You know us."

Shige felt oddly distant, as if he stood outside his own body. He considered that traveling the rift now would mean arriving at Tanegawa's World several weeks early, which would do his mission no end of good. And yet the logic of it felt like thin paper being wrapped over a conclusion he had already made and didn't recall making.

"We will help you," Mr Yellow whispered, and stepped away.

"Our orders are clear," Shige said. *We will proceed, Captain Jiang. Prepare for rift transit.*

In front of him, Mr Yellow stepped into the rift control nexus. The filaments quaked around him and came alive, brushing against his skin like cilia before sinking in. Around them, the ship shuddered.

"Shit." The engineer slapped one of the controls on his panel. A klaxon sounded through the ship. "Emergency shutoff on the network!" He turned his horrified gaze to Shige. "You just fucking killed us."

The emergency shutoff was like suddenly losing one

of his senses. The absence hit Shige like a blow, and he staggered. He caught himself on the edge of one of the panels and glanced wildly up. Perhaps that disorientation was why he did the one thing he knew to never do: he met Mr Yellow's eyes.

And fell

into the black-on-black depths, the space between stars, the color-noncolor that was the rift, the place where all things and no things existed at once. There was no sound, and all sound, and music that tore his marrow down to its individual atoms and boiled his blood. He couldn't move, couldn't do more than gasp for breath and try to hold on to the simplicity of his name as possibility tore at him. There were other Shiges, infinite ones, ones that had come screaming and wet into the world from between their mothers' legs rather than slipping from a silvery, impersonal tube. There were other Shiges that smiled with blood on their teeth, that wore the blue TransRift suit without irony, that raced across dunes with their brother and called themselves Samedi and drank whiskey straight from the bottle, and they all tore through his skin, fighting to be free.

He felt Mr Yellow sink his invisible talons into the fabric of the universe and part it between his hands. Light that was taste and color and sound flowed from the scars around Mr Yellow's face, hanging in the air like a bell-tone, a soft counterpoint coming from Mr Red. Mr Yellow stirred all of those possibilities, the infinite timelines and points of space, and selected one point, one moment, one life, one *song*.

He felt the universe shift around them, slide, and it was something no one could know and remain sane, because no person should feel the fabric of reality unwinding to threads in their hands.

Distantly, Shige felt his knees slam into the floor, his chin hitting the panel with a sharp *crack*.

Suddenly Mr Yellow's eyes were just eyes. The ship was solid around them all again. And slowly, Shige became aware not of music, but the klaxon, and the engineer retching against the deck plates. His chin and tongue throbbed in time with his too-fast heartbeat. Blood filled his mouth.

"Status report," Captain Jiang demanded over the audible intercom. "Status report, engineering."

Since the engineer seemed unlikely to recover in the next few seconds, Shige felt for the intercom with a shaking hand and triggered it. His words came out clumsy around a swollen tongue. "All right down here, captain. Is all well on the bridge?"

"You son of a bitch," Captain Jiang shouted. There was a pause, then she continued in a more reasonable tone: "We have arrived in Tanegawa's World local space."

Both of these things were impossible, Shige knew. Rifts could not be opened so close to the gravity well of the planet. That had been a hard-learned, early lesson for the company. And yet. He looked up at Mr Yellow, staring at his chin at the last moment. He didn't want to fall into those eyes again.

Mr Yellow's thin, colorless lips curved into a smile.

CHAPTER TWELVE • *52 DAYS*

"Come on. I'm serious," Coyote said.

"I know you're serious," Hob said, eyeing him. He'd popped into her office, like he had so often before he'd gone missing. It felt eerily right and wrong at the same time. This was the best he'd looked in the two weeks since they'd hauled him out of the desert, which wasn't saying a hell of a lot. He was still stick-thin, and while his eyes had their old focus back, there was a hectic gleam to them that she really didn't like. "Don't make it any less goddamn stupid."

"I'm going mad, seeing nothing but these walls. We always have more work than we have people. I know that can't have changed."

"You ain't in any kind of shape yet. Davey says so." A transparent attempt to get him to go bother Davey instead, but she wasn't above trying it.

"Davey worries too much. And so do you."

Hob snorted as she fished a cigarette out of her coat pocket. "Yeah, that's me. A bundle of fuckin' maternal instincts." But maybe there was something she could have him do. TransRift was looking for the blue mineral, the source of witchiness. As someone passing witchy herself, she had a mighty interest in not wanting them to succeed.

Coyote eyed her expression. "I recognize that look. You're attempting to think again."

Hob rolled her eyes. "And it's a right strain. But I'm thinkin'... this place you'n the Bone Collector talked about. This..."

"Well," Coyote said quietly. He didn't look so cheerful any more.

"He said it weren't a real place. But you been there, so then it has to be. And we know TransRift is lookin' for it. Best we find it first, don't you think?" And selfishly, she thought maybe it would answer a question or two of hers, like what this power really was. She was damn tired of not having answers for something so fundamental.

"You're getting very good at this logic thing," Coyote said dryly. "Have you been practicing?"

She ignored the taunt, not wanting to let him divert her. "'Stead of sendin' you out on a regular job, wouldn't it be better to put you in charge of the search?"

Coyote went very still. And then slowly, he hugged his arms around himself, like he was cold. Considering it was stuffy in the office, like in every damn room of the base, Hob found that hard to believe. "No," he said quietly. Then, "*No*." Emphatic enough that it felt like he was yelling, even though he hadn't raised his voice. Hob simply waited. She needed more of a reason than that.

He took a deep, slightly unsteady breath. "I don't think I can go there again. Not without going mad. Even getting close... please don't send me back there." He swallowed hard, meeting her eyes. "Please, Hob. *Please*."

Please wasn't something they used often on base. And coming from Coyote, when it wasn't a bit of passive-aggressive mockery, was almost frightening. For all his stillness, she felt like he was about to shake to pieces in front of her eyes. She'd killed her fair share of men, but she'd never wanted to disassemble them into their component parts. She wasn't about to start with Coyote. "All right," she said. He sagged with relief, a tension she hadn't even noticed leaving him. "Regular job it is."

Seeing him so shaken, Hob knew it needed to be something easy. A test like she'd give a pup, so he could prove to her – and maybe to himself – he had his shit together and wouldn't get himself or others killed when the bullets started flying. Hob shuffled through a pile of flimsies until she found the one she wanted. It'd been sitting for a while because she was fresh out of pups and no one had pissed her off enough to get a joke job. Perfect. "This ought to fit you to rights."

Coyote read it over, with all its creative spelling. The movements of his eyebrows were a full three-act drama, surprise to disbelief to even more disbelief. "You must be joking."

"This is my serious face," Hob said.

"Did you actually read this?"

"'Course I did. You wanted a job. There you go." Hob crossed her arms and smiled. At least that haunted look was gone from his eyes. "Think you can handle it?"

He looked down at the flimsy again and made an odd little choking sound that Hob recognized as a combination of disbelief and outrage. She hadn't managed to get Coyote to do that often before, and now it felt like even more of a victory because it was *normal* for him. She still needed to convince herself that it was real.

Voice a little strangled, Coyote asked, "And who's going to be coming with me? Unless you're planning to send me out solo?"

She wasn't sure what to make of his tone, but she didn't like any of the possibilities. The reason he'd died – she couldn't think of it any other way – was because she'd let him go out on his own, with no backup. She'd bought in to his line of bullshit about his own immortality, and she should have known better. "No more solo runs," she said. "That's a settled rule now."

His eyebrows arched up. "I suppose I'm honored to have brought about such change." His normally clipped central-world's accent seemed to have cranked up to a new level of snootiness.

He was trying to piss her off, which was also hearteningly normal. "And I got everyone else runnin' around already, so you're stuck with me." More bandit hunts, more message runs between the towns and now all these new survey sites. The miners seemed to be chattering a lot these days, but she figured if there was something Mag thought she should know, she'd say. It was also a good way to keep their own maps updated.

Coyote must not have been expecting that. He looked surprised, then very wry. "You should save some honor for the rest of the company."

"They got plenty," Hob said. She pointed at the flimsy still clutched in his hand. "You're runnin' the show. What're we gonna do... *boss*?"

It had never been easy to fluster Coyote. Hob was glad to know she hadn't lost the knack entirely. He grimaced and said slowly, "Well, I suppose we start at the last known location and see where it takes us in pursuit of our... miscreant. Ah... get going?"

"She's still going!" Coyote shouted over the short-range radio. "How the hell is a tractor that fast?"

"Guess she's a good mechanic." Hob choked back a laugh. "You got an intercept plan?"

They'd gone to the last known location of the rogue farmhand they'd been paid to hunt down and found no tracks, which wasn't unusual. Tracks didn't last long in a place filled with sand and constant wind. But without prompting from Hob, Coyote had taken the lay of the land and headed off to the stubby shape of some rocks about twenty kilometers distant, just big enough to provide a single person some shelter.

She shouldn't have expected him to need prompting. This was still Coyote. He'd been doing this for more years than she'd even been on the damn planet. She hated the feeling that she was waiting for him to crack and show that he wasn't really him any more.

When they were a couple kilometers out from the rocks, Coyote caught sight of the glint of metal and glass that had to be the tractor. And it seemed like their target must have caught sight of them in return, because the tractor suddenly spun away from the rocks in a cloud of dust and started heading north, toward where the dunes rippled densely together.

And that was how Hob and Coyote had come to a place where they were chasing down a goddamn tractor and in danger of actually losing her as the shadows got longer.

"We're more maneuverable than her," Coyote said. "Bear east and keep along the top of the dunes as much as you can. So that she can see you. Try to get ahead of her. That will force her to turn, and I'll be circling in for the pincer."

Not a bad plan; Hob had been thinking along similar lines herself. And this was Coyote's job, so she was happy to play decoy for him. Let him show her what he could still do. "Gonna be some tricky riding in the shadows," she commented, already turning her bike to bolt up the long back of the nearest dune. Hell, she hadn't gotten to have fun on a ride in a while. It would do her some good to practice a jump here and there.

"I'm not that out of practice," Coyote said. He took a tight turn and vanished into the long, dark shadows that stretched below the slip faces.

Hob twisted the throttle up to full, leaning down over the battery stack. The motorcycle leaped forward – damn, Hati must have been messing with her motor again and not bothered to tell her – and the back wheel swerved before she got it back under control. Air roared over her helmet and she felt rather than heard the rising hum of the machine beneath her. She shot up the long windward face of the massive dune, keeping an eye on the glint of the tractor in the distance to her left.

Then there was just the edge of red-orange sand and the endless blue sky. She leaned back and hauled on the handlebars as the motorcycle shot over the slip face and into the air.

This was the closest any of them ever got to flying. She whooped as gravity took hold, pulling the motorcycle back down toward the ground. The wheels hit the sand with a bone-jarring thump and she wrestled it back steady, aiming for the next long, windward ramp.

"I think you're having too much fun," Coyote said dryly in her ear, his voice already a little fuzzed with static.

"Ain't my fault you gave me the best part of the job," Hob said as she leaned back down over her handlebars.

Three dunes later, the tractor had started to turn; she had to tilt her head to see it, so she drifted a little more that way to encourage him to keep going. "She's bearing west."

A moment later Coyote answered, "I've got her. Keep going."

Hob grinned, pushing the throttle back up to full. "Hell yeah."

A few more minutes, and she saw Coyote's motorcycle flashing through patches of sunlight, though he was hidden from the tractor since it had to lumber around the dunes or stick to the gentle slopes of the windward sides. Then Coyote cut out into full light, heading right for the tractor.

The farmhand tried to turn, heading up the windward face. Hob saw Coyote close in, get his feet under him on the seat of the motorcycle, and then jump onto the tractor. His bike kept going steady for a few seconds, then leaned and fell as soon as it was no longer straight on the slope.

And Coyote clung to the cab of the tractor. In the distance, she saw him rip the door open and swing inside–

–then the tractor went over the lip of the slip face. The edge of the dune poured down in its wake, collapsing. All she heard over the radio was Coyote's harsh breathing, which faded to static. Hob gunned it and headed for that dune. "What's your status, Coyote?"

A long pause, too long, and she bit back the feeling of concern. This was a bullshit job, and they'd both known it. She couldn't have gotten him hurt or worse again on something this stupid.

Then Coyote said, the transmission strangely dimmed, "Bloody annoyed."

Hob didn't quite sag with relief – she couldn't and keep control of the motorcycle at this speed, but she felt a little lightheaded with it anyway. "Be there in a flash," she said.

"Take your time," Coyote answered. "We're certainly not going anywhere."

The tractor was on its side, half-buried in an avalanche of orange-red sand. Part of the slip face of the dune had given way under its weight. Hob parked her motorcycle a safe distance to the side, just in case more of the slip face collapsed. "You need me to dig you out?" she asked.

"That would be lovely," Coyote said.

Hob took off her helmet and grabbed a folding shovel from her motorcycle. As soon as she'd cleared the door off, Coyote flung it open and popped out.

"Lookin' peppy," Hob commented. She'd had to jerk back to keep from getting hit with the door.

"It's a bit close in there," Coyote said.

"Our target alive?"

Coyote glanced down, then pulled his own helmet off. "Oh yes. She's just playing dead in the hopes we'll think a little fall like that killed her."

"No, I'm not," a sullen voice came from inside the tractor. "You almost took off my fuckin' head."

"Yes, well, you deserved it," Coyote said equably. "And the contract doesn't specify how many parts you're to be returned in."

"Returned to who?" the farmhand shouted.

"Whom," Coyote corrected.

"Fuck you! You gettin' paid by them fuckin' greenbellies?"

Hob raised her eyebrows and leaned down over the door. "You havin' problems with them?"

The farmhand, who Hob now saw was sporting a bloody nose and a split lip, glared at her. "They been crawlin' all over us. Askin' about the fuckin' miners. Tellin' us we better not help 'em, and we'll get more pay if we don't."

Well, *that* was interesting. Hob filed that one away to tell Mag at her next opportunity. "They scare you off, chickenshit?"

"Fuck you. This is my tractor, and I ain't letting that fucker Handley sell it."

"Guess you get to sort that out with Handley when we hand your ass over," Hob said. The farmhand gave a shriek of outrage and Hob slammed the door shut in her face. Then jammed it with her shovel for good measure. A fist pounded angrily on the inside of the door.

"I hope she doesn't kiss her mother with that mouth," Coyote observed. He stretched his arms and winced. "Little asshole got me right in the stomach. Or maybe that was the gear shift."

"Sure gave me a bit of a turn, watchin' you go over," Hob admitted.

Coyote looked at her for a long moment. "You're just going to have to get over it," he said, and hopped off the tractor. "I'll get some rope."

Hob tugged on the shovel to make sure it was secure, then followed Coyote. "Get over what?"

"I volunteered to go to Harmony by myself. Even though I knew it was a rather stupid idea at the time," Coyote shrugged. "Did you see where my motorcycle dropped?"

"I'll get it. Grab the rope off mine."

"No," he said firmly. "It isn't going to work, Hob, if you treat me differently."

She grimaced, stung, and started fishing for a cigarette. "I ain't."

"You bloody well are. When you aren't waiting for me to break, you're pulling your punches because… well, I can almost hear you thinking, *but I killed him*. You didn't. And I need you to believe that I'm still me so that *I* can believe I'm still me."

Hob tucked a cigarette between her lips and lit it with a snap of her fingers. It bought her time as she tried to sort those words out. Had she been doing that? She'd sure been painfully aware at every step that Coyote was a dead man. "You sure talk enough to be yourself."

He huffed something too angry to be a laugh. "Well, thank you for that."

Of course he was. And he was also one of the people

she'd trusted to always be there. He'd outlived Old Nick, who she'd always thought was too damn mean to die. And then he hadn't outlived him any more, and it had been her fault. But, Hob reminded herself, Coyote wasn't the only one whose life was in her hands. All of her people were in that same spot. He'd just been lucky enough to come back, somehow. And she'd been looking at it as a chance to make good on some kind of cosmic fuckup – but it was also Coyote's goddamn life. That was more important than her guilt, by a long shot.

Like he was reading her thoughts, Coyote said, "Am I a Wolf or not?"

She reached out to clap him on the shoulder. He still felt too slight under her hand, but she assured herself that was another thing time and trust would cure. "'Course not. You're a fuckin' Coyote."

CHAPTER THIRTEEN • *48 DAYS*

The air on the landing field tasted like lightning and felt heavy against Shige's skin in a way that had nothing to do with humidity. He was almost certain that it hadn't been like this before, not even when he'd first arrived on Tanegawa's World with Ms Meetchim to find Mr Green in an induced coma.

Mr Yellow swayed lightly from side to side next to him, face tilted up, eyes closed. The Weatherman raised his hands, thin fingers spread like he'd grasp the air. It was behavior Shige had never seen in Mr Green, and he found it a relief to see the familiar saloon car moving silently across the landing field to pick them up.

"Come along, Mr Yellow," Shige said, when the car stopped in front of them. He opened the door to the rear compartment.

"We are ready," Mr Yellow said.

Ready for what, Shige couldn't begin to guess. "Of course. But you're not quite home yet. Come along."

Mr Yellow tilted his face down to look at Shige, and he had a strange urge to meet the Weatherman's eyes. Because then, it would make sense. He didn't need to understand the words, really, just see through to the intentions. At the last moment, he forced himself to look at the Weatherman's shoulder. He had more self-control than this – and it disturbed him immensely that he needed to exercise that self-control. "Into the car, please. It's far too hot to walk."

Shige saw him secured with a seatbelt before taking the other side. He set the thick stack of flimsies on the seat between them, like a pathetic wall. It would be a profound relief to transfer Mr Yellow and the instructions for his care to the team at headquarters.

But first, he had to introduce the new Weatherman to Ms Meetchim.

She was waiting in her office, which necessitated a long elevator ride with Mr Yellow – the high-speed cars seemed to have been slowed considerably. Mr Yellow insisted on standing at the exact center of the elevator, face toward the ceiling. The lights were dim, shadowing the Weatherman's face and softening the dark pits of his eyes – until he turned abruptly to look at Shige, who had chosen to lean against the wall.

He felt himself slipping, on the brink of an icy precipice, pulled by a gravity well that wasn't physical. Perhaps if he looked again, he would understand some universal truth that had escaped him before. Shige dug one fingernail deeply into the palm of his hand and focused on Mr Yellow's shoulder. "Nearly there now," he said, and tried not to notice the strain in his voice.

"We are already here," Mr Yellow said. Mercifully, the elevator doors opened.

In Ms Meetchim's office, which took up the entire top floor of the building, there were no lights at all. She had the privacy curtains open to allow in the harsh daylight. Jennifer Meetchim was a woman of medium height, her blond hair cut short and neat, her blue executive suit impeccable. She rose from behind her desk as Shige stepped from the elevator, Mr Yellow at his shoulder.

"Ah, Mr Rolland. I'm afraid you caught us a bit off guard."

They'd had four days to prepare for their arrival, Shige knew; that was how long it had taken them to get into orbit and then land – nothing compared to the scheduled three weeks. He was glad that he'd doctored the documents for Ms Meetchim first thing. He hadn't had time for anything else, and the files he'd acquired from Dr Ekwensi's office remained unopened. "Yes, well, Mr Yellow was very eager to start work."

"That, I am glad to hear," Ms Meetchim said. She made no move to come around the desk or get any closer to Mr Yellow and Shige, but that was to be expected. One did not shake a Weatherman's hand. "It has been... challenging to be completely without an on-site Weatherman."

"I'd noticed the lights," Shige offered.

"Lights, most of the laboratory equipment, just about every bit of civilization. The supposedly secure electrical grid has proven to not be as advertised."

"I am very glad for our early arrival, then. And I can assure you on behalf of the program director that Mr Yellow is... state of the art and one of a kind."

"As it should be," Meetchim said.

Shige divided the stack of flimsies he carried and set them on Ms Meetchim's desk. "These are the documents for you from Corporate. These are the care instructions that are to go to... I'm sorry, I've forgotten her name." He'd done nothing of the sort.

"Kiyoder," Ms Meetchim said, picking up her stack. "You'll have to escort Mr Yellow down to the basement level yourself, I'm afraid. The intercom isn't currently working."

"Hopefully that will soon be corrected. Would you like me to do that now?"

"Please do," she said, not looking up. "And once you've seen him settled, I'll need you back up here. Things have gotten rather disorganized in your absence."

Disorganization meant opportunity, and he was eager to start on that. Shige was aware of the short span of time he'd been given. He ushered Mr Yellow back into the elevator. The Weatherman hummed as they descended into the sub-basements, and Shige felt simple relief that he did not speak, or try to look at him again.

"Ah, Mr Rolland. That was quick."

Shige offered Ms Meetchim a practiced smile. He felt far steadier now that there were about forty floors between him and Mr Yellow. "Dr Kiyoder was very eager to get started, and so was Mr Yellow."

He took a seat across from Meetchim at her desk and fished a notebook and pen out of his pocket. The routine, for all it was a routine belonging to a persona, felt very comforting. Ms Meetchim was methodically going through the documents he'd brought for her. "I know that your correspondence doubtless needs my attention, but is there a place you'd prefer I begin?"

Not looking up from the flimsy in her hand, she opened one of her desk drawers and offered him a folder from it. "Nothing so pedestrian, I'm afraid. The miners have gotten obstreperous in your absence."

Shige took the folder. A glance at the first page showed unauthorized buying and selling of firearms, reported by a redacted source. This had to involve some local company agents, he imagined, since the firearms that had existed on the planet before TransRift's takeover were getting very long in the tooth. "I see." He kept his tone carefully neutral, though he found the news heartening. It was so much easier to start a revolt if people were already heading in that direction on their own.

"Mariposa is ready to seize the weapons and the would-be rebels, as well as find and sack the few greedy idiots in our own ranks who have enabled this nonsense, but I want the HR documentation in line first. I want them and their entire families on the blacklist." Meetchim turned a page. "That ought to set an example."

It would, Shige thought. And if played properly, that would definitely be the declaration of war that he needed the inspector to witness. The problem was timing. It was too soon. He needed to find a way to delay the fuse and yet not jeopardize the work he'd already done here. Mind racing, he thought over the historical reading he'd done while on Earth, looking for inspiration. "If I may, Ms Meetchim?"

She glanced up, one pale eyebrow arching. "Is there a problem, Mr Rolland?"

"While I understand these people must be dealt with, I feel I must remind you that they are always looking to make themselves out to be martyrs. Recall the case of the miner from Rouse?"

She frowned. "Remind me."

"Philip Kushtrim. He was severely contaminated and thus blacklisted, and his family removed. He had been very popular with the miners, and they took exception to this. There were protests in several towns and this probably led to the bandit attack in Rouse."

"All the more reason to make an example of these people."

It was dangerous, but he had to hope he could thread this needle. "With all due respect, Ms Meetchim, the witch hunt was supposed to accomplish that as well."

Meetchim set the document down on her desk and leaned back in her chair. She eyed Shige coolly. "Mariposa has had a free rein in keeping these ungrateful vermin under control for years."

"And I cannot fault them for it," Shige said smoothly. "Nor would I want such contemptuous activity to go unpunished. But in making an example, we risk making more martyrs. We are not dealing with rational, educated people."

"You obviously have an idea. Let me hear it."

He smiled, the picture of an eager underling. "We've been paying the miners with universal currency – but why is that necessary? There are no companies here but us. They can only purchase *from* us, or whatever trifling little handicrafts they make for themselves."

"Go on."

"If we pay them in company currency, that will cut off any sort of bribery at the knees. Corporate and security employees aren't going to want something that will be completely useless on the outside market, or in Newcastle. And we will of course punish those who took bribes before, but this will provide us with a solution going forward. Better, when we first roll out this new payroll system, we make the company currency monetarily more valuable than universal credits and offer the miners a chance to buy them up. These are not people who are known for their long-term thinking." This would provide him with a fuse as long as he needed, if he could convince Ms Meetchim. He could time the implementation of the pay system to ratchet up tension at the right moment.

Ms Meetchim sat quietly, expression thoughtful, and then began to laugh. "Why, Mr Rolland, you have a more subtle hand than I credited you."

Shige bowed in his seat. "Thank you, Ms Meetchim."

"Write up your proposal with a full financial analysis and I shall go over it with the head of Mariposa." She held up one finger. "*If* you impress me."

He bowed again. "I appreciate the opportunity."

Ms Meetchim smiled. "It's in TransRift's best interests to encourage talent within its own ranks. I'd have to be blind to have missed your efforts, Mr Rolland."

Another bow didn't seem amiss. "Would you care for a coffee?"

Ms Meetchim laughed as he rose to his feet. "Oh, it is good to have you back."

CHAPTER FOURTEEN • *38 DAYS*

Hob had just come in off a message run with Raff out to one of the survey camps; she could have done it on her own, but Coyote had started making up some damn song about hypocrisy and she couldn't stand the sound of him caterwauling. The camp had been populated with people from Primero, and they'd had some interesting news – like many of them not being miners, but cooks and launderers pressed into service. TransRift was going all in on this.

She hadn't even walked fully out of the garage, Raff abandoned behind her to take care of the motorcycles, when Coyote was on her. "Oh Hob, just the woman I've been waiting for," he sang out.

Hob squinted at him. "I remember that smile. I don't trust it."

"I'm hurt," he said.

"No, you ain't."

"No, I'm not. Would you like to hear a bit of gossip?"

Hob pulled her cigarette case out of her pocket. "Oh, ya know. I just love me some girl-to-girl jawin'. Ain't you back early?" She'd sent him and Lykaios off on another message run.

"We had a tail wind. Anyway, I heard in Walsen that

there's a new group of bandits that robbed one of the wildcat sites. Didn't hurt a hair on anyone's little head, but robbed them of all their cash."

"Bless their hearts," Hob said. She tucked a black cigarette between her lips and lit it with a snap of her fingers, outwardly calm. But she felt it coming: Coyote had the bit in his teeth, and she was always ready to wipe some bandits off the map – if there was a profit to be had. "And you just so happen to know where they got to?"

"I might have an idea or two," Coyote smiled brightly. "Though best we move quickly, yes? You know how these reprobates like to scurry about."

Hob grunted, sucking in a long drag of her cigarette. "Who all's come back? Just you'n Lykaios?" With her and Raff, that would be four. She wanted better odds than that on a bandit hunt when they were going in practically blind.

"Davey is here, and I think he could do with a bit of airing out. And Lobo. A little adventure will help him work those kinks out of his joints."

"Bala?" The man was still hobbling around on crutches, but if it was close enough that Coyote was proposing a single day roundtrip, they could put him on Lobo's supply cart with a gun. That was a fun thought, and she wondered why she hadn't come up with it before now.

Coyote considered. "It'd certainly put him in a better mood."

"Float it past Davey. See how loud he screams."

Coyote grinned. "You give me the best gifts."

Davey didn't scream, but he muttered. And he kept muttering over the shortwave channel, until Dambala told him to shut the fuck up. It couldn't have been comfortable, bouncing around in the little cart behind Lobo's trike, and it looked damned ridiculous considering he'd still put on his leathers and helmet so he had his radio and didn't get his tattoos sandblasted off. But Dambala didn't complain, just sat there patient as a mountain with his shotgun, the crest of spikes he'd put on his helmet going slowly orange-red with dust. A low black butte, softened by drifts of sand, humped up on the horizon.

"Found them," Coyote said over the radio. He and Raff had gone ahead to scout. He was barely audible over the static of distance, but good enough. "Bear southeast. They're camped on the lee of the butte."

"How many?" Hob asked. If it was a full camp, seven might not be enough unless they got really creative. It had taken the whole company to clear out the last one, and then they'd unknowingly had Coyote working as one hell of bloody distraction.

"All I got's two guards," Lykaios said. "Awful quiet in there."

"I'd guess that the rest are out doing a bit of work, since it's a sizable camp," Coyote said. "You know, how we tend to conduct ourselves."

"All right and proper of 'em," Hob said dryly. Maybe they were just really organized for bandits, but it stank of Corporate something fierce. "Keep your eyes on the horizon, case they come back in," Hob added. "Lobo, you bring that damn plow of yours?"

"I'm sittin' on it," Dambala answered. "Ass ain't ever gonna be the same."

"You bend it, I'll bend you," Lobo growled.

"Let's get it on once we're on the shadow side of that butte," Hob said. "Hope you're feelin' frisky."

Lobo laughed. "Always liked bein' a batterin' ram."

• • •

Electric motors were good for the element of surprise; no engine noise loud enough to sound over the wind to give them away. There was plenty of creaking and thumping from the cart still attached to the back of Lobo's trike, but that wasn't enough to be a warning until it was too late.

Lobo, the angled sand guard bolted onto the front of his trike, led the charge at the low humps of the bandit's camouflaged tents. He aimed straight for one of the sentries that Lykaios called out. The man or woman – impossible to tell which – had their back turned until it was almost too late, then screamed and jumped out of the way. Their fast reflexes didn't save them from taking a blast from Dambala's shotgun in the chest an instant later. Lobo plowed through one of the tents. A cloud of fabric, flimsies, and the shards of who knew what else exploded into the air.

Hob, Raff, and Davey had hunkered down directly behind Dambala's wake, so they weren't visible. Davey and Raff went left and Hob went right. The other guard, pants flapping open as he bolted from behind a tent, tried to draw a handgun. Davey, the machete he'd insisted on trading for in hand, arrowed past him. One cut and the guard went down. Davey slammed on his brakes and threw his bike into a skid, turned, and came back around to hit him again. Blood arced up from the blade as he drew his arm back.

"Think you got 'em good," Raff said, idling by with a pistol in his hand.

Hob braked to a stop in the middle of the small camp. "Check all the tents. We don't want any surprises." Out of the corner of her eye, she saw Coyote and Lykaios rolling in. "Oh, and good work, Diablo."

There was a pause as that got absorbed, and then the man formerly known as Davey Painter whooped. Hob had been meaning to give him his Wolf name at the last raid since it had been a damn sight bigger of a deal, but Coyote showing up out of the blue had turned everything on its head. She might as well make up for it now.

She left shiny new Diablo to get his back slapped and his arms punched black and blue by the other Wolves, and yanked open the flap of the first tent. Inside were the usual supplies – tins and ration packs, some of them marked as coming from the company store, couple of water bags, some personal items, and an ammo box. Hob ducked back out. "See how much of this stuff we can pick up and fit in saddlebags or around Dambala," she ordered. "Water first, that's what we need most. Then ammo. Lykaios, stay on watch."

"We waitin' for 'em to get back?" Lykaios asked. "I always got time to fuck up some bandits."

Hob paused and did a quick count of the tents. She could just about feel the others watching her, listening for her answer. "Don't like the odds, so no."

"But–"

Hob turned on her. "Don't fuckin' argue with me. We're dumpin' everythin' we can't take and I'm firin' the tents. You wanna go on a revenge that we ain't gettin' paid for, do it on your own time."

Lykaios took a step back, her solid form hunching in a little. Sullenly, she said, "You got us killin' all them bluebellies, sure like revenge."

Hob bared her teeth. "I got us a double payday for that. 'Less you got that in your back pocket, shut the fuck up and get to work." She turned and headed into the next tent, pulling out her cigarettes as she did.

Behind, she heard Dambala's amused rumble of: "Some day you'll learn to not try pissin' further than your CO. And them Ravanis got a mighty back pressure goin'." She'd got the impression Dambala and Coyote had known Lykaios in their previous life, but it wasn't the kind of thing you talked about.

Hob bit back a laugh around her cigarette and set into the routine of rifling through the supplies, tossing what she wanted outside the tent for the others to collect.

"Boss, I have something for you to see," Coyote called. She caught sight of him waving out the flap of the tent nearest the butte.

Inside the tent wasn't so different – except for several canvas bags. Coyote had one open next to him, and tilted it toward her as soon as she poked her head in. The bag was full of brightly colored, universal credit chits.

"That's more'n you'd get off one work party," Hob said.

"Even better, these bags are tagged." Coyote slipped a knife out of his boot and cut away a section of the canvas to reveal a familiar round, silver button: short range transmitter, recognizable as company issue.

Hob sucked at her teeth. "Startin' to think real bandits are a dyin' breed."

"Well, when one creature goes extinct, another fills its niche," Coyote said. He tossed her another bag. "We ought to be able to carry all of these. We're keeping them, right?"

"We ain't a charity." She had ammunition to buy and mouths to feed. Hob felt the canvas of the bag he'd given her until she located the hard round button of another transmitter. She drew her own knife. "Though mayhap I'm a good enough citizen to warn Mag there's some new fuckery afoot."

"I never doubted," Coyote said piously.

CHAPTER FIFTEEN • *36 DAYS*

"Clarence, I got somethin' here you need to see." The miner poked her head in his kitchen door. "Oh. Didn't realize you had company."

"You ain't interruptin'," Odalia said. They'd been having another meeting, working out supply plans, going over information from other towns.

The woman nodded. "Y'all lookin' better at least. Last I saw, you was half dead."

Clarence smiled, lopsided out of his new habit to hide the teeth the greenbellies had broken. After three weeks, his bruises had faded away to nothing. "You know we're tougher'n that. Come on in, Rosa. You want some lemonade?"

The miner closed the door behind her, then shook her head. Pores on her cheeks were darkened with the rock dust on her brown, round face; the areas around her eyes, nose, and mouth relatively clean where she'd been protected by her goggles and bandana. She waved away the glass of thin, vaguely lemon-scented water that Mag offered her. "Gonna head on home after we have us a talk. My girls are missin' me fierce, I bet, and I wanna make sure their other mama didn't spoil 'em too bad."

Mag realized then that she had to be one of the miners

that had volunteered for the newest survey crew. The exploration promised to pay more money even if it had bigger risk, and they were still playing it quiet in town, gathering their strength. It also meant they had people out there who could tell them what was going on.

"I'm sure she didn't. What you got?" Clarence asked.

Rosa dug a handful of something out of her pocket and deposited it into Clarence's palm.

"What the hell are these?" Clarence stirred the little bits of plastic with one finger. He glanced up at Rosa. "This some kind of play money for your girls?"

Mag leaned over to look herself, and picked up one of the chits. They were almost the same shape as the denominations of credit markers she knew, but the colors were wrong and the plastic felt too light. She turned the chit over and frowned at the TransRift logo raised a bit unevenly on its surface rather than the normal FUS logo.

"Payman on the site said it's company money," Rosa said. "In numbers, it's twice as much as we were promised for bein' on the wildcat crew…"

"But what the hell is company money?" Clarence finished.

"Payman said we could use it regular at all the stores, so it's more valuable 'cause we're gettin' more and the prices ain't changed. And they'd be happy to buy up our credits for twice their value."

Of course they would, Mag thought grimly. She already saw where this was leading. Greenbellies and bluebellies didn't deign to buy anything from the company store. They had all their stuff brought in on the supply trains. "They say you could buy a ticket off world with company money?" Mag asked.

Rosa's gaze flicked to her. "Said we could. And we could use it to send money off planet still too, one for one." Her expression was dark. "Got only their word for that."

Because of course, few people heard much from their families, once they got to Tanegawa's World. The only things that ever made it through were old-fashioned letters written on flimsies. People often got data cards they had no way of viewing. It was an act of faith, trying to send anything off on the rift ship.

"Y'all just take it quiet?" Odalia asked.

Rosa's lip curled. "Payman said that's all he had. So it was that or nothin'. One of the boys they brought in from Primero, he tried to stir things up. Cussed 'em out good. They took his pay envelope back, then took him when he threw a punch, and we ain't seen him since. Another one, he got his nose broke." She shrugged. "I got babies waitin' for me and needin' to be fed."

"How much diggin' you do?" Mag asked.

"One shaft, five hundred meters. Didn't hit nothin' but a trace here and there of that blue dust. They were excited about that for a hot minute, but got real quiet after when even the dust went out. Then they did a survey at the end of the shaft and said it weren't worth goin' further." She rubbed the back of her hand over her nose. "That blue stuff ain't showin' right on their surveys, I'm thinkin'."

Mag didn't like the sound of that. It meant the company was flailing in the dark, hoping to hit on something. That was dangerous for the people doing the work. And now the bonus pay wouldn't even go for any kind of good use.

Clarence nodded, and offered her the chits back. "You go see your kids, Rosa. Give 'em a hug for me."

The air in Clarence's kitchen felt thick and close as Rosa closed the door behind her. No one seemed to want to speak, though Mag wasn't certain why. Maybe because this was an unexpected tactic from the company. They were used to threats of blacklisting, and bullying by the greenbellies. From a certain angle, this looked *almost* reasonable, which was why she distrusted it profoundly.

She'd been trying to keep her head down more than usual, with how Odalia had reacted to her before. Quiet and efficient, rebuilding the trust seemed the way to go. But fine, she could start this. "This is gonna make it damn near impossible to pay off anyone from the company."

"I know," Clarence said.

"They been asking too much anyway," Odalia said.

"If we want guns and... anythin' else we can't get in the company store, we need to be able to do that," Mag pointed out. They'd been building up their stock slowly out of necessity, since they had to buy scrapped or broken guns and fix them. This was going to stop even that in its tracks.

"There's gonna be plenty of people like Rosa, who don't like it but can do the math," Odalia said.

"Gonna be others ready to fight," Clarence said. He rubbed his face with one hand. "Just had payday. That gives us, what... twelve days?"

"Yeah," Odalia said. "And we don't know for certain the towns are going to get that... that *play* money."

"And we don't know for certain we aren't," Mag said quietly. "So we get out the word. And... we tell people we need all the regular credits they got. I'll keep tight records. We can reimburse 'em with the company money one for one, and return the credits later if we don't end up needin' 'em."

"More'n that," Clarence said. "We ask the workers in all the towns if–" He raised his voice over Odalia's protest "–*if* that's what we get in our pay envelopes, what do we want to do about it. Because whatever it is, we all do it together. They been beatin' us and killin' us with accidents, and now they ain't even gonna pay us proper. There's gotta be a line, and I think we come to it."

Mag could have kissed him for voicing what was on her own mind. Though she felt a shiver of doubt, because that had been almost exactly what she was thinking. Did they just agree, or had she somehow unwittingly made him agree with her? No, she couldn't go down that path, not without making herself crazy. "Knowin' we got some action we're workin' toward will keep the hotheads at a low simmer," she offered.

"We gonna be ready in twelve days?" Odalia asked darkly.

Both she and Clarence looked dead-on at Mag. She hadn't realized until that moment that Odalia had been avoiding looking at her. How did that make her feel so small, so uncertain? Because she was small and uncertain, and she knew that there was a lot riding on this. They'd worked so hard to keep everyone restrained because she'd claimed they needed time, so that they even *could* get ready. "In twelve days, we'll be ready as we can be." She kept her voice steady and firm, somehow. Like she really believed it.

Clarence nodded. "I'll draft a note callin' for a vote on this. Not just the majority in a town, but the majority *of* the towns. That's the only way this is gonna work. And we gotta give people some time to chew it over, so... I'll ask for the vote back by ten days. Then we'll know which way we're jumpin'."

Ten days wasn't a long time, Mag knew. And ten days was also more than a lifetime. She'd lived it both ways. She set her shoulders, holding the determination that in ten days, she'd be ready. No matter which way it went.

"This one's from the Chadha family."

Mag saw the envelope, which was really a grimy,

folded-up flimsy, out of the corner of her eye, and took it. She popped the flap and did a quick count of the chits inside, then noted down the amount in her little book. "Got it."

"We had a bit of our water ration too, and I added that to the barrel."

Finally, she looked up. The man in front of her, Omar, was large, with a saturnine complexion and a face that seemed meant to be mysterious and brooding. His shaggy black hair hung around his brown eyes; his mine-pale brown skin pocked with black rock dust. He gave her an eager smile, revealing a chipped front tooth. "How much?" Mag asked.

"Dunno. About a third of a liter?"

Mag swallowed down her annoyance. With the break point coming, she needed the numbers precise, so they could figure out how to ration, and know how long they could hold on. Every drop of water, their most precious resource, needed to be accounted for. "I need a more exact amount than that."

"Sorry," Omar said, and he did sound sorry at least. Everything the man did was painfully earnest, to the point that Mag sometimes found herself wondering if it was an elaborate act.

"Next time, measure it," Mag said. "This is important."

"Yes, ma'am."

Omar made no move to leave, so she asked, "Something else?"

"Also found this at the message box, out in the gulch? No name or nothin' on it, but... Guess it might be somethin'?" He handed over a crumpled flimsy folded into its own envelope.

Mag untangled the flimsy and smoothed it out, instantly recognizing the awkwardly formed letters: *bandits from the company robbing yall of credits bagging to send back to newcastle and farmer told me company been tellin them to not help you*

Punctuation. Some day she'd sit Hob Ravani down and make her go over her punctuation.

From one angle, she supposed the information about the credits was almost... not good news, exactly, but useful. If she handed word of this around, more miners would be willing to add their credits to the fund in exchange for the company money, since better that than having them stolen the next time one of them got out to visit another town or was sent on a wildcat crew. And that seemed to be more and more common these days, people in and out of the mine for a few days at a stretch, only a skeleton crew actually working the veins they had. She wondered how much longer it would be until they'd pulled everyone out. Maybe they just hadn't found enough test sites yet.

But it was also bad, really damn bad. TransRift *knew* what they'd been doing, and this confirmed it. They knew the miners had been putting in bribes, and were cutting that off. Clarence's two crooked greenbellies in the armory had disappeared. Another, in Tercio, had laughed at the handful of company money one of the miners there tried, saying, "You can't get real bullets with fake money." The farmers had already wanted to ignore them, and this made it worse.

"Did I do right to bring that to you?" Omar asked.

"Yes," Mag said, and tucked it away in her skirt. "You see somethin' like that again, it's from the Ravani. Should come straight to me."

Omar's face lit up. "So we gonna be hirin' the Ghost Wolves again, with all this money?" While TransRift had been claiming to anyone who'd listen that the Weatherman had died in a tragic train derailment accident – while at the same time raising the price on

Hob's head like it was completely unrelated – the story had spread. The Wolves were on their way to being folk heroes whether Hob liked it or not. The kids and people Mag's age – though hell, she felt so much older these days – ate it up. Most of them seemed to have dreams of impressing Hob somehow, joining her crew. Mag didn't have the heart to tell them that Hob wasn't easy to impress, even if she had wanted to admit how well they knew each other.

Mag was fairly certain, though, that Hob really did like it, in her secret heart that beat thick with rebellion. Uncle Nick, on the other hand, was probably turning over in his grave. "I hear they got other matters on their plate."

The money probably would go to Hob, eventually. But she was keeping that under her hat for now. It was a strange sort of push and pull, between needing to keep all the workers together and make sure they were all on board, while not saying too much because there were company spies everywhere.

"I figure so. But… you know 'em, right? Do you think I could ever meet 'em?" he asked.

Which brought her back to Omar's bright, inquisitive brown eyes. Maybe that was hero worship shining out of them. Maybe it was an intelligence a lot more malevolent. She could feel him, right in front of her, like his mind was a tangible thing, his thoughts a pressure against her skin. It would be easy, very easy, to just empty him out of everything he knew – if he did know anything.

Mag swallowed down that urge. She didn't want to become what Odalia already assumed she was. "You got more errands to run," she said. "Scat."

She turned her attention back to the numbers until they swam in front of her eyes; really, she shouldn't have bothered until Anabi got home. While Mag had a good head for math, Anabi was even better when it came to keeping inventories organized.

The sound of the kitchen door and a breath of cool night air heralded Anabi's return. She smiled brightly and slid around a chair to sit next to Mag, hooking their legs together. She twitched the notebook out of Mag's grasp and wrote a quick sentence in the margin: *Next time I'll keep the books and you go to the warehouse.*

Mag had sent her to watch the miners trying to train, knowing they'd have a real fight on their hands eventually. "That bad?"

This time, Anabi did fish her slate out of her pocket. *Worse.* She wrinkled her nose and added: *I'd think they were drunk, only none of them smelled like it.*

Mag sighed and rubbed at her eyes. Anabi kissing the corner of her lips got her to smile at least. "They might fight better drunk, anyway. Could pretend it was a saloon." But she felt Hob's note crinkle in her skirt pocket, the reminder that they did know people who could fight and did fight for their entire living becoming a grain of an idea that bounced in her thoughts, like sand blown along a dune face by the wind. "We ain't mercenaries, and we ain't had their time to practice, or their teachers. But mercenaries'll do whatever you pay 'em for," she said slowly. Anabi nodded encouragingly; she was long used to Mag thinking out loud at her. "So what if we offer to pay 'em for doin' somethin' other than killin' for once? What if we pay 'em to train us? To find us a safe place to learn to use our guns?"

She certainly couldn't think of anyone else in the world better than Hob's people when it came to shooting. Hell, they could hit things while screaming around at top speed on those damn motorcycles.

The dead or alive price on Hob is getting pretty high, Anabi wrote.

"You're right about that," Mag agreed. "Couldn't be Hob doin' it, nor any one of her people's got a price on their head. But still." It was better than nothing. And who knew, maybe Hob knew a way for people to practice with guns that didn't require a lot of noise or wasting bullets. It was worth asking, and maybe worth paying for.

She won't like that.

She smiled wryly at Anabi, who smiled back at her. "We don't pay Hob to be happy. We pay her to get shit done."

CHAPTER SIXTEEN • *36 DAYS*

It was nearly midnight before Shige felt the full rollout of the new payroll system was adjusted to his satisfaction. He'd made certain to have some of the new chits sent to the wildcat sites early, a carefully introduced clerical error that Ms Meetchim would not care about if he was careful with her correspondence. To ensure the rest was as big a disaster as possible was more a piece of art. Breezy Corporate memos about the benefits and efficiency, the gratitude of workers on other worlds, would prime the company personnel to feel exceptionally stung by the almost certain rejection and pushback from the miners.

He sent the memos to the flimsy spooler, then sat back and rubbed his eyes. From his intellectual remove, he almost enjoyed this work, just as he'd always enjoyed classic games like chess, Diplomacy, and Systems United as a child. There was an art to laying out the board so that, whichever way the pieces fell, he'd achieve his victory. But should he also remind himself that these were people, not inanimate game pieces? Blood would flow before this had all ended, and at least some of it would be on his hands. He had to keep the only faith he'd ever had, learned on Ayana's knee: the blood of the few watered the tree that sheltered the many.

And here, the sacrifice of lives now would save future generations of miners locally, and many more exploited people on a multi-system scale from the depredations of a corporation that had little interest in anything but its own profit.

Shige was Ayana and Hamadi's own personal sacrifice, he'd been told many times after the abrupt revelation of his un-birth. He'd also never been able to bring himself to ask if his older brother had been intended for his role and hadn't wanted to play along. He'd been too angry at Coyote at the time, for all his horrible truths.

He sighed and swept aside those unproductive thoughts. He was tired, and he couldn't return to his sparsely furnished company apartment until he'd collated yet another set of reports Meetchim had happily dumped on him before she'd left for the night. Another stack built up during his absence, fallen by the wayside.

Shige fetched himself another cup of coffee. As he watched the thick brown liquid dribble into his standard TransRift-blue cup, he considered briefly the microinjectors he had hidden about his person, loaded with a range of poisons and drugs. He had a few with strong stimulants, and as exhausted as he felt, it was tempting. But with no idea when his next resupply would be, better to save those for a true emergency.

At his desk, he went over the latest reports from the wildcat sites and surveys, and meticulously updated the map for Ms Meetchim's consideration the next morning. The amritite veins – assuming that they'd correctly identified them in the surveys – were extraordinarily thin or nonexistent in the towns. Perhaps the mineral was simply that rare, though considering the effects its incorporation had on Mr Yellow, Shige had little doubt that TransRift would throw itself into chasing down every last grain. But as the surveys began to move outside of the towns, particularly to the north of Newcastle, there was some sign of the veins thickening, becoming more numerous – and beginning to curve deeper.

Satisfied, he turned to the last report as his wristwatch let him know that he'd need to be up in three hours to get to the office. The final flimsies were rather crumpled, a field report no one had bothered to retype. Initial transmission from an undercover security team – Corporate code for Mariposa officers embedded in and controlling bandit groups – about a "witch" having been found in the desert and prepared for pickup.

And then no follow-up. Shige checked the dates to find this had occurred while he'd been on Earth, weeks ago. The initial report receipt date was only yesterday, so there'd been a delay in transmission. That didn't speak well of the retrieval of the witch. Or perhaps it had been a false positive. There was no way of knowing, from this.

Frowning, he marked the report to be sent to security, to have a detail check up on it. Certainly not his top priority, but he had an interest in the witches of Tanegawa's World after what he'd seen during the attack on Mr Green's train.

Then, with his desk at last clear in front of him, he headed home. Or at least that was his intention. Instead, Shige found himself in the sub-basement, turning down a particular hallway. One wall was synthcrete and punctuated with doors; the other was glass, revealing a plain set of rooms: bedroom, dining room, playroom filled with reels of multicolored string and bits of construction frames.

The Weatherman ought to have been asleep, if sleep was something Weathermen even did. Instead he was up, dressed, and waiting at the door.

It was only polite, Shige rationalized as he swiped his security card and opened the door, feeling curiously like his hands belonged to someone else. Only for the best that he maintain his contact with Mr Yellow. All of those rationalizations fell away when he felt his gaze dragged upward to the Weatherman's face.

Fatigued and mentally muddled, he didn't have the will to stop. It wasn't until the Weatherman's dry fingers closed on his chin that he felt in control again. Gasping, he jerked back, though it was useless against the Weatherman's strength. But he was able to force his gaze down, to Mr Yellow's chin.

The Weatherman sighed, leaning in. Shige's back met the smooth glass wall, as breath that tasted like blood flowed over his lips. "We know," the Weatherman whispered.

"What do you know?" Shige asked, feeling hollow.

"We know you want to kill us," Mr Yellow said, his voice a bare whisper. "And we know you wanted to kill Mr Green. We know because Mr Green knew." Cold, dry fingers combed through Shige's hair.

He pressed his palms flat against the glass wall, as if the solid touch would make him feel less disoriented and trapped. "I didn't kill him," he whispered. Not a lie, though he bore some responsibility and had no regrets.

"We are not angry. We know you." He leaned yet closer.

"What do you want?" Shige asked. He turned his fingers, easing a microinjector, one of the few weapons he always carried, between two of them.

Mr Yellow's hand closed over his, pinning it firmly against the glass. "You don't want to hurt us."

For all the terror gnawing at him, the thought sounded clear in his mind: it was true. Mr Yellow hadn't hurt him, after all. Mr Yellow had gotten him here, quite early. There was so much work still to do. "What do you want?" Shige asked again.

"We are thirsty," Mr Yellow said. He tilted his head, and Shige felt lips press against the hot pulse in his temple. "We have always been thirsty. All we wish is to drink."

He knew that the Weathermen drank blood, and ate far less neat things. Shige shuddered. Some strange thing in him said *yes*, that might be rather nice. That *couldn't* be a part of him. "No."

"Not you," Mr Yellow said. "Not yet."

"Then what?"

"The water of this world flows in one direction. Take us there. Promise."

He would have promised anything, if he thought it would get him out of this moment alive. "I promise," Shige whispered.

"Mr Green thought we should keep you." Mr Yellow turned his head so their foreheads rested hard together, and then there was nothing for Shige to see but the darkness of a universe without stars. "We will."

Shige jerked as his head met the hard wall of the shower. The water streaming over him had gone tepid, when he usually preferred his showers close to scorching. He was lucky he'd leaned that way as he fell asleep, rather than toppling over.

It said a great deal about his fatigued state that he didn't recall leaving the office or returning home. Perhaps he ought to have used one of those stimulants after all.

As he watched the water swirl down the drain between his pale brown feet, he saw threads of red uncurl in it. Frowning, he brought his hand to touch his nose – his fingers came back bloody. Lovely, he'd even managed to bump his face. Hopefully there wouldn't be a bruise.

Annoyed, he turned off the shower and stood,

shivering, though it didn't feel at all cold. Fatigue and hunger, perhaps. Without the network at his call, he checked the wall display to see what time it must be – right, he had an hour before he had to be back at work.

Shige scrubbed his face with his hands, grimaced at the reminder of the bleeding nose, and took a deep breath. Now was not the time to lose focus. He had too much to do, particularly a better analysis of those survey reports. Perhaps, the thought came unbidden, this was a job for Mr Yellow.

CHAPTER SEVENTEEN • *35 DAYS*

"And how are we this morning?" someone sang out, loud and disgustingly cheerful.

She recognized that voice, Hob thought blearily through the endless, red-hot-spike throbbing of her skull. It was the voice of Satan. And here, she hadn't even thought he was real. There was a thump that echoed through her goddamn teeth, and she smelled... coffee. Satan had brought her coffee. How nice of him to be hanging around the base after a night of celebrating Diablo gaining his Wolf's name.

Hob grunted and hoisted her head up enough that she could fumble to locate the cup. She didn't open her eye yet. She was pretty sure if she did, her brain would slide out her empty eye socket and then she'd die. Maybe that wouldn't be such a bad idea.

"Really," Satan continued in clipped, amused tones. Satan spoke like a snooty offworlder. Huh. "I would have thought you'd go to your bed instead of curling up in your office. It smells like... stale beer and vinegar in here. What on earth were you drinking?"

Oh, she realized as she scalded her tongue on the first blessed sip of coffee. No, it was worse than Satan. It was Coyote. "I don't know," she croaked. Talking did not make her head explode or her stomach empty, to her vague surprise. "Lobo gave it to me."

"Oh. That was your first mistake."

"Startin' to realize." The next sip of coffee was more tolerable, or maybe she'd just burned out all the nerves in her mouth and throat already.

"Are you alive enough to accept a message?" he asked with relentless cheer.

"No."

"Good!" He slid a flimsy in front of her.

Hob stared down at the wavering letters and couldn't make any sense of them, though she at least recognized the handwriting as Mag's. Her eye throbbed. The goddamn ends of her hair throbbed. She shoved the flimsy back at Coyote and took another determined haul of her coffee like it was a cigarette. "You read it." Thinking of cigarettes had her hand automatically searching for her case, which was... not there.

He picked the flimsy back up. "Your coat is on the floor in the corner, presumably with your cigarettes in it. I've no idea why you left it there."

She stared at him as best she could. It must have still made an impression, because he grabbed her coat and handed it over. Hob fished a cigarette out. "Comfy?" Coyote asked.

Hob grunted in answer. She hadn't found an ill yet that a sufficient amount of tar-black coffee and cigarettes couldn't beat into submission.

Cheerfully, Coyote read: "Got a job proposal. We need training to fight, and a safe place to learn shooting. Send three people who don't have a price on their head and you can spare for a week." He regarded the flimsy. "The price she's offering is... to the low side of decent. Family discount?"

"Somethin' like." Though Hob wasn't sure how she

felt about teaching the miners. Felt a little like trying to put themselves out of a job.

Coyote made a noise that Hob wasn't quite certain how to interpret in the back of his throat. He thought it was his job to needle her, she reminded herself. He flipped the flimsy over idly. "Oh, and there's a postscript: *yes, and this means you, Hob.*" He checked the original message. "Ah, yes, the bit about having a price on one's head is underlined. Twice."

"Fuck that," Hob muttered. "I been in Ludlow plenty of times."

Coyote shrugged. "Not for any length of time, let alone using that time to try to beat a bit of skill into some raw recruits. So who will you send?"

"Ain't said I'm gonna send anyone yet." The look of disdain he gave her was eloquent. Hob rubbed her temples. "Well, go on."

"Hmm?"

"Go on an' tell me who I'm sendin'. That's why you're here, ain't ya."

"Well, I do have a few suggestions, if you'd like to entertain them."

Like she could manage to remember her own name right now, let alone figure out the few people in the group who had the skill to teach and the patience to go with it. She flapped her hand at him, *get on with it.*

"Lobo, of course. He's the best knife man you've got. Geri isn't bad, and also isn't nearly as much of an asshole when he's standing somewhere you can't see him."

Hob grunted, not willing to rise to the bait.

"Lykaios will round out the team decently. And of course, you'll be sending me to lead it."

"Will I, now?"

"There's no one better to send onto hunting grounds than a known corpse," Coyote said primly. "And you know if you send Geri along without someone to play moderating influence, he'll have far too much fun being in charge. Oh, and–"

She held up a hand. She didn't know how long the list kept going, and didn't want to find out. She had a feeling he'd thought of every argument she could make if she'd had a clear head, and already come up with a counter. "If I say you can go, will you get the fuck out of my office?"

"It would be my pleasure."

The sun was high in the sky before Hob felt human enough to venture forth. The base was damn quiet; Coyote had already collected his crew and got the hell out before she could change her mind. Freki and his crew of twelve were on their way to get past Shimera, trying to locate another pack of raiders with a thirst for Federal Union credits that had mysteriously sprung up.

The garage was warm and silent, but for the building shifting and the faint snoring of Hati in the corner. Hob quietly pulled out her motorcycle and checked it over, loaded it up with camping gear and a few days' worth of supplies, and walked it out to the gate. While most everyone else was working or down, she might as well make herself useful.

Hob headed away from the base, from the hardpan and rocky ravines that must have carried water in some forgotten age, into the drifting sands. There, she parked her motorcycle in the shadow of a dune and drew one of her knives. She put a cut on her thumb, right alongside a line of old scars. Nothing dramatic, just enough to squeeze out a few drops of blood. The Bone Collector had always claimed that was all it would take.

He'd also disappointed her before. He'd probably disappear entirely one day, and she'd never know when to stop waiting. She hated that feeling.

A great eagle moved in to circle overhead, its shadow stark whenever it passed between her and the sun. Hob's stomach sank more with each minute. Sweat trickled between her shoulder blades.

Then she felt it, a shifting in the air rather than any kind of sound above the breeze that sighed over the sands. She turned, and there the Bone Collector stood on her blind side, the hem of his coat flapping around his calves. He hadn't brought his staff today. "'Bout damn time," Hob said, stuffing all her worry under a blanket of temper.

"Did I keep you waiting long?" he asked.

"Long enough I was thinkin' 'bout leavin'. I got better things to do with my time than cool my heels while I'm waitin' for you to make an entrance."

He approached, his feet leaving no tracks in the sand. She held her ground against the urge to back up a step and resented it. "Time doesn't pass the same for me as it does for you," he said, like that was an apology.

"Ain't the first time you told me that. But that don't change how time is passin' for me, now, does it?"

He spread his hands. "I am sorry."

That disarmed her. She wasn't used to many people telling her they were sorry, unless they were either Mag – and that was damn rare, since if anyone was wrong between the two of them, it was almost always Hob – or someone looking from the wrong end of the barrel of her bone-handled revolvers. "Apology accepted," she said, somehow feeling like an asshole for it. "You busy right now?"

One of his eyebrows arched up. "If I were busy, I wouldn't be here."

When the hell had talking to him gotten harder? She was Hob Fucking Ravani, and this was ridiculous. "Good. I got a project you get to help me with."

"Get to?"

She ignored both the words and the tone. "That well you and Coyote talked about. Where all the witchiness comes from. Sure as shit that's what TransRift is lookin' for, so we're gonna find it first." And after, she'd come up with a plan once she knew more.

"I told you, I don't think it's a place like you understand places to be."

"It's gotta be somethin', if Coyote's been there. And the idea of ever goin' there again scares him shitless. Don't sound like some kind of... woo-woo thing to me."

"Woo-woo thing," the Bone Collector repeated, tone disbelieving.

"You got somethin' to say?"

"No. Just marveling at your way with words."

If she wasn't going to let Coyote bait her, she sure as shit wasn't going to let the Bone Collector do it either. She dug the map she'd been making out of her pocket, the one with all the wildcat sites marked on it. "If you're right and it ain't a real place, then we won't find it but they can't either. If *I'm* right, then we all got a big damn problem. You know the shit they do to witchy ones. So let's go lookin'."

"This map shows where they are," the Bone Collector pointed out. "It doesn't mean that they've found anything."

Hob shrugged. "You ain't givin' me any better ideas. And these sure look like they're movin' in a direction." There was a trend going to the north, she was sure of that. She'd had the good sense to write down the dates about when the sites had opened and closed.

"If you say so," he said, in the tone she'd come to interpret as him humoring her.

She folded the map back up and shoved it in her pocket. "You got any better idea, I'm listenin'."

"A better idea might be to not embark on a fool's errand."

"That ain't a real idea," she snapped, and then jabbed her finger at his chest. "You go actin' like you know everythin', but we both know that's bullshit. It took me'n my whole pack helpin' for you to kill that Weatherman. You as much as said that what the company's doin' right now ain't good. Think you're gonna stop it all alone any more than you did last time?"

He held up his hands. "That isn't what I'm saying at all."

"Good. Then start bein' fuckin' helpful. We're on the same side, an' I seem to remember you callin' us friends a time or two."

"Yes," he said. "That is still true."

"Then get on the back of the goddamn motorcycle."

They spent the rest of the day doing a modified search grid in sections of the dune sea, always moving north. Hob checked the map often and plotted it against what the simple computer on her motorcycle could tell her about course, speed, and time. And at every stop, she asked the Bone Collector if he felt anything. He'd make a show of sitting on the ground, eyes closed and palms flat on the sand, then shake his head and say, "No."

She kept them going into the night, not ready to stop too early. This wasn't something they needed that much light for, anyway, and it was almost nice, the moons washing the normally orange dunes into something pale and ghostly. The Bone Collector wasn't warm against her back, but he was solid, his hands ever-present at her waist. It also wasn't nice, because there'd only been one other time she'd gone riding around like this with some man on the back of her motorcycle, and that hadn't turned out well at all.

Not knowing how she felt made her prickly and short about everything when they finally did stop. She did her best to just ignore the Bone Collector as she set up the little camouflage tarp tent she'd brought. She didn't need a fire, just pulled a couple of flat rocks out of her saddlebags and heated them up in her hands, then cooked her dinner on those.

She'd figured out a lot of small, useful skills since Old Nick had passed. There was a joy in experimenting, and none of the Wolves gave a damn any more. Lobo had been the one who suggested this trick.

Every second, she was aware of the Bone Collector's piercing blue gaze on her. He squatted down next to the tent while she finished heating up some coffee, rubbing the smart camouflage fabric between his fingers like it was some kind of precious silk.

"You hungry?" she asked. Her voice sounded loud, in the cool silence of the night.

"Should I be?"

"Shit, how would I know?" Most people would be. He wasn't most people. They'd established that plenty long ago.

He sat down next to her with barely a sound, so she offered him the cup of coffee anyway, and then a shallow bowl of beans with sausage cut up in it. Not exciting food, but enough to go on.

"We're gonna have to share," she said. "Just brought my personal kit."

The coffee he seemed to know what to do with. He sipped it, smiled, and handed the cup back to her. He inspected the plate like it might bite him.

Hob took her own drink of the coffee. "Figure tomorrow, we'll keep heading north. I got enough food an' water to be on the trail another two days. 'Less you got a better idea."

"If I did, you know that I would tell you." Ignoring the fork, he delicately picked a single bean off the plate with his fingers and ate it.

Did she? It had felt like this whole time, he was just humoring her. It wasn't a feeling she liked at all. "You ain't been that helpful."

He sighed, and pinched another bean between his fingers. "If you saw as I did, you'd know it isn't so simple."

"Then show me." She said it like a dare she expected him to wave off.

The Bone Collector regarded her, sucking the gravy off one of his fingers. He didn't have a right to look that normal, she thought grumpily. And she fucking refused to consider his lips in this moment. "All right," he said.

"All right?"

"Yes, all right."

Well, she'd never backed down from anything before. "Fine. What I got to do?"

The Bone Collector set the dish aside, then reached out to rest his hand under her chin when she automatically followed that movement. He kept her face toward him and started humming, quietly, under his breath.

"What—"

"Listen," he murmured.

His fingers were so cool against her skin, and hard, though still like flesh and bone rather than the rock he sometimes became. But there was that feeling of intimacy again, like he was too damn close and about to lean in more.

"I won't hurt you."

Defiance had gotten her a lot of places before. She ticked her chin up a little and looked him dead in the eye. "Don't think you can."

"Bigger things than me have tried and failed," he

said softly, lips curving in a smile that she couldn't quite decide was affectionate or mocking. She was about to retort again when something changed in the world, shifted. His eyes, bright blue irises like lakes she'd only ever seen pictures of, black pupils, swallowed her up.

She felt every grain of sand, humming and shifting beneath her, and then that awareness expanded outward, into the currents of magnetism and electricity that churned in the dynamo of the world's heart, the other energies rushing back and forth in blood made of viscous stone. She felt every capillary and vein and artery and heartbeat, but didn't feel their locations because the brain wasn't wired to understand these things. Every sensation transmitted, every pulse of that thicker-than-blood ran through her and dissolved her and carried her and bathed her in so much power that there wasn't room to be Hob anymore – except no, goddamnit, she was Hob, she'd always been Hob, and she wasn't gonna stop being Hob for anything–

She felt like she was falling, except the ground was abruptly beneath her, and the endless black sky of Tanegawa's World above, sparked with untold stars.

"Shh," the Bone Collector murmured, his hand moving slowly over her hair. Then his face came into view, pale as the moon. Like she was daring him to try to make her dissolve again, she looked him in the eye. He smiled. "Bigger things than me have tried and failed."

Hob reached up, a vague notion that she was going to slap him on her mind, but her hand came to his cheek soft and slow, and then he turned his face into her palm in a tiny angle of movement that made her heart clench so hard she couldn't breathe.

She rolled to the side before she had a chance to be any more dumb and moonstruck. "What *is* it?" The blood that wasn't blood, the power that was more than fire, that was everything.

"Change made manifest."

"How? Why?"

He laughed softly. "How and why are you?"

Hob cussed at him, and it only made him laugh harder. She'd get her answer, dammit. If he couldn't tell her, she'd figure it out when she found this place. You couldn't feel from the inside where your heart was in your body, but it was still a point that someone could put a bullet through. "But fine. I see what ya mean. That it ain't so easy."

"Does that mean I am freed from riding on the back of your infernal machine?"

Hob reached for the coffee cup, which sat beside him: empty. She glanced at the plate: also empty. "Son of a bitch," she murmured. Then said, louder, "No. Just means you're gonna have to keep tryin' till you find something that works. And quit your bitchin' about my bike, until you're more useful than it is."

Of all the asshole things, he laughed. And she laughed with him.

CHAPTER EIGHTEEN • 34 DAYS

It felt like years since he'd been in Ludlow, though intellectually, Coyote knew that wasn't the case. He'd been there only a few months before, for some meeting or other that involved Mag. Oh, but they'd all been so young and beautiful then, he thought at himself with bitter amusement. Joking and laughing and drinking, and no one watching him from the corner of their eye, waiting to see if he went mad and tried to rip out their throat.

It was a good thing no one but him could feel that thirst still living on the bottom of his tongue. It was manageable now, something he could ignore most days, but it still crawled through him like an itch he could never scratch quite enough. In bed late at night, listening to Dambala snore, sometimes. Standing in the yard in full daylight and sniffing the air, like he could catch the scent of wet iron like the eagles. At least he smiled through it.

The best thing about Ludlow now, backwater shithole town on a perennial backwater shithole planet, was that none of the townspeople gave him that look. They tumbled around like puppies, tripping over their own feet as they tried to understand the rudiments of hand-to-hand fighting. They watched him with soft, open, earnest eyes like he was some sort of hero, and he was happy to let them keep thinking that. They were eager, most of them took it well when he knocked them over for their own good, and none of them seemed to think he'd bite.

He also engaged in a little mental back patting on his hand-picked teaching squad. Lobo had always been a no-brainer – he'd taken all of the most timid would-be fighters and coaxed them through their awkward smiles into slashing and feinting at each other with grim determination. Geri really was less of an ass when he wasn't trying to impress Hob and convince himself that her authority was meaningless. And Lykaios rounded things out well, forming a sort of tag-team with Geri so that neither of them got too frustrated.

"You're doing good work, Coyote," Mag said, next to him.

He smiled. Maybe the self-back patting hadn't been entirely necessary. "They're no longer unconscionably terrible, at least." Three days really wasn't enough time to produce a miracle, so he'd take what he could get. "Do keep them practicing the basics. So they'll be ready when we come back." That was the compromise they'd worked out – instead of seven days straight of teaching, they'd do three then two then two, to give the miners some time to practice between.

"I think they'll surprise you," Mag said.

"I noticed you haven't been joining the fray. And don't give me that nonsense about Nick having taught you. I knew both him and your father, you realize."

Mag sobered. "I got other things," she said quietly, then gave him a sharp look. "Like you."

"Oh, that bad, is it?" he said, though he felt rather alarmed at even that oblique reference. Mag hadn't been treating him like an animal, but he didn't like the feeling that Hob had been free about his business.

Mag's lips curled in a little smile. "Maybe not so bad as that. Don't want to make you feel like you gotta try harder."

"I'm certain Hob will thank you for that."

"Was that right, sir?" a large young man who looked like he'd been born scruffy – Omar, that was his name – asked.

"Duty calls," Coyote said, excusing himself to attend to his own set of students. "Almost, but there's one more thing…" He grinned as his group, the most advanced of the students – which wasn't saying much – groaned. He corrected Omar's grip on his knife and then tapped his knee lightly with one foot. "If you're going to commit, you have to commit. Halfway doesn't win fights. Neither dos silly things like honor and rules."

"Can't eat honor," a woman muttered.

He pointed at her. "See, I knew you were the smartest and best looking out of the bunch when I picked you."

She swatted at his hand. She had to be old enough to be his mother, though presumably unlike his mother, she actually looked something approaching her age. "Now," he said, "get back in your pairs, and let's see that again."

For all that he smiled the most out of the teachers, his students were utterly wrung out by the end of the two-hour lesson. He released them with a wave of his hand and an admonition that they ought to practice hard, or he'd be able to tell when he came back. "And we all know what happens to the lazy around here," he said conspiratorially. That summoned up a chorus of tired laughter.

Omar hung back as the group filtered away. He seemed to be trying to twist his big hands into knots. "Um, sir…"

"Looking for private lessons?" Coyote said, and gave him a cheerful wink. "I don't think you can afford me." There were no rules against flirting.

Omar blushed beet red. "No. I mean… yes, but no. Me'n a few of my friends are gonna drink'n'party a bit. Think you… I mean, all of you… would like to join us?"

Partying normally meant gambling, and Omar *definitely* couldn't afford him in that case. Coyote had also never believed in mercy when it came to cards. He also didn't really believe in sleep when there could be cards, either, and he'd always been disposed to like tall men and women, though Omar was a bit miner-pale for his tastes. "If you give me a moment, I'll check."

He tucked his thumbs in his belt and swaggered over to the other Wolves, smiling in a way he knew would make them nervous.

Lykaios took one look at him and said, "Hell fuckin' no."

"You haven't even heard what I'm going to say."

Geri eyed him. "We know that fuckin' smile. That's the one that means you're gonna end up with our paychecks in your pocket."

"Swore off gamblin' same time I swore off drinkin'," Lobo said.

"I'd forgotten you swore off fun," Coyote said. Lobo's answer was a rude gesture. "It won't be the same without any of you there," Coyote complained. He ought to have brought Davey – no, excuse him, Diablo – and Raff instead. Neither of them had learned better yet.

"You mean your pockets won't be as heavy," Lykaios said.

"We're still headin' back to base. Early, afore it starts gettin' hot," Geri said. "We ain't waitin' for you."

"I'll be waking all of you up, fear not." He gave them a little wave and headed back to Omar. "They're all terribly old farts who have no sense of fun. But you've got me, if that'll be good enough."

"Sure," Omar said. "I mean, I'm glad you're comin' at all."

"Where shall I meet you?"

Omar gave him directions to one of the houses near the walls, belonging to his friend Luis. "You any good at cards?"

"I barely know how to play, so I may need you to remind me of the rules," Coyote said sweetly. "Try to go easy on me."

Twenty minutes of shuteye and a change of shirt later – something that flattered his eyes a bit – Coyote wended his way through the night-cool streets of Ludlow. The streets were quiet and dim, only every other sodium-yellow street light on. As he turned into an alley, heading toward the walls, he caught the faint echo of footsteps. Coyote cursed himself – how long had he been followed? And how had he not noticed? Stupid. Who would have thought there'd be off-duty miners or Mariposa men hard up enough to try robbery inside the walls?

But he was Coyote. He had a ready tongue and a very ready knife, and thankfully people tended to underestimate him too. Probably because he was a bit on the short and slight side. It was so useful he'd stopped feeling annoyed about it years ago. Coyote ducked around the next corner and turned, keeping his hand close to his knife but not drawing it yet.

Ah, two of them, dressed like miners. Only their boots were way too nice – typical Mariposa issue. Apparently this was to be a covert operation. "Oh, you startled me," he said, breathing out an apparent sigh of relief.

"You lost?" one of them, a woman, asked. "I haven't seen you here before."

"As a matter of fact, yes," Coyote said. He liked it best of all when people opened his escape routes for him. "I'm trying to find the hostel, you see, and I think I took a wrong–"

That was the point where someone tackled him from behind. Had they already been waiting here? Had they been even quieter than the first ones? It didn't matter. Coyote drew his knife and managed to slash someone's leg – there was a satisfying scream – before a knee ground his face into the rough synthcrete of the street. His mind working a mile a minute, he went limp, thinking that he could fake them out perhaps, and then–

Something sharp and metal dug into his back. He smelled ozone and scorched cloth, and his muscles locked into rigid agony. And as if that wasn't enough, he felt a needle tear through the wire-tense muscle of his arm, felt the burn of something injected and forced through the already screaming fibers.

Some people had no sense of proportion.

The electricity cut off, and for a moment, he just lay still, muscles spasming. The moment he had any kind of control – too long, this was taking too long – he tried to push himself up, instinct demanding something.

He made it halfway onto his elbows before the ground rushed up to meet him again and he blinked–

–his eyes open to see a blur of steel gray and blazing white light. The world shook around him. Voices babbled in his ears. Oh, and it was bloody cold. His ass and shoulders were smashed flat against an unyielding plane. And – his arm jumped uselessly – yes, those were restraints.

It wasn't bloody *fair*, was Coyote's first coherent thought. Hob wasn't going to ever let him off base again at this rate, and he hadn't even gotten drunk for this trouble.

He felt a vicious pinch at his elbow and rolled his eyes down to see past the naked expanse of his chest – lovely, they'd stripped him completely – to someone in a light green medical smock, their face covered with a full breather mask, bent over his arm.

Over his head, a muffled voice said, "Get at least six tubes. The interference is off the scale."

He rolled his eyes back, but couldn't see the speaker. But he could smell his own blood, being drained away for who knew what reason. And with every drop, he could almost feel the cells of his body shrinking. Water was life, blood was thicker than water, and his blood was thick as stone.

Coyote shut his eyes and tried to organize his thoughts around the steadily growing panic and thirst. He'd expected to get beaten, maybe wake up in a detention cell. He felt another vibration shiver up through the table – a train. He was on a train. Hell. There was only one place that might be going: Newcastle.

He had to get out of there, somehow. And considering they'd already trussed him up and were sucking out his blood, he wasn't going to be able to talk his way out of this one.

There's a way, the thirst whispered to him.

"Shut up," Coyote muttered. But if given the choice between living to fight another day and going to whatever laboratory-experiment death awaited him, he knew which he'd pick every time.

"Did he say something?" the muffled voice said.

"Impossible. We gave him nearly enough to kill an ox." Muffled laughter.

Coyote opened his eyes. "Well, I'm not an ox. I'm a bloody coyote." He felt the thirst that lived in the back of his mind, that ran down the center of his spine, and he stepped back into it like sinking into a warm, wet pool that wasn't water.

Things became strange, slow and fast at once, like he was there and yet watching from a long distance. He felt restraining straps burst around him like overused violin strings. He heard screaming, saw his hands tear away respirator masks and eye shields, and yes – oh yes, felt his fingers sink into yielding flesh. Hot liquid kissed his mouth, but it wasn't very satisfying at all. *More.*

No. He didn't want to be quite that, even though his teeth itched and his tongue curled. The thirst howled in him, but he was still enough Coyote and not *coyote*. He could wait to drink for safer waters.

But we will drink. I promise. We will drink.

He sank his fingers into the metal skin of the train car and tore it like he would tear fabric. It screamed and bent, rending to let cold night air wash over his naked body. One moon smiled at him while the other half-hid her face from the sight of what he'd left in the train car. The stars called out and laughed. Ghostly dunes flashed by.

With a yelp of something like joy, Coyote launched himself into the night and hit the sand running.

CHAPTER NINETEEN • *29 DAYS*

Hob had elected to ride for a bit into the night, since one moon was full and the other at half and that was more than enough to see by without the headlight. She promised herself a good rest on the other side of it, and then dinner from her next-to-last ration pack. She needed to fortify herself to ignore the Bone Collector and his endless, steady calm that she wanted to take in her hands and break somehow. It wasn't fair, it wasn't right, and the least fair and right out of all of it was that she was still enjoying his company even if she wanted to snap at him every five minutes.

His hands suddenly gripped her waist tight, and she cursed him again for refusing to wear a helmet, because she couldn't just ask him what it was. She brought them to a hard stop and shoved her visor up. "You got something?"

"That way." He extended his arm, angled over her shoulder. It had been a long damn time since she'd heard that kind of urgency in his voice.

She checked the current stars and the angles on the moons against her map and made note of the direction – west northwest – then pushed the throttle again, turning them in a long curve. They headed straight for the dunes rippling on the horizon.

For a long time, he didn't speak or react again, but she figured that just meant she was going in the right direction. Going got slow as they hit the dunes, but she'd been doing this basically her whole life. The motorcycle had always taken care of her.

As she rolled up over the back of another dune, she saw movement in the distance, quickly lost as they dipped back down. She was looking when they came up the next. There, not quite dead ahead – was that a *person*?

If there was a person running out in the sands by themselves, they were either someone who needed help or someone who needed killing. And while Hob had been trained on Nick's knee that there wasn't anything free in life, she'd also been trained by life in the desert that you helped other people in the ways you could because some day it might be your turn to burn in the sands.

She edged their direction to intercept and flicked her headlight on. If they were armed, well, she was probably better armed. Once this was dealt with, she could check the direction with the Bone Collector again. For his part, he didn't seem to mind the diversion.

The headlight trick worked: the person stopped, standing at the top of the dune, a dark cut-out against one of the moons. They had their hands spread, so at least she knew they weren't getting ready for a fight. There was something disturbingly familiar about them she couldn't quite put her finger on. Hob took them halfway up the low windward face of that dune and then stopped, left side facing the person. Made her profile thin, and if things got dicey, she could drop behind the motorcycle. It also hid her drawing her pistol with her right hand.

"You're a long way from home," she said, her voice

booming through the helmet speakers.

Before the person could react, the Bone Collector got off her motorcycle and walked toward them, right through her line of fire.

Cussing, Hob threw down the kickstand as the Bone Collector drew even with the person, his tall form, not so thin when he was filled out by wearing his duster, hiding theirs. Still holding her pistol, Hob moved up the dune toward them. Hers were the only footprints left in the sand, and she liked that least of all.

Then the Bone Collector stepped aside, and she recognized Coyote, without a goddamn stitch of clothing on. He wiped his mouth with the back of his hand.

"What the fuck," Hob said, fervently, the closest she ever got to praying.

"Fancy meeting you here, boss," Coyote said, voice slightly breathy.

Mag opened the kitchen door to Odalia's house, feeling strangely divorced from her own hand as it twisted and pushed the knob. Listening to the story Coyote, now thankfully wearing Clarence's spare pants, had to tell while Hob sat grim-faced beside him in Clarence's kitchen had filled Mag first with horror, then with anger, then with some emotion that transcended both into a cold, killing distance. It was plain as day that the always-so-eager Omar had betrayed Coyote to the greenbellies. He was the one who'd gotten Coyote alone, got him walking to a different end of town where the ambush waited. She'd always known that there could be company plants or spies or sympathizers in with the miners, but she hadn't wanted to give in to paranoia about it.

Which meant she had to stop this now, she thought coldly. She had to warn Odalia and Clarence how badly compromised they were. And she had to find out who else was in league with him. No shying away from it.

There were three people in the kitchen, not the two she expected: Clarence and Odalia both standing over Omar, his face crossed with strings of tacky blood. Both his eyes were swollen almost shut with angry red bruises.

"What the hell is this?" Mag demanded. The three in front of her started and looked at her in alarm. Her gaze went to Clarence's knuckles, but his hands were clean. This didn't look like the two crew leaders had beaten her to the punch.

"Mariposa men jumped Omar," Odalia said tightly. "Beat him to hell, just for the fun of it."

It wasn't unheard of, especially with things on a razor edge like they were these days. But it felt damned convenient considering the part of the story she knew. She didn't trust this one bit. "Was that before or after Coyote met up with him?" She knew the answer, of course, but the point was to see what bullshit story Omar had spun.

"I was waiting for him," Omar mumbled through his swollen lips. "Just waitin'. We were gonna play cards."

"You were just waitin'," Mag repeated.

"At the corner, 'cause I thought maybe he got lost on the way to Luis's place. Then they come out of the alley and asked me what I was doin' outside. I said wasn't my shift so I could do as I pleased. The sergeant in the group said I was stirrin' trouble, an' too many of us were out when we shouldn't be. I said there weren't no law, and they said damn right, they were the law." Omar tried to cover his face with his hands, then seemed to think better of it. "Fuckin' monsters."

It was a convincing performance, Mag thought coldly. "Clarence. Odalia. I got to talk to you for a minute." She crossed her arms and waited for them both to nod, then

took them outside. She shut the door with her foot. This
close to the mine, the rattle and clank of the drive chain
would help cover them talking.

"Mag, what is–" Odalia began.

"I got Coyote and Hob in Clarence's kitchen. Coyote
said a Mariposa squad in plain clothes snatched him up
off the street when he was on his way to meet Omar.
They put him on a train – must've been a special one."

"Better ask if anyone saw the train leavin', and comin'
in," Clarence said. "If anyone was awake around there."
Unscheduled night trains happened now and then, and
the crew on them was always blue and green, with no
other workers called in. They were like damn ghost
stories.

"How'd Coyote get back here?" Odalia demanded.

"That's for him and Hob to know and us to pay 'em
good money for if we want one of their trade secrets."

"You thinkin' Omar betrayed him?" Clarence asked,
slow and thoughtful.

"How the hell else did they know who to snatch and
where to find him?" Mag asked.

"Anyone been in that warehouse the last three days
knew he was here. And that man's got a mouth a mile
wide. Why d'ya think they were lookin' for him?" Odalia
asked. "And what, they beat the hell out of Omar to give
him cover? That's a hell of a lot of cover."

Mag could admit, now that her anger was cooling
a little, that Omar looked like he'd been worked over
damn hard. And yet. Coyote had a big mouth, but not
for secrets.

"This town ain't that big," Clarence added. "If they
were lookin' for people to harass, could have just been
damn dumb luck."

"When did we start believing in coincidences? Why'd
they take Coyote and not Omar?" Mag asked. "There's

too much at stake. We know they got spies."

"Do we know that?" Odalia asked. "Ain't ever found one for sure."

"What're you suggesting, Mag? We beat him some more?" Clarence asked, expression going darker.

Tempting, Mag thought. Very tempting. But also unnecessary. "Let me at him."

"With your damn witchy powers?" Odalia whispered. "Are you insane? Want to turn 'em on your own?"

"Won't hurt him if he's got nothin' to hide," Mag said, though this turn of conversation grew a thread of sickness into her anger. She looked at Clarence, urging him silently to be on her side. He frowned.

"Maybe it wouldn't be a bad way to check…" Clarence said.

"Don't you go leanin' on Clarence either," Odalia snapped.

"I wasn't!" Mag said, shocked. She hadn't been, she was sure of it. Not consciously. She'd never had the thought cross her mind, not once she figured out what she could do. Clarence had always been good to her, and trusted her, and watched over her.

The look Odalia gave her wasn't one of trust. "This is just what they want us to do, don't ya see? Sowin' seeds of discord by pickin' on people here and there." It was an unsubtle reminder that they were less than a week from getting their answers on the vote, and only a day or so later would be payday.

"We got to be careful, though," Clarence said. "So you keep an eye on him, Mag. But only an eye."

Omar already knew so much, Mag thought with frustration. He was always volunteering for things, always ready to help. She'd been grateful to have that kind of help, even if he was too curious about her late uncle and his mercenaries. But how could she even try to compensate for this, when he had his fingers in damn near every bit of supplies they'd found?

That was her problem, she supposed. They'd put her in charge of it, and she had to figure it out. "What do you want me to tell Hob?"

"Tell her we're takin' care of it," Odalia said. "You think she's gonna make trouble? Like in…"

The unspoken name *Rouse* hung in the air. Mag shook her head. They'd all learned some hard lessons from that, and she knew Hob had taken them to heart. "No. I'll… make sure." Hob wouldn't like it, but Hob trusted her. She hated to call on that without having a real answer. But Odalia and Clarence had put enough doubt in her mind that she no longer wanted to just throw Omar to the Wolves. "I'll take care of it."

Hob hadn't been happy. She hadn't shouted, like Mag had been half-afraid. No, she'd just listened grimly and said, "Coincidence, huh."

It had made Mag feel sick all over again. And then Hob left without looking back, which always scared Mag. She remembered too well another time when Hob hadn't looked back, and then had disappeared for years. But Hob had also promised that would never happen again. No, Mag told herself, Hob was mad, but she'd also get over it, because she always did.

Feeling sicker, as if without somewhere for it to go she'd swallowed down that anger like a poison, Mag made herself a cup of coffee. Her head was starting to hurt too, but it was tension tight across her skull like a steel band, not the stabbing, burning pain behind her eyes that came from pushing her witchiness too hard. She ended up sitting, coffee cooling in front of her, elbows on the kitchen table and her face in her hands.

The kitchen door opened and she looked up, expecting

maybe Clarence, with something quick to say before he had to be up at the mine for morning checkthrough. Instead, Anabi slipped inside and shut the door behind her.

"I thought you'd gone back to bed," Mag said. "What were you doing?"

Anabi's beautiful face was drawn down in lines of concern. She sat across from Mag and stroked one of her hands lightly, then took out her slate. She wrote: *I followed you and eavesdropped.*

"What did you think?"

Anabi shrugged and wrote: *I don't know. Too many things to be suspicious about. But.* She erased the slate and continued, *Odalia talked after they sent Omar off.*

"Oh?"

Told Clarence you're getting more witchy. Getting more paranoid. She erased, then wrote: *"Is she really hearing what people think, or does she just think she is?"*

Mag put her face in her hands again. "Fuck," she whispered. Because some of it, she'd wondered herself. It was like Odalia had reached into the dark shadows of her brain and pulled out her own worst thoughts, then said them aloud to Clarence. There was always too much doubt. But had she been leaning on Clarence without meaning to? Was she influencing Anabi too?

She felt Anabi's hands, gentle on her shoulders. She covered one with her own. Anabi rubbed her other shoulder lightly for a moment, then leaned over to write something. She pushed the slate along the table so it sat in front of Mag's face. *I trust you no matter what.*

"Might be the only one." And maybe she shouldn't, Mag thought.

Hob does too.

"Not any more, I reckon."

Now you're being dramatic.

Mag laughed. "Don't I get to, now and then?"

Anabi kissed her on the part in her hair, light as a feather. *When you're different, everything is doubt*, she wrote. *If they can't hurt us directly, they try to make us destroy ourselves.*

Mag squeezed her hand. Anabi felt like a small, fragile point of stability in a world that was spinning out in all directions. Maybe if she just held on tight enough, something would make sense again. "Thank you."

CHAPTER TWENTY • *28 DAYS*

"The train is this way, sir."

Shige followed the green-uniformed security guard down off the station platform, leaving the bright lights behind them. They both snapped on their flashlights. His boots – he'd had the presence of mind to change out his office shoes before he left Newcastle – crunched on the crushed synthcrete that lined the tracks. Segundo was a large enough, old enough mining town that it sported something close to a proper railyard with multiple sets of tracks; most of the lines ran through it, claustrophobically close and squeezed by the canyon walls. Lights on those walls were few and far between, the further they got from the depot building.

"This far back?" he asked mildly.

"We didn't want to risk any of the workers seeing it."

Shige raised his eyebrows, but saved his breath. He'd see for himself soon enough. All he'd been told, when roused out of bed and sent out here by Ms Meetchim, was that there'd been an urgent problem with one of the special security trains, and that it was being held at Segundo for inspection. Which, to be fair, was all the report given to her had said. Shige was fairly certain his implied secondary task here would be to give the security people a little pep talk about writing reports that communicated useful information.

But it did stir a little hope in his heart. He'd been frustrated in the last week, at how little real reaction there'd been to the start of the pay change rollout. That could mean they were either more cowed than he'd feared – or better organized than he'd hoped. His preference was decidedly with the latter option. A terrorist attack on a train would be just what the doctor ordered, so to speak.

The train came into sight around the gentle curve of the canyon wall. Silver, dulled to gray in the dim light, and smooth with an enormous sand plow as a prow, the engine itself looked fine, as did the first few cars. At the third car, the security guard stopped and played her light over the siding. The metal skin gaped raggedly open, shreds curling inward, the frame of the car itself bent. Shige swept his light low to see that some of the car's wheels no longer properly met the rail.

"Explosion?" Shige asked. He already knew the answer to that question, however. He'd seen enough explosions to know what their wreckage looked like – bent outward, not inward. And how would a train car come to *implode*?

"You tell me," the security guard said.

Shige paused to pull on a pair of thick leather gloves before he cautiously climbed into the train car through that tear. The inside was a mess of torn metal, spatters and sprays of blood gone brown, shattered glass, and surviving items scattered in all directions. No sign of anything melted, no blackened chemical residue. "Bodies?" he asked the security guard.

"Four security, three medical. They're laid out in one of the warehouses if you want to see them."

"I will." He bent to look at one of the patterns of

blood, then glanced up. "Medical?"

"This op had a high probability of encountering contamination. They were on standby."

That hadn't been mentioned in the report either. "Any surviving records out of this mess?"

"A few things. You want those first, or the bodies?"

"Bodies first," Shige said, straightening.

All seven of the bodies were laid out on the gray synthcrete floor of a railyard warehouse, each in its own dark green body bag. The warehouse was guarded by grim-faced Mariposa employees, with one white-coat wearing doctor idling just outside the door, smoking a cigarette with shaking fingers. They all filed silently inside ahead of Shige.

As he walked the row of body bags, Shige kept his mouth covered with a handkerchief, trying to give the impression of a sheltered secretary disturbed by such a sight. All of the security guards were too grim-faced to smirk about it, as they unzipped the bags one by one, and he couldn't blame them on that account. They were the messiest bodies he'd seen in recent memory, though thankfully the smell was minimized because they'd been stored in one of the warehouse refrigeration units normally reserved for perishable food items.

He let the company doctor from Segundo point out the salient details: approximately two days post-mortem, bones snapped, limbs bent completely out of shape by whatever force had been able to tear the train car apart and bend its frame. More important were the soft tissue wounds: eyes plucked out to leave bloody hollows behind, great rends in flesh like claw marks, leaving trailing flaps of skin and muscle.

"So, not an explosion," Shige remarked, voice muffled behind his handkerchief.

"No," the doctor said, and dragged another cigarette out of her pocket. No one seemed to care that she might be contaminating the bodies with ash and fumes. "Wild animal attack, maybe."

"What animal, do you think?"

That was the question, of course. The biggest introduced species known to still survive were the great eagles, and none left damage like this. Shige eyed the teeth marks, plainly human, that stood out on the soft underjaw of one of the corpses in green. The doctor hadn't mentioned those, and he wondered if the oversight was due to overwhelmed horror or pure denial.

"Dune lion, maybe," the doctor said, not looking at the last body and its obvious teeth marks. "We still get reports of them now and then. Sightings."

"One wonders how a lion came to be inside the train. I'll see the records now," Shige said. He'd seen enough over the past months on Tanegawa's World that he did not disbelieve on its face that a human, or something human-shaped, could have done this. The question now on his mind was how he could use this to his advantage. It might prompt Ms Meetchim into another witch hunt, which could be useful if he pushed the timetable properly. But he'd have to find a way to keep the details from making the populace too cooperative. This sort of horror would make them much less sympathetic to the witches in their midst.

In the security office, someone shoved a mug of coffee, its surface skimmed with oily skin, into his hand. He ignored it in favor of the flimsies the chief of security spread across the conference table. "These are the notes we pulled out of there. Found other pages blown out along the tracks, but no idea what else has been lost to the wind," the chief said.

Handwritten pages, out of order. Shige turned them

over with care – some were badly torn and splashed with blood or chemicals that had made them brittle. Medical terminology, graphs that he could not decipher but might be able to use Dr Kiyoder at the office to translate, part of the security report about having obtained the "subject" due to an operative tip-off in Ludlow, a note that he was likely an as-yet undocumented associate of the so-called "Ghost Wolves" terrorist group.

He turned another page, to a grainy instant picture. The mug jerked in his hand before he could bite down on his own reaction, slopping mercifully lukewarm coffee onto his fingers. He'd know that face anywhere, though he had thought it impossible. When last he'd seen it, the cheeks had been flushed and puffy with wound fever rather than slack with sedation: his older brother, Kazuhiro.

Not impossible, he reminded himself. He never had seen the body. But he'd configured his life into that reality, where he no longer had an older brother because he was dead and not just disowned, and he couldn't classify his own reaction now. Anger? Hurt? Hope? The mix of it made a strange, sick little knot in his stomach, and he didn't have time for any of that. He recalled the number of times his father had whispered news of Kazu's continued survival on some backwater, and in some utterly compromising circumstance. He'd always turned back up, until this last time, and now… well, leave it to Kazu to not even die properly, he thought with a mix of grim amusement and annoyance.

He had a performance to maintain, he reminded himself. There was no room for any of this. "This was the subject?" he asked, to buy himself some time.

"And a fucking witch, too," the security chief spat.

"Maybe the witch summoned the dune lion," Shige said dryly. He was rewarded by a strangled guffaw from one of the guards, and a muttered "Fuck," from the doctor.

Kazu, what have you gotten yourself into this time? he wondered. The vivid crescent of teeth marks on the neck of the med-tech stood out in his mind. If he had his brother's dental records, would they match? Did he want to know? This was a level of animalistic brutality he did not want to think anyone capable of. And to think, Kazu had always said, in his least kind, illicit-drug-fueled moments, that Shige was the monster and Ayana the Frankenstein of the family.

By sheer force of will, he swallowed another, much less healthy laugh and made himself turn the page to another set of medical notes. Automatically, he skimmed over the words. He needed to maintain his calm. He needed to deal with the personal fallout – ridiculous that finally he could have something personal in this – later. "This says there were samples taken."

"Almost everything was smashed, like you saw. But we did find some unlabeled blood vials," the security chief said. "We've got them in a cooler, to go back to Newcastle with you. Figured your lab would want them."

And those were no doubt already documented, Shige thought. The entire room, with its grim-faced security contingent, knew about them, and that they were being given into his care. He could destroy them and doctor the records later if necessary... No, he couldn't do that. Out of the question. The thought of destroying something so precious as blood filled him with an alien horror. He rationalized the strange feeling as best he could: even knowing the source, that blood was far too precious to waste, filled as it was with whatever oddity fueled this world. "Good thinking, chief," he heard himself say. "I'll take all of this and the bodies back to Newcastle with me immediately. Destroy the train car."

That would take care of the optics problem, if Ms Meetchim did decide she wanted another witch hunt. He could defend the decision by saying they didn't want to rile the workers if she took exception to it. "What happened to the agent who delivered this terrorist to security?" he asked. Another person to track down himself, later, if he had the opportunity and deniability to do so.

"They're Ludlow security's problem," the chief said, then shrugged at the sharp look Shige gave him. "Up to them to keep the cover story going."

"I'll be certain to inquire. But it is of great import that their cover is maintained, since we cannot assume one of the witches will have simply died from running off into the desert." He couldn't even make that assumption about his own brother, it seemed. "And I will convey to Vice President Meetchim that this mess is not their fault and we're certainly not looking to blame anyone."

"I'm sure that'll be a great comfort, sir," the security chief said bitterly.

CHAPTER TWENTY-ONE • *28 DAYS*

"If I'd known getting abducted by Corporate security would put you in this much of a snit," Coyote, now properly wearing his own clothes, drawled, "I wouldn't have done it."

Hob glared at him from across her desk, and he offered her only a bland smile in return. Really, it hadn't changed all that much other than to make her pissed at Mag. She'd given Ludlow back the two-thirds of its money so she didn't have to send her people back there. Didn't trust it, and didn't think anyone would blame her for it.

Hob curled her lips back to snarl at him. "You ain't near as funny as you think."

"I'm not trying to be. Do we already have to re-litigate the fight you had with Nick before he died?"

It had been about Nick being paralyzed with caution after he'd overstepped badly and gotten a fair number of his people killed, all out of rage for a personal matter – the death of Mag's father, Phil. "It ain't like that," Hob said.

"You've got your foot on that path."

Hob held up one finger. "Not wantin' my people in a position to get picked up by the greenbellies ain't even half the same. We still got plenty of stupid shit to do that don't involve stayin' overnight in a town."

He rolled his eyes.

"Or are you just mad you can't roll in and take everyone's paycheck?" Hob said.

He held up his hands. "This isn't about me."

Hob sat back in her seat and took a long drag of her ever-present cigarette. "Yeah, it is. And you don't want it to be."

"Hob..."

"You think they knew what you was, when they snatched you?"

"A Wolf? Yes–"

"No. A witch. Fuckin' say it."

He closed his mouth in a grim line, then wiped that away with a hand over his face. "No."

"Think they do now?"

They both knew the answer to that one, but Hob stared at him until he said it out loud: "Yes."

"Ain't a safe place out there for those like us," Hob said, satisfied. "An' it's gettin' less safe."

"None of us are here–"

"–to be safe. Yeah. I know. But that don't mean it's fun bein' hunted, either." Hob rolled her cigarette meditatively in her fingers. They all knew who their enemy was at this point, and it was much too big of an enemy for the Wolves to go at head on.

And that circled back to her wasting three days tooling around in the desert with the Bone Collector clinging to the back of her motorcycle, and nothing to show for it. Might not have been a terrible vacation, if she looked at it sideways and skated over the other implications, but she was not someone who wanted, needed, or could afford a goddamn vacation just now.

Coyote still watched her. Hob took the butt of her

cigarette between her fingers and focused on it. The paper vanished in a white-hot burst. "TransRift's bigger and got more money than us. An' this shit is what they do. So maybe it ain't a surprise that we can't just come around at it from the side and get ahead. Maybe we got to follow in from behind and just be ready to jump in." Which was, in a way, what they'd done before with the Weatherman. Strike when the TransRift machine had its momentum going in one direction, and they'd know where to land their punch.

"We need more intelligence," Coyote said.

"Got as much as we could, lookin' at the busted wildcats," Hob said. "Ain't nothin' there. That's why they're bust. So we gotta find us one that ain't bust."

"Have there been any?"

"Don't know," she said thoughtfully. "Since the ones I hear about are the ones that fold up in a few days and the crews go home till the next site gets spiked. Damn." And trying to find a location she didn't know about was damn near impossible. The desert was a big place.

Coyote made a thoughtful noise.

"What?"

"I know it's not really your style, to go after solutions that don't require bullets or punches…"

Hob snorted. "Spit it out."

"You think of handing this one over to Freki and Geri?"

"No. Why?" She frowned. They wouldn't have any more information than her.

"When companies do an exploration pattern like this, they don't do it at random. They try to place their bets on where things are most likely to be in their favor."

"They got a lot of information we don't."

"Yes. But we can look at what they've done, and do our own analysis." When she still looked at him uncomprehendingly, Coyote said, "Numbers, Hob. Those things. Use the resources you *have*."

Suddenly, it all made sense. Of anyone, Freki and Geri were the best with numbers on the base. "And Geri was even bitchin' this morning that he was bored."

"Silly man," Coyote said. "He ought to know by now that's the incantation that summons work."

25 DAYS

"You sure it's somewhere around here?" Hob asked as her tires left salmon-pink saltpan and hissed once more onto undulating, orange dunes. The cloudless blue sky stretched long to the sharp horizon where it met land.

"No, we ain't." Geri's voice came back, fuzzed with static over the shortwave. "We fuckin' told ya, *likely* ain't near the same thing as *sure*."

"Keep goin'," Freki said. "Eagles."

And there were, ahead, two eagles circling. Hob's stomach sank slightly at the sight. Sure, it could mean what they were looking for – a mining camp would mean a lot of water – but it could just as easily be another body in the desert. She got tired of playing undertaker, sometimes.

After Hob had handed over all the maps and notes she had, with Coyote grinning evilly behind her shoulder all the while, the twins had come up with three different "likely" possibilities. Hob had split her available crew into small parties to check them all out. Coyote had begged off leading one of the other scouting parties; he hadn't said why, but seeing the look in his eye, Hob hadn't needed to ask. He was still running scared.

She'd taken the furthest, least certain of the possibilities for herself, and brought Freki and Geri along since they were the ones who had figured it all out. They were just about done with the "window" the twins had come up with, though, and nothing to show for it but a powerful hunger and a drained-off water ration.

Geri turned his motorcycle up the slope of a dune and paused. "Shadow on the horizon."

"Give us the bearing," Hob said. She turned that way, with Freki not far behind her. Geri would catch up. "This still in the area?"

"Barely," Geri admitted. "But we done told you it was fuzzy."

If it worked, it could be any texture it goddamn wanted to be and Hob wouldn't complain. She kept the motorcycle on a steady course, weaving along the gentle swells of windward dune slopes, the electric motor a soft hum felt in the bones rather than heard.

The shadow turned out to be a small, humpy outcropping of black rock, so small it hadn't even been marked on Hob's map. She made sure to note it down as precise as she could, so everyone else would get the landmark. As short as it was, it might end up getting buried in drifting sands anyway. The base of the rock swarmed with activity: a mining camp.

From a safe distance, camouflaged in the shadow of a dune, the three of them stood in a huddle, helmets off and looking through scopes at the distant activity. People and vehicles, the blocky mounds of mining equipment surrounded the rock and stretched its silhouette.

"Likely is lookin' pretty fuckin' likely," Geri crowed. He thumped Freki's shoulder. "We fuckin' win this one."

"Sure is," Hob agreed. "Guess you get all the numbers from here on out."

"Joke's on you. We love that shit."

The wildcat mine was little more than a pit at the base of the rocks, which a person went in or out of every few minutes. A portable drive chain rigged to one of the solar vehicles brought up large buckets of waste rock that got dumped to the side in a continual stream.

"Now what?" Geri said after they'd watched for a while.

"Guess we'll see if it calms down some at night. I don't think they run 'em twenty-four hours. Least that's what the miners I talked to told me." Too much surface lighting when there wasn't any sun, they'd said. Too expensive to haul out that many battery banks. "Mayhap send one of you back, get the others. We can run a distraction and then snatch and grab when there's more of us."

"What's around the perimeter?" Freki asked.

Hob had been wondering that herself. It wasn't a fence, precisely, but a set of wire lines and tripods with some kind of... unit at the top. From the distance, Hob couldn't tell if they were speakers, lights, or something else entirely. Opened crates sat haphazardly nearby, marked with a symbol Hob didn't recognize from any standard cargo load. "Maybe I was wrong about it not being a twenty-four hour op," she offered. "Don't look much like lights, though."

"Anti-wildlife fence?" Geri guessed. "Ain't seen any of these sites before."

"Might be something to keep the eagles away," Hob said. The two circling overhead had been joined by a third. Watching the three circle at different rates, weaving around each other, felt strangely hypnotic. An odd sort of dizziness washed over her, a feeling like she was far away from her body, falling up into that sky.

"Somethin's goin' on," Geri said, nudging her.

She brought her attention back to the ground, the black maw gaping in the orange sand by the rocks. But the far-off feeling persisted, got worse even, the sound coming to her ears starting to sound hollow. In a corner of her mind she wondered if she was about to faint, for the first time in her goddamn life, and just how many years it would take for Geri to let her live it down.

Two miners came up in one of the buckets. Excitement rippled through the little camp. The drive chain paused as they climbed out. People in green and blue suits moved in, and it got damn hard to see what was going on, and why did her mouth fucking taste like lightning just now? Why was her skin prickling, a low hum – like music, like something she should know – sounding in her ears?

Something blue, so blue, winked in the bright sunlight. It was a blue she'd seen before, touched, and turned into a burst of flame. She knew it, like she knew a perfect shot lined up or the moment when gravity took hold at the top of a jump. She *knew*.

"Oh," she breathed out. "*Shit.*"

CHAPTER TWENTY-TWO • *26 DAYS*

The air in Clarence's kitchen was thick and hot, even with the night gone cool outside. Mag and Clarence sat watching each other, silent, ignoring their long-cold cups of coffee. Mag jumped as the door opened to reveal the scruffy face of Omar.

"Runner from Rouse just come in," Omar said. The bruises on his face, now five days old, had gone purple to green and yellow. He hadn't been a pretty man before getting beaten, and this wasn't an improvement. He offered Mag a piece of stiff canvas that had been folded into an envelope.

Mag took it, looking at Omar from under her lashes as she tried to hide her suspicion. But the crew leaders at Rouse had followed their directions and sealed the envelope with wax. Mag knew it wasn't a foolproof way to keep out spies and tampering, but it was better than nothing.

Instead of leaving, Omar only retreated a step to stand by the door. His posture was eager, shoulders leaned forward. Like a dog waiting to jump. Mag was tempted to tell him to leave, but what would be the point? The result of the vote would be known, for good or ill, by all the miners within hours – and by the company on payday in two days' time. Maybe earlier if there truly was a spy.

"That's all of them," Clarence said.

Mag set the envelope down in front of him, to join the others already waiting. "Looks like." They'd agreed – Mag, Clarence, and Odalia before she'd had to depart to take over her shift – to open all of the vote tallies at once after the first two had come in three hours apart.

Clarence took the first envelope and split apart the wax, which was a mottle of colors – probably several candle stubs in the making – and then pulled out a crumpled flimsy. "Shimera," he read. "By majority, the vote is *strike*."

A shiver passed through Mag. She realized, then, that no one had used that word before, not out loud. They'd talked about work stoppage, about real work for real pay, about all coming down sick at once. But no one had ever said *strike*, a word from the depths of history passed down by the miners and completely absent from the curriculum in the company-run school. The word seemed so archaic, so impossible, and at the same time heavy with power. Clarence had written the word in his proposal to the crew leaders in the other towns, but even then, no one had said it out loud, like it was some kind of black magic that couldn't be taken back once spoken.

Mag made a note on her own flimsy, which was the margin of an old receipt. She had to fight to keep her fingers steady. "Next."

"Walsen," Clarence read after opening the next envelope. "By majority, the vote is *strike*."

She wasn't going to be scared, because this was *their* black magic. If the witches were on anyone's side, it was the miners. They *were* the witches. They were the lifeblood of the entire goddamn world.

"Tercio," Clarence read. "By clear majority, the vote

is *strike*."

Omar clenched his fist and thumped it against his leg, but remained silent. He was smiling, though. Was he really happy?

"Rouse," Clarence read. "By overwhelming majority, the vote is *strike*."

If any town would be racing to light the fuse, Mag knew, it would be Rouse. That was still her home, even if she hadn't crossed the gates since her parents had been killed. They knew what was at stake there. They wouldn't falter.

"Segundo," Clarence read. "By... simple majority, the vote is no."

That felt like running into a fist face-first. She shouldn't have been surprised, she knew. Segundo was a big town, an old town. And if they were going to go that way, then...

"Primero, by majority, votes no," Clarence finished, setting the last envelope aside.

Mag made herself breathe out. "Them two is what we thought." She looked at Clarence. "And how goes Ludlow?"

A small, unnecessary formality. They'd had their own vote days ago, a count of hands in the different cells the workers were broken up in. Mag had stood for each one. She'd seen those faces, eager, determined, grim, scared, jubilant. All of those things, mixed together as the hands shot up in a human forest blackened with mine dust.

Clarence said, expression set, "By clear majority, Ludlow votes to *strike*."

From the corner of her eye, Mag saw Omar raise his fist, like a salute to the other miners, unseen. Breathe, she reminded herself, breathe. But they had spoken that word. They had made their choice. And there was no going back – but had there ever been going back, from the minute the greenbellies shot her papa dead in the desert? Not for her. And maybe she was dragging them all to hell at her heels. "I'll copy up the statement so it can be run back out tonight to the other towns. So they'll know they ain't alone."

"So they know who ain't standin' with us," Omar said darkly.

"And we'll be ready?" Clarence asked, looking at Mag.

"We are ready," Mag said, like that was another kind of magic and her conviction would make it true. "We got our ground. It's time to stand."

Mag's fingers were stained with grease pencil after writing up the results to send back to the other towns. She always ended up taking care of messages because she had the best handwriting, the easiest for the half-literate to puzzle out. With bitter amusement, she thought her mother would be pleased, if she'd lived to see it. Irina had always told her to practice more and try harder, had kept pushing her back to school instead of letting her go to the breakers because she said Mag needed an education more than they needed the extra pay.

Anabi sat on her bed, her feet tucked up under her skirt. It had really become their bed now; there was still a pallet on the floor in case anyone got nosey, but it hadn't been used in weeks. She glanced up from the book in her lap as soon as Mag opened the door, her eyebrows arched up in query.

"Everyone but Primero and Segundo," Mag said. Anabi had known what this was all about, even if she'd chosen to absent herself from the meeting. As someone who had grown up in a farm town instead of with the miners, she still didn't feel quite at home. That, and she was still afraid of bringing attention to herself. That kind of caution didn't die easy.

Anabi took up her bit of slate and wrote, *Do you think it will happen?*

"Ain't in our hands, that. All in what the company puts in the pay envelopes."

And if they do?

"I don't know," Mag said. "We never done anything like this before, not really." They'd stopped work for one day after her papa died, but this was different. Then, they'd said it was just one day, for a funeral. To remind the company that even if they controlled the blacklist, they didn't control anyone's hearts. But now it was stop, and no start until they had their proper pay back, and some other demands besides – better safety inspections, shorter hours, no blacklist without a trial.

It all depended on them standing strong and holding their ground. Clarence said it over and over again like a prayer: the company was nothing without its miners, and they needed to be reminded of that. But how the company would react? Mag doubted it would be good. She'd already seen how itchy those greenbellies were to fight, and she remembered the result of their one-day work stop: her mother dead in a fire set by company hands. "But we gotta draw a line sometime."

Anabi rose to her feet and reached out to take Mag's hands. Mag smiled and squeezed the woman's warm, rough fingers. "Whatever does happen, we'll stick together. Like we did before. I promise."

Anabi leaned forward to kiss her. Her lips were soft and tasted a bit like coffee and a bit like cinnamon. Mag squeezed her hands lightly again. "Sleep if you can. We both got early mornings tomorrow. I need to think a bit."

After Anabi had gone quiet in sleep, Mag went over to her clothes chest. She dug down through the layers of plain work coveralls and skirts, well-worn and patched. She went past the thin strata of mementos she had, mostly things that Hob had saved of Uncle Nick's and passed along to her. At the very bottom of the chest, resting on the cheap, thin, synthetic wood, was a small, silver pistol that Uncle Nick had pressed in her hand a lifetime ago.

It felt heavier than she remembered when she picked it up. Mag hadn't wanted to use it when Uncle Nick gave it to her, had refused to even touch it until now. It had seemed such an ugly thing, full of the same kind of death that had killed her father. That disgust felt like a luxury she couldn't afford any more. Mag slid the pistol into her skirt pocket, where it hung heavy and cold against her thigh.

CHAPTER TWENTY-THREE • *25 DAYS*

The Bone Collector sat at the heart of the world and waited, listening to the ceaseless song spun by the vortices of its core. Too complicated to be expressed mathematically, but he knew the melody by instinct, could sing in harmony with it. And maybe, he thought, if he found the right harmony, he would be able to talk to it. There was a presence there, a mind of sorts, more alien than his, speaking its thoughts into a place just beyond his perception. It was infuriating. All he could see was the mirror surface of the Well, the alien stars within – and then he shied away from looking deeper, because in that reflection, his eyes were black in black.

But where? There was no *where* in a place where space and time twisted back in on themselves. He had tried to tell Hob that, again and again, and she'd still dragged him around the desert, looking. He'd told her, after leading her to Coyote, that he would continue to consider the problem, even if he thought it had no solution. That had brought him here, to these ceaseless permutations, to a cycle of continually almost losing himself and drawing back at the edge of dissolution. There was part of him that almost wished to let go, escape the flesh that caged him, flow into the blood of the world and cease to be himself. And yet he doubted that Hob Ravani would forgive him a second time, if she called and called and he did not come. If he ceased to be, it would no longer trouble him of course, but he still existed now, and the thought slipped into his mind like a needle through skin. Not so painful at first, but more wrong with each passing moment.

He felt and heard a change in the harmony around him, a creeping wrongness that shattered all his attempts at spinning in just the right way. He stopped, stilled, listened.

And recognized. Oh, he knew that wrongness, bile at the back of his throat, blood flowing out between his hands, the inhuman scream that threatened to burst his eyes like ripe fruit. When had it come here? How had it hidden itself from him? Still so fatigued from the injuries he'd taken, had he just not felt its cursed feet burning the ground?

It was still far away, but it searched. It hunted. It sniffed the air and lapped at the surface with a rough tongue, trying to find the blood beneath.

He hated it. He hated the black eyes, the scalp laced with silver scars, the wrongness of all of it. The Bone Collector flung himself outward, searching, hunting. If he could destroy this as he – as *Hob* – had destroyed the last one, then maybe, maybe…

He found the Weatherman at the surface, where the sand grains sang their distress as the breeze parted around him unnaturally. And the Weatherman saw him, his gaze piercing as knives. He sang a question in a language that the Bone Collector almost understood, and hated himself for understanding because it was unnatural, it was wrong. There was something different about this one. He was stronger than the last.

He reversed those words, wrapped them in on

themselves, reformed them into something new like a thin-bladed whip to lash out.

The Weatherman recoiled, turned the world ninety degrees, and came in again, trying to engulf him and trap him. Somehow, the Weatherman sang harmonies with himself, layer and layer and layer, louder until the sound of the world seemed a distant thing and the Bone Collector felt weak, trapped, grasping. A different, strange world welcomed him as this world had, warm and tasting like captive lightning, but he did not want this.

No, he asserted, reaching for stone and the hint of fire he'd tasted in Hob's blood, *I am me. I cannot be encompassed.* With a burst of energy, he flung himself to the four corners of the world, too great for the Weatherman to entangle.

You've been away too long, the Weatherman sang, and there was that curious harmony to his voice again, familiar and repugnant. *You should really come home. We miss you.* And by centimeters, using the confusion of that sound, that message, he began to drag the Bone Collector back in. The Bone Collector felt the thread of power from the world, dragged out like blood into the mouth of a parasite, flowing to the Weatherman.

The press of that power, those alien and hideous thoughts, was too strong. The Bone Collector felt himself losing his grasp again, ready to disintegrate as he tried to escape in a way that could not be followed. In desperation, he reached out, searching for help.

Distantly, he felt the heat that was Hob Ravani, banked in sleep. He tried to call, but she wasn't the sort to hear like that. She had a different kind of power.

But someone else heard.

He felt confusion, the sharp suck of an indrawn breath. And then it was like hands against his shoulders – no, the side of a mountain at his back, cool in the night and unmoved by ages. He leaned on that strength and used it as a second, stronger foundation, somehow more certain than his own sense of self, of the body he always felt so distant from, and lashed out at the Weatherman. He freed himself from some of those entangling lies, while the Weatherman sang more into existence with his discordant voice-within-voice.

The mountain listened, waited, understood. He felt it – her – shift, over a millennium, in an instant. She started a new sort of song, something simple and almost childish, but he felt the internal logic of it, rhythm building rhyme by rhyme.

> *My love has hair as black as night*
> *Her breast soft as the moonshine light*
> *She skips upon the sand and laughs*
> *While her skirts sweep out my lover's path*

The words didn't matter, only the emotion, the steadiness of it with a low pulsing beat that he recognized and didn't. He wove himself into the cracks of that song, built on it, harmonized, made it into a wall. She fumbled a little, following what he did, but joined eagerly as he pushed back the Weatherman, further and further away from the state of dreaming.

You don't belong here, he built into every part of that song. *Leave. You do not belong.*

Together, they gave one last mental push, and the Weatherman burst into sand the color of dried blood and blew away. He was still there, of course, a cloud of greasy smoke burning the horizon. The Bone Collector felt him like a boil on the skin of the world. But he'd been thrown out of his own dreaming, disrupted.

His relief was so great, he didn't realize for a moment

that he still leaned upon that mountain until he felt her recognition and surprise. They touched, exchanging feelings, snippets of memories rather than words.

The mountain was Mag; he knew her, had known her since she emerged from the labs beneath the scab called Newcastle. He'd drawn her through rock and sand, into safety. And she knew him as well, though her recognition came more slowly, after she cautiously felt around his edges and fixed his shape in her mind.

He felt her fatigue, stress, and fearful excitement, and with reluctance she offered him a memory by way of explanation: a gun weighing heavy in her pocket, the anticipation that she would soon use it to kill.

There seemed only one answer to that, a phrase that echoed in his memory in Hob's voice: *Don't go borrowing trouble when you've got enough on your own.*

Laughter rippled like a breeze over the sand. And he felt a warmth from her at the recognition of Hob's voice, similar but of a different tone than what he himself felt and still did not entirely understand. He shared that back, not intentionally, but as part of the ebb and flow of this odd sort of contact that was for once not combative.

Where? she asked in feeling rather than words. Where was he?

He drew her down to the world's heart. He felt her recoil, then her wonder at the music of it, the rush and hum of endless energy, that to her became like cool water, like all the water flowing down to one point: the Well. She did not threaten to unravel, so certain in the shape that was *Mag*.

The dynamic between them shifted, and she sheltered him with that foundation that was her own sense of self, remembered his shape when he felt he might begin to lose it. He showed her the harmonies he had learned, that mirror of stars. And when he shied away from it in fear, Mag stepped into the cool un-water and drew him past the dark image he saw reflected back.

For one perfect moment, they stood hand-in-hand, on the black sand beach of an alien world, with stars no human had ever seen hanging over them. Cool water lapped at their feet. Something shifted within his blood, within hers, a thing recognizing *home*, drawing strength and sustenance from it. Above them, the water of their world poured through the bottomless Well and onto these alien shores, and in exchange dream and blue blood made of change and will flowed back and manifested as the impossible.

Mag looked at him, and in this world she was a titan of living stone, each of her eyes its own well of stars. "Is this where it all comes from?"

He felt the answer, just as she did. And he wondered how she saw him, in this new place, one step removed from their world, where different forces governed the universe, where fire and stone and water lived and light sang itself into being, where will governed the planets rather than something so weak as gravity. "Yes."

This *was* a place, now, he knew. Hob had been right. A single point in their world where the umbilicus of this… magic attached and altered everything. And if he found that place, if he kept from unraveling with this certainty of self Mag had showed him, he would have a foot in each universe. He would be this heart, become this power, and he would move worlds.

CHAPTER TWENTY-FOUR • *25 DAYS*

"It was, indeed, another witch," Shige informed Ms Meetchim as he handed her cup of coffee over. He'd had to come straight up to her office after returning from Segundo; stimulants and determination kept him from looking in the least bit tired. "The damage was quite... disturbing."

"Mmm." Meetchim sipped her coffee. With her unoccupied hand, she turned the page of a report. From his vantage, Shige saw another survey map, the lines of the seismographs drawn in thin and red. "That sounds very messy."

Shige's expression of disgust wasn't entirely feigned. All he had to do was recall that apparently his brother had been involved in order to make it quite heartfelt. "It was."

"I'll take that under advisement. Thank you for traveling to look at it, by the way," she said, as if she hadn't all but ordered him to do so. "I don't think the distraction of a witch hunt is advisable right now, however."

A relief that he hadn't needed to lead her to that conclusion. "Of course. How is the exploration faring?" Poorly, he would guess, which was good. She knew she had to have results for the home office, and there'd been a demand for reports along with a monthly schedule of courier stops to pick those reports up.

"The seismic surveys are far too hit or miss. The geologists haven't been able to come up with any sort of provenance theory that makes sense of the data. What we have found isn't following the established tectonics and seems completely unrelated to the known stress mechanics."

"That does sound difficult."

"I'm going to have to request more personnel, to be certain. We need full-time exploration crews, and we'll need to still operate the current mines. We can't afford to lose all of the production indefinitely, no matter what potential there is in the new resource. We still have a business to run."

Shige gestured toward one of the maps, and after a moment of hesitation, Ms Meetchim handed it over to him. He looked at the drawing with little comprehension; no pattern that he could sense, and he was very good at finding patterns. He shrugged and offered it back. "This is obviously not my area of expertise."

"You are an excellent secretary, but no."

Shige smiled, not at all stung. "Have you considered putting Mr Yellow on the problem?" The thought had been constant in his mind for days, strangely: Mr Yellow was thirsty, and this could provide him some relief. Let him find the place to drink. It was odd compared to his other trains of thought, but he couldn't shake it or ignore it, so it must be important.

Meetchim opened her mouth as if to immediately dismiss the idea, then sat back. She tapped her fingers idly on the surface of a map, her pale nails obscuring the wildcat symbols in sequence. "A Weatherman has never been applied to mineral exploration before. His purview is atmospheric and local space conditions."

"Yes. But Mr Yellow is the first Weatherman to have been partially built with amritite-derived products."

"Is there reason to believe this will give him some sort of affinity?"

Shige opened his hands, palm up. "I don't know. But the Weathermen have always had an... affinity for the contaminated locals."

"Of a sort," Meetchim murmured.

"Of a sort." The sort that involved them consuming portions of said locals in a process that Shige devoutly hoped he would never witness in more detail. "Dr Ekwensi's theory on the amritite is that it's directly related to the contamination. So it isn't out of the realm of possibility that the Weatherman might have an affinity for that as well."

"Hmm," Meetchim said, noncommittal. "And your proposal for utilizing Mr Yellow?"

He was treading on more dangerous ground now, Shige realized. While he had not been at all blamed for the death of Mr Green, if anything bad were to happen to Mr Yellow while under his care, that would begin to look like a pattern – not that he would want anything bad to happen to the Weatherman now. He also needed to calculate if this exploration would be to the advantage of the Federal Union, though that butted up strangely against the duty he felt toward Mr Yellow. On the whole, he tended to think so; as long as the Union inspector arrived and they were able to take over before TransRift could fully exploit the new resource, it would be of use for the government. But this was a razor edge to walk, a level of industrial espionage to go with his other responsibilities. "Send him out to one of the wildcat sites that's shown the most promising traces. See if he can sense anything, and express it in an actionable way. We won't know what results we might get until we try."

"And how do you propose we take him to the site?"

Always before, the Weatherman had been transported on a special train, with a full contingent of guards. There were no tracks built to the wildcat sites; there wasn't a point when they weren't producing. "Do we have any sort of air transport?"

Meetchim's eyebrows went up. "There are cargo ospreys, left over from the settlement days, and a few attack helicopters belonging to Mariposa. They are almost never used due to the atmospheric hazards."

"Ah, but if Mr Yellow is traveling with the flight, that will protect them from the atmospheric problems, will it not?"

"Security would be rather thin..." But Ms Meetchim had shifted from trying to pick his silly notion apart to detailing a potential plan, he could see.

"I doubt the rabble here are prepared for anti-aircraft measures. I wager Mr Yellow would be safer in the air than on the ground." He frowned, considering the one truly loose cannon that still might be aimed at his plans. "Though there is the problem of the witches. I recall the one that showed itself at Primero when Mr Green went out there. It seemed to know we were there without being told."

Meetchim smiled, a secretive expression. "Dr Kiyoder might have the answer to your prayers there. Without a Weatherman to keep her occupied until your arrival, I gave her free rein with some of her odder research projects." She slid the maps across to him. "Pick the site you think might be promising for your experiment."

He'd begun to look over the maps, focusing on the newer locations, when the elevator door at the far end of the office slid open. A man in the green Mariposa uniform stood there, looking very displeased: Security

Chief Lien. Lien was shaped rather like a bullet, his head shaved. White scars stood out starkly on his brown-yellow skin, now flushed with anger. "Emergency report, sir," he said.

Meetchim held her hand out, steady as a rock for the entirely too long time it took Lien to walk across the floor, boot heels clicking, and hand a flimsy over. She read it quickly. "The mining towns are voting to strike on payday. It seems some loose lips have leaked the currency change and they're upset. I hope your feelings aren't too hurt, Mr Rollins."

"I'll try to survive," Shige said. He kept himself relaxed by force of will, waiting to see which way to jump on this. Would she blame him?

But Meetchim seemed more amused than anything. "You seriously overestimated their capacity for gratitude when you try to make their lives better. Any change will cause a tantrum, and I suppose the previous management gave them far too free a hand if they think this nonsense will stand."

"The garrison is ready to mobilize," Lien said stiffly.

"Send reinforcements out. But let them have their tantrum. The troublemakers will be known, and those will be the ones sent out to the next wildcat sites in chains. Let them be defiant when they remember they're a speck in an ocean of sand."

"You're not concerned about a work stoppage?" Shige asked, a little surprised.

"We were already looking at mothballing the mines to focus on the new exploration until I receive the next personnel transfer. Break them up over a hundred dig sites where they're stripped of resources and they'll remember that they owe us their very lives. Like all tantrums, this is a performance, Mr Rollins. And there's no one but us here to see."

Shige smiled, thinking about the ever-approaching ship that would bring the inspector. "How right you are, Ms Meetchim."

The basement lab was cool and lit steadily with bright overhead light strips. Both things were a marked improvement from when Shige had first delivered Mr Yellow down here.

Shige walked down the silent halls, his shoe heels clicking dryly on the perfectly smooth synthcrete floor. Dr Kiyoder's office waited at the end of one such hall, walled off in glass in an otherwise barren gray room. She'd decorated the walls of her office with decals and transparent diagrams of the human nervous system and neural networks, beautiful dendritic representations in bright green and blue.

The interior of her office was one-half pristine, a perfectly organized desk and table. The other half was a chaos of equipment, loops of wire, tripods and what looked like transmitters and receivers, though Shige couldn't guess for what. Radio and other wireless data transmission worked very poorly here; the equipment itself looked to be old, with new modifications.

Dr Kiyoder herself, a brown-haired woman golden-pale in the way that indicated she never went outside, sat at her table, drawing out something that he recognized a moment later as a neural circuit interface with neat lines. He rapped lightly on the glass panel that functioned as her door.

She looked at him and then offered him a cautious smile, waving him inside. "Mr Rollins! What brings you down here? Wanting to visit Mr Yellow? He was rather restless last night, though I can't figure out why from the diagnostics."

"It would be my pleasure, after we've spoken. But I

actually came to see you."

"Oh?" She waved a hand toward her table; he saw part of the stack of flimsies he'd delivered to her. "Thank you for all of the documentation from Dr Ekwensi, by the way. This will keep us busy for years. I'm already working on some correspondence for her."

"It's my pleasure to help. But... Ms Meetchim said you've been developing a possible solution to the witch problem?"

"Witch problem...? Oh, the contaminated individuals! Yes. After I studied the notes you were so good to take about Mr Green's encounters with them. You are very good at taking notes, by the way, Mr Rollins. Have you thought about a transfer to a more technical specialization?"

He bowed his head. "You do me great honor, but I'm afraid I have no talent for science."

Dr Kiyoder gestured toward the equipment that occupied the other half of the room. "There are known effects for the disruption of a Weatherman's neural network. I springboarded off of those to see if similar transmissions could deter contaminated individuals. I've had some success working on the subjects we gathered here before Mr Yellow's arrival. And I think I've found a balance where it will deter them, but not interfere with Mr Yellow. At least, the tests haven't bothered him at all."

"What about the subjects?" Shige asked.

Dr Kiyoder grimaced. "They were handed over to Mr Yellow shortly after his arrival so he could acclimate."

Shige imagined that all too well: a white room, a person pushed inside with Mr Yellow waiting, a brief crunch and a slurping sound. He kept his expression smooth. "I see. Ready for field testing, then?"

"Why, yes! I've already sent a few units out to the

wildcat sites on the offchance that there's an intrusion."

He raised his eyebrows. "How do you know they're not just acting as a general deterrent?"

"Oh, a negative like that would be so difficult to prove. But they draw so much power that they can't be run constantly on a site with such limited resources. The idea is that they'll turn them on if there's an intrusion." Kiyoder smiled brightly. "Is it terrible that I almost hope these so-called witches will try to attack a site? We can't prove my work unless they do."

"It isn't terrible at all," Shige said soothingly. He went over the rest of the details with Dr Kiyoder before excusing himself, already mentally composing his site proposal for Ms Meetchim. He very much wanted to see the success of Kiyoder's experimental equipment as well. A means to control the contaminated population would be important for the future.

Perhaps he ought to try to point that Ravani woman toward his test site and see what happened. Give her a reason to think she'd be poking a finger in the eye of the company, and he had little doubt she'd be eager to do it. But he had to be cautious about how he used that particular weapon.

Shige turned down another hall, to Mr Yellow's rooms, though his feet hesitated strangely at the start of it. No, he did want to see Mr Yellow. It was important to stay in his good graces, or what passed for those with a Weatherman – and perhaps he might even be lonely. For all Dr Ekwensi's cautions, he did not think Mr Yellow a mere tool. He followed the wall of windows to find Mr Yellow in the "play" room, slowly weaving bright pink yarn around a set of wires in a tangle Shige couldn't begin to understand.

This was how the Weathermen lived, when they weren't piloting ships or in the core of planetary buildings, doing whatever mysterious thing they did to control the local space. They lived under glass, like curiosities in aquaria. Shige wondered if they minded, when this was the only life they'd ever known. He easily recalled, with his overly keen memory, Kazu shouting at him in a fit of temper that Shige belonged under glass, as shards of a shattered bottle crunched under their shoes in that terrifying, stinking alley – though he'd apologized for it later, in the dark of the night, saying he'd been afraid Shige would report him to their parents again.

Mr Yellow looked up as Shige paused outside the door, his eyes like black pits in his head. Shige tried to look away, but he felt that undeniable tug. Mr Yellow smiled, lips moving to form words Shige could feel: *We miss you.*

CHAPTER TWENTY-FIVE • *24 DAYS*

The evening pay line outside the TransRift office was so quiet that the squeak and clank of the drive chain at the mine seemed loud, the sound of the wind brushing past the buildings in the full street a roar. Every miner from the day shift waited, silent and tense.

Mag stood under the awning of the company store, not quite part of the line that crowded the street. She didn't exist on the TransRift payroll; she'd gotten what little money she had since arriving in Ludlow from the miners and other workers, in exchange for mending their clothes and sewing them new ones. Mostly she'd lived on Clarence's charity, though he said she worked for him.

She wasn't the only one not on the payroll watching the street, though. She saw, peeping from alleys and windows, standing back-up to buildings, other people who lived on the underside of the town, officially unnoticed by the company: cooks, medics more affordable than the company doctors, the informal veterinarian people took their pets to, those who cleaned houses and did repair work and crafted things the company would never sell. Their two musicians, their single artist who hand-drew portraits in exchange for food, their tailors. Many of them had been miners, once, before they'd been injured. Others had been kept out from the start by their families and found another way to survive.

They all had a stake in this too, even if no one but the miners had gotten a vote.

A stir went through the miners as the door to the pay office opened and a line of green-uniformed Mariposa security guards filed out. They pushed back the miners at the front of the line to make room for themselves, forming a wall around the office with a gap just big enough for one person at a time to get to the pay window.

Mag stepped down off the store's porch and grabbed the sleeve of Omar, standing in the street. "Go up to the mine," she said, keeping her voice low. Even then, it felt like shouting in the street. "Let the night shift know to walk out."

"We ain't seen the pay yet," Omar said.

"Think they'd be comin' out like this if it was a normal payday?" Mag asked. "Go."

Omar wriggled through the press, elbowing here and there as necessary. A miner had her eyes fixed on Mag; she must have been listening in. "I don't like this," she said. "Pay's pay."

Mag opened her mouth to reply, but another miner cut her off. His tight black curls were plastered to his forehead with sweat and a skin of rock dust. "And a vote's a vote," he growled. "Pick your fuckin' side."

"We stick together," Mag said, firmly. She stepped back up onto the porch so she could see over the crowd. She picked out Clarence, moving up to the pay window; the miners had agreed he should go first and stand for all of them.

Mag found herself leaning forward as he signed for his pay envelope and took it. The whole damn crowd felt coiled like a spring. They all knew what was coming, and had known since the first man in green had stepped out of the office.

Clarence took one step away from the pay window, enough to put him on the right side of the line of guards. He ripped open the envelope and then poured the brightly colored company scrip chits out onto the ground. The angry rumble that followed was a snarl of human voices.

"Company don't want to give us real money," Clarence said loudly. "Then we ain't gonna give 'em real work."

Mag saw movement from the corner of her eye; it must be the night shift, coming down already. Omar must have sprinted the whole way... no, she saw green. Nothing but green, more of it, blocking one end of the street like a bottleneck. She heard a shout to the left and turned to see more security men. The whole damn garrison must have turned out for this.

She clenched her jaw. They'd known it was impossible to keep anything like this a secret, but she still wanted to find whoever had warned TransRift and wring their neck with her own hands. This was going to get people killed.

Down the street, someone moved to shove one of the guards, but two other miners caught him and pulled him back into the group. This was another thing they'd talked about, argued over in meetings. Make them strike the first blow, Clarence had argued firmly, and Mag had backed him up. Don't break the line. Most of Mariposa were scum who would be happy to wash the street with blood. But the pit boss, Bill, he wanted to believe he was a good guy, and he was still in charge. People who wanted to be able to keep believing their own stories might take the barest excuse to let things get ugly, but they still needed the excuse.

"There a problem?" came the familiar sound of Bill Weld's voice. He stood in the doorway of the company office, only the shiny top of his bald head visible over the line of guards.

"You know there is," Clarence said. "This is the last time I'll repeat myself: You want real work from us, you give us real pay."

"The company–" Bill started, and then was cut off by a wave of shouts from the miners, one Mag added her voice to so hard she felt like her throat would tear. His mouth moved a few sentence worth's more, but then he stopped.

Clarence crossed his arms over his chest and waited for the crowd to simmer down. They'd talked about this. They'd practiced. They'd planned. They'd drilled it all together, like it was a performance. In a way, it was. "We ain't here for your sales pitch. We're here for our pay. Our real pay."

Another roar that they all gave voice to. Mag saw the others like her, the people off the payroll, shouting too.

"We're all gonna go home now," Clarence said. "And the night shift too. And when you got our real pay, you tell us. We'll come get it, and count every goddamn credit, and *then* we'll talk."

Almost as one, the crowd turned to face the greenbellies at either end of the street. Mag could have cheered. "We're goin' home!" someone shouted. "Let us out!" The shout repeated, became a roar. Mag looked at Bill, at his dough-pale face, and wondered if this would be the moment where he ordered the guards to fire.

They'd talked about that, too. And there was a reason so many of the miners were wearing their mine coats, even in the oppressive heat of the evening. Mine coats hid a lot of things. Mag felt the little pistol weigh heavy in her own pocket. They were trying to avoid bloodshed, but they weren't stupid.

The woman who'd spoken before tried to move

forward, toward the pay office. Her neighbors grabbed her. Mag stepped back down from the porch to get a firm hold of the back of the woman's jacket. "We stand together," she shouted in her ear. It was the only way to be heard over the crowd. "You break, you're killin' us. We ain't gonna let you."

They had to police their own, and she hated the thought. But it was sides now. Either stick with the other miners, or go stand with their enemy.

The woman stopped struggling. Around them, the crowd went quiet. Mag looked up to see Clarence had raised an arm. It was a signal they'd all been waiting for. She fixed her eyes on that spot behind the wall of green fabric and muscle that hid the pit boss, and willed him to not be an idiot.

"There's no need to get nasty…" Bill began, and was silenced by another roar.

"You let us out," Clarence said. "You let us go home. And we'll come back to work when you meet our terms. Real pay. Real safety inspections. Decent hours. You think you got enough greenbellies to follow each and every one of us down into the mine with a gun to our heads?"

Stand down, Mag thought, teeth closed around just screaming out the words.

"Of course not," Bill said, his voice strained. "Don't be dramatic. I'll… I'll let the company know your concerns. I'm sure we'll get this cleared up quick."

Relief flooded through her like a wave. Not today. No one had to die today. And they'd taken their one step, so maybe they could get another. But there was a sick feeling in the pit of her stomach as well, a little voice asking if Bill had said that on his own, or if she'd made him somehow, even that far away. She felt stronger now, after that strange, fading dream of not quite talking with the Bone Collector. Did it matter?

The crush of people began to relax away, miners moving down the streets. Mag went with the flow of them, watching the guards still lined up along the buildings. Most of them looked ready to kill, and she half-expected to hear a shot, shouting, someone picking a fight. But maybe the greenbellies had drilled on this too.

Beside her, one of the miners let out a quiet whoop. "We fuckin' won."

"We drew our battle line," Mag said as they continued to walk. She saw, streaming down the hill now, the miners of the night shift stark against the red-purple sunset sky, come to join in with the day shift. There were some sounds of celebration, but most were like her: waiting for the ax to fall, wondering if they'd be able to catch it. She'd better write a note to Hob, let her know what was happening. She wished she'd done it when the strike decision had been made. "Now we gotta hold it."

CHAPTER TWENTY-SIX • 23 DAYS

In the nearly two days Geri was gone, run back to base, Hob and Freki had a chance to get the rhythms of the little mining camp, map out chow times and break times, and note which of the small contingent of guards was the laziest. It was also ample time to see another round of excitement go out, for Hob to feel that blue shine crawl up out of the ground and lick along her skin. She didn't like it one bit. Not long after that, a company man in a dusty blue suit and a greenbelly got into one of the solar-powered trucks and hightailed it out of there quick, in the general direction of Newcastle.

The sun was low in the sky when Freki spotted a dust cloud in the distance, oblique to the camp. He confirmed there were four riders in the cloud, and recognized them all by profile when they were still just specks in the distance: Geri, Dambala, Maheegan, and Coyote. They met a safe distance out from the mining camp.

"Diablo know you're out here?" Hob asked Dambala.

"My leg's fuckin' fine, and I don't need you motherin' me," he rumbled. But he tilted his head slightly toward Coyote and murmured for her ears alone: "He didn't want to come."

Hob nodded. After everything Coyote had said, she

was damned surprised Geri had managed to drag him out here. "From what we seen, camp really quiets down a couple hours after dark," she told the group, once they'd all got settled down into the lee of a dune. "We go in quiet-like then for a look."

"This big of a group isn't terribly quiet," Coyote observed.

"Most everyone's gonna be waitin' out of sight. We'll fire off if we need help, then we make like it's a raid. But I'd rather get in and get out with no one the wiser." She looked at Coyote. "You're the best at quiet we got. Think you can take down whoever's on watch?"

"I'll need to have a better look at the situation," Coyote said. "But provisionally, yes."

The rest of the crew they parceled out jobs to, with thin, dark brown Maheegan going to find himself a good vantage for sniping; it was his specialty. Not something that would come into play if things didn't go sideways, but he was one hell of an insurance policy.

As the sunset faded to purple-black, Coyote bellycrawled to the top of a dune to overlook the camp and Hob followed him, still curious as hell about his presence. She noticed his hands, normally rock steady, fumble out the small pair of binoculars he'd stolen from a Mariposa guard shack years ago.

"You need a smoke?" she asked dryly.

Coyote shot her a narrow-eyed look, then blew out his breath. "I can *feel* it. Like ants crawling all over my bloody skin. Like someone whispering in my ear."

She didn't have to ask what, though she hadn't noticed a damn thing yet. The mine works had stopped at sunset; they weren't bringing anything up to the surface. "You think this is the place?"

"I don't know." He finally got his binoculars out, lens caps off, and looked down through them at the camp.

"But I don't like it."

Hob fell silent. She fished her cigarette case out of her pocket and tucked one between her lips, but didn't light it. That would be too easy for the guards to spot. "Think I should call up the Bone Collector?"

He frowned, still focused down on the camp. "I think... I'd feel better if you did."

Hob realized that she trusted Coyote more than he trusted himself right now. "All right. We'll see if he shows up."

"I thought he always showed up for you."

"Watch your fuckin' tone."

Coyote grinned, like needling her had put him back on an even keel. Hob slid back down the dune, standing once she knew she was well out of sight from below. It was dark now, and dark hat, dark coat didn't tend to show up too well. She was just a shadow against the endless sky. But she wasn't going to count on that. Bold and stupid were two different things.

To her surprise, Coyote followed. He shrugged when she looked at him. "It isn't that big of a camp. I've had enough of a look."

And he kept following her, past the Wolves who were talking quietly amongst themselves, barely audible over the ever-present wind, and sharing a cold dinner. "What're you doin'?" Hob hissed.

"I'm curious."

She drew a knife out of the sheath in her sleeve, and Coyote took a step back, his hands coming up. Hob smirked, half because it was damn funny, and half because it hid her own sudden uncertainty. There wasn't anything weird or private or embarrassing about this, but it felt that way. Maybe because this was her one moment where the Bone Collector was *hers*.

Well, she didn't need anyone to be *hers*, she told

herself. That was some fool thinking, right there. She
drew the knife across the pad of her thumb, enough to
make it bleed freely. She squeezed a couple of drops into
the sand. "Now we wait and see if he shows up."

When Coyote didn't answer right away, she looked
at him and didn't like what she saw. His eyes were fixed
on her hand.

"Get your head together," she said, sharper than she
intended. She pulled a handkerchief out of her pocket
and wrapped it around her thumb.

He blinked, swallowed, and took a measured step
back. "How long does it usually take him?"

"Depends."

"On what?"

"On somethin' he ain't ever bothered to tell me."

Maybe twenty minutes later, she felt that subtle shift
in the air. She turned to find him at her blind side, orange
sand still rolling off the pale gray shoulders of his duster,
draining from the empty eye sockets of the small animal
skulls that decorated his buttonholes.

"I didn't expect you to call me again so soon," he said.
His gaze went down to her hand, thumb wrapped in a
less-than-white handkerchief. He reached for it, but Hob
caught a look of curiosity and amusement on Coyote's
face. She stuck her hand in her coat pocket.

"Got something you might be interested in," Hob said.
"Little wildcat mine."

The Bone Collector's head snapped up, face turned
toward the camp like that had been the cue. His eyes
narrowed, head tilting slightly like a man who was
trying to make out whispered words at a distance. Then
without saying anything else, he started walking toward
the camp.

"Hey," Hob hissed, alarmed. Which went to pissed off
as he kept walking and just ignored her. "You fuckin'

asshole!" She reached out to grab his sleeve; the dusty, well-worn leather of his coat slid downward out of her fingers as he sank below the sand in the space of a few steps. "Oh, you gotta be fuckin' *kiddin'* me."

"What in the hell just happened?" Coyote said.

"I don't fuckin'…" A waving mote of light caught her attention: Maheegan, from his vantage looking down at the camp. Something big had to be going on to get him to light up like that.

Cussing under her breath, Hob ran back toward the wildcat site, her boots sinking ankle-deep into the sand with each step. Coyote didn't even blink, keeping up with her, but she'd noticed he didn't leave footprints any more just like the goddamn Bone Collector. She tore back through the temporary Wolf camp, and heard the shuffle as the rest of the group dropped what they were doing and followed.

She crested the final dune, the cool, dry air of the night tearing at her throat, just in time to see the Bone Collector walk through the center of the wildcat camp, pretty as you please.

Geri fell in next to her, not breathing nearly as hard since he hadn't had to run half as far. "Are you fuckin' kiddin' me?"

"I wish I fuckin' was." It was possible, Hob supposed, that the Bone Collector would keep walking, and whatever charmed, ridiculous luck had kept someone that fucking stupid alive all this time would save him from being noticed. But with each step he took toward the open shaft, that humming she'd almost learned to ignore over the last two days got louder. She felt it in the roots of her teeth, in the ends of her bones: they were fucked.

"Get on the motorcycles. We're gonna make like we're bandits, be a distract–"

Too late, already. She heard the shout of the one goddamn sentry she'd been planning to have Coyote take out. And then a pop, a loud retort, as he suddenly went silent, his head disappearing in a dark spray. Maheegan, thinking quickly. Maybe too quickly.

"Go!" she shouted.

Below them, the camp came alive, the security guards scrambling to hit the floodlights. Hob shielded her eye as the area went yellow-white, even as she drew one of her revolvers with the other hand. When she could see again, she saw a man in green aiming at the Bone Collector.

It was like the goddamn train all over again, him just not paying attention. And this time, he didn't even have the Weatherman as an excuse. All thoughts of going back to get her own motorcycle fled Hob's head and she slid down the steep slip face of the dune. Fire wreathed her hand, bright and sudden and fierce, roaring up like it felt that same hum coming out of the ground. She saw Coyote right next to her, a knife glittering in his hand, and had a vague thought that at least he was planning on that instead of his goddamn teeth.

She pointed at the aiming Mariposa man and slung the fire at him. It leapt across that long distance in an instant, easy as breathing, far easier than it should have been. He burst into white-hot flame.

Ahead in the camp, people started screaming. Miners and more security guards boiled out of their tents in a confused mass. Which might have been useful, for the confusion of it, if the Bone Collector weren't sticking out like a sore thumb and still just walking like he didn't have a care in the world.

I'm gonna fuckin' kill him myself, Hob thought, as two guards came in, finally organized enough to have their rifles. One of them shouted at the Bone Collector, his words lost in the general confusion.

And then–

And then.

The perimeter of devices that had been puzzling Hob and Freki – definitely not lights, it was obvious now – came alive. Hob saw an aura around them, something sucking and black, and then it felt like two knives had been jammed into her temples simultaneously. The pain was instant, splitting, and killed all thought. She fell to her knees, clutching at her head even with her revolver still in hand.

Dimly, she was aware of Coyote pitching forward into a limp heap. Dimly, she saw the pale shape of the Bone Collector crumple, writhing, to the smoothed-out ground. She started struggling to her feet, even though a sound that wasn't a sound but was somehow gravity and the absence of light and a scream of unearthly agony sought to smash her flat, smothering the fire she held to nothing.

Then she saw lights, moving, weaving in and out of her wavering gaze. A hand grabbed the back of her coat, then a familiar voice said, "Got you." Freki dragged her over the battery stack of his motorcycle.

Hob managed to tilt her head enough that she vomited into the sand that flashed past rather than onto his boot, and then they were away, into the darkness, and she could think again. Sort of, over the residual pounding agony in her head.

"I," she ground out, more to convince herself she was still capable of forming words, "am gonna fuckin' kill him myself."

CHAPTER TWENTY-SEVEN • 23 DAYS

Consciousness came back in a series of snaps, like his senses restarting one by one. First a sickening sway and jolt that he recognized, after a dizzying moment of confusion, as the regular movement of one of Hob's infernal machines as it skated over the land surface. That artificial separation between him and the sand, as small as it was, left him feeling ill and disconnected.

Why, then, had this happened? When? He didn't recall steeling himself to get on the back of Hob's motorcycle, and the next snap of awareness told him he was head-down and feet-down toward the solid pressure of the world below, bent limply over the machine as it moved.

Next, the hum of electricity came into place, to go with the sensation of the steadily spinning, tiny whirls of magnetic and electrical fields that tickled his skin and fluttered along his spine. Hum, electricity, hum, sand against chainmesh tires, the hum and rush of air across ears.

He smelled metal and electricity, sweaty bodies, blood pulsing beneath thin skin, gunpowder, mineral-rich oil astringent against the back of his tongue.

His own blood as well, he tasted that thick on the inside of his mouth, heavy with a different kind of mineral load. Then he finally remembered: a sound that hadn't really been a sound, more like a physical blow that shocked every fiber of his nerves at once, and then nothing. He'd been switched off, short-circuited like some kind of human-made machine.

There were other sensations to consider, though, another sense snapping back into focus. There, the tone and heat that he knew to be Hob, like a flame of music burning steadily in the night. The lesser sound and feel of the other Wolves, so dim they were like ghosts in his perception, but present – not like the person-shaped holes in the fabric of the world made by the TransRift outsiders, who kept themselves so carefully sterile. And the new, liquid golden growl shot through tendrils of the world, always reaching and trying to find themselves again, that was Coyote and his endless thirst.

Oh, but he was tired. Going from sinking into the warm song that was the world, then suddenly finding himself face down on the back of a machine was a fantastic disorientation. He felt as if his blood had drained away, like it had before from the hole in his side that still ached in a distant way that he barely acknowledged.

Nearby, Coyote screamed. Then another person screamed.

The Bone Collector opened his eyes to the blur of sand, yellow-gray in the shadows of the night, flowing beneath.

There was the slam of machine against ground, metal skidding on sand, and more shouting. He felt rather than saw Coyote running off, and then the motorcycle beneath the Bone Collector screeched to an abrupt halt.

"What the fuck?" another Wolf shouted. Geri, that was right, he remembered Geri from long ago, from blood in water.

"Where'd he go?" Hob's voice was oddly slurred, but

no less emphatic than normal. That's what he'd always liked about it, what made her a point of stability in an endlessly flowing world, in ever-branching futures. There were certain things for which one could always count on Hob Ravani.

With the motorcycle stopped, and then bouncing slightly as Geri got off, the Bone Collector slid to his own feet. Out of habit, he brushed his hand over his waistcoat, a gesture that always felt like it belonged to someone else. The exhaustion pulled at him, urging him to become tireless stone. Now was not the time. All things in this moment were too critical; he was lost in possible futures, unable to calculate their course with everything in such flux. Which meant he really did need to do something.

Hob or Coyote – the easy answer was Coyote, because he'd run off and the Bone Collector had little doubt what had caused it. He turned to walk in that direction.

Someone – Hob – grabbed his sleeve. "The fuck you goin'?" she demanded harshly.

"I am going to fetch Coyote," he said, wondering how that wasn't self-evident.

She bared her teeth at him. "I ain't done with you."

The Bone Collector smiled. Because of course, he wasn't done with her either; there was too much happening around them both. If anything, that seemed to make Hob angrier, though he wasn't entirely certain why. "Of course not. I will meet you back at your base, with Coyote."

"I'm goin' with him, lemme just get my damn bike..." Another man, the one who smelled a bit like Coyote.

Hob growled a curse and let go of his sleeve. "You ain't doin' shit, Bala..." she began, turning away.

And the Bone Collector let the gravity he always felt take him, pulling him beneath the sand. That alone cured a little of his fatigue, leaving him cradled and encompassed. But it was still not time to rest. He listened to where he could hear, much more clearly now, the sound of Coyote, and followed.

The man got a respectable distance before he stopped, his knees and hands pressing into the dune face hard enough that the Bone Collector felt like it might bruise his own skin. He pushed himself back toward the surface, rising out into the cool night.

Coyote jerked at the soft whisper of all that sand and looked at him with eyes that glinted amber-brown. Then he curled in on himself, hugging his arms around his belly, tearless sobs jerking from his throat.

The need was obvious, necessary. The Bone Collector saw those threads of the world like torn-up roots, reaching and shriveling through Coyote's skin. He pushed up one sleeve and drew a knife made of black glass. The blade sliced through his thin, frail skin, making a line of red next to the vein of blue in his forearm.

Coyote jerked as the smell reached him. He curled away, then one arm reached out. The Bone Collector dropped to one knee and wordlessly offered. He stayed still as, growling, Coyote sucked the blood from that wound.

It was the roots he watched, expanding, uncurling, becoming whole. When that energy was full and right, Coyote released his arm and flung himself back.

It hadn't been so much blood, but he was already tired. The Bone Collector sank back on the sand and then lay on it, wanting the comfort of that familiar touch, warm as one of Hob's hands.

Coyote, panting, wiped at his mouth with the back of his hand. "Is this how it will always be?" he asked, despair black in his tone. "I can't keep doing this."

The Bone Collector closed his eyes, trying to visualize

the futures that branched out before them. It was too tangled and uncertain for him to even offer a small comfort beyond, "All things change." That was the truest thing he knew.

Coyote laughed humorlessly. "This was already quite a change."

The Bone Collector opened one hand, sweeping it palm-up over the sand. "You've touched the heart of the world in a way even I haven't, and torn yourself away before you'd fully grown into it. You aren't one thing or the other, and it is an unstable sort of half-life." He opened his eyes to see Coyote scrubbing at his face with one hand, the other curled to press against his chest.

"I remember more now. Every time, I remember a little more," Coyote said. "I remember seeing stars, reflected in the water. Stars that weren't these stars. Water more real than water can be." He closed his eyes, struggling with some thought. "It's the window to another world, isn't it? Another place."

The words didn't quite fit, but humans hadn't invented the necessary language. This seemed close enough, ideas that the Bone Collector had struggled to describe now simplified and flattened. "Yes. The place from which all change comes. The other side we cannot touch." He felt it, sometimes, like pressing his hand through thick fabric and taking an impression of what was on the other side. He felt too, sometimes, like he might be able to rend that fabric, like he should be able to, but he lacked the raw strength to do so – and it did not feel right, either, to reorder things to his suiting with force. He was part of the world. He did not want to destroy it.

"Guess I'd better tell the boss," Coyote said, not sounding terribly happy. "I don't think it's going to help her in a practical sense, however."

"And Hob is nothing if not practical." With a sigh,

the Bone Collector sat up. It would be too easy to fall into deep sleep otherwise. He rolled up to his knees and leaned forward, to place a kiss on Coyote's forehead.

"What the hell was that, anyway?" Coyote asked.

For a moment, the Bone Collector thought he meant the gesture, but realized instead that he referred to what had happened in the camp that sat like a wound on the world. "I don't know. But I have little doubt it will happen again." He might have said more, but he felt something shift, in the distance, a discordant hum in the air. His lips curled back to show his teeth, not unlike Hob had done earlier. He didn't know the precise arrangement of sound, it was new and disturbing. But he knew what it meant.

"What?" Coyote asked.

"The Eater of Worlds is coming." This had been inevitable since that monster had climbed down onto the planet; interrupting its dreaming was little more than an annoyance to it, he was sure.

Coyote stiffened and tilted his head, like he was listening for something barely on the edge of perception. His head turned, unerringly, so that he faced that great numb spot that the humans called Newcastle. "That's certainly a fancy name for a Weatherman."

CHAPTER TWENTY-EIGHT • *22 DAYS*

The desert below rolled and undulated, dark as a sea with no breaking waves. The massive electric engine made a thrum that Shige felt rather than heard, coming through the frame of the military-surplus light attack helicopter. He had done more than one training mission on the genuine article himself; he could tell that Mariposa had sacrificed quite a bit of speed and maneuverability for this much soundproofing – but who would they be trying to outmaneuver in the air, on a planet they wholly owned?

The paling of the sky that promised dawn showed on the horizon, the black of night fading almost imperceptibly to purple-gray. Kiyoder hadn't wanted the Weatherman overly exposed to the harsh light of day, a precaution she'd assured him and Meetchim had only been necessary with earlier models, but better safe than sorry. They would arrive at the wildcat camp just as the sun began to lumber over the horizon.

He turned back into the comfortable, if still cramped, passenger compartment of the helicopter. There were several seats that were rather plush at the middle of the compartment, one of which was occupied by the spidery form of Mr Yellow. The Weatherman leaned to press his hands and face against the window nearest him. All of the security guards had crowded out of his way, a few of them standing rather than risking the seats nearest to him.

And because of that soundproofing, Shige heard Mr Yellow humming, though not any of the songs he'd come to recognize from the Weatherman. He sounded… cheerful. "That's a new sort of tune," he offered.

He saw, from the corner of his eye, Mr Yellow turning toward him. "We like flying. Like space."

"It is a bit, isn't it. Do you miss being in space?"

"We like to fly," Mr Yellow said, and went back to humming as the pitch of the engines changed, the forward momentum slowing in preparation to land. Out of habit, Shige put on his seatbelt. He'd been in some rough landings before.

"We will not fall," Mr Yellow remarked. "We would know."

"How?" Shige asked.

"We see the branches," Mr Yellow said, as the descent began. "We see everything."

There was a strange smell in the air; Shige caught it as soon as the main door was opened. Electricity and ozone, something else metallic that he couldn't put his finger on. That already had him quietly on edge as he took the folding stairs from the helicopter to the ground. The camp itself had him more alarmed.

He'd expected some sort of ragged receiving line, at the most. The three helicopters that made his little convoy must have been visible from some distance, and about twelve hours earlier, a messenger had been sent with news that they would be coming. But the camp was in disarray, the miners huddled together on one end away from the tents, with green-uniformed guards standing over them, rifles in hand. Every light in the camp was on, another unusual thing when energy drain for the short-term batteries was always a concern. He recognized, as well, equipment like that which had been in Kiyoder's office, ringing the campsite.

And, Shige realized, the temporary drive chain was silent. He'd been to enough mining sites to always expect that clank and creak, like the mine breathing.

He spotted the lead guard from his helicopter, already in intense conversation with an unfamiliar woman in Mariposa green. Shige insinuated himself into that conversation expertly, not speaking quite yet.

"–fucking raid," the camp guard finished saying. "Bandits, I guess. Pack of 'em, on motorcycles."

Shige's focus took on a razor edge. Of course, that mad Ravani woman wasn't the only one on the planet with a set of cobbled-together motorcycles. But they were the most proficient he'd encountered. "Was anyone hurt?"

The camp guard looked at him, and then her eyes widened as she took in his suit. "I lost six of my men," she said, voice harsh. "Fucking sniper."

"Sergeant…" the Corporate guard began.

"Begging your pardon, sir. It's been a bad night."

Shige nodded. "I'm certain it has been, and I'll immediately have reinforcements sent to you. How did you thwart the attack?"

She waved at the ring of cables and transmitters that surrounded the site. "Steimez remembered the instructions that we should trip the experimental system if we came under attack. Quick thinking on his part, and I want him commended."

"Of course," Shige said. "I'll make a note of it."

"Anyway, he triggered the system, and the next thing we knew, three of the bandits had dropped. The others rushed in to grab them and then ran away. Damndest thing. I still don't know what this stuff is supposed to do, but it saved our asses."

"Did you get a look at the ones the system stopped?" Shige asked.

"I was a little busy," the camp guard said. "But a couple of the guys have been saying that one of them was a really pale guy, in a gray coat. For what that's worth."

It wasn't enough of a description for Shige to make a positive identification. "Who saw..."

The camp guard pointed past him. "Is that...?"

Shige turned to see Mr Yellow stepping slowly onto the sand, like he expected it to swallow up his foot. "Yes, it is." The guards shouldn't have let him off the helicopter before they were certain the area was secure, he thought grumpily. He left the conversation to join Mr Yellow, and instead found himself following the Weatherman, who walked unerringly toward the entrance of the mine.

For a dizzying moment, Shige entertained the mental image of Mr Yellow diving into the shaft and vanishing. He hurried forward, reaching out to catch the tail of Mr Yellow's coat. And then he found himself pulled along, which didn't help his worry at all. "Mr Yellow!"

Mr Yellow stopped, so abruptly that Shige ran into his back. The Weatherman was rock solid, strangely so, and something about touching him even through his clothing left Shige disoriented. He stepped back, fighting the urge to scrub his hands against the front of his own coat. "Mr Yellow?"

The Weatherman held his hands out in front of him, palms down toward the ground. His fingers curled, grasping, a tension coiling through his arms and furling down his spine. And then he drew his hands back, like he pulled on a physical object rather than thin air.

The ground beneath them cracked. Something blue and sparkling in the harsh floodlights began to flow up to the surface.

Mr Yellow relaxed and bent to sink his fingers into it, like it was soft as cake. He pulled up a handful, a strange smile on his lips. First he tilted his head, as if listening to it, then he bent, wet red tongue coming out to lick.

"Mr Yellow…" It struck Shige that he really ought not to let the Weatherman put strange things in his mouth.

Mr Yellow dragged his tongue slowly over the blue handful and then stopped, that red flesh still lolling beneath his lips. The blue mineral dribbled away between his fingers like sand, turning black as ash when it hit the ground and blowing away in the wind.

Then Mr Yellow let out a long scream, not human enough for Shige to place any real emotion in it. He clutched at his head with his hands and collapsed, with just as little warning.

Shige lunged forward and grabbed his coat again, saving him from hitting his head on the rocks. Grunting with the effort, he lowered Mr Yellow down to the ground.

The security guards pounded up behind him. "What the hell was that?" the Corporate man demanded.

Shige glanced back at him and saw an echo of his own horror: had they just unwittingly killed the Weatherman? Feeling disoriented, he rolled Mr Yellow over, resting his hands on the Weatherman's chest. Mr Yellow's eyes were open just a slit, nothing but black showing between the lids. But he felt the rise and fall of the Weatherman's chest, the thump of a strong heartbeat.

He sagged with relief, and didn't care if he showed it. It was only natural for someone in his position. "I don't know, but he's alive. He's still alive."

CHAPTER TWENTY-NINE • *22 DAYS*

No one had to tell Hob when the Bone Collector and Coyote arrived, just as the sky was starting to go light for dawn. She hadn't moved away from the window of her office since she'd gotten home and left her motorcycle, rescued from the dunes by the mining camp, to be dealt with by Hati. Her ashtray, a twisted piece of metal that had once served the same function for Old Nick, had come with her and was half-full of white-gray ash and the bent butts of black cigarettes. No matter how much she smoked, her goddamn headache still wouldn't go away.

The first thing she felt, seeing the pale, ghostly shape that was the Bone Collector and the shorter shadow that was Coyote, was relief. Then she reminded herself that she was pissed as all hell at the Bone Collector. He'd made the entire op into a giant fuckup, and maybe it was technically her fault for calling him in the first place, but it wasn't like she'd known he'd do something that ass-and-tits-up stupid.

She clamped her lips around her half-finished cigarette and headed down into the yard to meet them. She was surprised when the Bone Collector still stood there, a hand against one wall. If he'd had any goddamn sense, he should have run for it. She stopped in front of the two men, hands braced on her hips.

"You don't have to wait up when we're out late, you know," Coyote said.

She glared at him. "You all right?"

"Of course."

That was an argument to have at a later time. "Then get. Bala's probably worried sick about you."

Coyote looked at the Bone Collector, and shrugged. "It was nice knowing you."

A bare bit of red-orange sunrise light caught the wall in front of her, just at the top. That marked a whole night without sleep, which just pissed her off more. She was through worrying that much about anyone who didn't collect their paycheck from her. Hob turned her attention back to the Bone Collector.

The man looked... worn out. No. She wasn't going to think anything even that nice about him. If he hadn't wanted to get worn out, maybe he should have thought for three fucking seconds before waltzing into a goddamn mining camp like it was a dance hall. She crossed her arms. "And what the fuck was that?"

His eyebrows went up, graceful curves that she found herself itching to punch. "I fetched Coyote for you."

Was it possible for a human being to be this dense, even one that spent most of his time being a rock? She snarled, "Before that."

He opened his mouth, and so help him, it better have been to say something not stupid. But then Hob felt the world shift, impossibly, because they weren't anywhere near one of the damn camps. There shouldn't have been anything to make the air around them vibrate, prickling at her skin like a thousand needles. It was like what had happened before, but only a little. Like this hum ended not in some bone-deep harmony, but in an agonized scream.

Yes, someone was screaming. Hob found herself on her knees for the second goddamn time today, but her teeth were clenched. It wasn't her. That hoarse, terrible sound was the Bone Collector, bent with his forehead pressed against the dusty ground. His hands clutched at his hair and… those were words. A single word. Just "No!" endlessly.

If it was hitting her and the Bone Collector… Hob turned her head, and the motion felt strange, detached. Like she was moving through something thicker than air, because all things were wrong. There was Coyote, also on his knees, but thank any god if one existed because he wasn't losing his shit this time. He looked scared and confused, but he was still resident in his own eyes.

And then as quickly as it had come, the sensation went away. It had only, Hob realized as she glanced up at the little line of sunlight on the wall above, been a few seconds. Not even a minute, measured by how the sun moved so fast in the morning. It had felt like a damned eternity.

The Bone Collector had gone silent. She tried to stand and thought better of it, with her bones still feeling like they'd been melted. She crawled to the Bone Collector and pushed him onto his back. All anger forgotten, she sagged with relief to see him breathing.

"What the hell was that?" Coyote whispered hoarsely.

"I don't fuckin' know," Hob said. "And I'm getting goddamn sick of not knowin'."

The unholy racket the Bone Collector had raised dragged nearly everyone out of their bed – except for Lobo, because he slept like the dead, and Hob thought he was starting to go a little deaf besides. Freki and Geri, bless the both of them, took one look at Hob and went to pick up the Bone Collector. Geri took his feet, Freki took his arms, and he hung limp as a sack of meal packs as they carried him off toward the infirmary.

Hob waved off Maheegan and Akela when they tried to steady her. "I ain't dead or even hurt."

"If I didn't know better, I'd think you just come in off a bender," Akela remarked. He rasped at the gray stubble on his round chin with his fingers. "The hell was that?"

"Witchy stuff, I reckon," Maheegan said laconically, like he was just observing the sky was blue. His wide mouth curved in a faint smile.

She glanced toward Coyote. He was up on his feet now, one of Dambala's enormous hands steady on his shoulder. Most everyone was still giving him a wide berth – fuck, but that pissed her off – but as she watched, Raff came up, arms crossed awkwardly, and asked: "You gonna be all right?"

"Right as a dust storm," Coyote said lightly.

"That don't sound so right."

"Best I can come up with in a place where it doesn't rain." He smiled tiredly as Raff laughed.

"Maheegan, you go tell Lobo to send my breakfast up to the infirmary, and Coyote's too, and somethin' for our guest," Hob said. She could take a nap there just as easy as in her office or in her room.

"Will do," Maheegan said. He made an approximately salute-like gesture toward his short, wavy black hair that seemed a matter of habit for him – no one else in the outfit had ever saluted except for Coyote, and he did that just to be an asshole – and sloped off to the kitchen.

"You sure–" Akela started.

"Do I look that fuckin' bad?" Hob snapped.

Akela sucked at his teeth; he was missing more than a few. "You sure don't look good."

Hob scrubbed her face with her hands. "Don't recall you assholes ever gettin' this concerned about Nick."

Akela grinned. "I like you more'n I liked Old Nick."

That stunned her into silence as he turned and headed back toward the garage. All she could do then was shake her head and walk, her legs still frustratingly weak, to the infirmary. Coyote patted Dambala's hand and fell in behind her. "Breakfast?" he asked.

She shut the door to the cramped room Freki and Geri had laid the Bone Collector out in. There was a pause as they both stared at the one chair in the room, then Coyote shrugged and perched on the end of the Bone Collector's bed. Relieved, Hob sank into the uncomfortable, rickety metal chair. "Comin'. Figure you got one hell of a report to give me."

Coyote grimaced. "I wish I could disagree." He gave her a surprisingly unemotional recitation of what had happened the night before, which echoed what she'd felt. Then he added: "I remembered a bit more, a few more snatches of how it had been, before I really lost my mind."

Hob leaned forward, elbows resting on her knees. "What you got?"

"Have you ever seen a real well?"

Hob snorted. "Ain't many of those around here."

"Looked in a water barrel, then. Down onto some surface of water, where you can see yourself and the sky above reflected."

She thought hard about that image, and recalled the underground lake where she, Freki, and Geri had first met the Bone Collector so long ago. She'd never found that place again, and still wondered if it really existed. "Something like."

"Imagine instead of a reflection, the water was just a surface between you and some... mirror world. That's what I saw. That this Well is the border between here and... somewhere else."

She raised her eyebrows. It sounded like one hell of a fantastic proposition, but then again, she could form fire on her hands with the power of her will alone. "So, what's that actually mean?"

A knock on the door paused Coyote's answer: Maheegan with a battered plastic tray in his slender hands, precariously containing three plates of flapjacks and sausage. Hob relieved him of it and shut the door in his face.

Coyote went on between stuffing his face with bites of his breakfast. "I know you didn't have much formal schooling, but have you picked up anything about the first Age of Stellar Settlement? Before TransRift." Hob was weak on history, just knew scraps really, so she waved at him to continue. "Earth sent out massive generation ships, and then sleeper ships, that traveled hundreds of years to reach the worlds they settled. That's why advanced technology is still a bit… unevenly distributed, between the worlds. The ships, which were state of the art at the time, could only go fractions of the speed of light, which was thought to be the absolute speed barrier of the universe. Then Tanegawa's World happened. Or rather, the early settlers were somehow able to cobble together an engine that could do the impossible: circumvent space. From here to Earth in only a few months, most of that in-system maneuvering around gravity wells. Near-instantaneous travel. TransRift grew out from that."

This part, she knew a little. "And only TransRift knows how."

"They certainly aren't sharing, and no one's ever successfully copied one of their engine designs and gotten it to work. No one's yet figured out the physics of it either. But what if it's something unique to this world that allowed them to do that? To circumvent the laws of physics as we know them." Coyote shrugged. "But if Tanegawa's World is somehow connected to another... world... Oh, but this is quite silly."

"Think we got beyond silly a long time ago," Hob said dryly. "Say it."

"If there's another place out there, an entire other universe parallel to our own – which has been theorized, mind you, that there are really infinite universes, it gets very surreal and academic and that's the part where I became bored and stopped listening. But if another universe is connected to Tanegawa's World, perhaps in that universe, the speed of light is more of a suggestion rather than an absolute limit."

"And... the blue stuff is... solid other universe junk?" Hob rarely regretted her lack of formal education, but right now she did. Maybe all of this would make more sense to her if she'd done schooling like Coyote had. Or maybe she'd know it was total bullshit. But she could cut through that confusion to modify her initial assessment to: *it would be* really *bad if TransRift got its hands on this*. That, she could work with.

A soft sound from the bed drew Hob's attention. "That is... something close to the truth," the Bone Collector said. "You were right, Hob. It is a discrete place, the world's heart. But not one I can place on a map for you, for my own limitations."

Hob wished she could take a moment to savor having been right for once, but there was too much damn else to untangle. "Glad you got around to tellin' me that."

"I had only just come to that conclusion when you called me." He grimaced, scrubbing at his face with one hand. "*It* was there," he said, voice hoarse. Hob had only heard him sound like that about the Weatherman, and the thought made her blood run cold. When the hell had a new one come in?

"Where? *How*? We killed him," she said.

"At... the scar where you called me. And the vessel is different, but what it carries is always the same."

Hob considered the implications there. "That's a mite disturbing. Does that mean where we were was–"

"No. Merely a..." He looked down at his arm, the blue veins showing through pale skin, as if grasping for the words. "...a small vein as opposed to the capillaries. But... *it* touched the lifeblood of the planet. It tried to drink of that strength."

"You think they're gonna keep looking for the motherlode, if it was that bad?"

"Why settle for only a little world-altering power when you could have it all?" Coyote said.

"If it finds the heart, we will all be destroyed. That cannot be allowed to happen."

Hob blew out a long breath. "Well. Nice of you to offer to hire us again. You were a fair enough employer before. But you better have a pile of fuckin' credits left over now."

The Bone Collector rolled up on one elbow, frowning. "I'm doing what?"

"You're hiring us again," Hob said. Really, she should have thought of this a hell of a lot earlier, when she was fumbling around on her own. "If you can't tell us where we're goin', then we're gonna have to be up TransRift's ass. We're gonna have to follow 'em, and spy on 'em, and be ready so that the minute they find this 'heart,' we can jump in before the Weatherman gets there. And... I don't fuckin' know. Blow it up?"

"Certainly not," the Bone Collector said. "You will bring me there."

"If those're your terms, fine. How many cash boxes you got left?"

He blinked. "Six or seven."

"Bring 'em all here tomorrow and we'll get started. That'll be enough money to keep us goin', since we'll have to turn down all the other jobs while we're workin' on this, you realize."

"I... hadn't?"

It felt damn good to have turned the tables so for once, *he* was the confused one. This was something that would keep her warm at night if she lived to be even half as crusty and old as Nick had. "Well, that's the fact of it and my final offer. Deal or no deal?"

A long pause as she could almost hear the Bone Collector trying to gather his scattered wits. "Deal?"

"That a question or an agreement?"

"Deal," he said, more firmly.

"Deal, then." She looked at Coyote. "You feelin' a mite steadier now?"

"Everything looks better on the other side of breakfast," he said, then tilted his head toward his half-finished plate. "Or from the midst of it."

"Then get, and take it with you. Go finish it with Bala."

"If I take it near him, I might have to fight him for it," Coyote grumbled, already standing.

"Be good for ya. Build character."

He flipped a hand at her, then shut the door on his way out. Hob turned her attention to the Bone Collector. Pleased as she was with herself now, she was also still mad as hell. "We ain't done yet."

The Bone Collector lay back down with a sigh, which grated directly across her nerves. It was almost a relief. "Oh, am I borin' you?" she asked, voice dangerous and low.

"I'm not one of–" he began, with tired irritation.

"You ain't mine to order around, but you're my problem when you're gonna get my people killed," Hob cut him off. "That fuckin' stunt you pulled at the camp, that ain't ever happenin' again or I'll shoot you myself."

He half sat up, expression dark. "I–"

Hob cut him off again. "You can walk off a goddamn cliff for all I fuckin' care when you're on your own. But when you're in there with my people, you act like you understand the rest of us ain't fuckin' stone. Or you take one more walk, out that there door, and you don't ever fuckin' come back in."

There was a long pause, while Hob bit back some more choice words. Let him say one fucking thing and she'd let them loose. His jaw worked like he was chewing on a few things to say himself, brows drawn in. Then his shoulders slumped, and the Bone Collector said in a shockingly small voice: "I am sorry."

She really wished that he'd fought with her. She knew how to handle that. That's all everyone ever did with her, was fight. It was how they communicated. But apology? It wasn't natural. "Good," she growled, for want of anything better to say, even though it didn't feel right.

He lay back down, his eyes directed at the ceiling. "Will you come here?" he asked quietly.

She thought about that, how much she still wanted to just coldcock him. "Once I don't feel like breakin' your face no more, reckon I might."

"All right."

Silence fell on the room, just the two of them breathing. Hob took out a cigarette to give herself something to chew on, but didn't light it. Staying mad was easy, once she'd gotten her temper twisted back up. Familiar. And she didn't believe much in forgiving, let alone doing it quickly. Most of the time people apologized, they did it to make themselves feel better, get themselves out of trouble, not because they were really sorry. Hell, most of the apologies she'd ever spoken were like that. And maybe this was more of the same.

Well, she supposed, she might as well give him a chance to fuck up all over again. She'd gotten enough chances of her own like that in the past. And part of her, a much bigger part than she would ever admit out loud, wanted to go over there.

"Fuck," she muttered, and levered herself out of the chair. She felt the Bone Collector's eyes on her immediately. She sat down on the narrow edge of the bed, realizing now just how much her bones ached with the want to sleep. Maybe she was getting too damn old for all-nighters. At least ones that involved that much worry. "Scoot your bony ass over."

He did, and she stretched out next to him. It felt less awkward this time, having her legs rest against his. His hand, cool and smooth, found hers, and she let him weave their fingers together, and tug their joined hands to rest on his belly.

"I'm afraid," he said quietly.

"Means you're alive," she said. Her throat felt oddly thick, every inch of her too aware of where he rested.

He turned his head to look at her fully, and his nose brushed against hers, two blue eyes looking into her one. She felt his thumb move slowly over hers, and did her best to pretend she didn't feel that simple, stupid touch echoing down her spine.

"What d'ya want from me?" she asked quietly.

"I don't know," he said. "Do you know what you want from me?"

To kiss him. To just put her goddamn head on his shoulder and fall asleep. To be a million kilometers away where she wasn't thinking these stupid things. To not be always thinking about blood spraying a fine line on a ceiling, and the blackened buttons of burnt, melted short range transmitters pouring into her hand like an accusation. To fuck him until she could stop thinking about anything else. "I don't know either," Hob said. It was a lie, and wasn't a lie, both at the same time. Because she knew, if she did give in to that want, everything would change. The thought should have been exhilarating, but just made her even more tired. She had too much shit to do.

"Then I suppose that's all right," the Bone Collector said. Awkwardly, like he wasn't quite sure how the motion should go, he slid his other arm around her shoulders and pulled her more snugly against his side. "You look tired."

"You look more tired," Hob said. She rested her cheek on his shoulder.

"Will you sleep?"

"Reckon I might, if you shut up."

He laughed softly, enough to bounce her a little on his shoulder. She laughed too. That felt the best out of anything. He smelled like sun and sand and a little bit like blood, but all of those things were old friends. With his hand resting on her back, with their breath mixing, with the sound of his heartbeat echoing in her ear, she did the impossible and fell asleep.

CHAPTER THIRTY • *22 DAYS*

It was a quake, a shaft collapse, rumbling death under the ground. She saw Papa strap on his harness, slip a coil of rope over one shoulder and smile at her. "Stay here. I'll be right back."

No, she thought. *No, you won't. You won't ever be back.* That rumble was also the sound of an automatic rifle, firing from the deck of a helicopter, and Papa fell. And the rumbling continued, the shaft collapsing in on itself infinitely, until the earth under her feet buckled like the synthcrete slab in the TransRift lab basement, swallowing her down.

Mag thrashed, trying to swim out of that rumbling maw of sand and rocks. One arm hit something solid, something not right, and she realized she was laying down, she was in bed, she–

She'd just hit Anabi. She sat up quickly, sucking wind. "Oh no. I'm sorry."

Anabi sat up as well, the blanket falling away from the curve of her shoulder, a graceful line in the thin light of dawn that slipped between the curtains. She cautiously put her arms around Mag, pulling her in close after a moment, and rocked her like a child.

The ghostly feeling of the world shaking beneath her,

of something that shouldn't be anything but solid shifting and squirming like an animal trying to cringe away, still echoed through her. But it couldn't be a shaft collapse, Mag reminded herself. The mine had been silent for over twenty-four hours. After the first two, the pit boss had shut down the drive chain. The absence of that sound had made getting to sleep even so late, after a long day of organizing people and chasing down stragglers, strangely difficult.

"Do you feel that?" Mag asked. "Something wrong. Something... I don't know."

Anabi rested her hand over Mag's heart briefly, and she felt her nod. But even as she tried to find a way to describe it more, the feeling drained away. A shared bad dream, perhaps. Maybe that was the hazard of sleeping with someone who could read minds.

Mag leaned back more solidly against Anabi's smooth, flat chest, one hand finding the woman's hair as Anabi rested her cheek on her shoulder. Her breath tickled Mag's neck. It made her feel better, anchored, but her skin still itched with that strange feeling. Something was wrong, outside the shelter of the room.

"Don't think I can go back to sleep," Mag said. "Might go check on people. Just make sure everythin' is still OK." She felt Anabi nod again, then the woman released her. Rather than curling up back under the blankets, Anabi slid out of bed and started picking up their scattered clothes, parceling out which bit belonged to each of them.

That made Mag smile, at least, knowing that she wouldn't be going alone. It eased out some of the tension.

The eerie sense of quiet pervaded the streets. People were up and about, going everywhere in twos or threes, but no one talked above a whisper. There were two greenbellies at every corner, glaring at them all like they were scum, or just looking bored, like none of this had meaning. The miners glared back, shoved their hands in their pockets, and kept moving. Anabi kept tight hold of Mag's hand, her palm damp with nervous sweat.

Most of the houses she passed by had their doors closed tight, but a window open at least a crack. Mag had done the same at Clarence's house, making sure the windows were open so they'd be able to hear any shouting. Most of the houses also had a red handkerchief or scarf hanging from the window, the color they'd settled on as their own. Close to opposite of green and blue as they could get, really. And red stood for anger, for the blood they'd all spent in the mines, for the blood spilled by the fists and guns of the security men.

The feeling of wrongness still in the back of her head drove Mag slowly toward the warehouses. They'd hidden a few supplies there; maybe re-counting the water and food set aside would reassure her that disaster wasn't fully on their doorstep.

"Where do you think you're going?" a guard demanded as Mag and Anabi walked past.

"Walkin'," Mag said.

"You can't be out," her partner said, moving to block them.

"We ain't workin' right now," Mag said evenly. "So we can be out if we want."

The first guard spit. "This town doesn't belong to you."

Arguing would be stupid. The Mariposa guards were trying to pick a fight. But they needed to push against this, because it *was* their town, they'd built it and paid for it and it ran on their backs. But she also felt pitifully small against this. Two against two, but she and Anabi didn't have guns and god knew what other weapons. She could lean on two guards. She'd done it before. But that wouldn't fix it for anyone else the greenbellies harassed.

There weren't just two of them, Mag reminded herself. There were the other miners going quietly about their business, and even more in their houses. Why hang back like prisoners? If they let the guards be all through the town like this, then it was easy for them to divide the houses up, or harass miners like they were doing now.

This had to stop.

She squared her shoulders, her fingers curling into fists. "Yes, it does."

"The fuck did you say?" the second guard snarled, taking a step forward.

"I said this is our town. We live here." Mag raised her voice. "This is our town. These are our streets. This is our home. This–"

His fist cracked across her jaw. She reeled back to be caught by Anabi. She tasted salt and metal and lightning. But Mag wasn't going to stop. And she felt rather than saw people drifting toward them, windows opening a bit wider. She had their attention.

"Get back to your house," the guard said.

Mag straightened, stepping up again. She felt Anabi's hands clutch at her shirt. "This is my house. All these are my houses. You go back to yours."

The guard raised his hand again as his partner watched. Mag saw the female guard's eyes widen a moment before a large, rough hand snatched around her partner's wrist and yanked his fist back.

"The fuck you doin'?" the miner growled. "She ain't done nothin' wrong."

The guard jerked his hand free and stepped back. They were going to shoot, Mag thought with sudden horror. And like her thought put it into their heads, both guards raised their rifles.

Another hand rested on Mag's shoulder, and she felt

more come in, miners running out of their houses to join the rapidly expanding crowd. "You don't want to do that," she said to the guards. And finally, she leaned on them with her will, making them move their fingers away from the triggers of their rifles. Little things. She would protect her people. "This is our town. These are our streets. You don't get to come in here and tell us where we can and can't walk."

Around her, miners murmured in agreement. A few took up the ragged chant of "Our town" and "Our streets." The words multiplied as she continued to lean on those guards. It would have been a damn fool thing for her to do, if she hadn't had her witchiness to rely on – and in a crazy moment, she realized that she would have done it anyway. They had drawn their line. They would hold it.

Frustrated by something she couldn't put a finger on, the first guard hauled back her rifle and hit one of the miners with the butt.

The crowd roared around Mag. They piled onto the two guards, though Mag shouted, "Don't hurt 'em! Don't kill 'em!" The guards' rifles were passed back through the crowd to disappear. More miners grabbed the greenbellies' arms, lifting the screaming and yelling guards off their feet.

"Get out of our town!" a woman shouted. More people took up the cry.

"Take 'em back to the company office," Mag said. "That's theirs. We don't want that." And somehow, they still heard her over the shouting, and took that up as well. "Company men for the company office!"

More people were coming from their houses, the street filling. Mag saw Clarence and Odalia move by – the look Odalia shot her could have curdled stabilized milk. But they were doing what they always did, finding their crews, and moving them out – up and down the street. The sound of shouting filled the town, and the sharp retort of isolated gunshots. Mag felt each of those like a blow, but there wasn't time to wonder now if someone was hurt or dead.

Because if they pushed one set of guards back, they had to push them all back. She was bound to be in trouble, later. She hadn't talked this out with anyone, and it hadn't been a plan. Then again, she hadn't planned to get bullied either.

Mag let the crowd carry her along, though she felt Anabi's hands still tight in the back of her shirt. She'd have to go look at the warehouse later. They carried the guards back through the streets, toward the company office. The entire town filled with the roar of voices, covering up the absence of the drive chain. She saw the pale, doughy shape of Bill Weld's face in the windows of the office for a second before he ducked out of sight.

A line of guards surrounded the office. They leveled their rifles at the miners, though didn't fire. It probably had something to do with the multiple guards now held at the front of the crowd like shields.

"Disperse! You will disperse!" one of the guards in front of the office shouted.

The big miner that had saved Mag from getting hit again yelled back: "You stay here, and there won't be no trouble! Ain't no one been hurt yet but ours!"

Mag wondered if she'd done the wrong thing, then, waiting for the rifles to spit fire. The tension of it made her teeth ache. The crowd shoved around her as she saw more people come into the street. More guards got dragged up to the front by the office, put in front of the rifles.

Finally, the door of the office opened, and Bill Weld poked his head out, to jeers and shouts from the crowd.

"The guards are here for your safety…" he started to say, as more jeering drowned him out.

Captain Longbridge, the yellow stripes on his shoulders vivid next to his rage-purpled face, moved up to Bill's side. They seemed to be having an argument, an ugly one. Then his lips moved in something that had to be like a curse and he stepped back.

"The guards will stay here," Bill said. "But the first rule-breaking we hear of, I'll send them back into the town."

"We can police ourselves fine," the big miner growled. "Your'n picking the fights, not us." The crowd released the guards.

Mag waited to see if the greenbellies would fire then, as the frightened guards scrambled back. She felt them wanting to, felt fingers starting to tense on triggers, a massacre in potential. Well, she was angry too. Everyone around her was angry. She drew off that anger, and cast it over the greenbellies like a blanket of stone – let them know what it was like to be afraid. She felt Longbridge fight her, saw his lips curl in a snarl – but he didn't shout the orders he wanted.

And the crowd slowly moved back. Somehow, Clarence found her as they filtered through the streets. He grabbed her elbow, bruising tight. He had blood on his knuckles. "The hell were you thinkin'?"

Mag felt strange, floaty. For once, her witchiness hadn't made her head hurt. She felt strong, capable, ready. "Was thinkin' they don't got a right to bully us in our town."

He looked like he wanted to shake her – because he was scared, Mag thought. Maybe she'd feel scared later. "We're gonna have to get us some guards of our own." But even scared, he was thinking of the best way to organize things. "If there's an 'our side of town' now, we gotta keep it that way."

Mag couldn't help but laugh, still floating, maybe hysterical as she thought about the blood, the gunshots, what this really all meant. "Figured we needed somethin' to do, since we ain't got the mine to take up our time."

"God help me that I sometimes forget who your uncle was," Clarence muttered. "And this is my punishment."

CHAPTER THIRTY-ONE • *22 DAYS*

Shige prowled around the exile of his small apartment, wondering if he'd finally taken one gamble too many. Ms Meetchim had been angry enough to send him home once he'd delivered all of the news, including Dr Kiyoder's assurance that Mr Yellow would be just fine once he'd had a day to "reset." The chill ultimatum Meetchim had given him was that he might return tomorrow to see Mr Yellow wake up, and then he'd better have something good to go with her morning coffee.

It could have been worse, really. As upper management went, Ms Meetchim had a cold rather than hot temper. But he had little doubt that she'd hang him out to dry if things went poorly. This was what he got for taking the sort of mad risk that had made Kazu an infamous embarrassment for the family – he recalled multiple times he'd watched around a corner, as the security services had brought Kazu home in handcuffs and had tense conversations with their father about *favors*. He was supposed to be so much better at calculating the odds than that. But it seemed particularly unfair, since apparently Kazu still hadn't run through his luck, even as he'd turned his back on the family.

Shige fixed himself a drink – it had been a very

stressful day – and decided to use this downtime as an opportunity to finally comb through the massive dump of files he'd stolen from Dr Ekwensi's office.

With his feet comfortably up, he started reading. Mercifully, even unconscious, Mr Yellow still controlled all of the local fields. The lights were steady and there were no problems with his data card reader. He hadn't wanted to risk printing all of the files onto flimsies.

He began with the specifications for the recent generations of Weathermen. Most of it was supremely technical, data about particular genetic alterations. Some bits here and there he recognized as being similar to his own alterations. He'd made it his business to educate himself thoroughly once he'd come to terms with what he was. The information about the neural implants was less useful, in that he couldn't make head nor tail of it.

It would be nice, he thought grumpily, if there was some sort of primer for non-technicians on how the Weathermen worked. He found hints here and there, like the theory that the Weathermen could predict the future, at least in the short term, and that was what allowed them to safely bridge the vast distances. Through whatever means, they were able to place ships spatially so that they wouldn't collide with debris. He found out also that half of the neural network design – the earliest half of it – was to allow the Weathermen to interface properly with the ship engines, to use the power plants to do whatever mysterious twisting of space occurred entirely within them. On that point, no one seemed to know quite how it worked, other than it didn't make sense with any established science. There was a lot of that in the reports – this or that feature being counter to all current, established knowledge of physics, with no sign of any reconciliation.

What a comforting thought. No one knew how it

worked, just that it did, and their entire commerce system and most of the government was now based on it. Shige got up to fix himself another drink.

After floundering in detail, he decided to go back to the earliest files, the first experimental Weathermen. Understanding the root could mean finding understanding of the current state of things.

Only he found a strange gap. The earliest of the genetic experiments were there to be seen, and no problems at all. But the neural network research was far in advance, at that point. The genetic alterations had, in fact, been made to suit that generation of the neural networks, and then the two had evolved side by side from then on.

What, then, had come before?

And there, he found files hidden in the gap, code-locked on a different level than what he'd deciphered before. Shige downed the last of his drink, long since watered by melted ice. Whatever was in there must be interesting indeed, he thought, if it was so well hidden.

He set up a new codebreaker with the most current Corporate security keys he'd liberated from Meetchim's office, only a few days before. To his dismay, that wasn't the immediate solution. It would take time, and brute force.

What the hell had he found?

21 DAYS

A strange sound filled the air, almost like the shriek of a hunting bird, but it was a scream, and it came from Mr Yellow's lips. Shige wondered idly what the sound would be like if he was actually in the room with the Weatherman, rather than watching him from the other side of presumably soundproofed glass. He felt the scream like pressure against his eyes and the skin of his cheeks, a wordless, endless *want* that he needed to silence. "How long has this been going on?" he asked Dr Kiyoder, who stood beside him.

Her mouth was a grim line in her round, sallow face. "Since he woke up, about ten minutes before I called you."

He ought to be more worried than this, but Mr Yellow wasn't really hurt, was he? He merely… needed something. "Has this sort of thing happened before?"

She shook her head. "Not at this scale. It's normally caused by insufficient acclimation. If we were anywhere else, I'd just keep him in a dimly lit room, turn on the white noise generator, and give him a bit of time. They normally calm themselves after a few hours. But the conditions here are… more difficult." She rubbed her eyes, which were bloodshot and surrounded by dark circles. "More native material to consume would be our best bet, but he processed all of the subjects we had in holding. That should have been enough."

Shige grimaced at the phrasing of "processing," though he trusted she interpreted that as annoyance at the situation. "There's serious unrest occurring in most of the towns. They ought to be cleaning up the problem workers soon, and I imagine there will be no small number of them contaminated."

"Likely," Kiyoder said, though she didn't sound all that cheered. "I really don't understand what they have to complain about. But I'd rather not have Mr Yellow in this state for however long that will take to sort out." She frowned. "I might have to put him in stasis."

He didn't like the sound of that at all, Mr Yellow going away until they could get replacement parts of some sort on the next rift ship. The thought sparked an odd quiver of panic in his chest, one that would be unproductive if he allowed it to flourish. "If that's the best you can do…"

But it wasn't right, he found himself thinking. This wasn't a situation that meant poor attunement. Mr Yellow had been well settled for some weeks. This was a different problem, a different kind of imbalance, though it became harder and harder to think the longer the sound went on, the longer he stood in this room and felt the simple, elemental nature of Mr Yellow's *need* pressing against the backs of his eyes. *Thirsty.* The words drifted through his mind, *We are always thirsty.*

He could almost feel that thirst, thick on his tongue, and the haunting trace of the hot mouthful that would give relief. "Dr Kiyoder... do you still have those blood samples I recovered from the attack?" Part of him found the thought revolting. Kazu was still his brother, even if he'd become something monstrous. But that blood, it would be full of the so-called "witchiness." Mr Yellow *needed* it, and that sudden conviction could not be shaken.

Kiyoder's expression shifted to something more thoughtful. "They are... quite remarkable. Highly contaminated, more than anything else I've seen – though with similarities to subject 64539."

It took Shige a minute to recall why that number sounded so significant – that was the designation given to Magdala Kushtrim during her brief stint in the Corporate lab. He'd committed her records to memory before he went looking for her after her escape. And she was somehow similar to what his brother had become? Tone carefully uncomprehending, the desire for information warring with a sudden urge to scream at Dr Kiyoder to get on with it because Mr Yellow was dying of thirst, couldn't she feel it, he said, "Oh?"

She nodded, not really paying attention to him now as anything but a source of affirmative noises. "I revisited that data set with the new, if inadequate information you brought me about the amritite. And I think there might be a connection. Which makes Mr Green's interaction with that subject even more interesting. So perhaps..."

"Perhaps?" he prompted.

Kiyoder waved vaguely at him, then disappeared down the hall. He considered following, if for no other reason than to escape the unearthly noise Mr Yellow still made. It was more in character to wait. Dr Kiyoder had been prodded into motion, and that was what mattered most.

He wasn't kept waiting long. Kiyoder returned with one hand covered in a translucent safety glove, and a vial of blood held in her fingers. She let herself into the room with Mr Yellow; the moment the door was opened, the inhuman screaming became startlingly loud. Shige watched as she unscrewed the cap on the vial and waved it under Mr Yellow's nose, like one might do with old-style smelling salts on someone who had fainted. When that elicited no reaction, she tipped the vial to let a dark, viscous drop fall into the Weatherman's mouth.

The screaming stopped instantly. Mr Yellow blinked his eyes, then a pale, thin hand lashed out to yank the vial from Kiyoder's fingers and bring it to his lips. He slurped the blood down – Shige felt a shiver of relief that he couldn't hear the sound – and then looked at Kiyoder. His lips moved into a word that Shige felt like it had been written directly on his nerves: "More."

Shige turned and ran down the hall to where he recalled specimen storage being. He recognized the vials he had brought and took the entire cold case to bring back to Kiyoder. She relieved him of it instantly, and this time he followed her into Mr Yellow's room to watch the Weatherman drink them all down, one after another, so like a university student downing shots that Shige had to choke back a near-hysterical laugh. The Weatherman dropped the empty vials on the floor, heedless of their shattering.

When he'd had the last and licked every red trace from his lips with his tongue, Mr Yellow smiled. Shige's knees went weak with a relief he did not want to question, and a strange thread of pleasure.

And then Mr Yellow said: "We hear it clearly now."

CHAPTER THIRTY-TWO • *19 DAYS*

"Mag, you got a second?" A small, white-haired man, his back hunched, caught Mag's sleeve with his hand as she passed by. His fingernails were clean – it took her a moment to remember he was one of the town's tailors, and hadn't been in the mine for years.

"Of course." If she had a second to herself right now, she'd be using it to sleep.

He stared down at the cracked leather slippers he wore. "Can I trouble you for a few days' worth of water? I saved much as I could, but somethin'… a rat, maybe, it chewed through one of the bags."

"You all out?"

His shoulders jerked. "Didn't have much to begin with."

There wasn't anything to be done about that, even if the thought of already breaking into their supplies filled her with dread. This moment had been coming, and she should feel positive it'd taken this long; the store had been refusing to sell since the strike had started, out of sheer spite. "I'll bring you a day ration. But put it in somethin' sturdier."

"Thank you. Feel like a damn fool, I do."

She ought to comfort him. Maybe it was fatigue that

made the words stick in her throat.

Mag walked to the furthest warehouse through quiet streets to find the building empty – too empty. Mag went through all of the crates that remained, ones they'd cribbed from supplies that had been shipped in years ago and never touched. They were empty now: the supply cache was gone.

"Do you think someone grabbed it?" Mag asked Anabi, who if anything looked more distraught than her.

No one said anything to me, Anabi wrote on her slate. And since she'd taken over bookkeeping, no one was supposed to touch the caches without letting her know.

Mag took a deep breath, trying to wrestle down the paranoia that jangled at her nerves. Maybe Clarence had things moved. A hell of a lot of their water had been hidden in this warehouse, and water was more precious than anything, even bullets. "Gotta be an explanation," she said. She could go check one of the caches outside the walls, but that should be a last resort. Instead, she led Anabi back across town, cutting over fences and through narrow alleys between houses until they reached the church.

Mag hadn't wanted to trust the preacher in Ludlow at first, remembering all too well what the preacher in Rouse had done, according to Hob. Most of the preachers in the towns were in the pay of the company in some way. Brother Rami was a different sort – the part where he insisted everyone call him "Brother" instead of anything else was a start – and he'd gotten in deep with the miners and their meetings quick. And since he kept the church and preached the company sermons with a wink and a nod, the company mostly let him alone.

He opened the back door of the church after a minute of quiet, frantic knocking. Brother Rami was shorter than Mag, and wore a plain brown bathrobe, his hair in long locks pulled back from his face with a piece of twine. His wide-set brown eyes were round in his dark face when he took in Mag and Anabi. "Is somethin' wrong?" He craned his neck out, trying to look behind them. His voice was high for a man's, husky.

"I don't know. Maybe. You been out of your church much, last twenty-four hours?"

Brother Rami frowned, even as he waved the two of them inside. "I was out yesterday. Wanted to be able to grab anyone got hurt, if it came to that. And I was out again in the night. Tilly Grant got her ass beat proper because they caught her tryin' to sneak to the pit boss's house." He clicked his tongue. "Can't say I approve as a man of God, but also can't say I approve of her bein' that damn dumb."

Mag nodded. "Can you show me the cache?"

His frown got even more dire. "Expectin' trouble?"

"Might already be there."

He waved them along to the back room where extra books and candles and the like were stored. He moved a pile of boxes and knocked the false back off a cabinet. Mag peered inside and breathed a sigh of relief that she caught the glint of metal. "OK. But..." the space seemed small. "That all of 'em?"

He shook his head. "Had to split it up. You want to see the other parts?"

Mag nodded, and followed. He showed her another hidden cache in his kitchen, and then stopped at one of the pews, looking thunderous. "Didn't notice this before since we ain't had a service in the last day..."

"Notice what?"

He pointed to the floor; there were pale streaks like scars in the worn wood, blackened with years of tracked-in mine dust. "Someone scratched up my floor." He pushed the pew aside and pressed on the board until it came under his hand, then pulled it away. Beneath was empty. "What in God's name…" he breathed.

Mag felt like her entire body went cold. "Anyone know where that was, but not the others?"

"No one but me knew about the others. Boy who brought me the last load helped me stow it there, though. Omar… yes. Him. Do you think…?"

It was bad, to be so angry and yet so calm. Because of course, who else knew about the other caches? Just her, Omar, Odalia, and Clarence. And who was the latecomer to that, the eager helper? She'd been stupid to talk herself out of her distrust, and it wasn't going to hurt just her. "Thanks for your time, Brother."

Brother Rami observed her silently for a moment, then said, "Remember that murder is still a mortal sin."

Anabi clutched Mag's hand even tighter. "I'll keep that in mind."

Mag had Anabi take a message to Omar, asking him to meet her back at that first warehouse. She was too angry to be able to face him herself and keep up a facade. She waited, arms crossed. The small rear door of the warehouse opened after only ten minutes; he must have hurried.

Omar glanced around, looking surprised that she was alone. "Mag, what–"

"*Stop.*" She didn't want to hear another damn thing out of his mouth. She put every bit of power she had into that word, crashing over him like a wave. She felt him crumble. His mouth gaped, his eyes going all unfocused. It would have almost been funny if she weren't ready to choke him with her bare hands. "We're gonna have us a talk, Omar. You're gonna tell me everythin' I want to know."

"Be happy to," he mumbled, staring through her. A

thin ribbon of blood began to trickle from one corner of his eye. She found she didn't care.

"What did you tell the company men?" she asked.

Of all things, he still managed to look confused. "I didn't tell them nothin'."

Leaned as she was into that strange space that was his thoughts, she could smell that he wasn't lying. Or thought he wasn't lying. "Who did you tell about the caches?"

"You, Clarence, Odalia. Brother Rami, just for the one."

This couldn't be right. Couldn't be. She felt doubt suck at her will, and tamped it back as best she could. She had stepped into this with both feet. No choice but to see it through. "Who did you tell about meeting Coyote?"

"Didn't tell no one." Had it been bad luck after all? She began to feel sick, and felt her grip on him slip a little. Omar swayed back a step, his expression like a man in a dream. "I feel real shook about it. Didn't want no harm to come to him. Not after Odalia said he'd been havin' a tough time and needed some friends."

Mag froze. "Odalia said *what*?" He repeated himself, which wasn't useful. What could that even mean? "Tell me all of it," she ordered, pressing in on him with her mind so he'd understand what she actually wanted.

"Told me to talk to him. Told me where me an' my friends could meet up with him. Just for drinkin' and cards and she said he liked his men funny and I was funny," Omar said, slowly. "And she knows I been powerful lonely since I transferred here."

Mag took a deep breath and let it out slowly. If Odalia had set all of that up... it was a thought too horrible to contemplate, after how deep in she'd been with everything. "Has Odalia told you other things?"

"She's been real helpful," Omar said. "Checked over messages for me, 'cause my readin' ain't so good.

Checked behind me to make sure everythin' was hidden proper when you gave me supplies to take care of. Oh, an' when I was gonna put all those credits away, she said she'd do it, so they'd be safe." He continued on, more details, a hundred little things that on their face were innocent, helpful, all for the cause. But it meant there wasn't anything Odalia didn't know. And she'd done it without ever breathing a word to Clarence and Mag, through someone who just thought he was being helpful.

And she'd done her level best to always make Mag question herself, to make her seem unreliable and dangerous. Mag knew that too.

Feeling sick to her stomach, Mag took out her handkerchief and wiped away the blood seeping down Omar's cheek. Carefully, she let his mind go. He blinked like a man waking from a dream. "Mag?"

"Shh," she said. "You done a good thing today. You go on home, and have a good sleep, and be ready. Things're gonna happen sooner rather than later." The words were a gentle push compared to everything else, and he accepted that just as readily.

She waited for him to leave, then carefully folded the handkerchief so it was blood-side in. She still felt his mind, so close, his words and confusion echoing in her own skull. She did her best to shake the sensation away and focus on what he'd told her rather than how it had felt, the reality of betrayal.

It let her find her anger again, and she needed that like the air that filled her lungs as she made her way back to Clarence's house. Anabi waited for her, but silently stepped aside. Clarence sat at the kitchen table, cup of coffee in one hand, eyes still red with sleep.

The tiredness in his face seemed to both fall away and grow infinitely worse as he took in Mag's expression. "Mag."

She pulled up a chair and sat. "I got a thing or two to tell you that you ain't gonna like. About Odalia."

He put his cup down so slowly, so carefully that the surface of the coffee didn't even ripple as it touched the table.

CHAPTER THIRTY-THREE • *19 DAYS*

Once more, Shige found himself in the surprisingly plush cabin of the helicopter, desert rolling out beneath them. Only this time, the helicopter was one of a much larger convoy, complete with two heavy Mariposa gunships. Shige still wasn't certain why the security chief had ordered their presence; what had happened to Mr Yellow before wasn't something that could be shot from the air. But it meant that the expedition was happening, so he wasn't about to complain. The assurances, if cautious ones, from Dr Kiyoder that Mr Yellow was unlikely to experience a similar shutdown again had probably helped. But Shige thought what had truly tipped the balance was when Mr Yellow turned to Ms Meetchim, addressing her directly through the one-way glass of his room as she observed him. He'd said, "Let us go to the heart. We will eat it."

No one had quite known what Mr Yellow meant by the "heart", but considering the push for a more producible source of amritite, Ms Meetchim had been easy to convince afterward that it was worth exploring.

The Weatherman sat stock still in his seat now, when he'd never been so quiet during any kind of transit before. His head tilted like he was listening for a far-off noise that he could barely hear. One of the Weatherman's thin hands rested lightly on a pressure control that he could turn this way and that, which communicated the direction he wanted to the pilot. It was easier than trying to get him to finetune direction verbally; they'd mercifully figured that out before the convoy had taken off, when he'd physically acted out the direction he wanted them to go rather than being able to answer the question coherently.

They flew for hours, the orange-pink undulating desert below giving way to stretches of hardpan, and even a very rare field of spiky, gray-green native plants. Shige noted the coordinates of that sighting down, since they were always looking for sources of water that didn't involve expensive imports from other planets.

Then they were over a vast, light pink stretch of saltpan that extended out into the horizon. Shige had seen the aerial surveys of Tanegawa's World, pictures of sadly low resolution since the surveys had to be completed from beyond the worst interference of the planet's magnetic field. There'd been wide basins, the skeletal remains of long-extinct oceans, though no one seemed to know where all that water could have logically gone, just as the source of the moisture for the intense and shockingly short rainy season made no sense to any planetary climate model yet to be devised. The endless flat beneath them was one of those extinct oceans, he was sure of that before he even checked his map.

He would have lost all sense of time from the sameness of the flat that stretched beneath them if he hadn't had a watch to check. The time elapsed told him they had to be at least four thousand kilometers into the ocean basin when Mr Yellow sat bolt upright and said: "Here." He pounded on the pressure plate with one hand.

The pilot had no difficulty finding a place to land,

homing in on the exact spot Mr Yellow wanted. A salt flat like this was nearly as good as an engineered landing pad for lighter vehicles.

Shige slipped on a pair of dark glasses as the outer door opened again. The day was nearly blinding even with that consideration, the light and heat reflecting up ruthlessly from the pale crust of the salt flat. There was nothing remarkable about where they'd landed.

Mr Yellow, hands covering his eyes, walked out onto the flat. There wasn't anything for him to trip over out here, so Shige let him move as he wished, though he stayed close by. Three security guards and the copilot followed a little behind, while the gunships hovered overhead, their rotors shockingly loud in the stillness.

About a hundred meters from the helicopter, Mr Yellow came to a sudden stop. He crouched down and rested his hands on the burning hot surface of the salt, his eyes squeezed shut. "We hear."

Shige made careful note of their distance and bearing from the helicopter, which would have a much better estimation of location thanks to recorded velocity, bearing, and time information. He also had thought to bring a can of paint with him, which would probably be more useful. There wasn't sand to cover a mark quickly out here.

"I don't see anything," the copilot said, stopping next to Shige. "Or hear anything."

"We're looking for a mineral source, so it might be quite deep below the surface," Shige offered.

Mr Yellow's face contorted into a grimace. A thin whine escaped from the Weatherman's lips as he clenched his hands against the ground. Shige saw his shoulders tense and strain, as if he tried to lift up the land itself.

"What's wrong with him?" one of the security guards asked.

A thin rivulet of crimson ran from Mr Yellow's nose, drops falling bright onto the salt surface. Shige was half-surprised that they didn't sizzle on contact, though they already seemed to have dried when he crouched in front of the Weatherman. But he didn't feel alarmed, somehow, like he could hear Mr Yellow calling into the ground, searching for an answer – though obviously to no avail. But this was it, this had to be it, the place Mr Yellow needed. "Mr Yellow, stop. Please. Before you hurt yourself." When there was no response, he cautiously touched the Weatherman's arm.

"Too deep," Mr Yellow moaned. "We cannot reach it."

"That's all right." Shige took a handkerchief from his pocket and carefully wiped the blood away from Mr Yellow's nose. It would take some time, of course, since they'd either have to build tracks out here, or a landing pad suitable for a suborbital transport; he knew they had a few of those waiting around for use. But now that there was a location to be explored, he had little doubt that Meetchim would move fast. *Good*, he thought, then disagreed with himself: *bad*. TransRift couldn't be too entrenched when the inspector arrived... but no, he rationalized, wouldn't it be better to have this as a distraction for Meetchim for the last few weeks before the inspector arrived? Wouldn't it be better to have this mystery mostly uncovered – *Mr Yellow's thirst satisfied* – and waiting for capture by the FUS? "That's what miners are for."

18 DAYS

"I trust this latest outing was more of a success than the previous one?" Ms Meetchim asked, her voice dangerously cool.

Shige clasped his hands loosely in front of himself,

head slightly bowed. The security curtains of Ms Meetchim's office were drawn again, leaving her a lone figure in dark blue, seated at a glass-and-metal desk, against a black background. It made her pale face and blonde hair seem to float, disembodied.

"Very much so, Ms Meetchim. Mr Yellow is in fine shape and more eager than ever to continue to work. He led us out to a point he claimed was the source of the amritite." Not quite what Mr Yellow had said, but a useful interpretation.

"Show me the map."

He grabbed the cylindrical case he'd set next to his foot and shook out the map he'd had made just an hour ago. It was a beautiful rendition of the area from Newcastle to the point Mr Yellow had found, with the flight path of the helicopter in much higher resolution thanks to them having taken pictures as they flew. He tapped the red triangle that sat on the flat expanse of the salt plain, nearly due north. "This is the precise point."

"Far away, isn't it?"

"Further than I'd like. And Mr Yellow indicated that the source was deep underground."

She grimaced, measuring the distance between Newcastle and the point with her fingers. "I didn't particularly like having Mr Yellow off site, but I think we're going to have to utilize him in that capacity for the time being. Make a memo to let management and labs know that we'll need to shut down all non-essential systems, since Mr Yellow won't be able to monitor as closely as we'd like. Speak with Dr Kiyoder and find out if he'll have to be with every convoy, or if he can be stationed in such a way that we can have a free flow of supplies."

He took dutiful notes. "Will you want a rail line constructed to the site?"

"Yes. Built from both ends, though it will take quite some time." She tapped her fingers on the desk. "Until then we can mobilize the old fleet of cargo ospreys. We'll need the labs to switch over to full-time fuel conversion for them, I think. They were never retrofitted."

"The supplies will be simple to organize. Do you have a preference in regards to where the personnel should come from?"

Ms Meetchim looked at him for a long moment, then laughed sharply. He fought down a shock of alarm, wondering what he'd missed. "I suppose you have been busy over the last several days," she remarked. "All but two of the mining towns have made good on their tantrum threat. Convenient for all of the troublemakers to have sorted themselves out. We needn't play nice anymore."

"And so... put the non-striking towns and the farmers on the rail line, and–"

"–the rest down in the pit, yes," Ms Meetchim said. "They can go down there willingly or at the end of a rifle, I don't care. I'll put in a second request for personnel when the next ship comes in. I think... yes, the last round of news you brought indicated there was civil unrest on Tai-Yen. I'll ask for a recruitment drive there to sweep up as many refugees as we can get. They ought to be appropriately grateful for a new home and meaningful work."

Shige nodded as if her suggestion was brilliant rather than horrifying. "Shall I head out to the towns once I've completed the transfers ready for the wildcat sites and the supply schedules for the ospreys?" This might be his last chance to get information in some way to his contacts there. If nothing else, it would add another useful element of chaos to make certain Hob Ravani knew where all the resources would be going. And it would be an opportunity to nudge the conflict in a useful direction, since the miners had all seemed rather timid for their breed until now, surprisingly self-controlled for people who had grown up with so little education.

"Whatever for?"

"An operation of this sort will need coordination," Shige said smoothly. "If nothing else, we want to make certain that the towns aren't able to warn each other. A simultaneous crackdown will minimize the level of resistance and leave us with more able bodies."

Ms Meetchim tapped her lips. "This sounds like a task better left for the security chief Lien."

He pivoted smoothly: "While he must inarguably be in charge of planning the coordinated disciplinary action, I think he might benefit from managerial oversight, don't you? We need an able workforce, and he tends to be a bit..."

"Bullish," Ms Meetchim said dryly. "He has been itching to burn this infection clean. I can't say that I blame him."

He held his hands out, palms up in a helpless gesture. "We unfortunately must work with the reticent children we have available."

Meetchim snorted. "A sad statement of truth. Well, once we've got our new workers, we can deal with the disciplinary issues more permanently."

"Of course." His sag of relief was purely internal. "If I may be excused, sir?"

She waved a hand at him. "Certainly... oh, Mr Rolland?"

"Yes, sir?"

"Do fetch me a cup of coffee first. No one makes it up to your standards."

He made himself smile. "Ah, the real reason you don't want me running about the mining towns."

"I'm so glad you've re-found your competence," Meetchim smiled. "I'd be lost without you."

CHAPTER THIRTY-FOUR • *16 DAYS*

The afternoon sun beat down on Hob, the twins, and their squads as they squatted in one of the patches of shade in the exercise yard with plates of reconstituted mashed potatoes shaped into pancakes and smothered in chili. There was the bare whisper of a breeze coming over the walls, which made the yard a cooler place to be than the mess room. They were all still coated with orange dust from the desert, fresh off more scouting trips to the wildcats. Hob wasn't happy with her come-up-all-empty scouting jaunt, and judging by the looks on Freki and Geri's faces, she was about to feel less happy. At least Coyote was still out. Maybe that was some hope if he wasn't just getting his skinny ass in more trouble.

"You got that map handy?" Geri asked.

Hob pulled the folded-up flimsy – actually a series of flimsies taped together – out of her pocket and handed it to him. With her other hand she shoveled a spoonful of Lobo's tearjerker chili into her mouth.

Geri unfolded the map and tried to smooth it over one broad thigh. "You ever fuckin' heard of rollin' maps instead of foldin' 'em?"

"You volunteerin' to ride around with a fuckin' map case strapped to your bike?"

He grumbled under his breath, thick fingers touching the locations she'd marked on the map so far. He dug the stub of a grease pencil out of his pocket and made his own marks, then traced lines out from them in a pattern that probably meant something to him but might as well have been magic to her. "Everythin' this side is empty."

"Had a fuckin' feelin'," Hob grumbled.

"And there ain't anythin' new, least this far out, I'd wager." He traced a rough shape around the camps they'd checked. "We'd've seen a dust cloud risin'. We didn't see shit. Not even eagles."

Freki, mouth occupied with chewing, grunted agreement. He plucked the pencil from Geri's fingers and made his own marks.

"So we're talkin' a whole new area. One that you ain't picked out in your figures. Fuck." It would be back to the drawing board, and she was already damn tired of being bumped back to square one.

"Like they only stopped long enough to take the mining machinery. Didn't clean nothin' up," Conall confirmed. His bright red hair stood out from his head in uneven spikes. "Weren't signs of bandits or nothin', that we could see. Two days' worth of sand blown in if the wind was constant."

"Think our... *employer*'s gonna have something useful to say about that?" Geri asked. It wasn't any kind of secret, where the money for this job had come from.

"S'pose if we run totally dry, I could call him up, see if he can witch up some answers. But I doubt it." She wasn't looking to avoid him, exactly, and she wasn't shy about wasting his time, but it wasn't a thing to do lightly. "So what the fuck changed to make 'em pull up stakes everywhere so sudden?"

"Figured it was all bust real quick?" Raff offered from past Freki, but didn't sound convinced.

"I'd feel better if I thought that was true," Hob said.

"So would I," Geri agreed. "Shit."

From above, on the guard walk, Lykaios called down, "We got two riders comin' in."

Hob frowned and called up: "Just two?"

A pause, then Lykaios answered: "It's Diablo and Akela."

"Huh. Early, ain't they?" Geri said.

According to Hati, the two had gone off to Primero this morning, to barter for some medical supplies since they'd have the best stuff. Hob had been expecting that and given them permission ahead of time. Diablo had a fresh face and wasn't wanted by security, and he knew what the hell he needed for his own infirmary. Akela didn't mind cooling his heels and reading one of Hati's novels outside the walls while he waited for business to get done. Primero was far enough away to be an overnight trip, even a two day if no one was in a hurry. They'd been gone a hell of a lot less than a day. "Yeah, real early. Guess we'll find out what's got their asses on fire in a minute."

The two men still shed orange dust in clouds when they blew in through the garage door. Diablo's dark olive cheeks, brushed with black stubble, were clean thanks to his helmet. He headed straight for Hob, Akela on his heels. "Ospreys," he said.

Hob frowned. The last time she'd seen the company fly an osprey was when they'd been bringing new heavy equipment in to Shimera, stuff that wouldn't fit right on a train, years ago. And that had been only one. "In Primero?"

Akela, at Diablo's shoulder, shook his head. "Never made it that far. Doc spotted the ospreys before we hit halfway."

"They must've been coming out of Newcastle," Diablo

said. "A whole group."

"How many?" Geri asked.

"Five of 'em. Flyin' together, in a big V." Diablo shook his head. "I didn't even know they had so many. When my town flooded out and they sent in help, there were only two and we thought it was the third coming of the savior."

Hob tried to imagine being from such a place, where a flood could happen, and where the coming of the greenbellies might mean salvation instead of trouble. Her brain couldn't wrap around it at all. The farm towns might as well be from a different planet. "Which way were they going?"

Akela took out a scrap of flimsy and offered it over. "This is the bearin', best we could figure."

Hob spread her map out again; Freki and Geri leaned over it with her and together they traced the line, assuming it came out of Newcastle. It didn't head anywhere near the old wildcat sites, or any of the towns.

Geri whistled between his teeth. "Where the fuck they goin'?"

"Don't know," Hob said. "But we're gonna find out."

An hour and a half later, Coyote and Dambala leaned over the same map, now freshly marked with all the busted wildcats they had seen, and eyed the neat red line that Freki had put on it. Coyote glanced up at Dambala, an unreadable look on his face. "You know what they use on wildcat sites, right?"

"Much as any of us do," Dambala said.

"Think they'd be able to fit it all in a few ospreys?"

Dambala shrugged. "If you were askin' twenty years ago, maybe I'd know."

"Guess," Coyote said. "I have faith in you."

Hob watched the exchange with interest. She felt the

edge of a past here, something normally taboo. No one knew Dambala as well as Coyote did, and vice versa. If he was dragging history out in front of everyone, there had to be a damn good reason.

Dambala cleared his throat. "They usually move that shit in trucks. If we're talkin' cargo ospreys, they're made to carry and drop armored attack vehicles and full-loaded transports. So yeah, I guess so. If it's real cargo birds and not fast runners or gunships."

Coyote turned his gaze on Hob, eyebrows arched expectantly. "So you're thinkin' that they pulled out of all the wildcats and they're moving the equipment somewhere else in the ospreys," Hob said.

"It makes sense as a working hypothesis," Coyote said. "Even big cargo ospreys are an order of magnitude faster than a truck – and they have better range."

She glanced up at Dambala, feeling hopelessly out of her depth. They'd never talked air equipment, because people simply did not fly on this planet. "Can we follow 'em?"

He shifted a little uncomfortably on his feet. "Max air velocity's gonna be between seven and nine hundred kilometers an hour, boss," he said, apologetic. "Maybe more. Depends on the model."

Hob took a long, thoughtful drag of her cigarette. "Guess first we'll have to see if it was just the one convoy afore we get too excited."

"And if it ain't?" Dambala asked.

"We're gonna have to track 'em somehow." Hob glanced up from the map, met the eyes of the men around her. "And if they're sendin' out ospreys, then the Weatherman has to be with 'em or near 'em. Otherwise, that's a lot of money to have crash in the desert."

Coyote hissed under his breath, something in the tone so like the Bone Collector that she gave him a sharp look.

"Can't go fast enough to follow 'em," Dambala said. "And we ain't got range finders or anythin' like that. Trust me, ain't none of us that good at estimatin' distance, not even Maheegan."

"We can triangulate," Freki said. He nudged Geri, like that had been more than enough words for him to speak at once.

Geri nodded. "Easy stuff. Three teams in different places, where they'll be able to see the route. We got enough good watches that we can keep the times synced." He pulled a crumpled flimsy from one of his pockets as Hob looked at him uncomprehendingly, and liberated the grease pencil from his twin's hand. Coyote nodded slowly along, a little smile on his lips, his eyes glittering.

Geri put three marks on the paper. "The squads, right? Osprey shows up. Everyone checks their time every two minutes to keep it simple, writes the location of the osprey. So at 14:22, say, squad one sees it at this angle..." he drew a careful, dotted line, "and squad two sees it here," a second dotted line that crossed the first, "and squad three sees it at this angle." He added a third dotted line.

"Only need two squads," Hob said.

"Need three 'cause our maps ain't that great," Freki said.

"And we keep advancin', figurin' the route as we go," Geri added. "Ain't gonna just be a straight line on a map if it's any kind of distance."

"Sounds slow," Hob observed. Freki gave her a shrug that wasn't exactly an apology. "But better'n nothin'." She took a long draw of her smoke, eyes half-closed. "Get provisions and campin' gear for nine set up. Five days' worth. We'll start for Newcastle before light tomorrow and see if we even got anythin' to be excited about, then go from there. Dambala, you're gonna be watchin' the base. Me, Freki, and Coyote each run a squad. Geri's with me, and Maheegan. Everyone else, pick two. The rest, Dambala, put who you think can pass to go into town and see if they can figure out what the fuck is even goin' on."

She continued to smoke as the men filed out. Coyote lingered behind; she'd expected that.

"Geri looks like you fed him a rotten lemon," he observed lightly.

"Must mean I'm doin' somethin' right." She eyed him. "You think this ain't fast enough."

"We both know it isn't."

"Got any better ideas?"

He grimaced. "Not yet. I'm… percolating."

"And now you're a fuckin' coffee pot," Hob snorted. "I hate this watch and wait shit."

"You weren't meant to be a spy," he agreed.

"Only thing I got to look forward to is shootin' someone on the other end of it," Hob said. And by then, she reckoned it would feel like a goddamn relief.

CHAPTER THIRTY-FIVE • *16 DAYS*

"She's home for the night now," Mag said, crumpling the scrap of flimsy Omar had just brought for her in her skirt pocket.

"Yeah, I know," Clarence said. He stayed sitting, his head in his hands.

It had been three days of them running around and dealing with their own jobs in the young strike. Clarence had gone to have another chat with Bill, and then check on their people door to door. Mag had been sneaking around to take a quiet inventory of their supply caches, and the results were grim: over three quarters of what they'd had was gone. All that remained were the things she'd hidden in private houses where someone was always home, and a few extra things she'd buried herself and not told anyone about. Those were safe in the church now.

And worse, there'd been the talking to people to corroborate Mag's story. It wasn't that Clarence didn't believe her; Mag trusted him when he said that. Clarence had always had her back. But they had to make sure that Omar wasn't mistaken, that it wasn't some kind of nebulous plot to sow dissent in their ranks.

Ultimately, Clarence was grasping at straws, trying to

find an impossible way for both Mag to not be crazy and Odalia to not be a damned traitor. And when she wasn't so angry she couldn't see straight, she had it in her heart to bleed a little for him. Odalia was one of Clarence's oldest friends in Ludlow, bound up by countless jokes about their shared family name.

But mostly, she wanted to shake Clarence by the collar and tell him to pull himself together. It was tempting, to give him a good witch power shove in that direction, but she refused to be what Odalia had tried to make her into.

This was an emergency, but it also wasn't. The damage had been done. They'd cut Odalia so quietly from the loop that she hadn't noticed. They'd even fed her a couple pieces of misinformation, just to see if that'd get the greenbellies to chase their tails a bit.

"They been digging up the east side," Mag said evenly. She was back to screaming angry, and screaming right now wouldn't do any good. "All the spots we said."

"I know that, too," Clarence said. "I watched 'em for a bit myself."

"Then you know we gotta."

"Don't mean I like it."

Mag slapped her hand on the table next to him. She was meanly gratified to see him jerk back. "Where's your mad at now, Clarence?" she demanded. "She had a side to pick. Us or them. She picked her side and then fuckin' lied to us."

"I am mad," he said, though he didn't sound it at all. "But I'm also fuckin' tired, Mag. This ain't the same as beatin' a stupid idea out of someone's head."

Maybe he could be sad around his mad, Mag thought grimly, because Odalia hadn't been trying to convince everyone that he was crazy. "And it's still gotta be done. We ain't takin' more of their hits. So get on your feet, Clarence Vigil. Freedom ain't ever been pretty."

Of all things, his lips curved into a little smile, and he pulled himself up out of his chair. "How you want to do this, then?"

It felt like he'd just dropped it all in her lap, and she didn't like that either. But maybe he knew that he didn't have the tough in him for someone who used to be his friend. Betrayal hurt, Mag knew. It made some people bleed to death inside. "I'll talk to her. Have it all out of her like I did Omar. You listen in."

His jaw set and grim, he said, "Then let's go, before she sleeps. Powerful rude to wake someone up like that."

They walked together to Odalia's house. Mag went to the front door and knocked, while Clarence headed around to the back to keep her from running. He also knew how to jigger the lock she'd put on her kitchen door, he'd told Mag, and he could do that quiet.

Odalia, not looking too fresh herself, opened the front door. She frowned. "Somethin' wrong?"

"Yeah," Mag said. "Can't talk about it out here, all open-like. Sorry to keep you from sleepin'." And somehow, she managed to summon up a little smile from the depths. Like this was some kind of normal day, like she didn't want to kill Odalia dead right on her front step.

"Sure, come in." Odalia led her inside to the kitchen, and went over to the counter. "You want a cup of coffee?"

"Not really." The thought of putting anything in her mouth made her feel sick.

"I'll make one for myself."

Mag felt Clarence nearby, hiding in the shadow of the narrow stairs. There was no reason to wait, and good, because all that hot rage burning in her stomach needed to be let out. "I know what you done. I know you sold us out."

Odalia went still for a moment. Mag expected denials,

maybe Odalia trying to convince her she was crazy again. But the woman turned – and instead of a cup of coffee in her hand, it was a gun, compact and black. She'd seen those kinds of guns on the belts of Mariposa officers before, normally ignored in favor of their much heavier rifles. "You don't know anythin', and you're gonna know even less after I shoot you in the head," Odalia said calmly. "They pay good money for dead witches, and get your sickness out of town at the same time. Sounds like a deal to me."

Mag heard Clarence start moving behind her and saw Odalia's eyes go a little wider, her finger start to tense. She didn't let it get any further than that. Mag slammed into Odalia's thoughts with every ounce of power she had.

Odalia froze, her eyes gone wide, staring, unseeing. Mag had to steady herself with one hand on the wall; she felt like she'd just jumped across a gully with no preparation and landed strange.

Clarence moved around her, his expression dark. He pried the gun from Odalia's stiff fingers. "She gonna shoot you?"

"She still wants to," Mag said. She could feel that too, the anger and hatred that she'd never known was there, under Odalia's nice expression. Her skin crawled in response. "You go on and tell us, Odalia. Tell us what you done."

That hate and anger kept pounding at her with each word Odalia spoke, giving lie to her toneless recitation of facts. It had never been like this before, but she'd also never leaned on anyone who hated her so personally before. It wasn't like the Mariposa guards at all.

But Odalia kept talking, a litany of things large and small, what she'd told the company at this or that time, how she met with Bill or with one of the shift sergeants for Mariposa, how much information she'd passed on to them. It was damn near everything she'd ever been told. "They got people they're lookin' for," Odalia said, when Mag pressed her about Coyote. "Them so-called mercenaries. They want your friend, but they'll take any of her people. I knew he was her right-hand man, and they'd want him too. Just like they want any witch we can give 'em without causing a fuss."

The only relief was that Odalia didn't know of any other spies. Though that might not mean a thing, since Mag figured you'd have to be damn stupid to let all your double agents know who the others were.

Clarence, who had listened to it all like a man getting gutpunched repeatedly, finally spoke up. "Why'd you do it, Odalia?" His voice was low and ragged.

"I earned what I got with my sweat, and I made sacrifices for my family. I want a better life for them. They said I could get another promotion, a place in Newcastle where my boy could go to a real school, not just the company school," Odalia said. And some of her hate finally managed to creep into her voice. "I ain't losin' that for a fuckin' witch. Should've gave her over to the Weatherman when we had the chance. Should've gave 'em all over and taken care of our own, not risked our families for the fuckups in Rouse."

"It's about solidarity, Odalia," Clarence said. And now there was something hot as blood in those words, like he'd finally found his mad again.

Mag felt the words before Odalia spoke them, and hated her for their mockery. "You can't eat solidarity, Clarence."

His lips curled back in a snarl and he punched her, a solid blow that knocked her over. Mag felt the echo of the pain, the sick crunch of fist connecting with the side of the head. It wasn't her, she reminded herself, trying to step back from it and still keep Odalia unmoving. It hurt, but she burned away any thought of pity with the fire of Odalia's own hate.

"What're we gonna do with her?" she asked. She knew what she wanted to do, she was so angry. But she'd promised herself to never go off half-cocked the way Uncle Nick had, that night so many months ago.

"If it was me, I'd fuckin' shoot her here myself. But we ain't the only judge and jury, and we ain't helpin' any of our own if we just make her disappear like we're the damn greenbellies." Clarence looked coldly down at Odalia, who had begun to tremble as she fought against Mag's control of her body. There didn't seem to be a drop of pity in him either. "Let her be judged by the people she was so happy to betray."

15 DAYS

Clarence's kitchen was utterly silent as Odalia finished her litany of traitorous actions. Only after the last word had been spoken did Mag ease up her control. Her head didn't hurt yet, somehow, and that both surprised and frightened her. The air in the kitchen was hot, close, almost humid, and smelled of unwashed bodies and rock dust. Miners were pressed in together like they'd been vacuum packed, the only clear space a tight circle around Mag, Odalia, and Clarence. Odalia was tied to Clarence's most solid kitchen chair, wrists and ankles. Mag hadn't wanted to take any chances with her control faltering and Odalia escaping.

This wasn't even a fraction of the miners, but it was a representative from each work gang, people to vote and stand in place of their fellows. When no one still spoke, Clarence said to the men and women squeezed into the room: "This is our decision. What do we do with her?"

Silence, then murmuring, though too much of a jumble of words for Mag to pick any one thing out with her focus elsewhere. Then one man, his cheek blackened with bruises, said, "I say we shoot her. We ain't got the time nor the supplies for mercy."

Odalia laughed sharply, if unsteadily. "You ain't got authority over me."

That drew a volley of yelling. "Like you think you got authority over us?" one of the female work gang leaders shouted. "Where's your fuckin' blue suit, Odalia?"

"I been a good crew lead–"

"You ain't thinkin' of anyone but yourself!"

Mag closed her eyes and listened to the shouts rather than the words, the sound of the miners working themselves up to the inevitable. But then she heard Odalia say, "And I ain't the one you should be shootin'. You got a damn witch makin' me like a puppet, you know that?"

It made her blood run cold for a brief, awful moment as the room went silent again. But she'd known this was coming, Mag realized. In some deep part of her soul, she'd known it would come as soon as she'd agreed with Clarence on getting the work gang leaders. She could have tried to stop it, by gagging Odalia, by keeping a grip on her mind and her mouth, but she hadn't done that either.

Her entire life had been hiding, ever since Papa had gotten killed. She'd taken his vision and run with it, and gotten them this far. And she was damn tired of hiding. She wanted to stand, and fight, and die on her own terms.

Mag opened her eyes to find the entire room staring at her. Clarence had shifted slightly, to cross his arms, but also to stand a little closer to her.

She'd survived the lab under the TransRift building.

She'd survived getting drowned in the Weatherman's eyes. She'd survived TransRift murdering both her parents. She wasn't going to flinch now. "I am witchy," she said evenly. "But I don't think you ought to go shootin' me."

"See, she admitted it!" Odalia crowed.

Mag ignored her and continued. The people in front of her were suspicious, she could feel that. But she'd also laid the groundwork for this already, when she'd fought to make them all see the company's witch hunt was a bad thing. "The witchiness I got lets me do things like make people tell the truth. That's how me'n Clarence got her to confess, after she pulled a gun on me."

"Or maybe you're just puttin' words in my mouth," Odalia screamed. "She's probably followin' orders off the company, playin' us all."

Mag snorted, staying calm in the face of the uncertainty she saw before her. When would she have to stop justifying herself? "That'd be fuckin' stupid, now, wouldn't it? Company kills witches, for one. Makes us disappear just as bad as they do anyone else." She bit down on the phrase "normal folk." No, she wasn't going to agree with them that she was broken or different in a way that meant it was okay to kill her. "And if I was puttin' words in her mouth, why the hell'd I be lettin' her scream about it now? If I was workin' for the company, why would I do this instead of just playin' you all one by one till you're waltzin' into their arms?" She huffed a sound too exasperated to be a laugh. "They think we're stupid. Well, we ain't. None of us are. Sure as hell ain't stupid enough to fall for a lie that can't even hold up to a few questions."

"She's manipulatin' you all!" Odalia shouted, desperate.

"If I was gonna be witchin' anyone right now, it'd be

Odalia again to get her to shut her damn mouth afore she gave me a headache," Mag said flatly.

A laugh rippled through the kitchen. A man in the back of the crowd said, "I trust you, Mag." More agreement came, and Mag felt her stomach unclench.

Next to her, Clarence said, "Then let's get back to figurin' what we're gonna do with the real problem." He raised his voice to be heard over Odalia shouting about how they were all fools who were going to die.

One of the gathered miners took a handkerchief out of her pocket, and moved into the clear space so she could stuff it into Odalia's mouth. The woman gave Clarence and Mag each a polite nod. "Couldn't hardly hear myself think."

"What are you thinkin', now?" Clarence asked.

"I'm thinkin' shootin's too good for someone who was gonna sell us out," she answered. "But it'll do."

"Make her an example," another man in the crowd said. There was a murmur of approval there.

"Vote it," Clarence said. "Show of hands. For betrayin' her people to TransRift, who agrees she should be executed?"

All but two people voted for it. Odalia made a muffled shriek around her gag. Mag wondered if she ought to feel happy, but what was there to be happy about, voting on the life of another person? She was angry, she thought Odalia had earned what she had coming to her, but that didn't mean she was going to feel good about it. Looking around, she might have been the only one that reluctant except for the two nay votes out of nearly twenty.

Mag crossed her arms over her chest. "We want her to be an example for our people, or for the bluebellies?"

"Don't rightly know what you mean," Clarence said.

It itched to have all that attention on her again, but Mag pressed on. "We worried about our own people goin' spineless, or do we want to make sure TransRift knows we're gonna find every last one of their spies, and that we ain't fallin' for it no more?"

Clarence looked around the room, reading the faces, the people nodding or shaking their heads. "My people are solid," a woman said. "I ain't got no worries about them."

They'd all thought Odalia was solid too, Mag thought grimly. Anyone could be wrong. But she didn't want to sow more paranoia. That would also do the company's work for them. "Then we send her back to them."

"In pieces," a man added, to grim muttering.

Mag took a deep breath and let it out slowly. "If'n you'll trust me, I can do you one better'n that."

Clarence turned his gaze on her, brows up. She offered him no answer with her expression. But he still said, "All in favor?" and raised his own hand first.

It was a smaller majority, but still a majority. Mag looked down at Odalia, feeling the weight of the room on her shoulders. "Last thing anyone in Ludlow will ever ask of you, and then you'll be free. You're gonna take a message back to your paymasters, from us."

CHAPTER THIRTY-SIX • *13 DAYS*

Shige felt the tension the moment he stepped off the special train and into the thin shade of the awning at Ludlow's rail depot. The hot, dry air of the morning still felt dense and electric, like he'd stepped into an active war room in the government offices on Earth. Then, as the deep thrum of the engine behind him stilled, the motors winding down, he noticed the silence: no drive chain for the mine, no murmuring voices typical of a healthy town.

The small depot platform was almost empty, except for the town's chief of security – Longbridge, according to the general Ludlow personnel summary he'd read on the way here. As Shige moved forward to shake hands with Longbridge and introduce himself, he noted a line of guards stretching down the street, rifles held at the ready. On the other side, he spotted a few of the miners, silently watching.

"Perimeter guard?" he asked, his hand still trapped in Longbridge's bone-crushing grip. He was more than happy to let the man flop his arm around like a dead fish.

Longbridge finally released his hand. "Something like it. Nine days ago, the rats made a major push. Weld let 'em have the ground because he didn't want any trouble.

Keep things calm until you got here." Cool disgust filled his voice.

"A move you disagree with, I take it?"

Longbridge eyed him warily. "Far be it from me to question Corporate policy."

"I think you misunderstand me, captain. Corporate policy cares very much about results." Shige smiled.

Longbridge didn't smile, exactly, but he relaxed. "Pit boss is dickless, and Clarence Vigil's got him running in circles. That fucker's pulling all the strings." He curled his lips around the clipped words. "You shouldn't even be here. I could've fixed this the day they tried to get it started, if he'd let me."

"Your restraint in following orders is appreciated," Shige said. "Let me assess the situation, but then I'd like to speak with you again before I depart. It is in the best interest of the company that this disruption is brought to a swift close."

"I don't have anything on my dance card but watching these lazy pieces of shit wander the street instead of working like God intended. You can be certain I'll have the time." Longbridge escorted Shige the short distance from the train depot, past the company store, to the Corporate satellite office. "We've ceded them the entire rest of the town," Longbridge muttered, as they walked. "Dickless."

Shige could make no guesses if Bill Weld still had all of his attendant parts when he laid eyes on the man, but he certainly looked like he hadn't been sleeping, surrounded by a chaotic avalanche of flimsies in his small office. He stood hastily when Shige entered the room, spilling his half-finished cup of coffee in the process. The brown liquid pooled on the uneven surface of his desk. "Sorry for your trouble. It's not nearly so bad as it sounds."

"Of course," Shige assured him. He located a box of

tissues and offered them over to Weld, then waited as the pit boss awkwardly mopped up the coffee. "And yours isn't the only town having trouble. I'm visiting each as a matter of routine. We must be uniform in how we address this... dispute."

Behind him, Longbridge made a rude noise. Weld seemed almost grateful, though, to be getting some sort of direction. He sagged down in his chair. "What's Newcastle want us to do?" Then he stood quickly again. "Let me get you some coffee, too."

"No need," Shige said. "Please, sit. And before we discuss my end of things, I'd like to know what the situation is here."

Weld blew out a puff of breath as he dropped back into his chair. "They were already riled because we had some surveying accidents. Didn't think it had been so long since we sank a new shaft that they forgot exploration is a risky business. And we gave standard bonus pay out for it."

"Your adherence to policy is commendable."

"Fuckers were just looking for something to be unhappy about," Longbridge said. "They don't like risk, they should've transferred to farming."

Weld shrugged. "Anyway, they didn't take the new pay system well."

"Even after you explained the benefits to them?" Shige asked, all wounded innocence.

"They didn't give me a chance."

"I'll wager they're upset because it interferes with all their black market nonsense they think we don't know about," Longbridge interjected. "Idiots. Should've let me put a few down on payday, and we wouldn't be in this mess."

Weld shot Longbridge a cold look. "They're decent workers when they feel like we're listening to them."

"Shouldn't need us to kiss their asses to get them to do their job," Longbridge growled back.

"Gentlemen." Shige raised his hands. "I am not here to judge the actions of the past. Though I will say, we're rather glad that your town is still peaceful. It's not in our interest to lose able bodies at the moment, not with the push from Corporate."

"Those able bodies aren't doing anything for you now," Longbridge pointed out.

Shige continued on as if he hadn't spoken, "Obviously, this work stoppage of theirs breaks the employment contract each and every one of them has signed with us. And as we are the only enforcement agency available…" he nodded to Longbridge, "…they will all have to be arrested. Rather than blacklisting, which would deplete the workforce too much at this time, Vice President Meetchim and Security Chief Lien have agreed that hard labor will do as a suitable punishment."

"You going to send us a train to collect the ones we arrest?" Longbridge asked, a sudden, wolfish grin on his face. "And you realize, they're going to resist."

"I'll arrange for trucks to bring the reinforcements in, and a train to follow. Less lethal means are preferred. This is a mental game, and we wish to cow them and remind them for whom they work," Shige said. "Your handling of this will weigh heavily in your performance review this year. We need living, able-bodied miners for the new push." Hopefully repeating that a time or two would get the security head to rein in his bloodthirst a little – though not too much. Either way, Shige won; if there was a massacre, the inspector would take a dim view of that upon her arrival. If all of the miners lived but were put on unpaid hard labor, that was also a violation of nearly every human rights code in the Federal Union, and she wouldn't be pleased with that either. Though he hoped for the latter, so there would be plenty of miners to dig for Mr Yellow. The Weatherman was so very thirsty. Shige felt it, even now.

"Can we offer them amnesty if they surrender and go quietly to their new assignment?" Weld asked.

"Of course. Do you think any of them will take it?"

"I can hope."

"Then you're a fool," Longbridge said. "It's my job to enforce policy, not coddle entitled workers who want a free lunch."

"Creativity is part of performance," Shige said, smiling at him. "A more subtle approach might be called for. If, perhaps, you let them think my presence means Corporate is willing to entertain their demands, that ought to relax them a bit."

Longbridge let out a bark of a laugh. "Sweep 'em up at night after they all get drunk on celebrating."

Shige spread his hands. "I'm certainly not here to tell you how to do your job. But the day for this action is set–"

He was interrupted by a knock at the door. A guard in green poked his head in. "Sir?"

"Thought I said we weren't to be disturbed," Longbridge said.

"I know, sir. But we just had one of the rats break their line and come through."

Longbridge's eyebrows went up. "*Break* the line?"

The guard licked his lips, gaze flitting to Shige and Weld, uncertain. "Not exactly. I think… they let her through. And it's not just any rat. It's one of the agents. Said she needs to talk to the boss who came on the train."

"Agents?" Shige asked Longbridge.

"Got a few reasonable rats who want to make a bit on the side. That's how we knew this was coming." He eyed Weld. "Not that we did anything to stop it. But thanks to her, we cleaned out a bunch of their supplies."

"Ah. Well, please send her in," Shige said. "It sounds as if she must have something important to tell us."

Longbridge frowned. "Don't know why she'd be breaking cover."

"It's probably really important, then," Weld said. He seemed to be as nonplussed as Shige about the spy in the miner's ranks. Shige wondered how much Longbridge had been doing under the table in this town. "Let's see her."

Longbridge jerked his head at the guard, who opened the door wider and let a woman in. She had a dark complexion, her brown hair shaved close to her head, as was common for the miners, making it easier to wear their helmets and get the worst of the mine dust out of their hair. But there was something off about the way she walked, a bit jerky and wooden, like she was being propelled forward or dragged by an unseen hand. One of her eyes showed a blood-red sclera, and the other was bloodshot. Dried blood crusted her nostrils. It all put Shige on edge, though he kept his expression bland. But his instincts told him, *this is dangerous, be ready for anything*.

Weld's eyes widened. "Odalia Vigil was one of your spies?"

Longbridge ignored him, his attention fixed on the woman. "What in the hell is going on, Odalia?"

And she ignored everyone but Shige, her eyes on his blue suit. Though for a curious moment he felt like it wasn't her looking out of her eyes at him, but someone else entirely. "You the boss from Newcastle?" Her voice trembled.

"Yes. What do you have to tell me?"

In a lightning fast movement, she lunged to the side and ripped Longbridge's pistol from its holster.

Immediately the weapon came up to point at Shige, the safety coming off in a click very audible in the stillness.

Shige raised his hands. "*Stop,*" he snapped, as Longbridge coiled to spring on her. She'd be able to fire before the man could get her down, and he really didn't feel like being shot today. Longbridge froze, and Shige continued, "I'm listening. There's no need to point that weapon at me."

She recited without seeming to hear: "We ain't your slaves. We ain't your machines. We are miners. We are people. Ludlow belongs to us. Rouse belongs to us. Tercio belongs to us. Walsen belongs to us. Shimera belongs to us." Her hand moved, and suddenly the barrel of the gun was pressed under her chin. A stray tear squeezed out of her blood-red eye. "No more traitors, no more spies, no more of your company lies."

Longbridge lunged at her then, with the gun no longer pointed at Shige. Her finger squeezed the trigger, and the sharp retort of the gun preceded the wet thump of Longbridge slamming into her. Blood and bone and brain misted the air. Shige remained motionless for a moment, all sounds distant to his overwhelmed ears: Longbridge shouting with his face gone purple in fury, more guards flooding into the room, Weld vomiting into the trashcan by his desk.

Yes, he realized, this had just happened. The witch hunt had never made it to Ludlow, and he had little doubt that this was the work of someone contaminated by the planet. And he thought: *This was really quite helpful of them. Longbridge is more than ready to kill.* He cleared his throat. "Well, you know what Corporate wishes of you already. If you gentlemen will excuse me, I'm going to change my shirt."

Shige ignored the look of uncomprehending anger from Longbridge, the gape-mouthed confusion from

Weld, and coolly skirted the spreading puddle of blood as he left the office. As the breeze in the street touched his face, he finally noticed the wet of blood sprayed on his cheek. With one hand, he reached for his handkerchief. The other, compelled by some urge he could neither explain nor deny, came up to wipe the blood away.

Before he could truly comprehend his own movement, he licked the wet, red line off his finger. The earthy metallic taste sat on his tongue, and the immediate horror of it warred with a much calmer thought somehow in his mind: *Disappointing*.

CHAPTER THIRTY-SEVEN • *13 DAYS*

Enough people had run out of water that Mag had decided they'd best set up a regular distribution in the church, Brother Rami gently but firmly counseling the few people who tried to sneak through the line twice. They'd also brought out some of the remaining food stores, what little there was. It might be time soon, Mag thought, to make another push for territory, and this time take the company store. That would solve a lot of their troubles.

"Hold back the stable milk for them has children," Mag said, as she handed over the pathetically small box of white-filled bags to Omar. "Think the rest of us can handle drinkin' our coffee black while that holds out."

"Ain't gonna be long till that, neither." Omar huffed a laugh, though when she glanced at him, his gaze skittered away. She didn't know how much he remembered about her walking through his brain, but she guessed it was more than nothing.

Mag pretended nothing was wrong at all. She couldn't make someone be comfortable with her, and it wasn't fair to ask Omar that, not after what she'd done to him. "Just means everyone'll be plain meaner if the bosses try anythin', right?"

"Right." He tapped his fingers on the back of a pew. "You're lookin' tired, Mag."

"I am tired." She rubbed her eyes. "You think… Could you take over here?" It was another apology to Omar. A reminder he was trusted. But she never would have offered it if he had been a fuckup. Mag tried to spare the feelings of others, but she didn't see the point in being stupid about it, and most everyone had figured that out by now.

His smile got a bit wider. "Sure thing. You go get you some rest."

It wasn't that she'd done so much today, at least nothing labor intensive. But she'd felt, as they'd started measuring out the precise amount of water a body needed to make it through the day, the minute Odalia blew her own head off. It had been exhausting, to hold Odalia endlessly with a corner of her attention, like clenching her hand tight around a marble for hours on end. And once Odalia was gone, she'd had a moment of blessed relief, and then another kind of fatigue had set in.

Mag was more than grateful to turn her feet toward Clarence's house. She could only hope that if there was business talk to be had, he was doing it elsewhere so she could sleep. Maybe after getting Anabi to rub her neck first. She felt so tense she might snap.

The house was blessedly quiet as she opened the door. "Clarence?" No answer, but she hadn't expected one. They'd been trying to work in shifts, so if she was overdue for sleeping, he'd be out and running from one end of the town to the other, checking on everyone, making sure their line against the greenbellies was still strong. "Anabi, if you're there, I'm home."

Her mouth was dry and tasted like electricity, so she headed for the kitchen first. Just a bare sip of water, and she could sleep.

Anabi sat ramrod-straight at the table, her hands clamped around a coffee mug. And a man sat across from her. Plain clothes, a face she didn't recognize: broad nose, skin that wanted to be dark brown if it ever got a chance at the sun, straight black hair in a neat cut. She looked down at his hands, resting lightly on the table in front of him: no callouses, no ingrained rock dust, no dirt under the perfect fingernails.

Mag went very still. She felt so tired, aching, the inside of her head raw. Too tired for fear, but also too tired for mad. She tried to summon up her strength anyway, like dragging herself up from a well, an inch at a time.

The man reached into his breast pocket and drew out a card, which he offered to her. "My identification," he said. The way he pronounced that word, all clipped syllables, was pure offworlder.

Mag moved forward just enough to take the card and look at it. She had some vague notion that she'd seen the seals and symbols on it before, maybe on her school reader, maybe on the paperwork when she'd tried to get a ticket off world. The most important information was a name, *Shigehiko Rollins*, and the title, *Agent of the Federal Union of Systems, Bureau of Citizens' Rights Enforcement*. She rolled those words over in her head a good long moment, thinking of all the things Hob had told her, before offering the card back. "So you're Hob's 'reliable source'." Her tone was flat. It wasn't a question. What in the hell had Hob gotten herself mixed up in? What was a government man doing here? Even the simple revelation that the government existed as something other than paragraphs in a history lesson felt strange indeed.

The man, Shigehiko, took his card back and stowed it. "And you're Magdala Kushtrim. It's lovely to meet you at last."

"Didn't know I was so famous as to be worth meetin'."

There was sure a part of her that wanted to channel Hob and snarl, *what the fuck do you want?* But that had never been her way. Mag got herself a glass of water and sat down between Anabi and the government man. "What brings you here?"

"I don't know how aware of my department you are..." he eyed her expression. "I see. The Bureau of Citizens' Rights Enforcement is charged with seeing that situations like the current one never happen. We're the ultimate advocate for ordinary citizens such as yourself and your fellow miners in the face of much more powerful organizations... like TransRift. The company has been trying very hard to keep us away from this world, and it's obvious why, now that I've been here. But that situation will soon change, and I want to assure you that the BCRE will be very eager to hear the grievances of all the miners and other workers."

"We been here a long time. Why y'all suddenly interested in our problems?"

Rollins grimaced. "As I said, TransRift has been trying very hard to keep us off this world..."

"You're the government," Mag pointed out. "You're supposed to be in charge." Something really wasn't adding up here.

"TransRift is the only source of interstellar travel, Ms Kushtrim. They, as I think our mutual acquaintance might put it, have us by the balls."

She had no doubt what mutual acquaintance he was talking about, and that did win a little smile from her. "And you're lookin' to change that."

"I'm looking to discharge my duty, which is to make certain that all citizens enjoy the full rights to which they are entitled by Federal Union law. And I believe we do owe the workers of this world an apology for having kept you waiting so long."

The words sounded good. Mag might have wanted to believe him, but she knew better. People in nice suits didn't just help mine rats out of the goodness of their own hearts. There was more they wanted, and maybe the miners would see a side benefit, but she found that very hard to believe. And besides, this Shigehiko Rollins was only one man. "But that ain't yet."

"Soon, but not yet. I did want to let you know that there is an end in sight, and you ought to be ready for it."

"How soon?"

"Approximately two weeks. A bit longer if TransRift really tries to fight off the inevitable, but I don't think they're that foolish."

Two weeks was no time at all and a lifetime. Several lifetimes, maybe, cut short with bullets or thirst. "Sure we'll be tryin' to hold out that long or longer. But you got any help more solid than that?" Help was help, and she wasn't going to turn that away on the principle of it. The temptation to lean on him with her witchiness was strong, but she was already so tired, she'd probably fumble it. She couldn't afford to have this man running off, knowing what she was or thinking she'd tried to do something to him.

"A little information that you might find useful. TransRift has a new, extremely large mine that they only just spiked. They plan to be moving all of you to that new site, forcibly if necessary."

Her mouth went dry. "How soon?"

"Within the next forty-eight hours."

A new site. It had to be… "It's the amritite, ain't it. The source." From all Hob and the Bone Collector had said, this was bad, far beyond all the miners' blood about to be spilled.

He smiled. "I really couldn't say." But then he stuck his fingers in his breast pocket again, and this time extracted a folded flimsy. He offered that to her – just a set of numbers that her brain parsed into map coordinates. "If you've a way of getting this message to Hob Ravani, however, I'd be most grateful."

Mag smiled tightly, and something in the expression made Anabi shift in her seat. "Reckon I could do that. With your compliments."

"And my gratitude." He stood and offered them both a strange little bow. "Have a lovely evening, ladies. Be careful."

Mag and Anabi both stayed seated until the kitchen door had closed behind him. Then Mag dropped her face to her hands, rubbing at her eyes with rough fingers. "Shit," she muttered. "Oh shit."

A soft scrape, and Anabi's slate came into her view, slid across the table by Anabi's graceful brown fingers. *He said he would help?*

"Ever known anyone you could trust, said something like that?" Mag looked up.

Anabi shook her head. Then her lips quirked and she took the slate back to write: *Other than Hob.*

Mag barked a laugh. "Ain't that the truth. And if there's an opposite of Hob, I'm thinkin' that man is it." She rubbed her eyes again. "I've gotta... find a runner for that message. Even if I don't trust any of this, Hob should see it and decide for herself. She knows him better'n me."

I'll do it.

Mag felt like her bones had melted with gratitude. She got a grease pencil and wrote out a quick note on the other side, to explain the situation to Hob. Then, after a moment's thought, she got her own flimsy and copied the coordinates on there. She'd never had a head for memorizing numbers, but it seemed like it might be a good piece of information to know. That one, she tucked in her skirt pocket, and handed Shige's to Anabi. "Thank you."

 Anabi leaned forward to kiss her lightly, just as good as *you're welcome*. Better, even. Mag still tasted that little kiss when she collapsed into their bed to try to snatch a few hours of sleep, too tired to even draw the blackout curtains against the fierce afternoon sun.

CHAPTER THIRTY-EIGHT • *13 DAYS*

"Another osprey sighted," Maheegan's laconic voice came, faint and crackling, through Hob's helmet speaker. The helmet sat overturned on the sand between her and Freki as they sat in the shade on the lee side of a dune. "Lookit that. Finally got one comin' back."

"Bearing?" Hob asked.

There was a long pause, punctuated only by the whistle of the hot breeze blowing across the dunes. "Seven degrees off the ship rock."

There weren't official names on the map they had for most of the rocks and spires dotting the visible landscape, but before Maheegan had gone up his own spire to start watching from under the shade of a camo net, they'd agreed on some names. Geri nodded to himself and made a note of the location.

Hob checked her watch. "Fourteen hundred hours, thirty-two," she told him. Another nod as he wrote that down.

Geri tapped his finger on the first line in his notes. "Been sixteen hours, thirteen minutes," he said. "If it's the first one we saw goin' out."

"Can you tell, Maheegan?" Hob asked.

"I'd need a better scope."

Hob frowned at the flimsy while Geri wrote down a few quick columns of numbers on the margin of it. "If that's the same one an' it's been flyin' that whole time and Bala gave me the right numbers, that's atween 7,200 and and 5,600 kilometers. One way." He twirled the grease pencil in his fingers. "But if it's cargo and not recon, they'd have to unload. Dunno how long that would take."

Hob grumbled under her breath. "That's a long-ass ride." While the motorcycles could be recharged just fine on the road, they could only really go sixty kilometers per hour on sand, up to one hundred and twenty if they had some good stretches of hardpan. And they couldn't go all night safely; even if the batteries held up, the riders wouldn't when they were talking about that kind of distance. "And a lot of supplies to carry for a round trip."

"Damn long. We're talkin' at least five days straight," Geri agreed.

Wherever the ospreys were going, it was one hell of a trip out into the wastes of the planet. The Wolves had always kept to the network of towns connected by rail lines, with even going to the far-off farming communities more travel than they were willing to do without a damn good profit already promised.

And just to make things a notch harder, if they were going to try to follow the ospreys, they couldn't do a straight-line path under them. The motorcycles and riders would stand out in the desert like a line of bullets in a bag of sugar.

"You got enough numbers for now?" Hob asked Geri. They were supposed to be heading back today anyway for resupply.

He looked over his list and shrugged. "Gonna have to do more scoutin' further out, but enough for here."

She'd figured he was going to say that, but still didn't

like hearing it. They had the Bone Collector's payout, so they could probably get the supplies together for heading further into the desert, but it would be one hell of an undertaking. Hob already didn't like how far they'd come from their base, like there was some kind of invisible leash leading back home.

"Send up the flare once the sky's clear, Maheegan," she said, louder, so the helmet mic would pick it up.

"Thought you were going to leave me up here until I was well done," Maheegan said, his tone amused. "I'm barely at medium rare."

"It's your lucky day."

Twenty minutes later, Maheegan fired off the signal flare, one that put out a bright puff of green smoke. Hob glanced up at it as she finished packing the last of her gear. "This actually gonna work, Geri?" she asked.

He shrugged as he checked the strap on one of his saddle bags. "The math ain't the problem. We'll find where we're goin. Your problem's figurin' how to get us there."

11 DAYS

Hob's group got in last, since they'd been the furthest out. Freki and Coyote waited for them in the garage, which didn't seem such an odd thing right off. But the expression on their faces wasn't what Hob had been expecting from either of them. And while Freki reached out to squeeze his brother's shoulder, they didn't immediately run off to go start having an incomprehensible talk about curvature and velocity.

Hob leaned slowly back against her bike, not sure if she wanted to stand after being on her ass so long, or sit because her legs weren't up to stretching out... after being on her ass so long. "What you got for me?"

"Message from our darling Mag," Coyote said. He held out a crumpled flimsy to Hob, and she took it without even glancing down. "All but two of the towns, and you can guess which two, are on strike. As of thirteen days ago."

"Fuck," Hob said. She stuffed the flimsy in her pocket. "Thirteen fucking days. How'd it take thirteen fucking days for us to hear about this?"

"You know the answer to that already," Coyote said.

And of course she did. Messages had to be carried, and left at drop points, then picked up. That slowed things down a hell of a lot. And they'd been away from base for most of those days, scouting out the camps and then the osprey flights.

"Fuck," she said again. If it was a strike, things were going to get ugly, and fast. Might have already gotten ugly, and the thought made her stomach turn. And here she was, not there again when Mag needed her. "Scramble the whole base. Everyone, thirty minutes. We're goin' to Ludlow."

Geri eyed her for a moment, and he didn't seem to like what he saw. Or maybe he liked it too much. He didn't smirk, didn't bitch, didn't do anything that he normally did. He might as well have been his brother in that moment, how he acted. "Yessir." He turned and headed out, Freki at his heels.

Coyote didn't move a muscle, and he wasn't smiling. "I suppose it's my turn to be the responsible adult rather than the crazy uncle," he said dryly. "We already have a job. Recall the pale fellow with the payroll boxes? He hired all of us for a specific purpose, and this isn't going to forward that particular contract."

"He can wait."

Coyote continued as if she hadn't spoken, "Mag didn't ask to hire us. Her message was purely informational."

Hob curled her lips back in a snarl. "You know they need us. They can't fight worth shit, and the hammer's coming."

"The hammer might already have fallen. You need to step back, Hob Ravani, and look at the larger picture. I understand that you have a thing about Mag. And–"

Her fist cracking into his jaw shut that line of reasoning up and sent him reeling back two steps. Hob shook her hand out. His head was harder than it looked. "Thing ain't the word for it. She's my blood. Closest I got to blood. And I ain't leavin' her to twist. So you shut your goddamn mouth."

Coyote straightened and wiped the back of his hand across his mouth, leaving a thin smear of red. There was an odd gleam to his eyes, a level of calculation she'd never really seen there before, and it made cold wash some of the anger away. He was looking at her like he wondered how her blood would taste. "And," he continued, in the same horrible, reasonable tone, "I thought we'd concluded that if TransRift found the 'Well' you've been driving me and everyone else into the ground to find, we'd all be in far greater trouble than we can imagine."

She hated him, she decided. She hated his fancy words and his snooty accent and his refusal to shut up. Most of all, she hated the fact that he wasn't wrong. But he wasn't right, either. He couldn't be. "We ain't gonna stay. Just gonna get Mag."

"You know she isn't going to come with you."

And he was right about that, too. She'd never gotten Mag to back off and take refuge before. The girl was more stubborn than her uncle. She couldn't swallow back the pleading note in her voice when she said, "I got to try, Coyote. I know your own brother's a goddamn shitbag, but you still gotta understand."

Coyote sighed, then huffed a laugh. "Oh, I understand. I'm here, aren't I? Blood is thicker than water." He rubbed one hand over his face. "Give me Maheegan. He's got the best eyes. I'll get the plan for the next step from Freki and Geri, and we'll take care of that while you're off breaking heads."

Hob sucked at her teeth. She didn't want to spare anyone, not knowing what they were headed into. But she could also feel Old Nick's bony hand on her shoulder, hear him hissing in her ear: *Contract's all that matters, girl. That's the only coin we got. You lie to the world, but you never lie with a handshake.* If they did that, it would be bending the promise she'd made over the money she'd taken, but it wouldn't break it. "In and out. You got my promise on that. My real promise."

He flipped a hand at her. "You don't need to tell me that. I'm just following orders." There was no humor in that statement, though. He rubbed his jaw again and turned away.

She wondered if she should apologize for hitting him, but the words stuck in her throat. And then he walked away, to get Maheegan and his resupply, and she wondered if she'd end up regretting this as much as the last time she let him go off on his own mission. She swallowed the apology down like knives. If he wanted it, he'd just have to come back alive.

CHAPTER THIRTY-NINE • *11 DAYS*

Ms Meetchim sat straight-backed behind the clean expanse of her desk, framed by the windows of her office. This time, the privacy blackout curtains had been drawn back. Today, the building lights flickered in a particularly bad atmospheric perturbation thanks to the absence of Mr Yellow. But Ms Meetchim's demeanor was considerably less cold, if not something Shige would ever be so foolish as to consider *warm*. She listened to Shige's verbal report in utter stillness except for one finger slowly tapping the glass surface of her desk.

"A shame," she said after he'd finished. "I know they're all pig-ignorant, but I would have thought they'd have a little more sense than this."

Shige shrugged helplessly. "Familiarity breeds contempt. An old saying, but still true."

Meetchim waved a hand. "I suppose we'll see how many Mariposa corrals for us. This will be their test. I need more workers on site, and now."

"Needing them alive unfortunately does limit the options."

"Annoyingly so. We'll see the numbers after tonight." She held up a finger. "Have the message sent out that any worker surrendering themselves to the company will be placed on probation, but after one year will be fully pardoned for their breach of contract."

Oh, he could imagine the choice words the miners in Ludlow and the other towns would have to say about that sort of offer. "Very generous, sir. And if they continue this self-destructive course?"

"Starve them out. All they care about is keeping themselves fed. And in the meantime, we can pull the farmers into the dig site."

"That may well spike the accident rate," Shige said. "They are wholly inexperienced."

"The fault of the miners for not wanting to do their jobs. But we'll backfill them into the above-ground jobs first. The tasks should be simple enough."

He bowed his head. "I'll draft a memo to that effect, to go out to the site with the next cargo run."

Meetchim held up a finger again. "You'll be going with it."

"Sir?"

"We're moving Mr Yellow from the halfway point to the site itself. The foreman says they're having too many problems with the portable equipment. Unusual levels of interference. Security Chief Lien has assured me that the pilots will be able to manage the intervening air space that opens up as long as we monitor carefully, and Dr Kiyoder has confirmed that Mr Yellow shows unusually apt control over the atmosphere. She has included a rift resonance generator in the next shipment, and is confident that with its use he'll be able to extend his control as far as necessary."

"I see…?" He made it a question, since there'd been nothing in her words yet to indicate why he needed to be there himself. This situation with the mining towns was fraught enough that he should be monitoring it closely. He had to be ready to act when the inspector arrived.

"Mr Yellow has been asking for you," Ms Meetchim said.

"Ah." He marshaled a new argument to his lips, about the amount of work Ms Meetchim now faced on her own, but no, he was *needed* by Mr Yellow. Who was he to argue with that? "When will I be leaving?" He pivoted his thoughts neatly to view the change in plans in a positive light; he'd be able to monitor the situation at this potentially invaluable new mine personally – and position it for the Federal Union to sweep up with little resistance.

"The next cargo flight departs at 0900. Be there an hour early to report to the flight commander."

He nodded again. "Yes, sir. May I go pack?"

"Please do," Ms Meetchim said. "I am keeping close watch on this for your next personnel assessment. Good work, Mr Rolland."

Shige leaned one hip against the spotless meal counter in his kitchen, inhaling the darkly aromatic steam rising off his tea as it steeped. Nearby, a small hourglass stood, pure white sand trickling down its neck one grain at a time.

It wasn't necessary to be quite this traditional about brewing, but it was a ritual he'd come to appreciate during his various assignments, a chance to simply breathe and be, and let the tensions of always wearing someone else's skin drain away. His modest assistant-salary level apartment, with the west side of the TransRift tower filling up his floor-to-ceiling windows and rendering them functionally useless, had proven to be an excellent refuge, and he did not expect to be back to it for some time. His travel bag sat fully packed by the door, the spare contents of his refrigeration unit ready to be dumped into the compost bin on the way out to the landing field.

Would he be greeted on the landing field with news of a massacre at Ludlow and the other towns? He sighed and drew in another breath of that soothing tea-scent. This was all necessary, but that didn't mean he had to feel *good* about it. Feeling good wasn't his job; getting results to turn over to the BCRE was. His reward would be a job well done, a duty discharged to the Federal Union. And who was he to want more than that?

Kazu had wanted more than that, and walked away without a backward glance toward the unwanted little brother he was abandoning.

This had been the entire trajectory of Shige's life from the moment Ayana had him created. He was her instrument. But that brief moment, when he had seen those other lives during rift transit, still haunted him. What would it be like, to ride under the moon at Kazu's – no, Coyote's – side? He found himself unable to imagine, and instead turned back to his duty.

The new site Mr Yellow had found would be a boon for the Federal Union... if they could take it over. Some odd, heavy feeling in his mind, the same that had wondered so keenly what the dead spy's blood would taste like, pointed out that Mr Yellow would no doubt do glorious things... He did his best to quash the burst of exhilaration that did not feel wholly his with mindfulness of duty. Duty did not care about glory.

His internal speculation over what Mr Yellow could or could not do given a potential new source of power drew his thoughts to the code-locked files. He'd nearly forgotten about them, so caught up in his other efforts. But they ought to have been decrypted a long time past, now. A little light reading before bed, then.

Shige took his tea and retrieved his reader. This time, those ancient, code-locked files yielded without a problem. He took a careful, aromatic sip as he spooled them back to the early history of the Weatherman program.

No computers could safely navigate the theoretical rift drive, the file informed him, and they did not know how the original inventors of the drive had operated it; all of those settlers had died within months of returning to Earth, their corpses curiously desiccated. Careful dissection of the remains had yielded no useful data. An organic, then human component was hypothesized to be necessary. Volunteers were sought, under the guise of an advanced training program. Neural aptitudes with an emphasis on mathematical and spatial reasoning were given priority. Ultimately, three subjects were chosen for the initial program.

Between the spare lines, he wondered how much those people, recruited at the cusp of the interstellar era almost two hundred and fifty years ago, had known about what was going to happen to them. Unfortunately, this sort of human experimentation, while highly illegal, was far outside its statute of limitations.

He continued reading, to find that two of the subjects had died, the implication being very unpleasantly. The third, retroactively dubbed *Weatherman 001*, successfully piloted the modified first rift ship. A small in-system jump, then between systems, then from the homeworld to Tanegawa's World, providing that vital link that had truly started this new age of humanity. A few more trips recorded to different destinations, and there were some notes he lacked the technical expertise to decipher about neural activity. More subjects were sought, partially successful augmentations made that allowed a limping sort of progress toward interstellar travel. Difficulties with neural and immune responses abounded. He read a few first musings made on the possibility of cloning their success story, since none of those who came after him proved to be as good even if they did at least manage to survive. This made him wonder if Mr Green and Mr Yellow were descendants of this first Weatherman, somehow. They didn't all look the same; they weren't just clones. But he'd gleaned enough from the other records to know they were always trying new genetic mixes in search of better stability and ability to bond with the neural networks.

Fascinated, he continued to read. Whatever those long-dead scientists had seen prompted them to try their prototype on the surface of Tanegawa's World – Weatherman 001 had been asking for it as well, it seemed. And who didn't want to go to the surface of a world, rather than just orbit? Even if the thought of a Weatherman *wanting* anything like a normal human seemed odd, now. Maybe the first Weatherman had been more *man* and less *weather*. He certainly hadn't been raised in the sterile confines of a lab.

Thus, Weatherman 001 was set down on the world. He was allowed the freedom of the small spaceport settlement with his handlers and a contingent of guards, excited notes made about his ability to calm the atmospheric perturbations and allow technology to be used. Perhaps chafing at the strictures of the tiny city, or fueled by some burn of exploration, Weatherman 001 began to ask persistently to go out into the desert. Speculation from the scientists, that perhaps more control over the world could be achieved, and they were willing to try it – after all, his initial request to be placed on land had worked out splendidly for them. And the desert, or rather its mines, was the place from which Weatherman 001's powers had come. It seemed

terribly incautious to Shige, but those had also been
different times, a sort of expansive, frenetic energy to
push the frontier.

And then – some nameless disaster, in emotionless
black and white. Bodies in the desert, the picture
accompanying the dry facts far more reminiscent of
what he'd seen on that train car than he liked. But no
body for Weatherman 001. He had simply vanished
into the sand without a trace. The handlers were
puzzled, as he'd showed no signs of mental instability.
Weeks of search logs showed no results. And then
the researchers realized that they were trapped on
Tanegawa's World until the home office managed to
manufacture a Weatherman 002, their reports long
years away from even being received. He could almost
feel sorry for them, considering what sort of despair
the heartlessly dry reports must have held.

Curious, Shige flicked along until he found the
attached medical file on Weatherman 001. He lacked
the expertise to make sense of most of it, until
he found the section that was the man's original
personnel file: Gabriel Chua, British and Malaysian
descent – how odd the old country names sounded
to him. Aged thirty at the time of his transfer to the
program, previously an eight-year career in the now-
defunct Earth Allied Militia, followed by four years in
the up-and-coming private security firm Martindale,
which later was renamed in a merger to Mariposa.
His field records were best summed up as decorated
and brutal. Shige wondered idly why someone with
these sorts of standardized test scores had ended
up as a skullbreaker, but perhaps it was an issue of
temperament.

Then he flicked over to the next part of the file. His
tea mug, still half-full, fell from his suddenly nerveless

fingers. He didn't feel the absence, overwhelmed by the pit of horror that opened in his stomach.

Staring out from the reader with cool hostility was a face he recognized. The hair was different, of course: military trim rather than long, black rather than white-blond, and eyes dark hazel instead of blue. But the bones of the face were an exact match. He'd seen this man twice: once, outside Primero during a brief confrontation with Mr Green; the second time at the Weatherman's death. That was the face of Hob's associate, the pale man who carried a staff topped with a wildcat's skull.

Impossible. No, he knew better than to dismiss anything as impossible, not on this planet. But that would make Chua – Weatherman 001, whatever he was called now – 276 years old, and he didn't seem to have aged a day. And it would mean he'd just handed over the coordinates of the wildcat site to those he now knew to be associates of Weatherman 001. The Weatherman who had gone mad and slaughtered his handlers before vanishing into the desert.

This was not a factor he could have even begun to guess at in his calculations, and it took the situation entirely out of his control. It would stand in Mr Yellow's way. He had to fix this before he lost his advantage entirely. But how?

Perhaps the answer was in Weatherman 001's associates. After all, Hob Ravani was the first and only person known to have killed a Weatherman. She'd technically almost killed Mr Green twice, even if the second time she'd needed a bit of help. He doubted she liked Weathermen very much in a general sense, beyond their association with TransRift.

And, he thought slowly, she didn't seem the sort of person who liked being lied to. If she didn't know any of this information, perhaps the best interference would be to simply give it to her. And then hope that her anger would fuel action. That seemed to be how she worked as well.

The situation was salvageable. It had to be.

CHAPTER FORTY • *11 DAYS*

Mag woke to the sound of shouting in the street outside her window. She scrambled out of bed, thoughts a tangle of terror and confusion until she realized that the voices sounded happy. Not enraged. Not terrified.

She made herself take a few deep breaths and scrape her tangled hair back from her face with her fingers before looking out the window. People were hugging each other. There was no longer the tension she'd felt in the air the last few days, like the warning crack of glass before it shattered. What the hell had happened? Why did she feel so unsettled, when it plainly had to be something good?

Mag went downstairs to look for Clarence and Anabi. She found Clarence first, standing in the narrow strip of shade that fell over the front step, his arms crossed over his chest. And he was smiling. She hadn't realized just how long it had been since he'd really smiled until the expression looked so unfamiliar now.

"What happened?" she asked.

"Bill had me in about an hour ago. Said the bosses in Newcastle have agreed to renegotiate our pay, with real credits." His smile got a little bigger, as he talked. "We won."

That seemed far too easy, as much as she wanted to believe it. "When?"

"Someone from HR will be out on a special train tomorrow."

She trusted that even less. "They didn't ask anything from us?"

"Well, we ain't started negotiatin' yet," Clarence said. "They pulled the greenbellies back from the street, to the office and the depot. Don't want to risk the hotheads pickin' a fight before we get a chance to discuss things."

That, too, seemed logical. But none of this added up. Was what the government man Rollins had told her true, or was it some lie for his own purposes? Maybe she'd been so set on spending blood for this, so ready, nothing peaceful felt right. "They say anythin' about wantin' to move us to a new work site?"

Clarence's smile finally faded. "No. Why?"

Mag gestured him back inside, then told him about the government man visiting, every detail she could remember. By the time she was done, his expression had gone downright thunderous. Mag felt bad, but also sickly relieved that she wasn't the only one worried now.

"You think this is a fake," he said.

"Maybe he was tryin' to twist us one way or another," she shrugged. "But I know I don't trust any of this."

"After what you said, I sure as hell don't either." She could feel his unspoken thoughts, because they echoed her own: they'd already had one traitor manipulating them. The company fought dirty, and it never showed its hand until it was too late. "I'll spread the information to the work gang leaders. We gotta be watchin' like eagles, ready for anythin'."

"What about them?" Mag jerked her chin toward the street, still filled with the boisterous sounds of celebration that she was about to kill.

"If people got it in 'em once the news is spread, we should keep dancin'," Clarence said. "Company ain't the only ones who can play this game."

They quietly doubled the guard on their section of the wall, on the streets that stood between them and the company buildings. Those not standing had themselves a picnic out in the street, pretending that everything was fine, that they really did believe there'd be a negotiator coming in the next morning.

Maybe it would be, Mag told herself. Stranger things had happened. She'd be happy if she was wrong. She should have been trying to get a few more hours of sleep – Clarence had basically ordered her to do it – but she felt every nerve in her body strung wire-tight. So she'd parked herself at one of the tables set up in the street, with a piece of pie she really didn't feel like eating in front of her, and a glass of lemonade she barely managed to drink.

Anabi touched her shoulder, and she jerked. Mag offered her an apologetic smile. "Mind was wanderin'."

Anabi turned her slate toward Mag: *Going to take some pie to the sentries.*

"I'll go…"

Anabi shook her head and wrote: *Sit. Or you'll fall over.*

Mag huffed out a humorless laugh. "Fine. I'll be waitin' here for you, then."

The answer she got in return was a quick kiss on the corner of her mouth. Then Anabi gathered up two untouched pies and a big carving knife and carried them away.

A burly, red-faced miner next to Mag gave her a gentle nudge, grinning. "Well, well. Ain't you lucky."

On that account, she managed a smile back. It felt good, normal. This man also hadn't been in the meeting when she'd told the work gang leaders what she could do. Maybe they'd been keeping their mouths shut. Or maybe some people were just good, and liked to see others be happy, and wanted to trust each other. She missed being able to feel that. "Very lucky," she agreed.

"My wife made one of those pies. Those sentries gonna feel damn lucky too," he said. And with a little prompting, Mag got him to start talking about his wife, who was back in their small house with their six month-old daughter, making more food to share out. She got the story of how they met, both on the same work gang, and him doing double time so she could stay out of the mine for a while, then their plan that they'd trade off so he could stay home with the baby. Mag didn't have to say much herself, just a little affirmative noise now and then to keep him talking, and she liked the listening. The words washed over her like a cool breeze on a hot day, or the water in one of those rare times she'd gotten to have a real bath, comforting and bolstering. Life went on, ordinary life, with good, ordinary people.

As they talked and she slowly nibbled her way through the pie she hadn't thought she'd eat, the sky went blue to violet to black, with the one moon near full and the other a crescent, stars winking out between them. The sodium-yellow lights of the street snapped on, the batteries feeding out the power they'd been drinking in from the sun all day. The town really was self-sufficient in most ways, Mag thought vaguely. Anything that could be done with electricity and a machine simple enough to survive here would tick right over until it got worn to death by sand. If left on its own, the town would keep going, empty but for ghosts, until the desert took it back. The real trouble was the people, because they needed food and water, and that was something they had to depend on others for.

Didn't matter, hopefully. Maybe Clarence was right, and the offer of negotiation had been genuine. Maybe for once, they could win without paying for it in blood.

A sharp *crack* jerked Mag out of her slow descent into relaxation, and stilled her new friend's words mid-sentence. "Was that..." he began, head swiveling back toward the walls.

Another *crack* and another, then a series of rapid *pops* – and a massive *tear*, a *crash*, like a building collapsing. People around the street bolted to their feet, Mag only slightly slower as she struggled to comprehend what was happening. But they all had their trained instincts, at least, something every miner knew: you heard a sound like that, you waited for the moment of quiet, and then you ran toward it. The lives of every person you worked with depended on it.

Then she heard the screaming, not so distant, and she didn't know how she'd ever mistaken the joyful sound this afternoon for this kind of anger and fear that moved over her skin like claws. First formless, then coming closer as the message carried: "Greenbellies!" "Attack!" "They're at the walls!"

Her first thought was Anabi. Maybe she should have thought about the others first; there were a lot of people on the wall. But the image of Anabi, terrified and still incongruously holding those two pies, jolted her into motion with the hectic energy of pure fear. Surrounded by miners, she sprinted for the wall. Uncle Nick's little revolver, which she'd kept in her skirt pocket since the day she finally took it out, banged a bruising tattoo against her thigh.

More people poured into the street ahead of her. Someone tripped, fell. Two other miners dragged them up by the arms and kept going.

Smoke poured into the street. First it tasted like

scorched metal and synthwood and rock dust. Then a
chemical stench came through it, something stinging
that sent tendrils of dizziness reeling through her. She
had to catch herself on the shoulder of the miner next
to her.

"Gas!" a man yelled from the side. "They're gassing
us."

The crowd drew up short. Then a few miners went
into the nearby houses and came out with their breather
masks, the ones they used during mine collapses. They
threw extras, belonging to siblings or housemates or
spouses, probably, into the crowd. Mag caught one and
pulled it on. It wasn't the right size; she still tasted the
smoke around the edges, but it would have to do. The
band around the back of her head yanked at her hair.
She shoved to the front of the crowd, with the other
people who had masks, and they kept going into the
smoke as it got denser. Yellow lights glowed dully in
the dark billows, people becoming nothing more than
shadows.

Then out of the smoke, more lights blazed, along the
ground. Truck headlights, Mag realized, and she made
out the high shape of the town's wall, but with a gap
through it. They'd blown or ripped or torn a hole in the
wall of their own town. Dark shapes moved in and out
of the light and smoke, and Mag couldn't make head nor
tail of it.

A hand grabbed her shoulder, someone pushing past
her. They – she – raised her hands, like she was going to
just push the smoke away. The breeze blowing into town
through that hole in the wall slowed, stopped, then
shifted to come from a new direction, directly at their
backs. It was weak, attenuated by too many houses and
the other side of the town wall in the way, but enough to
start rolling the billowing smoke and gas back.

The woman sagged back, and a miner who had to be twice her size caught her. Mag recognized the woman now, as one of the witches that Hob had brought into town back during the witch hunt, who'd taken a job in the mine and tried to just blend in.

She saw people in green uniforms, men made monsters in some kind of military tech armor moving in and out of the walls. Some of them carried bodies, not bulked-up ones – unconscious miners from the walls. At least, she hoped unconscious. It wouldn't make sense for them to be taking the dead, would it?

Anabi. She had to find Anabi. Miners charged in around her, brandishing what weapons they had, mostly picks and hammers. The greenbellies raised shotguns to fire at them, and another round of loud *cracks* and *pops* made Mag drop to the ground. A voice roared over some kind of speaker system, the words so overdriven it sounded like a howl, but she picked it out: "STAY DOWN. STAY DOWN."

Mag scrambled back up to her feet, desperate. Somehow, in all the light and noise and confusion, people shoving her this way and that, she closed her eyes and tried to *focus*. She knew Anabi. She knew what the woman felt and smelled and tasted like, the sound of her mind. She could find her. She had to find her.

There.

Mag turned, focused on one thing as the shotguns roared again, as people screamed, as the greenbellies howled like demons. Shapes twisted and blurred, and she saw Anabi, struggling to free herself as a man in dull black armor dragged her toward the hole in the wall. Metal flashed and she dropped to the ground, let go abruptly. The greenbelly reeled back, the carving knife sticking from the meat of his forearm. Mag ran toward them as another guard lunged in, his fist connecting with Anabi's face, the sound of it lost in the chaos. A fresh wave of chemical smoke washed over them, the breeze shifting again, and Anabi became a limp shadow on the ground, one the guards picked up and dragged.

"No!" Mag screamed behind her mask. She forgot about the gun in her pocket, about everything else. She reached out with her hands like she would crush the heads of those two guards between her fingers, even from fifty meters away. And she felt them, minds like tiny sparks in the melee, she smelled them out by their proximity to Anabi, by them touching her. Her throat raw with a scream she wasn't aware of, she threw the weight of the witchiness in her blood on them and watched them drop to their knees.

She could do this. She would do this. She was doing this.

So focused, she didn't see another guard raise something too big to be a shotgun and fire at her. She didn't see the gas canister fly through the air toward her. She felt an instant of impact against the side of her head–

–then nothing more.

CHAPTER FORTY-ONE • *11 DAYS*

Long before the shadow of its walls were visible against the horizon, Ludlow was a column of smoke boiling up over the dunes, lit from within by evil yellow light and the strobe of brighter, blue-white pops.

The shortwave radio chatter, which had been its normal mix of shit talking, shit talking, and more shit talking, stuttered to silence. Static popped, not quite in time with the flashes of light erupting through the smoke. Finally, Geri said, voice low and tense: "What the *fuck*."

It couldn't be the town burning, Hob realized after an instant of panic. She knew smoke from fire, and she didn't see anything in it that flickered like a living thing. She didn't feel it in her blood. "Don't know, but we ain't slowin' down. Guns at the ready." Mag was in there, somewhere. Mag was under that cloud.

They came up over a dune and the town wall was visible – what was left of it. Its shape went ragged in the uncertain light and blowing smoke. But Hob saw, too, the trucks parked outside the wall, headlights cutting broad white cones. The guard towers had their floodlights pointed at the ground, and the dark shapes of people moved in and out in a mass of confusion.

She still didn't know what the hell was going on, but a few things were plain: it wasn't bandits, and she'd bet down to her last breath it was Mariposa, attacking their own town. "Kill your lights," she said. With all the action around the wall, there was a good chance they hadn't been spotted yet. "Freki, what's your estimate on how many of 'em there are?" There were enough trucks arrayed outside the walls that she wasn't going to try to do that math in her head, not with her brain already buzzing up with adrenalin.

"Hundred and eighty," Freki answered quickly. "Maybe two-forty. Depends."

"Fuck me," someone said over the radio. Either number was bad, it was just a choice between really bad and really fucking bad. Without Coyote and Maheegan, there were only twenty-six of them. Not good odds – if they were going in head-on. If Ludlow was going quietly, which it sure as hell didn't look to be.

More confusion was going to be to their advantage, Hob saw quickly. And they weren't going to be able to make this a toe-to-toe fight. But if they could get Mariposa twisted around enough, maybe they'd retreat. And if the fuckers retreated, she could at least get into the town and look for Mag.

"Geri, take four. Go around the walls, and get the guard tower lights down. Make 'em think there's a shitload more of you, goin' for the rail depot." That'd force at least the town garrison to split off some of their people to protect that. "I want Lykaios and Diablo. We're goin' in one of the tunnels. Freki and Dambala, split everyone else atween you. Come at the trucks from either side. Make a lot of noise. Use them flash-bangs if we still got any left. Just leave a fuckin' clear path for 'em to retreat so we can make 'em think it's a good idea. Give us about a thirty-minute lead, then start makin' some noise if you ain't heard otherwise."

She listened with half an ear as Freki and Dambala quickly parceled out the other sixteen Wolves between the two of them. "Get all your hand lights out," Dambala said over the radio. "We're gonna string 'em together right quick."

"Flares, too," rumbled Akela. "Oldest trick in the book."

Anything to make it look like there were more of them than there were would help, Hob knew. The only advantages they had were surprise, and that it was already so chaotic, no one would be able to tell what the hell was actually coming at them.

She'd picked her people right. They'd do the best they could with what they had, and better without her breathing down their necks. She had her own job to focus on.

With Diablo and Lykaios close behind, Hob headed for the tunnel entrance Mag had shown her. Turned away from the town, she hazarded having her headlight on again. Maybe fifty meters from where she remembered the tunnel entrance to be, she caught the ghostly shape of a person running across her view and slammed on her brakes. Thankfully, Diablo and Lykaios were quick to react. Skidding across sand, they all came to a halt.

"Who's there?" Hob demanded, one hand going to her holster, though she didn't draw yet. She hadn't gotten a good look, but she was sure it was no security man she'd seen. "We ain't greenbellies. We're Ghost Wolves. Who the fuck's there?"

Slowly, the rustle and scrape of their steps over sand muffled through her helmet, one kid, then another kid, then a gangly teenager holding a baby edged into the bubble of light cast by their motorcycles. Then another, and another. There had to be thirty of them, kids of various ages, from babies being carried to ones almost old enough to be toting a gun and riding a motorcycle.

"Shit," Lykaios said.

"Y'all from Ludlow?" Hob already knew the answer.

The oldest of the kids, a rail-thin girl with her dark brown hair puffed out in an afro, nodded. "Mag's been teachin' us what to do, if somethin' bad happened. Makin' us practice. So we grabbed the babies and run."

Hob felt like a hand squeezed her heart, with fingers made of fear and pride. "Then you done right and good. You hunker down in this here gully and stay quiet."

"Yessir," the girl said.

"You know how to shoot?"

"A little," the girl said.

Hob reached back into the holster on her motorcycle and pulled out the sawed-off shotgun and held it out. "Seen one of these?"

The girl hesitated, then took it. She looked at it like it might bite her. "Somethin' like."

"Never aim it near someone you ain't gonna shoot. Keep it pointed at the ground. But you see a greenbelly comin', you shoot 'em. You understand me?"

The girl's expression twisted, firmed. She nodded. "Yessir."

"Stay outta sight. We'll come back for ya when it's safe." Keenly aware of the childrens' eyes on all three of them, Hob found the steep path down into the gully. They stowed the motorcycles down there. "Keep your helmets on. For the radio." Hob saw wide eyes in small faces from dark to pale watch as they armed themselves, especially Lykaios and Diablo with their hammer and hand ax respectively. It was a relief to get into the tunnel, away from the kids.

"What're we gonna do?" Lykaios whispered as they followed the narrow tunnel.

"Dunno," Hob said. "See what'll be most useful when we get there." Without knowing how bad things were in the walls, planning any further ahead seemed pointless.

The tunnel popped them out in a warehouse, far enough from the walls that they only smelled the smoke and chemical stink, enough to make them a little dizzy, but not enough to knock them over. "Fuckin' nox gas. Ain't smelled that in years," Lykaios said.

"Means they ain't tryin' to kill anyone outright," Diablo pointed out.

Hob led them around the side of the warehouse, then stopped them with a movement of her hand. The general roar of chaos was loud, but she thought she heard something closer. She ducked her head around the corner to see a group of four greenbellies clashing with three miners. One of the greenbellies had captain's chevrons on his sleeves, and he had a spring-loaded baton in one hand, a clear shield around the other, bashing at a miner who had three light-reflecting stripes on their helmet instead of one – a crew leader.

Hob stepped back and held out her hand for Diablo's ax. She drew one of her revolvers with the other hand and crept around the corner–

–in time to see the greenbelly captain drop the baton and snatch a pistol out of his belt as the miners tried to run. Even with the chaos echoing through the town, the snap of those shots was loud. The miner in the crew leader helmet went down in a limp tumble.

Cursing into her helmet, Hob snapped off a shot, not taking the time to aim. The greenbelly captain jerked, stumbled, but she saw it hadn't gotten through his armor, just given him a kick in the shoulder. She kept rushing in to swing the ax at the hand holding the pistol. She felt it bite, and grate, heard a muffled scream. Lykaios came around her side, hammer coming around to slam into the head of the second greenbelly. His helmet shattered and he went reeling, still on his feet. Diablo had the third, coming in with his own shotgun.

The fourth, Hob turned to shoot, yanking on the ax as she did to try to free it. By some miracle, her hasty aim got her lined up with the guard's neck, the only weak point she ever counted on in armor. The bullet sliced between breastplate and helmet, and the guard dropped, gurgling.

And the other two miners, who had slowed when their leader got shot, charged back in. One whirled a pickax over their head, narrowly missing hitting Lykaios to bury it in the back of the reeling security man.

Outnumbered, the greenbelly captain, blood running dark from his wrist, ran.

Hob emptied the revolver after him, but didn't chase. After an abortive jerk of a step, Diablo and Lykaios didn't either. They fell back to the remaining two miners, who knelt over their fallen comrade.

"He gone?" Hob asked, even as she knelt to yank the helmet off the guard she'd shot in the neck.

The miner looked up and pulled the breather mask off the fallen man. Hob recognized him instantly: Clarence Vigil, the man who'd taken in Mag.

"Fuck." It felt a little like getting the wind kicked out of her, but there wasn't time for that, and she was here for a reason. "Mag?"

The miner finally spoke, in a high, muffled voice. "Ain't seen her. We got separated every which way when we fell back."

"We better fall back too," Lykaios said. "We got more coming." There was a rumble coming down the street, formless light in the smoke and gas fog getting a lot more focused. The ground trembled under their feet.

The two miners started to pick up Clarence's body.

Hob shouted, "Stop! Ain't got time for the dead. Go!" She gave them a firm yank up for good measure, and got them stumbling down the street. They needed to find the rest of the miners, and fast, if they wanted a chance in hell to defend.

The fallback point was the church; they'd blocked off the streets with furniture and boards, and there were several greenbellies dead on their faces nearby. The rest of the security men were back a respectful distance, though Hob doubted that would hold long.

A tall, gawky man Hob didn't recognize – not that she could tell a damn one of them apart in their helmets and breather masks – met them in the press behind the barricades. "Where're the rest of you?"

"Outside the walls." Hob checked her pocket watch. "And we got ten minutes till they come in and make as big a stink as they can." She looked at the people around her, the smoke-smudged faces showing over rock dust-black breathers. "Y'all ready to make a push?"

"They got Clarence, Omar," the miner who'd been leading said. "Longbridge shot him in the back."

"They ain't been shootin' much with real bullets," Omar said. "Been takin' people off, instead."

"They made an exception for him," Hob said. There wasn't any time for this. "Where's Mag?"

"Don't know."

Didn't mean anything, she reassured herself. Shit like this got dicey. "Then guess you're in charge. You ready?"

Omar seemed to give himself a shake, a full body shudder to try to work the world back into some kind of sense. "Ain't got a choice." But his eyes were almost pleading as he looked at her. Hell, for all his size, Hob would have bet he wasn't even as old as her and Mag.

"Y'all got any fireworks or anythin' you can fish up?"

Omar squeezed his eyes shut for a moment. "Wait. We got the company store now. We can make... bombs with alcohol."

Alcohol wouldn't burn hot on its own, but it'd be a good distraction – and Hob could see about giving the fire more ferocity. They didn't have time to mix up anything fancier. "Grab it all, now."

Heads ducked low to keep safe behind the barricades, with the guards firing shots still and winging in gas grenades that the miners quickly threw back, they passed out every bottle of spirits they'd been able to grab from the company store. The miners stuffed dirty handkerchiefs down the necks to start soaking up the alcohol, though Hob caught more than a few prying up their masks to take a swig for fortification first.

Hob traded out her helmet for the Mariposa one she'd stolen – if the Wolves could manage a radio channel, she was damn sure the greenbellies would too. The helmet smelled like mint and garlic, but she did her best to ignore the sick tickle in the back of her throat as she tried to make sense of the chatter. She knew the minute Dambala, Freki, and Geri had started their part of the attack. One of the floodlights on a guard tower they could see blew out in a shower of bright sparks. And over the channel, she heard men shouting, "Lights, we have lights." "Reinforcements?" "It's bandits. Fucking bandits!"

"Lightin' 'em up," Hob said. She held her hand out, and flame popped onto the ends of those handkerchiefs in a wave. A few of the miners yelped, but they'd been warned. They held onto their bottles.

"Throw 'em!" Omar shouted, surging up over the barricade to sling the bottle at the momentarily confused security men. The bottle of cheap whiskey, its top flaming, shattered on the street. Glass and alcohol sprayed on the surrounding greenbellies, and there was enough spark left from the rag that the fumes caught in a rush. More bottles shattered on the street as the volley continued.

Hob closed her eyes, feeling all those cool little alcohol fires. It was too hard for her to make big fires out of nothing, but once the fire was already burning? She felt it in her blood. She fed it strength and pushed it, hotter and whiter, so it could burn more than just alcohol.

Security guards started screaming, the smarter ones dropping to the street to try to roll the flames out, as the miners poured over the barricade. Rather than waste limited bullets against heavy body armor, they attacked with their pickaxes and hammers, focusing on battering the guards down and yanking their helmets and breather masks off.

And Hob, standing on the barricade so she could see, her one eye squinted down to a slit, kept the fires burning hot, yanking them away from Diablo, Lykaios, and the miners, and fanning them onto the guards.

Between that and the howling confusion happening over the Mariposa shortwave channel, within minutes the greenbellies were into full retreat. They dragged their downed men, a few with shields bringing them together in the front to protect themselves from more thrown bottles, small hand hammers, chisels, and rocks. Hob kept the fire leaping from one guard to the next, her head swimming with the effort.

Diablo popped out of the crowd and scrambled up the barricade next to her. "Trucks are pullin' back. Bala asks pursue, yes or no?"

Hob read the surging mass of miners like a book. They could push, but they weren't an army. If they cornered the greenbellies, things would get a lot uglier a lot faster. She didn't know why the security men had been softhandling things, but if their escape got cut off in the face of a riot, they'd go full lethal. Even as she watched, a few of the guards abandoned their shotguns and pulled their service revolvers. Miners dropped on the street in dark pools of blood.

"No pursuit," Hob said, though it burned her. She still didn't know where Mag was. And if something had happened to her, there wasn't a hell deep enough for these greenbellies to hide in. Wolves were made to hunt. She'd get them later. "We got cleanup to do here."

10 DAYS

Once the greenbellies were driven off proper – and Freki's crew followed them, lights doused, for a good twenty kilometers to make sure – Ludlow's quiet weather witch, one of her teeth missing and her lip split, shifted the winds again to clear out the smoke and gas. Diablo went to bring the children back in and almost got shot for his trouble. And free of their masks, the miners took stock of the damage and started counting the bodies.

The Wolves, mercifully all of them who'd ridden in, if plus a few wounds that needed stitching or setting, did their best to help. Diablo, with Lykaios's steady hands, got the Wolves doctored and waded right into the crowd of wounded miners. Dambala put himself in charge of getting sentry posts set up, and clearing out the guard houses – when the trucks had fled, the rest of the garrison had gone with them. Lobo mustered as many able bodies as he could and they soaked up every bit of spilled water they could find at the miners' supply caches – somehow the company had known about these new ones and torn them apart. Geri set himself to getting the wall as rebuilt as it could be with the materials at hand, and he had plenty of eager workers for all everyone dragged with exhaustion. And Freki parked himself with Hob, helping the crew sorting and hauling the bodies.

Seven security guards dead, most of them by the church barricade, their heads beaten in. Twenty-two miners, including Clarence Vigil, were laid out with care on the church pews where their loved ones could find them and wash their faces. But more worrisome were the missing – at least forty by the rough count of the crew leaders, scrambling to check all their people off on their lists.

And Mag, Freki found facedown near the broken wall. He yelled for Hob and she came running. She saw him turn Mag over in his arms, her head lolling limply, and thought she'd never breathe again around the rock her heart suddenly became. Then Freki looked up and said, "She's alive."

One side of Mag's face was a massive bruise, though when Diablo checked her over, he said her skull wasn't cracked, and that was a goddamn miracle and a half. She'd probably just gotten dosed good by the nox gas Mariposa had been slinging over the wall.

Hob carried Mag back to Clarence's… to *Mag's* house and settled her into bed, then parked herself in the chair next to it. And fuck, she didn't care any more that everyone hated her filthy habit. She opened the window and started smoking her way through cigarette after cigarette. Considering the air from outside, still stinking of chemicals and burning, her cigarettes didn't smell so bad after all.

After an eternity contained in three cigarettes, Mag stirred. Hob flicked the half-finished butt of her fourth out the window. "Mag?"

"Hob?" Mag's voice was a whisper of sand and gravel. "My… head."

"Looks like you got hit real good with somethin'," Hob said. "Still didn't crack that damned thick skull of yours though."

Somehow, Mag managed a smile, though it had to hurt like hell around all those bruises. "You ain't one to talk." Suddenly her right eye – her left was too swollen to do much of anything – opened wide. "Where's Anabi?"

It wasn't that Hob had forgotten the woman, so much as she hadn't had room in her head for anything but Mag. She had to think a moment. "She weren't among the dead that I saw," Hob said. "Might be out there, helpin' out. Everyone's workin' 'cept for slackers like you."

Mag struggled to sit up. "No, I need to know – she'd be here, Hob."

Hob leaned forward to put her hand on Mag's chest. "Diablo said no fannin' around. You bide." She waited for Mag to nod and still. And, hell, she might as well break the other news now. "Clarence Vigil is dead. Greenbelly captain shot him in the back in the street. Weren't nothin' I could do."

Mag went silent and still, and for a horrible moment Hob wondered if she hadn't heard, if she'd have to repeat that news. She almost missed Mag cussing her out like she had when she'd broken the news of Phil's death. At this rate, she might as well be the angel of death, and she suddenly hated it. But Mag took in a shaky breath. "I'll see to him, then. He didn't have no family."

"He's gettin' his feet washed like one of them martyrs by the preacher man," Hob said. "You worry about yourself, 'cause you're still livin'. I'll go ask after Anabi." She headed back out into the street. Took her more time than she liked to hunt down the miner with the lists. She liked the news he gave her even less – Anabi was definitely one of the missing.

By the time she got back to the house, Mag had somehow crawled her stupid ass down to the kitchen and got a glass of water, though she didn't seem to have the strength to do more than sit at the table and clutch it. She took one look at Hob's expression and the color drained out of her skin, making the red of her new bruises as vivid as a burn. "Is she…"

"Not dead. But taken. We think. There's some forty-three people confirmed missing now. Bala said he saw them puttin' people in the trucks. At the time, he thought it was injured guards. Didn't get a good look, ya ken. But might have been…"

Mag let out a low, despairing moan. "He warned me. He tried to warn me. But…"

"Who? Tried to warn you about what?"

"He said they have a new site. That they were going to move us there, by force if they had to. He–"

"Mag," Hob interrupted. "*Who?*"

"Oh… Coyote's brother," she said. "The government man."

Hob sat down very carefully. "He was here?"

"Sittin' where you are now."

"How 'bout you tell me the whole thing."

Mag's story was stumbling and halting, but Hob got the gist of it at least. And then she fetched the copy of the coordinates that Mag had made so she could look at them herself, comparing them to the map she had. "I don't…"

"Get one of the big maps from the mine office. It's gotta be the standard stuff they use."

Mag didn't move in the short time it took Hob to run that errand. She spread the map over the table and looked it over, muttering to herself. Mag, who had her eyes closed, didn't seem to hear. Finally, she found the point, hell and gone away from Newcastle, in the middle of a great stretch of saltpan marked as an extinct ocean. "Fuck," she whispered as she measured the distance with her fingers. The already impossible distance Geri had estimated had been bad enough, and it looked like their assumptions had been wrong. Their Well was almost ten thousand kilometers away, over a week of solid riding into unknown territory.

"That good, huh?" Mag said, without humor.

Hob sat, rubbing at her face with one hand. Hopeless frustration welled up, threatened to choke her if she didn't scream it out. "That man's fuckin' crazy. We ain't got the resources to get that far out. Can't carry enough fuckin' water, for one. We–"

Mag slammed her hand down on the map, her palm covering the point that Hob had marked with grease pencil. "Yes, you fuckin' *can*," she said, her open eye blazing. She sounded so like Old Nick that it made Hob's blood run cold. Then Mag lunged across the table and grabbed Hob's hands, her fingers hot and strong as iron. "They took my girl, and they're gonna work her to death out there so the bosses can talk about how much fuckin' money they made. So you fuckin' *will*. You tell me why."

The pressure of Mag's fingers increased until Hob felt her bones creak. "'Cause I'm Hob fuckin' Ravani," she said, her voice hoarse with that small pain that seemed so stupid beside everything else. "And I ain't ever given up."

Mag sat back down on her chair, her hands going limp. "'Cause you ain't ever given up," she repeated. And then to Hob's distress and knee-shaking relief, she started to cry.

CHAPTER FORTY-TWO • *9 DAYS*

Heat rolled up from the saltpan in thick ribbons, a trick of the light making it look like the extinct lake still survived as a moat around Newcastle. Coyote tried to ignore the sweat rolling off his nose and stinging his eyes. It was still better than being cold, he reminded himself. Anything was better than being cold.

"They're bringin' another hydro-jack out," Maheegan said slowly. His skin shone with sweat as well, his loose black curls plastered to his forehead. They were huddled under a camouflage net together, the air inside thick and still. "Crates. Big 'uns."

"Can you see any labels on them?" Coyote asked, making another note on the flimsy spread out on the saltpan in front of him. It was a wonder it didn't melt, really. They'd been at this since dawn, watching the loading as a flight of ospreys went out and another, empty from what Maheegan had seen, came in. TransRift was not messing about.

"Waitin' to see if they'll turn it."

The list of what Maheegan had already been able to observe going on at the landing field through his scope was impressive. Heavy mining and earth moving equipment, enormous pallets of synthetic timbers for shoring up mine works, prefab housing of the most rickety sort. But that also wasn't the information Coyote was after – he wasn't certain what he was after, but he'd know it when he saw it.

"Caught the symbol. But… dunno what it is."

"Let me see." Coyote took possession of the scope, listening to Maheegan's annoyingly laconic directions on where to find these crates in the massive sweep of the landing field. Normally used for landed rift ships, the full, busy operation didn't even manage to cover a third of the area. He finally found the crates in question and frowned. It was a non-standard symbol, but he'd seen something like it before – at the wildcat camp where the Bone Collector had almost gotten the lot of them killed. Which had also been where that odd equipment perimeter had been set up.

"Any ideas?" Maheegan asked.

"A few, and I don't like any of them." Coyote handed the scope back and made another note.

"Next lot is… explosives." Maheegan *hmm*ed under his breath. "Don't seem right, puttin' those in an osprey."

"They aren't really any bumpier than a train, depending on the atmosphere." And he was certain, if they were flying with this sort of intensity, the Weatherman was going to be involved to smooth their path. He also had a feeling, though he couldn't quite explain the why of it, that the Weatherman wasn't currently in Newcastle. His skin wasn't crawling with the proximity, at the least.

"You think this is gonna tell us where they're goin'?" Maheegan asked after another long stretch of silence.

Coyote wiped a swath of sweat from his brow and flicked it onto the saltpan. He was surprised there weren't eagles circling over them yet. Newcastle probably had some sort of sonic deterrent that only the birds could hear, or they'd be getting no peace at all. "Of course not."

Maheegan looked over at him, thick eyebrows raising. He didn't look or sound upset, though. Maheegan wasn't the sort to be overly fussed by anything. "Then why're we here?"

"The Ravani wasn't thinking rationally when she told us to work on mapping on our own. It's a triangulation exercise. We could perhaps do it with two teams rather than three, but no lone Wolves."

"No lone Wolves," Maheegan agreed, and focused on the landing field again. "Think you illustrated that one all nice and neat."

Coyote huffed. "Will I ever live that down?"

"Nope."

"That's very unfair."

"That's what you get for not dyin' proper," Maheegan remarked. "Oh, they're fuelin' one of the ospreys."

"They have a fuel port on each wing." Coyote took out his own pocket watch. "Tell me when they change between each port." He watched the seconds tick by in silence, increasingly apprehensive. It was possible they only had low-flow refuelers here, but he doubted that. He'd never gone through pilot school himself, but he'd spent enough time on or around the heavy ospreys for other jobs over his checkered past.

"Finished with the second one," Maheegan said, nearly thirty minutes later. Without looking up, he said, "You ain't lookin' happy."

"How would you know?"

"Can hear it."

Coyote sucked at his teeth, pensive. "They've fueled them fully. Presumably they don't have a refuel depot on the way, since we haven't seen them shipping any tankers out. But they also don't put much in the way of extra fuel on those, to save the weight for cargo."

"What kind of range, then?" Maheegan asked.

"Twenty thousand kilometers round trip, give or take," Coyote said.

A pause for nothing but heat and sweat. "Damn," Maheegan said. "That's a long-ass ride."

"I daresay longer than we can manage. But I've an idea."

"You plannin' on growin' wings?"

"Don't be silly. Let me have the scope again." He raised it to his eye, looking through the wavering heat to that landing field. It was really damned impressive that Maheegan could see as much as he had. But then again, there was a reason he was their one and only sniper. Coyote looked over the landing field, re-counting the heavy ospreys, noting their configuration for loading, the spaces left for others. He noted, too, the guard towers at each corner of the landing field, the chain link fence with its thick coils of barbed wire at the top. Bless the high winds that tended to hit flat stretches of hardpan like this one, Coyote thought. It meant they couldn't really build up decent, solid walls without a major investment the company wasn't willing to make when it didn't have to. Newcastle wasn't as heavily fortified as any of the mining towns. Bandits didn't come this far in, because they were either under TransRift's sway already, or not stupid enough to try it.

"You gonna share that idea?" Maheegan asked.

"Do you really want to know?"

He felt rather than saw the man shrug. "I'm a curious fellow."

"Well, what I'm thinking is that we simply need an osprey of our own."

Maheegan guffawed in his own way, the sound almost silent but very emphatic. "Gonna steal us a pilot too, while you're at it? And a Weatherman, so them invisible storms don't just swat us out of the sky?"

"Haven't you noticed? We've got someone much better than a Weatherman on our side." Coyote swept the landing field again, noting one of the ospreys being towed over to a different area, toward the hangar. There'd be less security there, he thought, because only a fool would steal an osprey that wasn't in perfect flight condition. He'd always been happy to be a fool, and in this case, a fool with an extremely good mechanic available, if Hati could just be dragged away from his damned novels.

"Mayhap. Don't help with the pilot, though."

"Recall how, in a previous life that we all politely don't talk about, you were something that led you to being very good at shooting men in the head from over a mile distant?"

He sensed the sudden turn of caution in Maheegan, reluctance. This was always fraught territory. "Yeah?"

There were a million stories there, just screaming to be told, funny and terrible and *no shit, there we were*. But he'd taken this one bit of thieves' honor seriously. All of them were born mewling from the desert with their Wolf name. They had no history they acknowledged beforehand, at least not publicly. In private, they remembered very well indeed. No man ever escaped his past or the habits of a misspent lifetime. "Well, in that previous life we so politely don't talk about, I know someone who was a pilot. Not me," he added quickly.

Maheegan worked it through, then laughed again. "You know, you're finally soundin' like your old self."

Coyote looked over at him, noting Maheegan's shit-eating grin. "I wasn't aware I'd stopped."

"You been quiet, and morose, and downright spooky. For you." Maheegan rolled onto his back, still careful not to disturb the camouflage net they shared, even as he laughed more. "But this's gotta be the dumbest fuckin' idea I heard in years."

"Thank you. I think."

Maheegan slapped his leg. "Ravani's gonna love it."

CHAPTER FORTY-THREE • *9 DAYS*

Mag stood on the wall of Ludlow. The hammer blows from the repairs still underway echoed up through her feet, and pounded in her head. Hob's man Diablo – it was still hard to think of him that way, rather than Davey like he'd been a few months ago, hidden away in a train car with her – had thought she had a concussion and wanted to give her some pills and have her laying about. She'd said no, because she didn't have time for that.

There was so much to do, hurt people to help, families to be checked on, a defense to be organized. The water situation had gone from worrying to desperate in just one night. She was the last of the nominal leaders, and she hadn't ever meant to be that – it had been Odalia and Clarence making all the speeches and pushing the votes, and her just supporting them and giving them a kick when they went in the wrong direction. But now those two were a dead traitor and a dead hero, and people kept looking to Mag.

She needed that. She needed something to do to keep her hands from clenching into fists until her fingers broke. She needed work so that she wouldn't think about Anabi, abducted and afraid and in the power of people who would do god only knew what to her. So she wouldn't think about Clarence, stiff and cold and pale, laid out in the church and waiting for his turn to be burned on the hill by the mine.

Brother Rami had chased her out of the church and told her to lay down, and Omar had shooed her from the company store and told her to go lay down, and she wasn't fucking ready to lay down, because she might not ever have the will to get back up.

Dust bloomed on the horizon, an orange-red cloud. Mag felt the bottom drop out of her stomach. It was too soon for another raid, wasn't it? She'd sent Hob and her people out before dawn to go check on the other towns. Could it be them coming back? She opened her mouth to shout an alarm, but someone else beat her to it – good thing, she seemed to be taking ten times too long to work any thoughts through her brain.

Pounding feet echoed through the wall as miners piled alongside her, clutching a motley assortment of guns stolen from Mariposa and mining equipment, even lengths of chain. And blessedly, a pair of binoculars, lenses frosted with sand scratch. Mag elbowed her way over to the woman holding them. "Mind if I borrow those?"

The woman, tiny and spare with a face like a hatchet, seemed liable to argue until she looked at Mag. Then she handed the binoculars over without so much as a word.

The closer view didn't help that much, since all she saw at first were billows of dust, indistinct shadows moving in them. Then she picked out the bulky shape of... "Trucks," she yelled. "We got more trucks comin' in." A murmur swept through the miners, the strange creaks and squeaks of hands tightening on weapons.

Someone tugged at her elbow – the woman whose binoculars she'd taken. Mag ignored her, still peering into the dust cloud. She began to make out new shapes, smaller ones, darting back and forth between the bulk of the trucks: motorcycles. A motley enough assortment that they couldn't be spit-shined security vehicles.

Relief made her sag. She lowered the binoculars, not really strong enough to hold them up any more, and felt them be snatched away. "It's the Wolves. It's them. It's all right." This time, at least. A ragged cheer went up around the wall, and people moved back off to what they'd been doing. Mag stayed where she was at, watching and waiting until she saw the unmistakable, lanky silhouette of Hob, at ease on her motorcycle.

The trucks were full of people, many of them bruised and bloodied. Miners from Walsen, and the children that they'd hidden away when the raid started. "We're all that's left," their only work gang leader told Mag. She was a big woman, white skin now gone red from being in the sun, her shoulders broad and arms heavy with muscle. Dried blood covered half her face, run from a clotted cut on her forehead. "Lot of dead. Rest got taken in the trucks. We're the ones managed to breach the wall on the opposite side and run for it."

Mag looked at the little crowd, a bit shy of one hundred people, and tried not to choke on her despair. More mouths to feed and fill with water, and they'd brought nothing with them. Well, she'd always said over and over that the miners had to stick together. She wasn't going to change her tune now. "Hurt ones, go to the churchyard and see Brother Rami and Diablo." She had to swallow a hiccuping giggle of hysteria as that combination of names struck her. She felt almost relieved when someone in the exhausted crowd did bark out an unsteady guffaw. "Rest of you, a place to stay gets assigned at the company store. Food and water's strict rations." She pointed them in the right directions. Hob stood by, arms crossed over leathers fuzzed with rust-colored dust, and waited.

"You got more news?" Mag asked her, when the last of the people from Walsen had gone on their way.

"Mayhap. On the way around Walsen, Conall and Lykaios were dead sure we were bein' watched. Probably spies in camouflage blinds. No one tried to stop us."

It didn't take a whole lot of thinking for Mag to know what she was getting at. "They want us to gather everyone here. Run us through our supplies faster."

"Good news is, one of the trucks is about half full with shit we salvaged from Walsen," Hob said.

"I'll let Omar know."

"Bad news is, it ain't that much. And ain't no water." Hob had been running her small outfit for years, always on the ragged edge of starvation. She had a keen eye for supplies.

"Maybe we can hold out till the government man shows up," Mag said, though even to her own ears, her tone sounded bleak. "And get Brother Rami prayin' that the new boss ain't gonna be the same as the old boss."

"We both know what prayin' gets you." Hob sighed and ran her hand over her hair, sweat-soaked and plastered dark to her scalp. "Our crew that checked on Rouse met up with us too. Rouse held. Ain't as well organized as what you got here, but they're gettin' their shit together. They got survivors comin' in from Shimera."

Mag opened her mouth to ask about Tercio, the closest of them to Newcastle, but another round of shouting from the wall stopped the words in her throat. She didn't have it in her to run, so she walked a good clip, Hob at her shoulder like she thought Mag might fall over.

This new dust cloud was on the south, almost hidden by the black rocks of the mine. Mag found the woman with the binoculars and again took them off her, ignoring the dirty look she got for her trouble. "Think that's more trucks," she said, after a moment of trying to stare through the dust.

"An' more," Hob agreed. She had the scope off a gun held up to her one eye. "Those other things? Tractors."

Mag didn't fight the woman who snatched her binoculars back. "Tractors?"

"Don't ask me," Hob said. "But we know they ain't Mariposa."

This new group, twenty-two people by Mag's count, was from the town of Blessid. She recognized Tavris Meeks, the small brown man she'd once tried to ask for help, as he slid off the seat of one of the tractors. Bullet holes marred its fenders. Mag met him outside the town gates.

"We're lookin' for help," he said, not meeting Mag's eyes. "Heard y'all might have shelter."

"The hell happened to you?" Hob growled behind Mag. And bless her for it, because Mag didn't think she'd be able to say a damn word without screaming.

"Company man come," Tavris said, finally looking up. "Said they needed people for a special project. Minin' and buildin' a new rail line for the mine. Offered us a bonus, and a few went, but most of us don't want that. So we told 'em we ain't miners, and we got crops to tend and sent him packin'. Guess they didn't like that answer. Come back with trucks and guns and... we're the ones who escaped."

Mag let out her breath carefully and somehow her voice was even as she spoke. "I remember, when I came to you for help, an' you said our problems weren't yours."

"Company men come and told us again and again that we keep our noses clean and not help the troublemakers. That we was different, and they give us a bonus for keeping to ourselves." Tavris looked down at the ground, his shoulders taut as wire. "Guess we ain't so different after all."

She wanted to punch him. She wanted to shove him. And she definitely wanted to tell him to get the hell out of her town. And then, she thought, what good would she be? She made herself take another careful breath. "You brung any food or water with you?"

"Got some guns," Tavris said. "But they took everythin' else. Like they was expectin' it. And burned the silos." That last, he delivered in a tone of mixed anger and horror.

She felt Hob behind her, ready to jump whichever way Mag did. And suddenly, she felt too damned tired to jump. "Any of you hurt, go to the churchyard and find Brother Rami. Rest of you, go to the company store. Ask someone to show you the way. They'll find you somethin' to eat and a place to sleep."

Tavris swallowed hard and relaxed, like he'd been all tense for a blow that never came. "Thank you. We were wrong. I pray to God we get another chance to do it right."

She didn't have a response for that, and just waved him and his people in. Even angry and exhausted, she found herself wondering what could be done with the tractors, how they might benefit the town.

"Thought you were gonna deck him," Hob said, amused, once they were alone.

"Wanted to. Would've felt damned good, too. But not given us more food for our bellies nor water to drink." Mag swallowed against an upwelling of despair. "We gotta figure out water, or we ain't gonna last long enough to starve."

Hob sucked at her teeth. "You got enough credits to play with, we could mayhap do a raid on Primero or Segundo..."

Mag shook her head. "I don't want you hangin' here no more. You're supposed to be gettin' to that place the government man left for you. Work on figurin' that out. And get my girl back."

"Ain't gonna do her any good if you're dead by the time I get her back here. Don't be fuckin' stupid."

Mag rubbed her face, shying away from the massive bruise on the side after the lightest touch. "Shit."

"Why Mag, I do believe you're developin' a nasty mouth," Hob said, obviously trying to lighten the mood.

Mag waved the stilted teasing off, a grain of an idea caught in her mind – the Bone Collector. She remembered Hob telling her about how she'd met that strange man, years and years ago. It was a memorable story, really, but suddenly it felt more important. Because maybe… "Hob, tell me how you'n the Bone Collector met again."

Hob's eyebrows went up. "Right now?"

"I'm askin' right now."

Hob shrugged. "Me'n Freki and Geri was shit-stirrin'…" She recounted the story, about kids on their first motorcycles, going out into the desert and finding a cave that they were never able to find again. One that had an underground lake in it, so fresh and clear that they could see through to the bottom like it wasn't even there. And inside the cave, the statue of a man – the Bone Collector. She told about how a company man and a preacher man had shown up, one with some kind of gadget, one with a sledgehammer, and were going to take him away. How they'd made the snap decision to fight those two, killed their first men ever. And then the statue that was the Bone Collector had moved.

"A lake," Mag said when she finished. "Underground. The water's got to be somewhere. There used to be whole oceans here, to carry all that salt. Water don't just vanish."

"What you thinkin' – gonna dig for it?" Hob asked. "You got the equipment, I s'pose."

Mag shook her head. "It'd take too long, and we don't know where. No. Can you call up the Bone Collector for me? I seen you do it before."

Hob blinked her eye. "I can. Don't know why I didn't think of that before."

Because you're scared of him, Mag thought. Well, more Hob was scared of herself when she was around him. That was plain to anyone who had eyes and had known Hob as long as Mag had. But saying that out loud would just get an argument, and she didn't have time for that either. "'Cause you ain't ever had to ask him for something like this," Mag said, diplomatically. "But it don't hurt to try now."

"Plenty of stuff hurts to try," Hob muttered.

Hob put Mag on the back of her motorcycle and they rode out a few kilometers, to get into the dunes proper as the sun began to set. Then, as Mag watched, Hob took out one of those wicked silver throwing knives of hers and made a cut on her hand. A few crimson drops splashed down on the sand, and then Hob took out her handkerchief, already clouded with brown stains, and wrapped it around her palm.

Maybe thirty minutes later, Mag felt the shift in the air before she heard it in the sand. She'd touched him with witchiness. She knew him now. Felt his approach, like the sun creeping over the horizon. And when he stepped up out of the sand like he was coming out of a bath, he didn't look surprised at all.

He still reached for Hob's hand first, the one she'd cut, and smoothed his thumb over it. Mag watched, curious, feeling like she was spying just a little on a private moment.

"I'm surprised to find you here," the Bone Collector said to Hob.

"Had somethin' that needed doin'," she answered, defensive. "And worked out, 'cause I know where we're goin' now." Her gaze flicked to Mag. "Just gotta figure out how to get there."

"I asked Hob to call you," Mag said, even if part of her wanted to let Hob squirm a little more. "Hoping maybe you can help me."

The Bone Collector's pale eyebrows arched up. "Help you with what?"

"We got raided last night. Most of our supplies are gone. We need water. And... there's got to be water somewhere, right? It rains sometimes."

"There is," the Bone Collector said. "Even though much of it has gone to the heart. You saw that. But there are rivers that flow underground, and lakes to catch them."

"Can you make a well for us? I know you can... shape rock and such."

The Bone Collector seemed to consider this. "Why should I?"

That wasn't an answer she'd expected. A flutter of hope hit her, instantly crushed. The man's blue eyes were so cold as he looked at her, like they'd never shared that dream. "We're gonna die if you don't."

"What care have I for miners who do nothing but hurt this world and steal its lifeblood?"

No, Mag reminded herself, he might be human-shaped, but there wasn't anything human in him sometimes. It was just easy to forget when he was around Hob. But she'd felt the alienness of him, something still terrifying but less discordant than the Weathermen. "We're fightin' TransRift. That's how we got in this place. We got a common enemy."

"I have people I hire when I need something fought," he said, his eyes glittering strangely.

"Leave me out of this," muttered Hob.

"And they do not dig," the Bone Collector continued, ignoring her.

"Now look here," Hob started. "Maybe you don't give a shit about Mag, but I do…" She stopped when Mag laid a hand on her arm.

Hob would fight for her, Mag knew. To the ends of the world. And Mag would do the same for her. But this wasn't about just the two of them. A movement had to be more than one person if it was to breathe on its own. Her own life wasn't worth spit if she just let Hob hinge it all on her. "If you're on our side, we'll be on your side," Mag said. "We dig where TransRift wants us to dig 'cause that's the only way we got of surviving. Give us an alternative, and we'll take it."

"You'll stop mining."

She almost agreed to it that instant, because it was so easy. But what about when the government men came, and they still needed miners? Some people would take their chance to get off planet, but for many of them, Mag included, this was the only home they'd ever known. Even as the dry desert air tried to kill her by sucking every drop of water from her body, she knew in her bones she wouldn't survive without it. "It's more complicated than that."

"I think this is exceedingly simple," the Bone Collector said.

"That's because you ain't ever had to make a living," Mag said. "I can't make you care about us humans if you don't want to. But I think you're a fool if you're gonna turn your back on the chance to get a whole passel of us who'll listen to you and talk with you and deal with you instead of just tryin' to wipe you out."

"I survive," he said.

"Your one-man war can't be goin' that good, if you keep havin' to hire Hob," Mag said, and was rewarded with Hob snorting. She grimaced at the smell of cigarette smoke, then; Hob must have gotten one out. She wasn't even going to look, her eyes fixed on the Bone Collector's.

"You are not one of them," the Bone Collector said.

"Yes, I am," Mag said firmly. "I don't care how much witchiness I got flowin' through me. There's more in my heart than blood. We didn't let TransRift divide us, and I sure as hell ain't lettin' you do it."

He tilted his head, his expression taken aback. Then he glanced over her shoulder, toward Hob, and that flat pissed her off. "You don't look at her," Mag growled. "You're dealin' with me."

The Bone Collector looked at her again, really looked at her, and then nodded slowly. "I suppose I am."

8 DAYS

He made the well in one corner of the churchyard, after pacing back and forth until the sun had come back up, muttering and humming under his breath. Mag, Hob, and a crowd that had to be nearly everyone who wasn't on the walls or too hurt to move, watched.

The odd, colorless man stopped and crouched down to rest his hand on the black stones they'd used to pave the churchyard. Then he began to sing, a song without words – or at least words Mag could understand – that she recognized, somehow. She felt it flow in through her ears and the tips of her fingers, like she was leaning in and resting against his back, like it had felt when he'd somehow found her in that dream. She hummed along with him, then sang, the tune if not the words. Next to her, Hob stayed silent and simply lit her next cigarette on the smoldering butt of the one she was finishing. Nearby, she heard another voice come into the song – the weather witch. The miners around them drew back slightly.

She felt the rumbling beneath the ground, a shifting, a flowing. It moved with the words of the Bone Collector's song, coming closer and closer like he was coaxing an animal to his hand. To *their* hands, she realized, because she was in it, bolstering him again, letting him lean on her like she so often leaned on other people. But it was a different sensation, companionable, an asking rather than demanding.

Under his hand, the stones of the churchyard folded in on themselves and made a round hole, which grew slowly outward until it was half a meter across. The Bone Collector held one last note, letting it trail away, then stood. "Be sure to cover that before someone falls in."

Those casual words hung strange in the air, which now smelled dark and wet as that new hole breathed out. The churchyard sat so silent that the gentle, echoing splash of distant water on stone was loud enough to hear.

"Water," people began to murmur. "He brought us water." The Bone Collector smiled serenely, but Mag felt tension under that expression. He was waiting, just like her, for someone to shout out about witchiness.

And then there was shouting, but it wasn't angry. It was a cheer, a roar of approval. The sound of people seeing their deaths postponed. The crowd closed in around Mag, Hob, the Bone Collector, and buffeted them with claps on the shoulder and back, even a few hugs – though no one dared try that on anyone but Mag.

"Water!" the miners echoed. "We have water! We can do anything, we have water!"

CHAPTER FORTY-FOUR • *8 DAYS*

Hob found the Bone Collector leaning against the wall outside Ludlow, bright in the full sun. He had his head bowed, but looked up as she scuffed her boots in the sand. "You already tired?" she asked.

He huffed a laugh. "I don't think I've stopped since you woke me up."

Hob rolled her cigarette between her lips, then sat down next to him, an arm's length apart and downwind. "I reckon you can sleep when you're dead, same as the rest of us."

He laughed again, and then leaned his head back against the wall, eyes closed. "You have such a cheerful outlook on life."

"Came by it honestly." She let the silence fall, but it was too thick, too awkward. She didn't know why the hell she'd followed him as he'd squeezed out of the crowd. Only Mag hadn't needed her just then, and it wasn't her celebration. "Thanks, though. You done a good thing."

"I didn't do it for you, so there is no need to thank me."

"That's why it's a good thing." She hadn't liked it, when he'd looked at her instead of Mag for that second until Mag took his head off with a few words. Being in charge of someone's life because you paid out to them, and you watched their back while they watched yours was one thing. Having that kind of power over someone like the Bone Collector made her feel like a thing to be traded. He didn't owe her a damn thing, and she wanted to keep it that way. Even if she knew she would have used it in a second if she'd felt her back against a corner. Keeping Mag safe meant more to her than her own peace of mind.

As the silence stretched fit to snap again, she found herself looking at him from the corner of her eye. It seemed so easy, to let him be that little bit apart. It was sure as hell easier on her, because it meant not having to ask herself any questions, let alone answer them. But there was still that tug of *what do you want from me*, and it ran up against the shadow she felt coming on the horizon. There was always the chance, whether it was a big thing or a small thing or just riding off to get some goddamned supplies for Lobo, that it would be her last living moment. She didn't want regrets, and she didn't want to be Old Nick, dead-eyed because she'd killed too much of what she loved. She weighed those two wants in her hand: blood spraying indelibly across a ceiling, and the most infuriating person she'd ever known breathing softly against her hair.

She reached out and slid her fingers over his. The Bone Collector inhaled sharply, but he curled his fingers around hers, and pulled her hand in to rest against his chest. Hob frowned and tugged her hand away, long enough that she could pull off her glove. Aware of how intently he watched, she reached out again. And that was right, his skin as cool as ever against hers, no longer muffled by the glove. Maybe it had also been a mistake, because it felt too damn good when he stroked her fingers with his thumb. Something that small had no right to mean that much.

With her other hand, Hob flicked her cigarette butt away. It vanished in a shower of sparks. She got another out of her pocket, a little fumbling one-handed, and lit it with a snap of her fingers.

"I wish you wouldn't do that," he said.

"I wish you'd quit your belly-achin'." It helped, because if he hadn't said anything, she might have gone and done something real stupid and tried to kiss him.

The low hum of a motor, the sound of chain mesh tires on sand made her look up, yanking her hand away from the Bone Collector as she did. Two familiar figures rolled along around the wall. She would have known them by their size and postures even if she hadn't seen the paint and scratches on their helmets: Maheegan and Coyote.

They stopped a few meters off. Coyote pushed back the eye shield on his helmet. "Terribly sorry. Are we interrupting something?" The extra fruity tone of his voice was pure mockery.

Hob showed him her teeth. "I'm on a smoke break. The fuck do you want?" They were supposed to still be out, tracking the convoys. Just as well, Hob thought. She had those coordinates from Coyote's shitbag of a brother now anyway.

"I've got a modest proposal for you," Coyote said.

"Then I shall be on my way," the Bone Collector said, pushing himself to his feet.

Coyote extended a finger to point at him. "Not so fast. It's for you, too."

Hob raised her eyebrows. "This better be good."

The helmet muffled the sound of his voice, but Hob still heard Maheegan... *cackle*. "Oh, you betcha it is."

6 DAYS

"I don't see any fuckin' ospreys," Hob said, squinting out from under the camouflage net they all huddled beneath, out in the great saltpan around Newcastle. It was the dark of the night, and cold, which made her just a little grateful for them all having to be so cozy.

Hob had waited for the rest of her people to get back from the towns and handpicked her party carefully – Dambala, Coyote, Maheegan, Lykaios, Freki, Geri, and the Bone Collector riding on the back of her motorcycle and hating every minute of it.

"No, there's one," Coyote said. He passed her a scope, then extended his hand to point. "There, in the hangar." Thankfully, for all it was black but for the stars outside, the city and the landing field were a blaze of lights, like the glittering shell of some alien insect with its claws sunk deep into the hardpan.

Hob felt Dambala shift uneasily behind her. After she took a brief look – sure was a big fucking osprey, which was about all she knew about those machines – she handed the scope to him.

"Are you fuckin' serious?" Dambala said. "It's grounded for repairs."

She didn't like the sound of that. "You sayin' it's broke, Bala?"

"If it's in that there hangar, it sure as hell ain't at full operation," Dambala said.

"We watched it come in yesterday morning and it was flying just fine," Coyote said, a touch defensive. "Probably some backup system warning light that they have to inspect away."

"You don't know that," Dambala said. "This ain't some motorcycle with an overheat light you can ignore, you dumb asshole. I ain't flyin' somethin' just to have it fall out of the sky."

Hob still wasn't certain how Dambala had suddenly transformed into a pilot, or why Coyote had known this about him. She wanted to ask, but it definitely fell under the *no talking about anyone's life before they were a Wolf* rule. Stupid fucking rule sometimes, she thought.

"And," Coyote continued in an entirely reasonable tone, which meant he was at his most dangerous, "it's currently unattended. We'll never get this sort of opportunity when they're doing load and prep for the next flight."

"And how the fuck you plannin' on fixin' it even if it don't fall out of the sky?" Dambala demanded.

"Assuming it isn't just a silly failsafe light we can put a bit of tape over?" Coyote asked. "Come now, old boy. You must have more faith in our dear friend Hati than that."

"Coyote," Dambala said, warningly. "Night flyin' ain't a fuckin' joke either."

"Both of ya, hush." Hob took the scope back. It was true that there was a lull of activity on the landing field, because it was night, and because there was nothing there to load or refuel at the moment. She sucked at her teeth, thinking. "We get you in there, Bala, will you be able to tell pretty quick if you can fly it?"

"Maybe. Dependin' on the alarms, I'll sure as hell know if I can't," he said. "But they ain't gonna let us just—"

"I know," she interrupted. "But that's what Freki and Geri and Lykaios and Maheegan are gonna do."

"That so?" Geri said.

"Yeah," Hob said and offered the scope over. Freki took it before his twin could. "You're gonna make a ruckus and get them chasin' ya so we can get in. Then we'll make a bigger ruckus stealin' their fuckin' osprey so they'll forget about you."

"That's the dumbest thing I ever heard," Geri said.

Coyote laughed and punched Hob lightly on the arm. "That's my Ravani."

There were guards stationed around the Newcastle landing field, but compared to what they'd always seen at the mining towns, it was a joke. Punishment for the greenbellies who weren't enthusiastic enough, maybe. Hob and her three, now mounted up, kept under the camouflage net while the diversion crew went in. They got damn close to the landing field before anyone noticed, close enough that Hob wondered if maybe she should have tried a different tactic. The floodlights on several guard towers swiveled to fix on them, and a voice boomed out across the salt flat: "You are entering a restricted area."

Geri parked his motorcycle and climbed off it with a drunken swagger. He waved a middle finger at the nearest guard tower. "You don't tell me where I can go!"

Hob could all but feel the disbelief rolling off the guards. She nudged Dambala and Coyote, and peeled back the net to bundle it into the confused Bone Collector's hands. While Geri continued making a production of himself – he started picking a mock fight with Freki, she saw out of the corner of her eye – they gave that part of the landing field a wide berth and headed for the fence closest to that hangar.

This never would have worked at one of the mining towns, not in a million years. They had too many bandit troubles, real bandits that didn't work for Mariposa on the sly. But Newcastle had been untouchable for so long, Hob had figured they wouldn't know what to do.

"Cease and desist!" boomed out across the hardpan. They really, really didn't know what to do.

They made it to the fence line with their lights dark. A guard tower loomed overhead, though with them directly under it the person inside wouldn't be able to see. The plan was that everyone on this section of the wall, bored out of their goddamn minds, would be looking toward the fine entertainment cut by Geri's crew.

Coyote threw his jacket over the barbed wire and Dambala boosted him up. He was eerily silent, more than she'd thought possible, though he timed his move with more shouting from the other end of the field. Hob gave him a count of two minutes to go clear out the guard tower. She and Dambala pulled out wire cutters from their saddle bags and started working at the fence. There was no way in hell they were leaving their motorcycles behind. With each snap of wire under tension coming free, Hob expected to hear a shout, or the sound of a gun being fired. *Snap, snap, snap, snap, BANG.*

Hob and Dambala both froze, momentarily. But Hob's ears told her that the shot hadn't been that nearby. It was from downfield, where the others still were. Dambala cursed under his breath.

Geri's voice, attenuated by distance, raised up again. Hob didn't allow herself the luxury of relief. She went back to cutting through the fence.

Then there were more shots, the sharp retorts of rifles and then the bark of shotguns. Hob glanced downfield to see several lights down, sparking.

"One hell of a diversion," Dambala muttered.

"Gotta trust 'em." She wasn't sure if she was trying to reassure Dambala, or herself. The real secret of leading the Wolves was figuring out the person for a job and then just letting them do what they did best.

Coyote appeared on the other side of the fence, his previously helmet-flattened hair slightly mussed. Wordlessly, he held the section of fence as she and

Dambala cut it free, and pulled it aside. "Way's clear," he said, as he got back on his motorcycle. "They're all running for the west gate so they can have a go at Geri."

Was Geri still even there? Before Hob could ask, she heard shotguns roar. She just had to hope he'd have the gumption to get while the getting was good. Hob got back on her motorcycle and made sure the Bone Collector had a good hold around her waist before she gunned the motor and sent them flying through the hole in the fence.

She felt the moment her wheels went from saltpan to synthcrete, slippery and louder than she liked. It felt horribly naked to be moving under the floodlights that kept the landing field as bright as day. Their only hope was Geri's distraction as she headed them straight toward the hangar. And an even more important hope was that Dambala would be able to fly the osprey, because she hadn't given near enough thought to how the hell else they were going to get out.

They arrowed into the hangar. Hob started to slow, but Coyote and Dambala kept going, looping around the massive osprey that sat, nose pointed at the door. With a mental shrug, she followed them, to find the cargo ramp of the osprey down. Bemused, she kept right on their rear wheels, up the ramp and into the shockingly huge space of the cargo bay. How the hell something like this could even fly was beyond her imagining.

Hob nudged the Bone Collector off and laid down her motorcycle, copying what Coyote and Dambala did.

"Find some rope or chains. We don't want those sliding around," Coyote said, and then ran back down the ramp.

"The hell are you getting, then?" Hob called after him.

"Fuel pump!" he called over his shoulder. Then he was gone around the corner.

Well, she was glad he'd thought of that, because it'd never occurred to her. Vehicles that didn't run on solar – that was a hell of a thought. Hob ran down the ramp and out into the hangar. Feeling so small against the cavernous space took her back to her childhood, growing up in the belly of a rift ship under the rough eye of the cargo handlers. And that memory prompted her to the boards on a far-off wall where the cargo netting and chains hung. As she ran across the stupidly large space, she wished she'd had the gumption to grab her motorcycle. Too late now.

Back up the ramp with her lungs and legs burning, she threw one of the cargo nets to the Bone Collector. "Help me."

He unfurled it and then stared, like he had no idea what such a thing could be for. With a growl, Hob grabbed the net from his hands. "Go stick that hook in that eye there – no, that one. Fold it out from the wall."

As she worked to get the motorcycles something close to secured, glancing every few seconds at the ramp like she expected to see greenbellies with guns popping up, she yelled, "You got shit figured out up there?"

"I'm workin' on it," Dambala shouted back. "I ain't done this in near twenty years."

"Remember faster." She didn't know how many minutes had passed already. Every second felt both too slow and too damn fast, as keyed up as she was.

Coyote came barreling back into view. "Get the ramp up. We got lights coming at us. And grab the chocks! Get those first."

"What the fuck?" Hob looked around, not sure where to even start on that task. She'd already run through every similarity this machine had to a rift ship.

With an exasperated noise, Coyote gave her a shove toward the cockpit. "You go assist. I'll take care of this."

And he pointed a finger at the Bone Collector. "And you, sit. Out of the way. Over there. Belt in."

Hob ran up the second, much smaller ramp to the cockpit, her boots echoing loud on metal. She found Dambala in the pilot's seat, a headset looped around his neck, and his fingers moving over a control panel that was a goddamn light maze as far as she could tell. "Fuck me," she muttered.

"You and Coyote, you both thought this was a great fuckin' idea," Dambala said.

"It's still a great idea!" Coyote yelled from the depths of the cargo hold. "And hit the emergency line eject when you're ready to take off, I left a pump running on both wings."

Hob really wished that he'd go back to speaking English instead of whatever the fuck he was yelling about now. She glanced through the windscreen of the cockpit to see pairs of lights coming toward them across the landing field. "Come on, Dambala. Tell me you got this."

"Ain't even the same fuckin' model as twenty years ago," he said, flipping a few more pressure switches over. "Look at that dial on your right. Not that one. Two more up. What's it say?"

Numbers. She could do numbers. "1205," she answered.

"Well, could be worse," Dambala said.

"What's it mean?"

"That this machine's in here 'cause it's got a stabilizer out."

"That bad?"

"It ain't good," he said, but his fingers kept moving across the board. "I flown bigger death traps. Just ain't gonna be pretty. And if they chase us, could be trouble."

"Might be trouble, then." Hob looked out the

windscreen again. The lights were almost there, resolving themselves into several small cargo haulers, filled with people. Not friendly people, she was sure. "Bala, we're almost out of time. There a... there a gun on this or somethin'?" Visions of sitting in a big gun like some kind of action story hit her. That could work.

"This look like a fuckin' combat model to you?" he snapped. "Sit down."

She sat.

"Give me that number again."

Hob looked at the dial. "1460," she read.

"OK," he said, like that held some deep and important meaning. "OK." He stabbed a finger at another button.

Around them and beneath them, the osprey roared to life. Like the rift ship taking off, but the vibration kept growing, louder and louder. That was how motors sounded when they weren't running on electric, Hob realized. She tried to shout a question to Dambala, only to find he'd put the headset on. He gestured impatiently at another one near her, and she stuck it on her head. The noise blessedly cut off.

"All secure back there?" she heard Dambala ask over the headset.

"Buttoned up tight, darling," Coyote answered. Even odd and tinny with transmission, there was unmistakable glee in his voice. "I haven't had this much fun in years."

"God fuckin' help us," Dambala muttered. He leaned over and pointed to several buttons on Hob's side. "This one, this one, then this one. When I tell you. And keep an eye on that dial there," he pointed at a different one. "Tell me right smart if it goes below twenty."

"It says eighteen," Hob said.

"Fuckin' gorgeous," Dambala growled. There was a strange, distant pinging, then another. "Are they fuckin'... they're shootin' at us."

"Should we–"

He pressed a few more switches, slammed his fist down on a big red and yellow striped button, and gripped the small handles in front of him. "Fuckin' morons." One of those controls must have been the throttle, because the osprey started moving forward, rolling out of the hangar.

Hob saw greenbellies scramble to the side, and heard more of that distant pinging. Then Dambala shouted at her to do her damn job and she hurried to press those buttons and put her attention onto the dial. She felt the shift in acceleration going from *forward* to *up*, felt the vibration and rumble as the osprey's engines turned for vertical take-off.

Another volley of pinging went down the skin of the osprey as they rose into the air. On the panel, several lights suddenly went red, an alarm sounding over the headsets.

"Bala…" Coyote said from the back.

"I got it," he yelled. He half-looked at Hob, "2-F Cut. Find it, push it."

"OK…" She ran her hand over the switches, reading as fast as she could and cursing herself that it wasn't faster. She'd never been a quick reader, and the labels on the switches were tiny.

"Any day now!" Dambala yelled.

"I'm fuckin' lookin'!" She spied the switch, in a row of equally incomprehensible switches, and snapped it down. The alarm swapped out for a different, less urgent sound. All the while, the osprey kept shooting straight up. Then they came to a halt, just hanging in the air. Dambala shifted the sticks and they moved forward, weaving a little drunkenly.

"Come on, come on, there's a girl…"

For a moment, Hob thought Dambala was talking to her, but realized he was muttering to himself and the osprey. "You got it... come on... all right." His tone shifted, and he glanced at her. "Gonna go fast as we can, to get distance afore they can scramble one of their helicopters. Don't fuckin' touch nothin' 'less I tell you."

She felt so in over her head that she was happy to nod. Then someone grabbed her shoulder – Coyote. She tugged the headset off so he could lean in and bellow in her ear, "Go back. I can handle Grumpy McAsshole here." He laughed as Dambala, eyes still fixed ahead, swatted him on the side.

Grateful, she untangled herself from the safety belts and slithered around Coyote. He grabbed her arm and pulled her back for a second. "Smile, boss. We just stole a five hundred million credit flying junkpile."

Stunned, she didn't resist as he gave her a little push down the narrow cockpit hall. She turned the number over in her head, trying to make sense of it. No, too big. A little unsteady, bouncing back and forth on her feet as Dambala kept fighting the controls or the wind or his own temper, she made her way into the cargo bay. The Bone Collector was a huddle in a fold-down seat, his arms clutched around his middle.

Hob noted he wasn't wearing a headset and leaned over to shout in his ear. "You look like shit."

He said something, but she couldn't hear it at a bare whisper. She leaned down to try to get a better look at his face, then jerked back as he vomited a thin wash of bile onto the deck at her feet. With a grimace, she pulled her handkerchief out of her pocket and offered it to him. He clutched it in his hand and didn't do anything useful with it.

Better to leave him alone, she thought suddenly. Since he might be all that was really keeping the osprey in the air. She sat next to him, wondering if she ought to rub his back or some shit, but that had never been her thing. He solved that particular question by laying down with his head in her lap, his mouth in a grim line.

"You better not barf again," she shouted. His only response was his nostrils flaring around a snort. Hob pulled the headset Coyote must have abandoned on. "You knew," she accused Coyote.

He laughed. "I am familiar with that particular look."

"How're things looking?" she asked.

"We're still flyin', ain't we." Dambala answered.

"Can't argue with that. How about the bit where we go from flyin' to landin'?" Hob asked.

"Guess we'll all find out in an hour when we get there."

She'd never been the sort to want comfort, and knew better than to expect it now. But she stroked the Bone Collector's hair, and that made her feel a little better, even if it probably didn't do jack shit for him. "Hour ain't so long as that," she told him. Impossibly quick, considering how long the journey normally took on a motorcycle.

"Weren't the life expectancy I was lookin' for," Dambala muttered.

CHAPTER FORTY-FIVE • *5 DAYS*

The shaking hands that offered the folded flimsy to Mag showed the permanent black speckling of embedded mine dust, and new angry red of split knuckles and dirty brown runnels of dried blood. She steadied the man's hand with her own and took the message. "You're safe now," she said.

He shook his head. Black stubble bristled on his dark cheeks, marred with more dried blood, more bruises. "Ain't such a thing. They're all around you. Us. Took my partner. Soon as we were out of sight of Tercio. Took our daughter. I… I wanted to go with 'em, but they said I had to bring this message to you."

She poured him a cup of water, which he gulped down. His eyes widened with surprise when she poured him another, but he sucked that down just as readily. "You gonna try to go back out to 'em now?" she asked.

"I got any choice?"

"No," Mag said. "Not really. We ain't lettin' anyone leave. We all got to stand together, or none of this means anythin'." And now he'd seen too much. He knew they had water, and how many people, and how many guns. No more traitors. No more spies. She refilled his glass again. "I'm sorry. I know what it feels like. They took one of mine, too."

He buried his face in his hands. "Wish I'd never fuckin' voted for this."

Mag stood, brushing her skirts down. Dust drifted away from her hands in ribbons. "We ain't the ones who took your baby. Remember who the enemy really is. Remember what we're here to do." She rested her hand briefly on his shoulder, and he didn't push her away.

Outside the room, Omar waited. "Take him to Brother Rami once he's got himself back together," Mag said. "But keep an eye on him, hear? They got him deep."

Omar nodded, arms crossed, then jerked his chin toward the flimsy she had in her hand. "What's the shit today?"

"Same as yesterday," Mag said, and handed it to him. "Phony amnesty, tryin' to get us to surrender. Think they still don't know we got water, and that's good."

"Mag!"

She turned to see Diablo coming in, a dusty bandana pushed down around his neck. He and most of the other Wolves had stayed on while Hob took her small party off on their latest fool's errand, though she'd had Hati and one other go back to their base to wait. Mag was grateful for every experienced gun she'd left to ride herd on the miners. They were getting leaner and meaner by the hour, but they still had nothing on people who had been professionally harassing TransRift for years.

"There a problem?" she asked. There was always a problem, these days.

"Just got back from the run in to Walsen," Diablo said. "What's left of it."

"Anythin' useful?"

"Found a few things. Not much. Don't bother sendin' anyone back there." He reached into his pocket and offered her another flimsy. "Hit the message drops on the way back, out of habit. Found this in one of 'em. It's got your name on it."

Mag frowned and took the flimsy. It felt the same, slick and fresh, as the one she'd just given away to Omar. Another threat from TransRift, from a new place because they'd somehow managed to find a drop box? She unfolded the message, found another folded page within, and scanned the first few lines, neatly handwritten rather than in print type: *Ms Kushtrim, a matter of utmost urgency has come to my attention…*

No. This wasn't the same at all. She folded the flimsy back up before prying eyes could get any further than she had. "Thank you, Diablo," she said, her mouth suddenly dry.

"You all right, Mag?" Omar asked. Diablo was looking hard at her too.

"Nothin' y'all need to worry about," she said, and tried to school her expression. "Go on. I'll be back at the wall shortly, just need to read this."

She retreated to her kitchen. It still felt strange to think of the house as hers, and she'd made room for the refugees from other towns just like everyone else, so it was still full of people. But not Clarence. His absence was like a missing stair. She still expected to walk in and find him drinking coffee at his scarred and pitted kitchen table, slumped in a dust-stained undershirt.

The kitchen was empty now, so she took Clarence's place, and made herself a cup of coffee that was so thin as to be barely brown, the grounds on their eighth or ninth reuse. She didn't really notice the taste, as she unfolded the message from Hob's government man and read it with slow care:

Ms Kushtrim, I hope that this note finds you well, though I feel my subtle attempts at intervention on behalf of your

cause have failed utterly, from what I have gleaned. For
that I apologize, and offer a warning: Captain Longbridge
has requested more troops for another assault on Ludlow,
though the vice president has for now reined him in,
preferring to convince you of the error of your ways with
thirst. Longbridge has also requested an artificial limb
replacement, so I fear it is personal on his count.
However, a matter of greater urgency has come to my
attention. I have come upon information concerning an
associate of yours and Hob Ravani's. While I do not know
his name, his distinctive mode of dress – clothing decorated
with bones – should be enough to identify him. It seems
that he is in fact one Gabriel Chua, AKA Weatherman
001. He should be considered extremely dangerous and is
not to be trusted. I have attached a copy of the personnel
file I found containing this information. I regret being the
bearer of such news. Respectfully yours, Shigehiko Rollins

All the words were spelled correctly and well written,
but none of them made a lick of sense when strung
together like that. She knew Weathermen, in an intimate
way that had nothing to do with bodies. Her skin still
crawled with the memory of being shoved into a room
with Mr Green repeatedly, and what he'd done to her.
The Bone Collector, and she still felt him leaning on her
like she was a rock instead of a scared girl, was nothing
like that.

She unfolded the second flimsy, and found herself
looking into the Bone Collector's face. Only it wasn't
him, not really. The expression was wrong. The hair
was really wrong. The eyes were wrong – beyond their
color, it was what she saw in them. And she read over
the personnel record of this Gabriel, noticing that he
was over two hundred years dead. Maybe a great-great
grandfather, or something. It really couldn't be what Mr

Rollins said.

She folded the flimsies back up and tucked them in her skirt pocket. The temptation to throw them away was fierce. But better, she decided, to let Hob take a look at it, and see what she thought. Better still to bring Coyote in and grill him about his damned brother and see if he knew what the play was. She didn't know what game Mr Rollins was trying to set up, but she was long done with letting TransRift play her, and she wasn't about to let the government man start. She, and Hob, were no one's pawns.

4 DAYS

Hob and her small crew rolled back in surrounded by a cloud of dust, the sunrise at their backs. Dambala had a little trailer attached to his motorcycle, which Mag was used to seeing on the back of Lobo's trike. The big, one-eared man was already in Ludlow, making miracles that tasted shockingly good out of their patchy stores. If anyone could stretch food, she supposed, it would be a mercenaries' cook.

Even better, Hob laughed as she hugged Mag. That alone let her forget for a moment how grim everything felt. Hob laughing was a rare sight to be treasured. "Guess it went good?" Mag asked.

"Was a fuckin' disaster," Dambala growled, heading past them into town.

"Any landing you can walk away from…" Coyote all but sang as Dambala walked off. Geri and Lykaios followed, then Freki, but he stopped to clap Mag on the shoulder, startling a smile out of her. She noted the Bone Collector's absence, but maybe it was for the best.

"Rough landin'," Hob said. "And Bala was feelin' a mite… pressed. But we got the osprey. Hati's sure enough he can fix it. Gave us a list to see what spare parts y'all might have in the mine, if you'll give us that as pay for what we done here so far."

"It's yours," Mag said. They'd already cannibalized everything useful, and there was a lot of machinery that didn't do them any good as long as the mine wasn't running. She'd much rather Hob be able to do whatever she could to get to their missing people. "Not just the spares. Anythin' you want out of there."

"Good." Hob waved a hand at Maheegan, who'd been standing by like a shadow, silent and waiting. "Get on the list. Take all the help you need." She looked back at Mag. "If we're gonna do this, I'm gonna need to pull all my people out. This site ain't gonna be small."

This wasn't just about Anabi, Mag reminded herself. It was a whole lot more. It was about stopping the Weatherman from burrowing into the planet like a tick, with him and TransRift never to be removed. "Then you do it, and don't worry none about us. We'll hold out. This is the only chance we got to get some hand in if the government men do show up." She hesitated, then offered, "You want any of ours to go with you?"

Hob looked startled, then shook her head. "I ain't to the point where I'm lookin' for bodies to throw."

"They're a little messy to ride over," Coyote added, wisely. "At any rate, we'd best get on with the search–"

"Wait." Mag felt that flimsy from Mr Rollins, crinkling in her pocket. "There's somethin' else. Come on. Both of you."

Hob's eyebrows went up. "Where we goin'?"

"Somewhere with fewer ears," Mag said. She headed back toward her house. It would be good enough. "Bone Collector not with you?"

"Stayed back with Hati to sleep."

"He got hilariously airsick," Coyote added.

That was neither here nor there with what she had in her pocket, but Mag had a hard time imagining the Bone Collector getting sick at all. He always gave the impression like he didn't quite live in his own body, just sort of rode it around. "Hope he feels better," she said, to fill the space while she let them into her kitchen.

"Why you askin'?" Hob asked.

In answer, Mag took the flimsies from her pocket, unfolded them, and spread them out on the table. She stepped back to let Coyote and Hob look them over, though Coyote finished reading long before Hob did. "The fuck is this shit?" Hob said.

Mag had her attention fixed on Coyote. "How trustworthy is this?"

"Trustworthy isn't the right word to use around Shige. Mother trained him well. The question is what he *wants*." Coyote tapped the flimsies with one finger. "If it is true, why does he want you to know this? Because he's asking nothing in return. And if this is a fabrication, well, why does he want you to believe that falsehood?"

"Pretty fuckin' obvious," Hob growled. "He gave us those coordinates. He knows we're goin' there. And he doesn't want the Bone Collector with us."

"I'd agree." Coyote snorted. "Not that he is going to get his way. We certainly can't fly that distance without him keeping the osprey aloft."

"Right," Hob said, though she didn't sound happy.

"D'ya think it is true?" Mag asked.

"He ain't like any Weatherman I ever seen," Hob said. "Sure hates them."

"It's frighteningly easy to hate what you are," Coyote remarked.

"Whose side are you on?" Hob glared at him.

He gave her an even look. "The side of not dying, preferably. It's your call, boss." When she glared at him, he raised his hands in surrender and backed out of the kitchen to leave them alone.

Hob gathered up the flimsies, refolding them without bothering to look at the old creases. Mag's heart hurt for her. She didn't know what was between Hob and the Bone Collector, but it was enough for there to be betrayal. "Don't be hasty," she said, carefully.

"It's fuckin' typical. Really fuckin' typical."

"It ain't the same," Mag said. She knew they were thinking in parallel, about the preacher's boy and the transmitters.

"Close enough."

Hob flinched away when Mag laid her hand on her arm. "I know him, in my own way. I know the Weatherman we had before, and the one we got now. They ain't nothin' alike. And I don't know what the government man's game is, but ain't neither of us here to be played, Hob."

Hob covered her face with one hand. "He's been strange, lately. Passin' strange."

"He's always been strange from what you said."

"Different kind of strange." Hob rubbed her eyes. "We're this fuckin' close, Mag. Like maybe if I wasn't a chickenshit, I would've fucked him already. Or if he had the gumption to ask, I don't think I could say no. And he weren't like that before."

But he hadn't almost died before, Mag thought. And he might have known Hob for years, but it was only lately that they'd been practically in each other's pockets. People changed, maybe even people made out of stone. But she couldn't blind herself to other explanations, even if they were hard to believe.

And yet. She'd helped him fight off the new Weatherman. She'd felt him, felt a lot from him, all that hate and fear, and also that warmth for Hob that he didn't seem to know how to deal with. Idiots, the both of them. "If this is even true," she said, trying to order her thoughts, "*if* this is even true, then he still ain't like the other Weathermen. We both know that. And you need him. *We* need him. He's the best weapon we got in this fight."

"He ain't a weapon. He's a person. A damn stupid one, betimes."

Mag laughed. That sounded like Hob getting her feet under herself. "You do what you got to, Hob. You know I'm at your back no matter what. But this ain't the same as it was, and you gotta get untwisted. Don't get yourself tricked into doin' someone's dirty work."

Hob let her hand fall away, and revealed a crooked, painful little smile. "Maybe if I'd listened to you before, it wouldn't have happened that time."

"Can't know about then. Guess we'll see about now," Mag said. She squeezed Hob's arm again. Who would have thought, the same words were coming out of her for everyone these days. "Remember who the real enemy is."

CHAPTER FORTY-SIX • *3 DAYS*

They made a long train back to base, piled high with every spare part they could dig out of the mine and the warehouses nearby. Hob could admit that maybe they'd gone a little overboard on that, but what didn't get used now, they might have use for later. Seemed fair enough payment for what they'd already done and what they would be doing.

Damn, but she didn't know how she kept falling in to being double paid for jobs, but she hoped she could keep it up if they survived the next few days.

She made sure Hati had everything he needed, made sure all the Wolves were ready to go and knew the shape of the plan they had, which was damn vague indeed since they had no idea what they were heading toward if and when Hati got the osprey fixed. All the while, she felt Coyote's gaze weighing on her, waiting. She hated it.

"Still asleep," Geri informed her, as she walked by. "Don't look like he's so much as moved since we left."

Well, she'd told him not to go anywhere, in case they needed him on the quick. She couldn't fault him on that even if she wished him back in the depths of whatever hell he came from. She climbed the back stairs of the barracks, up to the empty room they'd given him. She knew each creak and pop of these stairs, just as well as she'd known them the night she was sneaking up and down with a boy stashed in her room, when Old Nick had ambushed her.

It's not the same, she told herself. *Not hardly*. But she expected to smell the blood and ash scent of Old Nick around every corner. The only fucking mercy of the whole thing was that they weren't so full up they had to stash the Bone Collector in her old attic room. He was one floor down, stretched out on the narrow cot with his coat and shoes still on, hands folded over his stomach.

No, Hob thought, he wasn't like the Weatherman she'd seen. But that didn't make him less dangerous. Just a different kind of dangerous. Maybe not the kind of dangerous that needed to hear Mr Rollins's truths or lies. Maybe–

He blinked his eyes open and turned his head to look at her. "What's the matter?"

The folded, now very crumpled flimsy felt like a brand in her breast pocket. If she never showed it to him, she'd never know. And she'd never stop thinking about it, or waiting for him to grow into a different, less familiar kind of monster. She'd done her fair share of lying, but not to someone she might be idiot enough to care about. Hob took the flimsy out of her pocket, unfolded it, and offered it to him. She should say something, she thought, but the words just hooked sharp in her throat and wouldn't come. Because what the fuck did you say, at a time like this? *Tell me this ain't true? Tell me you ain't one of them?*

The Bone Collector frowned, puzzled, and took the flimsies. She saw his eyes move as he looked them over, first uncomprehending, then... something else. His expression went from stone to wide-eyed horror when he flipped to the second flimsy and found his own face looking back at him. "What *is* this?" he whispered.

"Don't know," Hob said, her voice somehow even. It should have been impossible when she'd eaten her own goddamn heart years ago, but she felt something in her chest break a little. She'd seen dying men who looked less hopeless than that. "Hopin' you can tell me."

"It's a lie, obviously," he said. But one hand crept up to clutch at his own hair – no, to feel it, his fingertips probing. "It's ridiculous."

"Then why you lookin' like that?" She wanted to believe him, so badly. "Like I gone and shot you in the gut."

His lips curled back in a snarl. "If *this* is what you think of me…" He stood. "I don't think we need continue." The Bone Collector moved forward, toward the door.

Hob leaned in the doorway, blocking him. Something was obviously cutting him deep, but she needed to know now, how much of him had been a lie. She was tired of falling for lies. "We ain't done yet."

With a shout, the Bone Collector shoved her out of the way. He was stronger than he looked, she remembered that. She hit the doorframe hard enough to knock the breath out of her. Wheezing, she dragged herself to her feet, though not fast enough to catch him as he ran for the stairs.

She knew running away like this. She knew it meant you kept running until you evaporated into nothing. She still had no idea what the hell was going on in his head, but she wasn't going to let him disappear. He had a bad record of doing that at the worst moment, and her own feelings aside, they needed him right now if they wanted a chance in hell of getting to the goddamn Well. "Oh, hell fuckin' no," Hob muttered, and forced her legs into action.

She clattered down the stairs at record speed, seeing

the pale hem of his coat flitting around every corner. She didn't bother yelling at him, because he never fucking listened anyway if her fist wasn't involved, and she needed all her breath and concentration to not break her neck. She slammed out of the door a bare three meters behind him.

The Bone Collector looked up at the sky, his pace slowing. The ground at his feet began to flow away in a movement Hob knew all too well. He took his first step down—

—and Hob hit him in the back, hard as a ton of rolling stone. She popped him right out of the ground like a shallow signpost and sent them both tumbling across the yard. And she'd been ready for this. She'd learned this kind of fighting from Makaya the Knife and Coyote. She rolled them until she came up on top, straddled over his chest. Then she drew back her fist and punched him for good measure, a solid right across the face.

The Bone Collector went limp, stunned. Hob shook her stinging hand out. "I said," she snarled, "we ain't done yet."

She realized it might have been the wrong tactic when he grabbed her around the throat. Stunned or not, his grip was strong. Air barely squeaked through her windpipe, and she knew that he was holding back. He could crush her neck one-handed if he wanted. "Let me go," he hissed.

Her eye watered. It was the almost being choked, she told herself. Not that sick, horrible feeling in her gut. Now was not the time for tears. "No. Not till you tell me if it's true. If you been lyin' to me." She drew a strangled breath. "I'm goddamn tired of everyone I care about but Mag lyin' to me."

Something shifted in his face, the anger unraveling like his heart had turned inside out. Somehow, that hurt worse to see. His grip loosened slightly, and she sucked in a long breath. Out of the corner of her eye, she saw movement, and heard a door open.

"Boss…" Coyote began.

She didn't dare look away from the Bone Collector. Just held up one hand, the one she'd used to punch him, a few threads of red bright on her knuckles. "Get the fuck back inside," she bellowed over the new scratch in her voice. "All of you. An' stay there."

The door closed, and they were left in silence again. She rested her hand on the Bone Collector's and carefully pulled each of his fingers from around her throat so that she could curl them in her hand, and rest that bundle against her chest. "I want to believe you. But you gotta give me somethin' to believe first."

The Bone Collector looked away first, his bright blue gaze shifting to the side like he was hoping to find an escape. "I don't know."

"Then why don't you tell me what got you so shook, if you know it ain't true?"

He licked his lips. "I don't know, though."

"Then tell me what you *do* know." She wasn't made for this kind of patience. She wished Mag was here. Then again, Mag probably wouldn't have had it in her to punch him in the first place.

"I woke up in the desert. Near Pictou. That's the first thing I remember."

Pictou had been destroyed decades ago. But if that document was to be believed, he was a couple of centuries old. Who knew how time worked for someone like him, anyway. Hob wished she had a cigarette, but she didn't want to let go of him to do it. "Then why you runnin'?"

"Because I don't remember anything else!" he shouted. "Don't you see? Every one of those abominations has acted as if they knew me. This new one told me to… to… *come home*." His voice hitched with despair. "And when I see myself in the mirror of the Well, I *am* one of them."

That was plain disturbing, and something he hadn't bothered to tell her before. "Do you want to?"

"What?"

"Do you want to *go home*, whatever that means to them?"

"No!"

Well, that was something. "Mag said even if that's true, you ain't like them. She'd know if you were. And I know you sure do hate 'em."

"And yet I am one of them."

"Mayhap." She finally gave in to her need and let go of his hand, then moved sideways to sit on the ground next to him. He didn't seem liable to run any more. Hob got a cigarette out of her case and lit it with a snap of her fingers. Probably said a lot about the Bone Collector's scattered state that he didn't even make a face. "We got a rule here. Past is dead. 'Cause Old Nick told me, don't matter a lick what you are or where you come from. Matters what you *do*."

He was silent, then slowly rolled over toward her. She let him put his head in her lap, his lean body curling around her folded legs. She even let herself put her hand in his hair, and now she knew what to look for, she found what he must have been feeling for there, along his scalp: the faint, faded lines of crisscrossing scars. Not quite the same as what she'd seen on Mr Green, but not so different either. She made herself keep stroking his hair instead of curling back in revulsion, which felt like the bravest goddamn thing she'd done since walking into the TransRift lab for Mag.

"The past doesn't simply die for wishing," he said quietly.

"All I care about is, what're you gonna do?"

"Have you take me to the Well," he answered. "And keep it from them."

She combed her fingers slowly through his hair, and told herself that it was just to make him feel better, nothing to do with her. "This just about stopping them, or about us takin' control ourselves?"

"Would you rather it be the second?"

She exhaled a long cloud of smoke, thinking. Before she'd been thrown into doubt, she had her answer. Should it be different now? Did she still trust him? She looked down at him, the way his hand now curled over the top of her thigh like he thought *she* might go running off. "Yeah."

"Then it will be done."

"You ain't tellin' me somethin'," she said, still watching his face.

"I don't know what will happen."

"But."

"I've touched the power before. This will simply be more of it."

"Before as in when you went missing?"

"Yes."

She huffed a sigh. "Guess I can live with that, since in the end you come back." It felt like there had to be more; there was still a darkness to his expression. But maybe she didn't want to think it would be worse than that. There was already enough hell they'd be flying through. "If Hati gets the damn osprey in the air."

"If that, too."

To the side, she heard the door open again, but she didn't bother to look. "Go about your business," she called. "And don't be gawpin'."

"Wouldn't think of it," Coyote said.

One hell of a spectacle they had to make, Hob thought

grimly, her sitting in the middle of the yard with a man in her lap. And right now, she didn't give a shit. She kept stroking his hair, like this might be the only excuse she ever had for it, and noted the red swelling already marring his cheekbone. "Gonna have a good bruise."

"It won't be the first."

"Tell 'em you got in a bar fight," she said. "Have Coyote make up a good story for you." And it felt good to see the Bone Collector smile, even if it didn't make all the uncertainty disappear.

CHAPTER FORTY-SEVEN • *1 DAY*

Jennifer Meetchim, Vice President of Production for the Outpost, was not in a good mood. Her assistant, James Rolland, had been gone for a week, which meant her correspondence was notably disorganized and her coffees never on time, hot enough, or the right flavor.

Worse, five days ago, thieves – which seemed a very light name to put to criminals of this caliber – had stolen one of the cargo ospreys. She eyed another non-report about the incident that graced her desk with disgust. The head of the investigation was pushing the theory that the osprey, which had been in the hangar for mechanical problems, must have crashed. After all, the airspace outside the transit corridor was known to be extremely hazardous now – which was the justification for his lack of results in searching. The chances of there being a good enough pilot available to unaffiliated bandits to nurse the wounded machine any kind of distance were vanishingly small. But the investigation had also turned up no wreckage, which piqued her suspicions.

On the other hand, after four days, it was just as likely that the wreckage had been buried by the ever-shifting sands of this backwater nightmare of a planet. Jennifer would have liked that to be the case, but she hadn't climbed to her place in the Corporate hierarchy by letting loose ends flop about.

She set the frustrating lack of progress aside to take up the dispatch envelope that had been brought in with the recent return convoy from the Oceania wildcat. Mr Rolland's precise handwriting greeted her eyes, which told her that at the least, this report would be concise and coherent: *Thick veins of the amritite in evidence. The engineers believe we are about to break through into some sort of natural cavern, so have pulled back for twenty-four hours to shore up the shaft properly. Survey results, though garbled, indicate that this will likely be the tip of the major discovery, should you care to join us.*

For the first time in days, Jennifer allowed herself a small, tight smile. If this really was to be a breakthrough, it would be excellent to witness as her moment of triumph. Hitting this sort of major discovery would be the capstone of her career on the production managerial tree, and a kick into the more rarified world of the home office. It would be nice to get back to civilization.

But would the current situation be able to stand a few days without her eye directly on them? She refreshed herself on the reports from the security perimeters around the rebelling towns. The miners, apparently unable to strategize how to push their supposed advantage, had hunkered down in those confines. Let them, she decided. It would be easy enough to maintain the security lines for a few more days, at which point the filthy ingrates would realize just how much TransRift had always done for them as they began to die of thirst. They'd come crawling in for help then. There'd already been a healthy number of defectors from all of the towns but Ludlow and Rouse, which they'd shipped off to the wildcat site in chains.

Satisfied with this line of reasoning, Jennifer wrote up

the orders and set up her office for a two-day absence. She certainly wouldn't want to spend more time than that out at the camp. The facilities were no doubt primitive, though she wasn't a stranger to roughing it when necessary. She sent one of the lesser administrators to see that she had her minimal luggage waiting for her at the landing field, since the next convoy was set to leave in a little less than an hour.

As she was setting her desk in order, the elevator doors to her office opened and someone Jennifer recognized vaguely as a runner from the communications office puffed across the smooth expanse of floor toward her.

"Compose yourself," she said sharply.

"Yes, sir. Sorry." The tech stopped and stood up straight. "I'm sorry, but there's an emergency communication."

"From the Oceania wildcat?" What could it be now?

"No," the tech said. "From orbit."

The words seemed incongruent. There wasn't a major shipment due for some months, though she supposed a minor resupply could be due. Those were always subjected to the whims of scheduling, and were Mr Rolland's to track. "And?" she asked, for lack of anything better to say.

The tech held out a reader to her. "Rift Ship *Jentayu* sends greetings from Captain Santos." The tech took a deep breath and continued, almost steadily, "And Federal Inspector Liu Fei Xing."

Meetchim did not drop the reader, nor did she shout at the tech, though she felt unsteady enough for a moment to do both. "Federal Inspector?"

"The full message is on the reader. They dropped us a packet of data cards in a drone."

"How far out are they still?" she asked. Of course, the ship wouldn't be in orbit yet. They must have only recently arrived in system and sent the message drone ahead.

"Our calculations say they'll be entering the atmosphere in ninety-six hours," the tech said.

She would have to commend Captain Santos for getting her at least this much advance warning to clean house. And what a mess the house currently was – gone were her thoughts of letting the miners sweat themselves to death. A clean sweep would have to be made, and immediately. They could claim an epidemic, and that would be a good reason to keep the inspector isolated to Newcastle, just in case they were the sort to try to slip their leash. "Get me Security Chief Lien. Immediately. Have him meet me on the way to the landing field."

"Yes, Ms Meetchim." The tech seemed grateful to escape.

Jennifer turned her attention to the reader, to scan over the full text of the message. The normal formal nonsense, the demand for full cooperation, the reminder of duty and privilege. That mattered little to her. Then she caught one stray line in the form text – *I expect all documentation to be prepared, as you have had several weeks' warning of my arrival. See notice provided in data card packet and hardcopy carried by Rift Ship* Kirin *for exact requirements. Compliance on this ground is mandatory and expected.*

She re-read the sentences again, to be certain. Mr Rolland had arrived back on the Outpost via the *Kirin*, shepherding Mr Yellow. He had given her all of the paperwork from the home office, and she'd read it to the letter, as was her job. There had been no mention of an inspector incoming.

Jennifer ran back to her desk, heels sounding sharp on her office floor, and scrambled through the flimsies Mr Rolland had brought. There was nothing in any of them. And Mr Rolland was not the sort to forget anything, or simply lose a document. He was utterly reliable, and had been for years. That was why she had brought him with her to the Outpost, why she'd entrusted him with so much sensitive business.

Yet the document was missing. Had someone in the home office removed it as a power play? She paged through the flimsies again, searching for a gap in the numbering. Everything was in order. The document either hadn't been sent, or had been removed and replaced seamlessly. Either someone in the home office or–

–or Mr Rolland. The thought seemed almost inconceivable.

Meetchim considered the number of near misses her assistant had undergone since coming to the Outpost. The few times Security Chief Lien had said he had lost track of Mr Rolland, and she'd dismissed it as incompetence on his part – because Mr Rolland was a mere secretary. And had her mere secretary been here rather than the Oceania wildcat, he would have received this message, instead of it coming directly to her hand.

Had she been played for a fool?

The very thought shook her to her core, first with betrayal, then with rage. No, she would not be hasty. She had attained this position because she wasn't one to act foolishly. Before she decided what to do, she would find a way to prove once and for all if Mr Rolland was loyal and being played by the machinations of Corporate, or if he had betrayed her.

And if the latter, he would be disposed of.

Jennifer stuffed the reader and all of the documents into her briefcase and hurried to the elevator. The building intercom was down due to Mr Yellow's absence, so she simply ran. It was unseemly, but she needed to catch her security chief before he left the building. She was in luck; the doors of the thirty-eighth floor opened to reveal him waiting for the elevator, his briefcase in hand.

"Ms Meetchim?" he said, shocked.

She jammed her fist onto the door open button. She couldn't risk that the greatest breakthrough of her career was being overseen by a traitor eight hours out of her reach. "Tell the flight commander that the convoy is delayed indefinitely until you and I are on board. And I want a security team sent to Mr Rolland's apartment."

CHAPTER FORTY-EIGHT • *12 HOURS*

The osprey rose slowly into the air, massive engines putting out a growling thrum that Hob felt right through her bones. The ascent was steady, the wings so even that Hob was pretty sure she could be standing on them and drinking a beer without spilling. Dust whipped and tore up from the dunes, billowing over the camouflaged walls of the base. Hob squinted against the dust and the bright overhead sunlight. The osprey's shape cut a black shadow as it continued to rise and turn, a little too awkward to be one of the great eagles.

The massive net they'd pulled over the osprey the day they brought it back sat crumpled on the ground. Coyote had put a foot on it to keep it from blowing away. "Looks like less of a death trap," he commented.

Hob pulled up the shortwave unit Hati had cobbled together to talk to the osprey. "How's it feeling, Bala?"

A pause, then the answer came back. "Like flyin' a fuckin' bathtub."

"That means he's fine," Coyote said.

"Land it if you're satisfied," Hob said into the shortwave. "And we'll start packin'." She turned the transmission off and looked at Coyote. "He gonna be OK to fly that long at night?"

"Oh, he'll piss and moan, but he was one of the best night flight operators I ever knew." Coyote grinned. "It's like riding a motorcycle. You never forget once you learn."

"Thinkin' we get on the road soon as can be, that'll have us where we're goin' after full dark." Freki and Geri had calculated the trip as taking roughly eight hours. "We can land distant, get in close on the motorcycles, and have the day to get a real good look-see." If she was lucky, she'd even be able to scope out where Mag's girl was and get her the hell out before the lead started to fly. The bigger the camp or town, the more security holes it tended to have if someone was clever and didn't mind belly crawling.

"Fair of a plan as any," Coyote said. "I don't particularly enjoy charging in with no intelligence, despite rumors to the contrary."

"The world will be fuckin' shocked." Hob looped the large net up over her arms and waited for Coyote to grab the other end. Between the two of them, they dragged it back into the metal-flavored, hot dark of the garage. They left the net there in a jumbled heap, for whoever ended up on her shit list to take care of later, if there was a later.

In the yard, Hob rang the alarm bell. No one hurried or looked surprised as they filed into the yard; they'd all known what was coming if Hati fixed the osprey and Bala didn't crash it. Hob looked them all over, expectant and many of them grinning. If derailing the Weatherman's train had been a middle finger raised in salute to TransRift, this promised to be a double-barreled gesture accompanied with fireworks and artillery.

They'd all signed up for this, she reminded herself, looking at the bulk of Lobo leaning on the doorway to the mess hall. No one was here because they thought they were going to die abed at a ripe old age.

"I want every motorcycle, every bit of kit, every weapon, and all the emergency spares in the osprey. Coyote's gonna oversee the loadin'." She crossed her arms over her chest. "Don't know what we're headin' into. We'll see it when we get there. But they ain't invented a wall yet could keep us out, 'cause we got the fire in our bellies. And we're gonna leave 'em in the dirt and spittin' teeth. You ready?" They cheered, god help them all. Hob grinned even with that weight on her shoulders, because she felt it too. She was tired of sitting and waiting, of chasing her tail. They were going to make it rain blood. "Then get movin'."

There was a scramble of activity, Wolves going to their various assignments. As Hob watched, Geri stopped by her elbow. "No fence?" he asked.

She knew what he was thinking, because it was the same thing she'd been thinking the minute the words left her mouth: the strange electric fence at the wildcat site, that had knocked out her, Coyote, and the Bone Collector. "We're gonna do a scout out once we're there," she said. "If they got that damn thing again, we'll spot it. Bet it won't hold for spit against bullets."

Geri laughed. "Most things don't."

She found the Bone Collector outside the walls, sitting on a drift of sand and watching Dambala land the osprey for the Wolves who waited with the first rank of motorcycles and supplies. She was surprised he still hadn't done his regular disappearing act, after they'd had it out. She'd been all set to add another scar to the growing collection on her hand. But no, he'd stayed in his assigned room, picked at whatever food Coyote thought to bring him, and kept to himself.

"You about ready?" Hob asked.

He didn't turn to look at her. "I didn't think I could

despise anything quite as much as I despise your motorcycle," he remarked. "Until I met that thing."

"You'll have your very own bucket," Hob offered.

He gave her a sharp look, then snorted at her grin. This was good. This was easy. Needling someone was a hell of a lot more in her experience than soft words or caring. "You're very thoughtful."

"Old Nick raised me right." She sank down onto the sand next to him.

"I am surprised you're not in the thick of it," he said.

"Privilege of rank. Plus Coyote told me I'd only be in the way. He's got some grand plan about how he's gonna load everythin' up, and all the devil's tricks won't be enough to save a body that gets in his path." She let the silence stretch, aware of the solid, cool mass of him in touching distance. She'd thought about visiting him over the last few nights while they waited for Hati to figure his way around the mechanics of an osprey. She'd also thought about those crisscrossed scars under her fingers, and his hand on her throat, and the look in his eyes like he was dying. She wasn't sure if she'd wanted to erase those things, somehow, or run from them herself. So she'd stayed away. He hadn't seemed to notice. And it was easier to think about it out here, in the open, where doing something about all those urges wasn't a possibility.

"I think about it, at times," he said. And for a moment, she thought he'd pulled some witch trick, and read her mind. But then he continued, "If I really am one of you or not."

"Would that be so bad?" she asked. Not that humans were any kind of fucking prize.

"I still don't know." He finally looked at her, an odd little smile on his lips. "I am always between, and I wish I could flow out through the cracks in the world." He reached down to find her hand, and curled their fingers together. "But then there is this. And I would miss it."

And tomorrow they could all be dead, Hob thought, an odd lump in her throat. It would be damn easy, to bridge that little gap between them. Out here, where anyone could see, because who the hell was going to stop her? She was Hob Fucking Ravani. Unless she stopped herself.

She must have leaned in a little closer, because he turned to really look at her. She'd never seen his expression so somber before. But maybe he felt it too, that nebulous whatever hanging between them that scared her spitless. "What do you want?" he asked quietly.

She knew, then, that she did want it, whatever she could wring out of him. And she didn't have time for being distracted. Not with the osprey back on the ground and being loaded. Hob gave his hand a squeeze, then freed herself and stood. She retrieved a long black cigarette from her case and lit it with a snap of her fingers. "Ask me when we get back."

Seemed the best way possible to keep both of them alive.

THE LAST DAY

CHAPTER FORTY-NINE

Shige shielded his eyes against the bright smear that was the sun's last sliver, slipping under the horizon. Beside him, Mr Yellow hummed to himself, his whole body turned toward the mine pit that sank deep beneath the pale salt surface. Shige had come to notice that the salt here was not so perfect white-gray, but rather shot through with veins of pink and red. In this light, it looked more like blood-filled capillaries than he might like.

It was Mr Yellow's humming that put him in mind of grim things. He couldn't really place it or explain the difference in words, but something about the tone and resonance had begun to make his skin crawl. Like there was an unheard echo, discordant, coming up through their feet. He wished that Mr Yellow would find the right note to harmonize, because really he could sing quite beautifully when he wanted – in their days here together, he'd shown he could, until the mine started getting deeper and the disharmony became too loud to ignore.

"Are you ready for dinner, Mr Yellow?" he asked, hoping the Weatherman would respond to him this time. More and more lately, he did not, and he'd begun to feel quite lonely about it. It was only him and Mr Yellow here, because the security men were brutal nitwits and the miners were far too ignorant to understand what was going on. He'd really begun to enjoy the Weatherman's company.

Mr Yellow swayed to lean in close. Shige felt his gaze draw toward Mr Yellow's, inexorable with something that was want and loathing mixed. He shut his eyes tightly in confused response. *Never look them in the eye*, he told himself, though he could no longer remember why.

Over the hot rock and metal smell of the mine site, he caught the dry, bloody undertone of the Weatherman. "Will it be today?" Mr Yellow asked.

"I don't know," Shige answered. He felt steady enough to open his eyes and focus on Mr Yellow's shoulder. "But we must be patient. And you must eat, to keep your strength up for when the miners finish their work."

Mr Yellow took his hand – when had the Weatherman started doing that? It had begun to feel like he'd always done it – with his dry, cold fingers and squeezed them. "We're all coming home."

"Of course." And this time, it was Shige who leaned toward him. It felt like that curious moment of looking over a bridge, the thread of thought swirling that perhaps this time, he ought to jump and be free – no. Not even enough to be an impulse or an urge, but the musings of a mind that believed it was safely under control, he knew. He kept a firm hold of Mr Yellow's hand and led him toward the Corporate dining tent. While only a tent, it was still far superior to anything the workers had been provided.

The camp was the most massive of its sort he'd ever been in. The camp facilities, including the temporary barracks on the north side where the miners were kept imprisoned, sprawled three kilometers in diameter, with the open pit of the mine a ragged hole nearly half a kilometer across at its center. The tailings pile to the north of the pit was an ever-growing mountain in miniature. The mine works, with two drive chains and elevators, and the start of the train station that was being built toward Newcastle to meet the crew coming from that end crowded around the pit. Dr Kiyoder's defensive perimeter couldn't extend out to surround the entire extensive site, but encircled the mine works and the managerial portion of the camp. A surprisingly solid temporary wall had been built around the pit as well; they were taking no chances about sabotage, since most of the workers were conscripts. That no one particularly cared if something crawled out of the desert and ate the miners was implicit.

Shige paused as a group of miners was escorted past by armed Mariposa guards, heading from the mine back to their little prison camp. The miners clanked as they walked, shackled. One, a dark young woman whose hair hung lank around her head, looked hard at him as she passed. The ragged swirl of her now-mottled gray and black skirts hid the chains. Shige felt a shock of recognition that he quickly strangled: she'd been at the meeting he'd had with Magdala Kushtrim. He wondered if Mag was somewhere in the camp as well, or if she'd been killed in the raid. Either way, it would certainly light a fire under Hob Ravani, which would only benefit him – though hopefully she wouldn't show up until Mr Yellow had finished with the mine.

To his intense relief, the woman looked away and said nothing. He made a mental note to see if he could speak to her on the sly, later. She might have interesting information.

As she passed by, Mr Yellow leaned toward her, and Shige tightened his grip. "Is something the matter, Mr Yellow?" he asked, pretending to have noticed nothing at all about the miners.

Mr Yellow sniffed at the air, and then his mouth rearranged itself into a puzzled frown. "We thought we smelled the light, but…"

"You must be hungry," Shige soothed. It would be no surprise if an associate of the ragtag little resistance had some amount of blood contamination. "That sometimes makes things a bit confusing." He tugged at Mr Yellow's hand to get the Weatherman walking.

As they headed toward the dining tent, the low hum of osprey engines built in the air. Shige glanced back in the direction of Newcastle and picked out the moving lights in the sky. "The convoy's a bit late," he observed.

"There's a surprise," Mr Yellow said.

He hadn't heard the Weatherman speak in such a way before. Bemused, Shige asked, "One I'll like?"

Mr Yellow tilted his head, like he was listening to something only he could hear. "You'll be going home too." Then he started humming to himself again, and didn't seem to hear anything more Shige said.

He ought to be excited at the prospect, but it did mean he'd need to do his duty and dispose of the Weatherman. He was far too dangerous. Shige found he didn't have the stomach for it any more, perhaps because he'd really begun to feel the similarities between the two of them, beings created in a lab to be used as tools. And Mr Yellow was so good to him, so dear, so important. Curious and concerned now, Shige watched the convoy land on the saltpan surrounding the camp. The massive stretch of extinct ocean was effectively one endless landing field. They could bring the next rift ship down here if they wished, and easily, so long as there wasn't concern about native attacks.

He watched the crews begin to unload crate after crate of cargo, then saw Ms Meetchim, immaculate as always in her suit, exiting the final osprey. Security Chief Lien followed behind her, but headed in a different direction. Shige tugged his hand away from Mr Yellow's fingers and hurried forward to meet her.

"Ms Meetchim, it's lovely–" he started.

"Very good, Mr Rolland. I'm here to oversee the final breakthrough." She kept walking, not even really looking at him as he caught up. She headed straight for one of the cooled tents that had been designated for meetings. No doubt she'd studied the camp layout on the way.

Shige kept up with her doggedly. "Of course. How may I best assist you?"

"Find a tent for me. Not shared. And send the engineers and the camp security chief to meet me." They reached the tent and she stepped inside. "This will be a closed meeting, and I do not wish notes taken. Be about your business, Mr Rolland." The door, thick canvas on a metal frame, shut in his face.

He took a step back, both mental and physical. What had happened, to put her in such a mood? A tremble of apprehension and excitement ran through him – had the inspector arrived? But why, then, was he being shut out? There was little he could do to prepare, but he would do as directed to maintain his cover as he thought it over.

Mag saw Anabi, in the twisting confusion of smoke and gas and floodlights. A greenbelly had her by the skirts and dragged her across the ground as Anabi silently screamed and stabbed him over and over again with the knife she'd brought to cut those pies. No blood came out of the gashes and tears in the greenbelly's armor, just dribbles of blue sand. Anabi drove the knife into the ground, clutched it, and the seam on her skirts started to rip under the greenbelly's fingers, *pop pop pop pop–*

Not splitting threads. Splitting air around bullets. Mag threw herself out of her tangled blanket, her head whirling in confusion. Her room was caught in the soft place between light and dark, the orange-pink of final light edging in between her curtains. She'd been sleeping days since the first attack, little catnaps really, trying to be ready for the next.

Another crackling volley split the air. Mag pulled on her shirt and skirt, and habit made her tuck Uncle Nick's little pistol in her pocket. As she ran out of her house, she slapped every interior door she passed, shouting, "To the walls! Get to the walls! Everyone!"

She wasn't the only one tumbling into the street. More people spilled from their houses, half-dressed, carrying the few guns they had or pickaxes and hammers. Mag fumbled up Clarence's breather mask, which she'd grabbed on her way out. They'd all learned their lesson at the last attack. Right before she slipped the mask over her face, she spotted Omar, trying to run and buckle his belt at the same time. "Get the kids!" she shouted at him. "Get them out first!"

Because it wasn't the soft, faintly hollow sound of gas canisters they were hearing now. It was bullets, real ones. And then faint screaming. Omar turned on his heel, and ran off in the other direction. Mag kept going, breath loud and hollow behind the mask, running for her spot on the wall. *Why now?* she wondered, as her feet thumped the hard-packed dirt. *Why now?* They should have had time, while the greenbellies tried to force them to yield with thirst, according to Coyote's brother. It was too soon.

She climbed the ladder to the wall walk, right on the heels of the woman in front of her. Her heart sank as soon as she saw over, to the wall of floodlights and headlights that surrounded the town. A voice crackled and boomed over a speaker fuzzed with static: "I'm here to take my town back. Keep resisting!" She recognized it as Longbridge's voice, and then someone yanked her down as another volley of gunfire cracked. Chips of hot, shattered synthcrete cut her cheek as they whistled past. Someone nearby screamed, and there was the meaty sound of a body falling down, off the wall.

Didn't matter if it was too soon, Mag thought grimly. The greenbellies were at their door. Knowing the reason or not wasn't going to save anyone's life now.

"Keep your heads down!" Mag shouted. "Hard hats. Get your hard hats on." She didn't have one of her own, and had never been issued one. But there were extras now. She should have grabbed Clarence's. "They try to send a message in?"

"Nothing," the work gang leader for this section of the wall said. Mag recognized her voice, even muffled by the mask. "Caught a group of them heading for the wall with some charges and shot 'em." She ducked down lower behind the wall. "Guess they're mad we ruined their surprise, because then they all come up."

"Ain't the only shady thing they're goin' to try," Mag said.

"I know," the woman answered grimly. "Already passed it down the wall."

"Good." She didn't know what else to say. The bigger problem was that none of them were soldiers. They could crouch behind a wall and shoot back, but what happened if – *when* – the walls got breached? Longbridge was out for revenge, and he'd already murdered Clarence.

Mag waited for a pause in the fire and peeped up over the wall. She drew her pistol from her pocket, aimed it like Old Nick had told her, and… hesitated. She looked down the barrel at a greenbelly, their face obscured with a mask. But there was a person in there, she could feel it even at this distance. Killing a person was a hard thing, a big thing, a terrible thing.

The greenbelly looked right at her and raised their rifle. Mag squeezed the trigger. Her shot went wild, and she threw herself down just in time to avoid the return shot. She cursed herself a million times a fool for hesitating, and for not ever practicing with Coyote. Hell of a time to realize that for all her carrying the little pistol around, she had no idea what to do with it.

But there was something else she could do. She could feel them all, out there, all those minds, intent on Ludlow. Mag shoved the useless little gun at the work gang leader – she'd know what to do with it – and pulled herself up again. She focused down on the greenbelly she'd been going to shoot, who'd almost shot her. She felt them – him – felt his mind, felt him ready to bend as she put more and more pressure on his will. She felt his intent, felt the shape of his orders, felt the blood waiting to spill out on either side.

She'd done this to Odalia, and hated herself almost as much as she'd hated Odalia. But that no longer mattered. She could stand to hate herself a little if she was still alive to do it on the other side. If even one more of her miners was still alive because she'd done this terrible thing.

She felt rather than saw the greenbelly shaking and trembling. His name sat on the tip of her tongue, but she refused to acknowledge it. She didn't want to know. She just pushed and pushed, blood thundering in her temples, until he raised his rifle again, turned, and opened fire on the guard next to him.

CHAPTER FIFTY

Mr Yellow hummed in the full dark, with the stars drowned out by the camp floodlights – they had been going twenty-four hours here ever since the second shipment of battery stacks arrived. The Weatherman stood on the flat as close to the mine pit as Shige would allow him, gently swaying in time with his own music.

"Ms Meetchim wants to see you now," a woman said behind them.

Shige turned toward her, noting the green uniform, the rifle held less casually than he liked in her pale hands. He didn't recognize the security guard, which likely meant she'd come in with Ms Meetchim on the latest convoy. "Is she still in the second meeting tent?" he asked.

"Yeah."

Shige glanced at Mr Yellow. "Will you–"

"I'll stay with him," the security guard said. "Go. It's urgent."

"All right." Something about this didn't feel right at all, and he'd learned to trust his instincts on such things. "Do remember to not look him in the eyes."

"Yeah, yeah," she said, moving up to crowd him out of his place.

"Goodbye," Mr Yellow murmured.

The finality in that word, so uncharacteristic of Mr Yellow, made Shige feel bereft and stilled his feet. But the guard gave him a pointed look and he forced himself into motion again. Disquieted, he took a quick mental inventory of what he did have on him. No gun, because he never carried a gun – it was too easy to be caught with one. He had a garrote concealed in the hem of his jacket, which would only be useful if there was no audience. He also had a few microinjectors and darts. A pitiful defense. But he'd learned on his mother's knee that if it came to violence, the situation was too far out of control anyway.

The atmosphere inside the tent was thick with tension, and he knew he was in serious trouble the moment he stepped over that threshold. Ms Meetchim waited there for him, along with three guards and Security Chief Lien. All regarded him with looks ranging from uncaring to cold hostility. He fought the urge to run at the sight. No one had threatened him yet; he still might be able to talk things into a useful circle. Running would simply get him shot in the back.

"Ms Meetchim, I was told you needed to see me?" he said, with his usual studied pleasance.

Ms Meetchim held out a data reader to him, which he took. "Please read aloud what I've highlighted. I wish your opinion on it," she said.

He glanced over it, and the words washed across his skin like icy water. Why yes, he was in a great deal of trouble. But he would keep playing the game in the hopes he could salvage it. What other option did he have? So in his most neutral tone, he read the quote as if it was just another bit of business: "*I expect all documentation to be prepared, as you have had several weeks' warning of my arrival. See notice provided in data card packet and hardcopy carried by Rift Ship Kirin for exact requirements. Compliance on this ground is mandatory and expected."* He lowered the reader. "This is rather alarming."

"Don't bother," Meetchim said. "I had your apartment thoroughly searched."

Surprise. He ought to be surprised. Shocked, even. And he was, simply not in that way. "Did you find anything interesting?"

"A curious absence of certain things," Security Chief Lien said. "And unmarked data cards."

"I'd no idea that was a crime."

As if he hadn't spoken, Ms Meetchim continued on: "What I would like to know is for whom you are actually working."

There was no getting out of this, no lies he could spin quickly enough. Meetchim had already made up her mind, and Lien as well. Shige wasn't certain if it was more or less horrifying that they'd come up with something that was at least partial truth. The question now was how he would take this dive down. Protesting his innocence? He doubted that would save him from being thrown into the desert. Should he reveal himself as an agent of the Federal Union? There was the barest of chances that it might save his skin; with an inspector coming, who would want to have to explain the mysterious disappearance of the on-planet agent? But that would also compromise an investigation he'd put years of his life into, and warn them just how much the BCRE knew of their plans and actions. And what about Mr Yellow – no, that was a ridiculous thought, Mr Yellow was perfectly safe.

Shige was inclined to be loyal, perhaps programmed for it with genetic or behavioral modification, and even knowing that intellectually didn't make the urge to protect his mission any weaker. Going meekly to his death while casting up a smokescreen of corporate espionage would serve that purpose well. Ayana would want that, and while he was sure retired Prime Minister Hamadi Rollins would weep at his younger son's by-necessity secret funeral, neither of those things did *him* any good. He was an empty vessel, always filled with the purpose of others. How fitting that he'd end up as an urn empty of ashes.

"Well?" Ms Meetchim said, impatient.

And then he thought, of all incongruent things, of Kazu, the night he'd left. Kazu, face almost lost to shadow as he stuffed a few belongings into his backpack and prepared to abandon his precocious little brother to the mercies of the schooling he hadn't been able to handle himself. Kazu, reaching out to ruffle Shige's hair with genuine affection, his eyes dark with... yes, regret. Shige heard his last words clearly in that moment, as if Kazu reached forward from the past: *Sorry, kiddo, but they finally emptied me out on smiles and lies. All I've got left is "fuck it" and run.*

And of all things, the thought made a little smile quirk Shige's lips. "Fuck it," he said, trying it on for size.

"Excuse me?" Ms Meetchim said. Lien's thin eyebrows arched high on his smooth forehead. James Rolland wasn't the sort to use coarse language, after all.

What *would* Shigehiko Rollins want, if he ever managed to want something strictly for himself? He still didn't know, torn between duty to the Federal Union and his strange, ever more urgent need to care for Mr Yellow. But he'd never find out if he didn't try to live for it rather than die for everyone else's purposes. With a bare movement of his fingers, Shige brought out two of the microdarts from his sleeves. "I said *fuck it*."

Meetchim opened her mouth. Shige moved, muscles as fast as a human could be genetically tuned, and flung the darts. Lien slapped at his neck, like he'd been bitten by an insect. Then his mouth went wide and open, and he sucked in one final, strangled breath before he crumpled. One of the security guards hit the floor at the same time. And Shige was already thumbing out two more of the darts, hands whipping to fling those as well. Two more guards down. The last of the guards, the last of his immediately reachable darts. He reached to rip the garrote from his coat hem as nearby the sharp retort of a gunshot sounded, incongruously, because the guards were all down.

Oh, and what a curious sensation. He wasn't aware of pain for a moment, merely that he couldn't breathe, like he'd been kicked solidly in the chest. He staggered, fingers no longer so precise as he still fumbled at his coat hem. He caught sight of Ms Meetchim, wide-eyed and her hair disordered for perhaps the first time in her life. She held a small, snub-nosed revolver, and a corner of his mind made the complimentary note that she was standing quite properly with it.

She shot him again.

Shige dropped to the ground. He clutched uselessly at his stomach with one hand. He needed to move, he told himself, needed to move, she was *right bloody there*.

More guards burst into the tent. One ended that line of thinking by kicking him hard in the stomach, and oh, there was all of that pain, driven out from where it had been hiding. He sprawled back on the floor.

Ms Meetchim stood over him, her shoulders moving in time with her harsh breaths. Then the barrel of a rifle swallowed up his view. "Want me to?" someone asked.

"No," Ms Meetchim said from back behind that rifle. Her voice shook, then firmed. "He doesn't deserve such mercy. Take him out onto the flats and drop him there. Let the eagles have him while he's still fresh."

How… Promethean, Shige thought numbly as two

guards grabbed his arms and dragged him from the tent. His head lolled back and he saw, not so distant, Mr Yellow looking at him. The Weatherman tilted his head back, scenting the air, then bent to look the security guard next to him in the eye. She did not look away.

It hurt, a little, to think he'd been replaced so quickly. Why didn't Mr Yellow want him any more? He'd been summarily discarded in favor of some ill-educated brute in a green uniform, no longer useful. As the guards dumped him into one of the jeeps – oh, that hurt, quite a bit, he felt all tangled up both inside and outside – he heard a muffled rumble and shouting from the direction of the mine.

The Bone Collector flew over the shell of the world, and he did not like it any more this time than he had last time. But he focused, on the whispering currents of air, the lines of magnetic force that swirled from the vortices at the planet's heart, the other lines of nameless energy in whispering blue that spun out from entirely different vortices and poured forth from the Well. And he found, if he used his body as a stable point, with the ground no longer firm under his feet, the experience was at least slightly less horrifying.

The energy rippled, waves in a pool, more and more violent. They were close to the center of all things now, the lines thick, and trying to sort them all left him faintly dizzy. But it told him that something was happening, something that could not possibly be good. Still holding that link to his body, he slid close, rode those waves, and then heard the discordant sound. The Weatherman. The *thing*.

His brother/cousin/son. The thought sickened him all over again. He hid himself in the swirls of energy and watched the patterns, felt how they moved around the Weatherman, how close he stood to the center. Not quite there, too high, but in the scale of the world they overlapped.

And he felt the Weatherman reach. Felt one of the lines of power begin to twist into something discordant, suiting itself to the Weatherman's harmony.

And felt the roof of the world begin to crumble, cave in to reveal that beating, alien heart, ripe to be plucked out.

No.

He exploded into physical waking, his eyes flying open, and jerked against the restraining harness that crossed his chest. For a moment, a different sort of panic welled in him, one without name, and he fought to swallow it down. He still heard the world's song, the discordant note. He focused on that.

"You OK?" the man next to him – Raff, that was his name – asked.

The Bone Collector ignored him, scrabbling free of the harness. Legs unsteady, he made his way up the narrow ramp to the cockpit. All of the motorcycles and supplies the Wolves had brought had still left nearly half of the cargo hold empty. His steps might have echoed, but for the roar and hum of the wind outside.

He nearly tumbled into the cockpit, catching himself before he ran into Hob. She stood between the two seats up there, occupied by Dambala and Coyote. All three looked at him sharply, though Dambala just as quickly jerked his attention back to the front. Outside the cockpit, the sky was black, the stars brilliant overhead, but washing out toward the horizon in the light that blazed up from the new scar in the ground.

"What is it?" Hob asked, though she had to shout to be heard. She had an unlit cigarette between her lips, half-mangled from chewing. "Or, no. Can it wait? We're gonna set down in a few minutes."

"He's there," the Bone Collector said, loudly. It should have been obvious to them. How at least Coyote wasn't reeling with the sensation was beyond him.

"He?"

"The Weatherman. He's at the Well."

"Shit." She grimaced. "But we kind of figured…"

"More than that, isn't it?" Coyote asked.

"There's no time." He grabbed Hob's shoulder and squeezed, trying to convince her of the urgency in the only way he really knew. "They're breaking through. He's there. We have to stop him *now*."

Hob stared at him, uncomprehending, then began to swear as his words made the needed impact.

"Boss?" Dambala asked.

"How much time?" Hob asked, staring him in the eye.

"We may already be too late."

She bared her teeth. "I ain't ever believed that." And she leaned in to shout to Dambala: "We're goin' straight in. Guess we gotta hope the element of surprise makes up for the element of not scoutin'."

CHAPTER FIFTY-ONE

The bodies had been cleared away out of the tent and most of the mess cleaned up, though the bloodstains on the flooring material remained. Jennifer Meetchim tried to ignore them, from the irregular pool where the traitorous Mr Rolland had landed to the long streak showing where he'd been dragged out. She had no sympathy for him, and was already cursing herself a fool for reacting emotionally in anger and not thinking to have him interrogated. His outburst hadn't answered the question of who he worked for, though obviously he was highly trained and very well armed. The microdarts had been collected from the bodies of Chief Lien and the three guards, on the hopes analysis of them would yield some useful detail.

But now she was left in a tent that smelled of antiseptic and gunpowder, her hands shaking faintly, and in want of a coffee. Curse Mr Rolland anyway. All of this was his fault. Two guards stood watch over her in the tent, in case Mr Rolland had accomplices, and she was sorely tempted to send one out to find her something hot to drink. It would settle her nerves.

Another subterranean rumble rolled through the ground beneath her. A cavern, the engineers had assured her as they rushed out, after the first set of shocks. This was not unexpected. But would she please stay here, as it was too dangerous for her to approach before they had everything properly shored up. They'd seemed concerned over already having lost some miners and wanted to pull the rest back. The caution was so counterproductive, and she'd refused permission.

The door of the tent opened, and Jennifer watched a security guard step in. She recognized the woman vaguely as one of Lien's personal picks, who had accompanied them to the site. She'd escaped Mr Rolland's little massacre by being sent to watch Mr Yellow in the meantime. The guard stopped and looked at her, though it felt more like she stared through to a point beyond Jennifer's body.

"Yes?" Jennifer said, impatient. "Shall I come out to the mine?"

The guard did not answer, except to raise up her rifle in one motion. "We are no one's tool." A trickle of blood ran down from her nose. The barrel yawned wide, filling Jennifer's vision. It spat fire, roared–

And out near the mine, Mr Yellow, who seemed so intent on the open pit, smiled. A fresh wash of delicious blood scent filled the air as another rumble shook the ground, one more layer of rock standing between him and the meat of the world falling away.

The osprey lurched, tilting down even more. The Bone Collector's hands clutched tightly at Hob's waist. She didn't particularly blame him, since her own stomach rolled with the sensation of arrowing down while weaving and facing backwards. She gripped the handlebars of her motorcycle tighter. "How's it goin', Bala?" she asked.

"It's goin'," came his grim reply over the shortwave.

"Gonna put us down on the west side."

It would mean a lot more to her if she had any kind of idea what the west side of the camp looked like. Next to her, she felt all of the other Wolves, everyone but Coyote and Dambala, tense and waiting. Would have been safer if they'd all still been strapped in, but all they'd have going for them was the surprise of an osprey jamming down out of nowhere and them getting out as quick as possible.

"They're asking for flight codes," Coyote said a moment later.

"You got anythin' for them?"

"Of course not," Coyote said. "Get ready."

Rattles and pings went across the hull of the osprey in a wave. Hob recognized that now as gunfire. The osprey bucked, lurched. Diablo and Conall went over, their motorcycles half on top of them, while everyone else hung grimly on and stayed upright by grace of the strength in their legs.

"Change of plans," Dambala suddenly said. "They just fuckin' blew out our landing hydraulics. You're gonna have to jump it."

"Are you fuckin' serious?" Geri shouted.

"Slow it down as much as you can, then," Hob said. "Get the engines goin', boys."

Hati and Lykaios had hopped off their own motorcycles to get Diablo and Conall righted. They all scrambled to get back in order. The faint hum of the electric motors was lost in the roar of the wind, another wave of shots pinging and thumping off the armored belly of the osprey. Hob stared at the closed cargo door and wished like hell she was still up front so she could see where they were going.

The osprey shifted again, slowing abruptly. They all rolled a few meters backwards, scrambling to get their boots firm on the rough metal deckplates. Hob squeezed the brakes on her motorcycle and fought for balance as the Bone Collector's hands tightened another notch. "I can't fuckin' breathe, you keep doin' that."

"What?" Coyote said.

"Nothin'." Of course the Bone Collector couldn't hear her. He always refused to wear a helmet.

"Get ready!" Dambala shouted.

A metallic *crack* and then more wind, how had she ever fucking thought there was wind before, came howling up through the cargo door as it began to move. Amber alert lights swirled into life around it. Through the ever widening gap in the door, Hob caught a dizzying smear of pale salt, lit with a splash from the floodlights. The osprey lurched lower, swung crazily wide. She could about feel Dambala wrestling with the controls. Sure sounded like his teeth were gritted around the curses that streamed over the shortwave. The osprey banked harder, then evened out. The ground rushing past below still seemed damn fast, salt and salt and salt and then the bright white of the floodlights bouncing back.

"Good as it's gonna get!" Dambala shouted. "Go!"

Hob had made her life out of trusting her people. She didn't hesitate. She revved her engine to a pitch she felt squeal up through her bones, and let go the brake. Her motorcycle leapt forward, gathering speed down the ramp of the cargo door. Then she was out over open space, hanging, the Bone Collector trying to squeeze the breath out of her, maybe crack a few ribs in the process.

Well, she thought in that split second. This was one hell of a way to die. Take that, you old bastard.

Gravity arced her down and slammed her into the salt. Her teeth crashed together near shattering, her spine compressing like she'd be a goddamn half a foot shorter when this was all over. The salt wasn't as smooth as it looked, and that saved her, let the chain mesh tires bite enough to keep from just sliding out. She fishtailed, leaned, arms and legs tight to burning as she fought for balance, grasped it, held.

And then where the fuck was she?

Hob tried to make sense of what she sped toward: the blinding splash of light, the chattering mine works and fencing that reared up from where the pit had to be, the sprawl of tents, the boil of people. She hazarded a quick glance behind her, saw a ragged line of motorcycles forming up. She didn't have time to count, but she saw three down behind them, motorcycles broken to pieces. In the distance, she saw the osprey banking again, coming back. Good. If Dambala buzzed the site as many times as he could, it would add to the confusion. Had to be Coyote's idea, since confusion was his trademark.

She did a quick calculation of where she saw green and blue, where she saw the most machinery concentrated. That had to be the overseer side of the camp, since she bet they wouldn't trust the miners to be close to the machines when they weren't working. "South side," she shouted into the helmet radio. The channel was crystal clear for once – thanks to the Bone Collector's presence. "Right hand as we're facin'. South side. Go for the fuckin' greenbellies. Don't give 'em a chance to group up. Diablo and Conall…" she waited for confirmation from them that they'd made it to the ground "…head north. See if you can get the miners riled up."

They needed more confusion, more chaos, and she felt that element surging in her blood. Shouting with not effort, but some kind of wild joy because it was so damn easy, somehow, she felt almost drunk with the fire that surged at the hint of her calling, ripped a wave of fire up from deep beneath her feet like she was just the channel of it, not the source. White-hot flame burst into a halo around her hand, and she swept it across the distant tents like she'd wipe sand away from a window. The flame howled through the air, ropes of heat surging into shimmering being in a wave that flowed out from her. The people and tents directly in front of her smoked, sparked, burst into explosive flame. The osprey dove down over, Dambala shouting words in her ear when she couldn't rightly understand words any more, its propellers ripping up whirlwinds of flame and smoke.

A wave of howling boomed from helmet speakers beside and behind her. And ahead, a great gout of dust shot up from the mine pit as the ground below trembled. The dust curled and swirled around a lone figure standing still outside the wall, ignoring all that went on around him: the Weatherman.

"They've breached the walls! They've breached–" the miner's shout cut off with a gurgle, then a wet thud as she fell from Ludlow's wall.

Mag looked up, sluggish, her attention divided in a half dozen different directions as she tried to maintain control of the few greenbellies she'd found most vulnerable, to keep sowing chaos. One of them blipped out of her consciousness just like the miner had, felled by a bullet from his own side. "The walls?"

Brother Rami – when had he gotten here? – dragged her away from the edge, toward the ladder. Only then did she notice how many around her were dead, sprawled and bleeding. One of the survivors gave her a push from the other side. "Move, move!"

Her control on the greenbellies fumbled and unraveled. She felt slammed back into the confines of her own head, and it left her reeling.

"Come on, Mag, one foot in front of another, down the ladder," Brother Rami said, his voice urgent. "They've broken through on the west. We're dumpin' fire gel into the warehouses to slow 'em down, but we have to *go*."

Give them the walls? It was horrible, and impossible, and she didn't know how they'd win if that was their only option. Something tickled Mag's cheek, and she tried to ignore it as she felt her way down the ladder. Her head felt raw and stuffed with needles, but she wasn't ready to stop. She couldn't afford to stop. "Where are we going?"

"Back to the churchyard. Omar got the area barricaded. We can try to hold out there." Rami helped her down off the last few rungs of the ladder. Hand firm on her arm, he started pulling her down the street. The air was already so thick with smoke or perhaps gas that she couldn't see more than her hand in front of her. Through the mask, every breath was acrid in her throat. And the cracking of rifle shot never stopped, nor did the sound of running feet.

"Hold out for what?" Mag asked. They weren't expecting help. She'd sent Hob away, to go look for Anabi. To find the Bone Collector's Well. That had been the only way, hadn't it? Her cheek tickled again and she swiped her free hand at it, her fingers coming away slick with blood. She'd taken a ricochet or a graze and not even noticed.

"For a miracle," Brother Rami said grimly.

More running feet approaching, but Mag knew already that these were different, felt them, even as they burst out of the billowing smoke. Shields and armor and lights cutting beams in the dark. Their rifles came up, and Brother Rami shoved Mag behind him. She reached out a hand, like she'd grab the one in the lead, and yanked him to the side. The greenbelly lurched into his fellows. The volley of shots went wild, though Brother Rami grunted, something that sounded a lot like a curse.

While Mag had the greenbelly turning and whipping his rifle to bludgeon at his fellows, Brother Rami all but picked her up and ran. She half-heartedly moved her feet, but didn't get traction on the hardpan of the street until they were around the corner, out of sight.

Once she was under her own power, Brother Rami sagged. Mag hurried to catch him, get herself under his arm. Her hand, against his side, came up sticky. He hissed between his teeth. And she had to focus, now, not on the greenbellies bearing down on them, but just putting one foot in front of another, remembering which street to turn at. She'd never been the churchgoing sort.

"None of this," she gasped at him, using the words to anchor herself here, and not have her reaching back to those small, petty minds behind them. "You ain't goin' nowhere till you bring us that miracle."

Brother Rami gasped out something like a laugh. "I wouldn't dare."

The buildings on either side gave way, just as a dark barrier loomed up in front of them. Despair clutched at Mag's heart – had she taken a wrong turn, distracted and disoriented? Then there was the scrape of furniture being moved, and familiar hands took hold of her and Brother Rami and dragged them inside.

"See to Rami," Mag gasped, slapping the helpful hands away. She reeled back around to get up against the barricade and stare out into the smoke, waiting to see light beams cut through it. "I've got this."

And then she waited in silence, listening to the miners around her cough and murmur, the sound of rifle fire coming ever closer. There wasn't anything else to do. This was their last stand.

CHAPTER FIFTY-TWO

A bullet ricocheted off Hob's helmet, slamming her head sideways. Ears ringing, Hob got herself straightened. She drew one of her revolvers, keeping one hand steady on the handlebars. Most of the balance was in the legs anyway. "Scatter! Use the mine works for cover!"

The Wolves' line broke, weaving to put the mine structures and the security wall between them and the south part of the camp. Hob's attention fixed on the Weatherman, so damn near. She dimly heard the Bone Collector shouting behind her, but couldn't make anything useful out. She raised her revolver and tried to use the trick she'd pulled on Mr Green – there was so much fire all around her, just waiting to be born boiling in her blood. She pulled and pulled that power and packed it into one bullet, aimed at the Weatherman's back, and fired.

Light exploded around that thin form, swirled and mixed with the dust whirling around him, and fountained away. And the Weatherman did not move.

Another bullet screeched across her helmet. Hob darted out for a quick loop, taking aim at one security guard in the harsh floodlight and squeezing off a round. Flame spat toward a guard in green. They screamed as they started to burn. Bullets spit up chunks of more salt around her tires as she gunned it away. "Hati and Lobo, get us—"

A strangled scream over the radio, and she looked around in time to see a motorcycle spin out, the rider tumbling like a ragdoll with a crooked neck: Raff. The first to go, but not the last, Hob knew, if they didn't get the Bone Collector into the mine. And even then, who knew what would happen. They might all be sprawled out on the saltpan before dawn.

So she kept going, because that was all she could do, "—a hole in that wall. Top priority. Everyone else, keep movin', keep 'em confused. And watch the goddamn Weatherman!"

"'m at the wall," Lobo said. "Northwest, you can see one of the drive chain housings peepin' up. Get me covered. Hati, get your ass movin'."

The low hum of the osprey got loud again, too loud, wind whipping down over them as Hob turned her motorcycle toward Lobo's location. She could drop the Bone Collector off, and be able to move better after. Do some more damage, she figured. She hazarded a glance up to see the osprey going in low, bright orange flame licking out of two of its engines. She clutched at that flame with her hand and ripped it down out of the sky, driving it into the ground and the greenbellies nearest like lightning. Fire bloomed around more screaming, but that couldn't fix the damage done to the machine overhead.

The osprey aimed nosedown right at the cluster of tents on the south side, where the greenbellies were regrouping. People scattered away from it as with a ground-shaking crunch and tear, it plowed into the salt, flattening tents in its wake. The osprey's fuselage, already riddled with scorch marks and bullet holes, crumpled and tore like paper.

Hob had the presence of mind to keep her motorcycle steady, and even to take a wild shot at movement she saw from the corner of her eye, but she couldn't look away. "Dambala. Coyote. You there?"

Nothing. Dead, or their radios busted. Either way, Hob was sharply reminded as a shot grazed her arm in a line of fire, she didn't have time to think about it. Had to rely on blood and luck. Had to drop the Bone Collector off and then really wade in. She aimed toward where that shot had come from, and saw the black line of what might have been the barrel of a rifle, peeping around some crates. She kept her hand steady, feeding heat into the crates until they started to smoke. "Just show me your goddamn face…"

The air suddenly tasted of ozone and electricity, her mouth full of metal. The wall around the mine swirled black and inky with auras that sucked at her brain, emanating from – fuck, she'd forgotten about that, hadn't had a chance to look in the mess of equipment, she was a fucking moron–

Her last coherent act was to lay down her motorcycle, because that was better than letting it fall on her and the Bone Collector. The machine skidded across the salt on its side, Hob and the Bone Collector tumbling after it, but she didn't feel the rough surface tearing at her leathers, because she didn't feel anything but the knives in her brain.

There was a place beyond exhaustion and into numbness, mental and physical. Anabi knew it from her escape from Harmony, and she'd never wanted to feel that way again. But twelve lightless hours, fumbling at being a miner while just waiting to be prodded with a rifle for being too slow or too clumsy, day after day, had done it. All that sustained her now was anger, and that iron will to survive that had kept her feet moving as she climbed from Harmony's green, irrigated valley and out into the sands while a wildcat's scream tore ceaselessly at her lungs.

She hadn't given up then, when she'd had no promise ahead of her, and she wasn't going to give up now. Not with Mag waiting. She had to be waiting, because she wasn't here, and she couldn't be dead.

Anabi lay on the board of the lowest bunk bed in her assigned tent, listening to the sounds of misery around her. The tent stank of sweat and burst blisters beginning to go wrong. She mulled over the presence of Mr Rollins, Mag and Hob's government man, in the camp. She didn't think for one moment that he was looking for her, but she could threaten him, maybe. She knew who he was. Maybe he could get her out of here. She'd just need to find something to write with. After the attack on Ludlow, the greenbellies had searched her. They'd taken everything, even her slate. If she got desperate, she could draw words on people's hands, and there were some things that gesture was easy for. But she felt like she'd had her voice stolen all over again.

The low hum of an osprey coming in close filled the air, buzzing in the flimsy furniture and tent supports. One of the few people awake muttered, "Ain't they already come in tonight?" Another person shushed him. Deep in Anabi's throat, the wildcat's scream, which had been sullenly dormant for so long after she'd ignored it, stirred and scratched for a way out. Maybe she'd let it out, she thought. She was tired of having no voice to call her own. But she wasn't so angry yet, that she wanted to destroy everything.

Then the shooting started.

They were used to a few isolated shots here and there,

now, in a horrible way. Every day, a miner or two got dragged out and shot. There'd been a few this evening, after they'd been put down in their tent, echoing across the camp. But this was different, many of them, in constantly popping volleys, cascades, clusters of shots with a few cracks at random between them. The hum of the osprey went on and on, and there was a rumble deep below. Something was happening.

Anabi slid from her bed. She wasn't the only one. It was enough of a ruckus to wake even the most exhausted prisoners. Miners piled in at her back, confused murmurs giving way to grim silence. They must all feel the same thing as her, Anabi thought. Whatever attack was happening, whether it was friends or foes or strange creatures from campfire stories that would turn on them and eat them, now was the moment to fight back.

"If I end up as eagle food, least I'll be free," a woman muttered behind her.

Anabi pushed the flimsy door of the tent open. The guards normally standing on either side, ready to harass anyone who dared need the latrines in the middle of the night, had moved, drawn toward the other end of camp. They turned at the sound behind them, rifles coming up.

Two shots sounded sharp, and the guards dropped, one spraying blood and bone from his head, the other from her throat. Anabi cringed back, unsure of what was happening, then saw behind them the familiar shapes of two motorcycles. She recognized the helmets, the way they'd been painted. She stumbled forward, waving frantically.

Diablo stopped in front of her, so fast his rear tire lifted off the ground. The other – Conall, she thought – swerved around him and came to an uneven halt. Diablo shoved his face plate back. "Anabi? Shit."

She wished she had something to write with. Instead,

she simply pointed toward the mine. Hopefully it was enough of a question.

"Rest of the Wolves are doin' their best," Diablo said. He looked at the miners, flooding out of the tent around her. "Y'all in for a fight?"

Two miners scrambled to pick up the rifles belonging to the dead greenbellies off the ground. "Hell fuckin' yeah," one said.

"We're gonna clear—" There was the crack of a shot, and a miner dropped to her knees, clutching her shoulder. Diablo and Conall turned, drawing their guns. One of the miners beat them to it, firing the rifle and killing the greenbelly that had just come around the corner. "We're gonna clear out the rest of this side, then get to the pit," Diablo said, keeping his gun at the ready now.

"The hell you want with the pit?" one of the miners asked. "It's a fuckin' grave."

"Don't rightly know. But we got us a witch on our side, and the Ravani reckons he can put the screws to the greenbellies if we get him into the pit, so that's what we're gonna fuckin' do." Diablo pulled out a shotgun and offered it over, then a knife. Anabi darted in to take that. The blade was heavy in her hand, the hilt warm from sitting next to Diablo's body. "Do what you can."

Conall finished handing out a few extra weapons to eager hands. He and Diablo kicked themselves rolling again, and moved toward the rest of the tents. As Anabi watched, Diablo retrieved a wicked-looking hatchet from the back holster of his motorcycle.

No time to watch more. The crowd of miners began moving into camp, many of them breaking into a run. Anabi dragged her tired legs into a half-jog, wanting to stay behind the few people who had guns. She already knew how pathetic a knife was against all of that.

Ahead, the camp was a mass of confusion, dust and

smoke and fire, the small contingent of Ghost Wolves zipping around like heat-mad sand flies. Greenbellies massed on the south side, organizing themselves around barricades. Around her, miners tumbled and fell, taken with bullets from the right. More greenbellies here, hiding in the tailings piles, the equipment sheds.

Anabi set her jaw and went for the wall. She saw straight in from where she stood, a couple hundred meters distant, a massive man that had to be one of Hob's people. There was a trike near him. He attacked the wall near the drive chain housing with a sledgehammer. Anabi felt the wildcat scream churn in her chest and wondered if maybe, maybe...

A massive cargo osprey buzzed the landing field, so low that Anabi and the people around her threw themselves down to kiss the salt. It knocked the breath out of her, and she gritted her teeth around the scream, holding it in. Something bright like lightning from the flood-storms cracked from the sky and more fire exploded to add to the confusion of screams and gunfire. The ground shook and she looked up to see the crumpled osprey sliding through more tents, bowling greenbellies left and right.

Anabi scrambled to her feet and started running again, half aware of the others around her running, shooting, shouting and screaming. She saw the big Wolf with the hammer move to take another swing, and saw his head splatter out on the wall as he took a bullet that split his helmet in half. The air shifted, something distant and electric like the storms that blew from nowhere and rumbled across the farm valleys, and Anabi stumbled, feeling not quite right in her own skin. She felt sick, and like something she couldn't quite hear scraped at her anyway. Near her, two miners fell, unconscious without a mark on them. And ahead, a motorcycle she recognized as Hob's went down, the two people on it tumbling limply after the machine, coming to a stop. They must have been alive because they curled in on themselves, as if trying to escape an invisible beating.

Something slammed into her shoulder, and she stumbled, falling to her knees. Blood washed down her arm in a red flow, followed by the red, internal crunch of pain. She saw the greenbelly who'd shot her out of the corner of her eye, training another shot, and she dropped fully to the ground like she'd fainted.

The ground against her cheek shook and trembled with footsteps, with the endless growl of sand tires on salt flat. Anabi kept her eyes open, tasting blood from where she'd bitten her tongue, that pain somehow almost more present than being shot in the shoulder, and tried to breathe shallow. The scream boiled up in her throat, but she held it. It would do her no good now. The little tremor of nearby steps, and the barrel of a rifle prodded at her. She played dead. She felt rather than saw the greenbelly bend to look down.

Teeth bared, she whipped her hand up with Diablo's knife and stabbed him. Her first blow was glancing, a slice across his face. He jerked back, and she lunged to her feet, yanked up by the force she contained in her, and drove the knife into his neck. He fell, blood pumping out across her hand.

Breathing harsh and raw, Anabi yanked the knife out and looked around her. Another motorcycle went down, its rider tumbling. More people were on the ground, curled up like Hob and her friend. Anabi looked at the wall around the pit, the bloody spatter on it. She wondered about the machines they'd been made to put up around the wall; she'd heard the guards joke about it being an anti-witch fence. And she looked down at the knife in her red-cast hand as the scream boiled and boiled in her throat, shrieking for release.

She'd always told Mag she didn't know what would happen, if she let the scream out. If it'd kill her. It'd sure as hell kill everything in her way.

And it might just be enough to destroy the wall.

She stumbled forward, bent almost double with the effort of breathing, trying to angle herself so she wouldn't hit anyone she knew to be friendly. This was as good as it would get, she thought. She planted her feet. Blood pattered from her hand onto the saltpan like impossibly gentle rain. Anabi relaxed her throat, opened her mouth, and finally, after so many years, *let go*.

The world tore apart at the sound of her anger.

CHAPTER FIFTY-THREE

Dambala blinked blood out of his eyes, trying to orient himself in the sparking darkness. A strap cut across his chest, so tight he could barely breathe. What had–

Right. He'd crashed the goddamn osprey that his goddamn partner had convinced their goddamn boss to steal. He'd been around Coyote too fucking long, that was for sure. And... "Coyote?" he said. Right, his precious idiot had been in the cockpit with him. He tried to reach out, feeling for the copilot seat, couldn't hardly move with the safety harness trying to strangle him and break his back in half at the same time. Dambala changed tactics and grabbed for his knife – he always had a knife in reach, he'd learned that one in the service – and sawed through the safety harness. It took a damned eternity.

Then he popped free, or tried, only to find himself jammed between the control panel and more bent wreckage. Cursing under his breath, he squirmed out. He felt his way along with his hands, skating over sharply bent metal, until he found something soft and yielding and... yes, Coyote's hand. Had to be, there were those scars on his knuckles that he'd gotten off his jag of picking endless bar fights with his damn mouth. "Coyote?"

Nothing, but at least he was still breathing. Good enough. Dambala felt the shape of the situation, and by touch alone, untangled Coyote from his seat. If there'd been some hope in hell of a medevac, maybe he would have left him in place, since he'd gotten enough lectures in his day about spinal injuries. But that was a long ago dream thanks to their growing dedication to chickenshit outfits.

He found other things by touch – his shotgun, Coyote's helmet, and the door. He hung Coyote over his shoulder like a limp sack of laundry and felt his way out into the cargo hold. There was light there, a crack in the bent and warped door. It was almost blinding after the dark of the cockpit. The familiar smell of smoke and gunpowder and blood wafted in, carrying with it the even more familiar sound of a gun battle. More distant, he saw the wall around the mine pit. Damn, he wished he'd been able to hit that instead, but the angle hadn't been right.

Dambala hazarded a glance outside and saw nothing directly close but the wreckage field he'd made on the way down, torn tents and shattered crates and smeared, twisted bodies. He wedged himself into the crack in the door, put his back against the hull and got his legs up to push. He was too goddamn old for this, he was sure of it, the way his back was twinging. Slowly, groaning all the while, the door squealed open. Enough that he'd be able to get them both through it.

He dragged his limp partner out into the open air and started wondering where the hell to run to next, since he didn't want to survive the fourth goddamn crash of his career just to get his ass shot by a Corporate shitlicker, when the wind suddenly whipped up into an unholy, impossible shriek. Instinctively he dropped Coyote and slapped his hands over his ears, and it made no difference. The sound grew and grew until he thought his goddamn eyes were going to burst from the pressure, and then–

The wall around the pit shattered, metal and synthcrete barriers shredding into splinters, the tripods around it turning into chaff that spun through the air and blew out high over the camp. Hands still uselessly over his ears, Dambala huddled over Coyote, his back turned toward the swirling storm of debris. He felt splinters tear at the leather of his coat, a few sneaking under his collar to slash at his neck–

And then the sound was gone. The air was still but for a patter almost like rain, except he knew it was pieces of the goddamn mining camp.

Beneath him, Coyote squirmed, then gave him a solid shove. He made a muffled sound that Dambala, long used to translating Drunk Coyote Speak, made out to be, "I can't breathe!"

Dambala sat back, then yanked Coyote to a sitting position with one hand on his collar. "What the fuck happened?"

"They must have another of those anti-witch camp perimeters…" Coyote turned to look at what had once been the mine works, now scraped almost clean of the ground. Debris piled up in drifts. His eyes went wide. "… And it isn't there anymore."

Ahead of them, one of the piles of debris shivered and shook apart into Geri. He reeled up to his feet. After that moment of perfect calm after the storm, a gunshot cracked loud. With nowhere left to hide, they flattened themselves on the ground as more gunshots sounded – people still alive making themselves known. It wasn't even half over. "Where's the boss?" Coyote said.

"Don't know. Your helmet's busted." Dambala waited for a slight pause in the shooting and stretched up, looking. Dust choked the air. "Way to the mine's sort of clear if she and her friend ain't dead." Saying it like that was a way to ward off disaster, instinctive. Never assume. Always let them be alive and surprise you. He ducked back down.

Coyote bellycrawled to peer around the edge of the wrecked osprey. "Oh, bother."

"What?" Dambala demanded.

"They're getting organized. Whatever that explosion was, it didn't catch too many of them."

He looked at the wreckage. "Don't think it was aimed to." What would that have done to a group of people? And why hadn't it been used like that? Well, he didn't even know what the hell kind of weapon it was, though it stank of witchiness and no mistake. He didn't give a shit, because witchiness on their side was the best kind of witchiness there was. He felt another rattle coming up through the ground, knew it to be the drumming of feet. Through the dust and smoke and wreckage, a flood of ragged, black-smeared people burst into view, screaming as they came. After the sound that had torn apart the wall, it seemed damn thin.

A gunshot cracked and one of the people – one of the miners, he realized – hit the ground. Another raised a rifle, pointing at an enemy Dambala couldn't see, and returned fire.

"Think we should run for it now..." Coyote started.

Dambala saw another pile of debris shift and move. But what emerged wasn't a familiar face, but someone tall and thin in a blue suit grayed with dust. Dambala had only ever seen Mr Green from a distance when they'd helped kill the Weatherman months ago, but he knew. The same way he knew in the jungle that he was being watched, the same way his healed-up leg ached when the air was shifting. "Oh fuck."

"Oh what–"

Dambala reached out to yank Coyote back around. The new Weatherman brushed himself off and started picking his way over the debris with the deliberation of a spider, toward the open pit. Dambala didn't understand half of what was going on, and it wasn't his goddamn job to. But he'd listened enough to know that the Weatherman getting to that pit was a grade-A instance of bad shit, and their job was to not let that happen. "We got to fuckin' go."

Coyote scrambled to his feet and started running, faster than he had any right to. Dambala started hot on his heels, falling step by step behind. But they were both of them too goddamn slow. They couldn't close the distance even at a flat run, not with the Weatherman already near the lip of the pit.

Then Freki came barrel-assing out of nowhere and slammed into the Weatherman's side. He tackled the skinny fuck to the ground and went in punching. Somehow, Dambala found a little more speed to pour into his legs. Because he remembered, he goddamn *remembered* what it had been like before, and there was no way it was that easy.

The Weatherman grabbed Freki's face with his hands, holding it still. "No, don't look–" Dambala gasped as he ran, like Freki could fucking hear him.

Freki's fist stopped mid-blow, shaking, and blood began to slide from his ears, his nose, his eyes. Then the big man, who might as well have been Dambala's adopted son since he'd helped Nick pick him and his twin up off the street in Tercio, went limp. The Weatherman casually pushed his form to the side as if he weighed nothing.

Dambala squeezed that wash of horror and rage at the sight into a bullet that lodged in his heart. He brought up his shotgun and fired, both barrels.

The scattering of shot stopped like it hit a wall, half a meter away from the Weatherman. And the monster turned his goddamn head toward Dambala. But he'd done his time on the interstellar service. He knew the one rule was that you never looked them in the eye. Ever. He squeezed his eyes shut and fumbled for more shells, like those would do a bit of good.

He heard Coyote yell, a savage note to his voice that he hadn't uttered in years. There was a sound like meat slamming into rock, somehow audible over the chaos that had engulfed the camp. Dambala hazarded a glance even as he stuffed the shells into his shotgun. Coyote squared off with the Weatherman. Crimson dripped from his hands, and he wiped a smear of it across his mouth. A slash of scratches stood out vivid across the Weatherman's face, blood obscuring his eye. The Weatherman shrieked, covering his face with his hands.

That was when Geri hit him, slamming into his back and folding him in half with sheer weight. A knife flashed in his hand and tore a hunk from the Weatherman's sleeve, but left only the thinnest line on his skin.

"Don't look in his eyes," Dambala roared. He cursed himself for never passing along that lesson. But they hadn't ever needed it here. He hadn't wanted to admit why he knew, and now it was his goddamn fault–

The Weatherman half-threw Geri off. Coyote lunged in, striking at him again. Bullets chattered off the ground near Dambala.

"Pile in!" Coyote yelled. "We have to keep him down."

And hell, being on top of the Weatherman would probably keep the greenbellies from shooting at them too. Not that he expected to win this fight, but maybe it would buy Hob time. Dambala waded in, wielding his shotgun like a club.

• • •

Hob came back to awareness with gravel raining down on her helmet, and she couldn't breathe, she couldn't fucking *breathe*–

She ripped her helmet off and sucked in lungfuls of air. Her heartbeat thundered in her ears, the pain still stabbing through her head in time with it. But she could think. She could fucking think and move and... gunshots. And screaming, howling, pounding feet. She was in the middle of a goddamn battlefield and now was not the time.

She rolled to her belly, casting around to find the Bone Collector. Through the smoke and flickering lights that remained, she saw the shadow of motorcycles near them, and Wolves sheltering behind them, using them as cover so they could fire: Maheegan, Akela, Lykaios, Hati–

"The wall!" she shouted. Croaked, more like. But loud enough that the nearest, Lykaios, shouted back, "Ain't a wall no more."

Hob looked to see the wreckage, trying to puzzle it into something that made sense in her head. "The fuck..." No, she could get that story later. It didn't matter how it happened, just that it had happened. She felt fingers close on her jacket sleeve and looked to see the Bone Collector, his face haggard.

"Need to get... the Well," he whispered.

The gunfire around them was only growing. Hob made a quick mental calculation and then dragged them both to the side, behind the slim cover of Lykaios's motorcycle.

"Shit!" Lykaios said, trying to give them room.

"We're gonna take your bike," Hob said, leaving no room for discussion. There was no time, and she couldn't feel the fire any more, with her head pounding and numb by turns. They'd probably still get their asses shot if they rode, but at least they'd cover that insurmountable distance faster. "You cuddle up with Akela. Throw everything you got at them, buy us some time."

Lykaios cussed a blue streak and sprinted the short distance to hunker behind Akela's motorcycle. Hob checked what she could safely see on Lykaios's bike. It had already been shot to hell, but it'd run enough to get them a few hundred meters. She dragged the Bone Collector upright. He looked like he might vomit again. "I'm gonna get up first," she said. "Then you get in front of me. Gonna run you in. Got it?"

He nodded. "He's so close," he whispered. "I can hear him. Reaching."

Must be the Weatherman, Hob realized. Like they didn't have enough fucking problems. Well, she could only worry about one thing at a time. If she got the Bone Collector there fast enough, maybe the rest would take care of itself. He'd never been clear on what might happen, exactly, but it was the only chance they had. "I'm goin'. Get your shit together."

She reached up enough to get the motorcycle going, ignoring the unhappy, uneven whine of the engine, the sound of sparking. It didn't have to last long. She slid her leg over, then reached down and pulled the Bone Collector up, throwing him over the battery stack with brute force. She gunned the motor, almost running into Akela's bike in the process, and swerved them out of there.

The first bullet hit Hob in the shoulder. That wasn't so bad. It hurt, it felt like getting hit with a hammer, but she didn't need her goddamn shoulder. The next one slammed through her leg. The third lodged in her gut.

Her hands stopped working quite right and she lost control of the motorcycle. Somehow, she shoved the Bone Collector free before the bike crashed down, pinning her leg. Oh fuck, everything hurt. Everything fucking hurt and she couldn't hardly breathe around it. She turned her head to see blood pooling under her already, and her legs had gone numb, which seemed like an improvement. She looked at the Bone Collector, still sprawled where she'd shoved him. It'd taken him damn longer to recover than her before, and they didn't have that time. "You motherfucker," she yelled. "Ain't this enough of my blood yet?"

He rolled, uncoordinated, toward her. Bullets dug tracks through the salt, tore trails in the dust. Hob fumbled one of her revolvers free of her belt and dragged herself around enough to fire a few shots in the right general direction. So close. They were so goddamn close.

The Bone Collector came to her, the idiot, he should have been going toward the Well. He cupped his hand in the pooling blood and raised it to his lips. Then he reached toward her.

She slapped his hand away with the butt of her revolver. "Ain't time for your nonsense," she shouted, even though every word ached and burned deep in her gut. "Fuckin' *go*!"

For once in his goddamn life, the Bone Collector listened to her without her having to punch him in the face. He stumbled to his feet, and limped for the Well.

Hob pulled herself up to sitting, leaning against the downed motorcycle. She balanced her arm on the battery stack and half-turned to squeeze off a few more rounds in what she hoped was the right direction in all that confusion. The revolver clicked empty, and she fumbled a quick loader from her pocket.

Another bullet tore through her chest and embedded itself in the battery stack.

"Fuck," she gasped, but didn't have the breath anymore. The Bone Collector was forty meters from the

Well. She knocked the shells out of her revolver and somehow got the quick loader lined up.

Another bullet. She knew it from the impact. She couldn't really feel anything any more, or even hear anything over the roar in her ears. The Bone Collector was twenty meters from the gaping, steaming pit. She dragged herself around to fire toward the southeast, since that's where the last shot that hit her came from. She saw Maheegan sprawled out across the salt, making weak swimming motions in his own pool of blood. She saw miners, still streaming in from the north of the camp, cut down into limp tumbles. More streamed past like ghosts in the swirling smoke, mouths open to howl.

Ten meters. In her periphery, she saw a shape surge out of the billowing cloud like a thing of nightmare – the Weatherman, his suit torn and gray with dust. Two men – Geri and Dambala, oh, it was nice to see Bala was still alive – tackled him to the ground.

Hob dragged her revolver around to train on the Weatherman, just in case. She tried to stoke up the fire in her blood, searching for that roaring flame that had helped her kill Mr Green before. But she didn't have an explosion waiting in her belly, just lead and her life draining slowly away. She saw Coyote rise up from the melee, slick to the elbows with blood and grinning his damn fool grin. He opened his hand and flung away a chunk of something red and wet. An unearthly scream cut the air, the Weatherman now slick and red still crawling toward the edge of the pit.

The Bone Collector paused at that edge, heedless of the bleeding horror crawling toward him, to look back at her. His lips moved into some message that she didn't fucking care about because he needed to *move*–

He spread his arms and fell forward, like he was diving.

Then he was gone.

Well, Hob thought with a sick mingling of horror and hysterical amusement, what the hell else had she expected to happen? One-handed, she fumbled her cigarette case out of her pocket and opened it. A bullet cut through her bicep and she dropped it, all of the cigarettes scattering. "Cocksuckers," she muttered with lips that tasted like her own blood. Painfully, she transferred her revolver to that hand and managed to reach one of the cigarettes. She tucked it between her lips and lit it with the last flickering spark in her blood.

Another unearthly, shattering scream came from the Weatherman. Geri's arm came up, combat knife black with more sticky fluid, slammed down. The Weatherman thrashed unsteadily under the onslaught of the Wolves and went still. Coyote sat up, his round face a half mask of blood from nose to chin.

Maybe he wouldn't be so damned thirsty all the time after this, Hob thought numbly. Now if only she could actually inhale and enjoy her last damn cigarette. "Never wanted to die abed anyway," she muttered, beginning to droop forward over the motorcycle. No one needed to be in bed to sleep when they were this damn tired.

The crackle of gunfire strung out, blurred, and at first she thought it had to be death clouding her ears, but it was a rumble in the deep, a rumble made of time and space and pure witchiness.

A spark of light – a bullet – stopped bare centimeters from her cheek.

And then the world *sang*.

CHAPTER FIFTY-FOUR

The church's doors boomed inward, splintered, and still held, somehow. Mag leaned against the pew that she and the other miners held, every bone in her body aching from the blows of the battering ram. In the pitch-black back of the church, in the odd silences, she heard Brother Rami praying with a small group of the injured. His words were a blur she could not make out, but she still found them comforting. Maybe she'd been wrong to avoid Ludlow's church for so long.

Boom. The doors shuddered, held.

Omar, next to her in line, laughed sharply. "Keep trying, assholes. We could do this all day and all night too." A ragged bubble of exhausted, near-hysterical laughter echoed through the church.

Boom. They dug in their feet and pushed back.

The flavor of the air coming through the cracks in the doors changed, to something more chemical. She couldn't quite place her finger on it; Papa had always kept her out of the mine and away from the blasting in particular, and Clarence had done the same. But the miners recognized it. A low moan swept through them.

"What?" Mag whispered.

"Ignition gel," Omar said. "They're bringin' it out. I

don't know if they're gonna try blastin' the doors…"

One of the miners on a pew abandoned her post, and scrambled over another pew against the wall to look out the window, just peeping over the edge. "They're sprayin' the walls," she called back. "I see… Longbridge. That fucker. He's sittin' and havin' him a drink while he watches."

Mag didn't need an explanation for that. "They're going to burn us alive," she whispered.

"They still working the ram?" Omar called.

Before the woman could even answer, another *boom* shook through them. A man stumbled, collected himself, and lunged back in to put his shoulder against the pew.

Mag closed her eyes. There wasn't any death out of this that would be good. But perhaps the worst would be burning. Like what they'd done to Mama. "Then we let 'em in," Mag said. "We got the timing. Let 'em run on through. Slam the doors behind them. Then we got some of their people hostage."

Omar laughed sharply. "You're as crazy as your friend."

"Learned it from her."

Omar counted them off, and they waited for the doors to shudder one more time. Then both teams of people pulled back, ready to catch the doors as they swung open and slam them back shut with reinforcements. Every other able-bodied person waited with a weapon, ready to spring. And the woman at the window slipped down to pull the bar from the door.

It worked too well. The doors burst inward, shattered beyond recognition, not enough there for them to catch and put back together. The waiting miners jumped on the battering ram team as they slowed in confusion, beating on them with hammers and shovels. More greenbellies came into view, and Omar shoved the pew forward to block them. Not twenty meters away, Longbridge rose up from his chair like it was a goddamn throne, a glass held in one shining metal hand.

And somewhere, in the distance but approaching like a roar, Mag felt the world shift, change, in a seismic wave as fast as thought. As the ground moved under her feet, she screamed and surged forward with Omar.

Longbridge raised his revolver. The greenbellies in front of him raised their rifles. The muzzles flared and spat fire.

The world stopped. A voice that was not a voice, that was bells and shifting tectonic plates and an ocean – how did she know it was an ocean, there were no oceans on Tanegawa's World, but she tasted the salt spray in her throat – said in words that were not words: *No. These are my people.*

The bullets, hanging in the air centimeters in front of Omar, puffed into dust. A fresh breeze, impossible to imagine after hours of drowning in burning and chemical stink, blew the billowing smoke back, carrying the orange-pink dust with it. As the dust touched the greenbellies, the color spread across them, until they weren't Mariposa men at all, but statues of orange, red, and pink. They burst into gouts of sand on the wind and spiraled up into a sky just starting to go deep purple with the promise of dawn.

A soft noise behind her in the frozen world where only wind and sand existed made her turn. The Bone Collector stood at the center of the church, his staff in his hand, and regarded her with eyes as blue as that impossible ocean.

"What did you do?" Mag whispered. It was a stupid question, but she couldn't find anything else to combat all the impossible things she'd just seen.

He smiled, that damn mysterious smile that Mag

suddenly knew was the one Hob had once punched off his face. "This is your moment, Mag. What would you have me do?"

Shige came back to himself in a pained rush, like layers of gauze had been lifted away from his awareness. It cleared away the remnants of improbable sadness he'd felt, seeing Mr Yellow turn his back – what had that been about? He'd been a tool, Shige realized coldly. He'd been built to be a tool, and the Weatherman had used him as such. Had twisted his thoughts, had been the source of those strange urges, and Shige had never quite picked it up. Perhaps because he believed he could not be suborned, perhaps because the call had been coming from inside the house and all else had seemed impossible.

But he had greater problems to face than his emotional upset, and the unbearable vibration and jolting of the jeep under him brought that into intensive focus.

Another jarring thud echoed through the bleeding rupture in his body, but Shige bore it. He didn't dare shift enough to call attention to himself, from where he'd been stuffed in the cargo space of the vehicle. There wasn't anywhere he could have moved to that was comfortable, anyway. All he could do was press his left hand against the hole in his chest and struggle to breathe. With his right, he extracted the rest of his small arsenal of weapons and took stock.

The garrote was unlikely as a solution. He might be able to summon up the pure desperate strength to take down one of the guards, but the other two would kill him in the meantime. Same problem went for the knife. More promising were the four microinjectors he'd retrieved from the cuffs of his trousers. They weren't made to be thrown like the darts, but he'd have his opportunity to use them when the guards came to pull him out of the back of the jeep. He could just pretend to be nearly dead and limp, and sneak in a hit of poison with a little theatrical flopping.

Though really, who was he kidding? He wasn't nearly dead yet, but he was on his way there. He'd done the field medical classes and self-first aid as required. He knew that he was likely developing a pneumothorax, and could only hope that they'd consider themselves far enough away from the camp to dump him before it fully incapacitated him.

The plan was simple: kill the guards, use the onboard medical kit to its best advantage, and then steal the jeep. He'd have to take a look at the vehicle and its onboard supplies before he could decide his best destination, since his only options were either far-off Newcastle, or the camp – which was an iffy prospect for obvious reasons. It was a plan made entirely of holes, and held together by a thin web of wishful thinking. It was also the only plan he had right now, alone and bereft of resources.

An extra vibration seemed to pass through the jeep, and Shige gritted his teeth. There was a sharp whine from the engine, a jerk, and the vehicle rolled to a stop.

"What the fuck?" one of the guards said.

"I don't fucking know," another, presumably the driver, shouted. "It just fucking jinked."

With much cursing and swearing, the guards opened their doors and piled out. Shige rearranged his microinjectors so he could reach them easily and readied himself.

More cursing and slamming around outside, probably them puzzling at the engine. "Fucking radio is on the fritz too."

"They know which way we were headed," the third guard said. "Even if we can't raise them or fix it, they'll send someone after us."

The voices started coming closer. "Let's just dump the traitor here, then. Don't want his corpse stinking up the jeep if we're to be hunkering down in it."

The one he'd identified as the driver laughed sharply. "Give us a bit of entertainment when the eagles show."

Shige went carefully limp, eyes half-closed and head lolling, as the door to the cargo space opened. He stayed dead weight as the guards stared at him, poked at him. "Think he's already dead," one said.

"Does it matter?"

"Not really."

One grabbed his legs to start dragging him out. He let his hand fall to brush over their wrist and trigger the microinjector. They didn't even seem to notice. As the guard started to drag him, grunting, "Come on, some help here?" Shige let himself be pulled over. There was a moment of red, distracting pain, and then the second guard grabbed his wrists. Before they started pulling, he tagged them with the second microinjector.

Because after that point, it hurt too much for subtlety. Over the ringing in his ears, he heard the third guffaw, "C'mon, little back office wimp like him can't be that heavy."

"Yeah, fuck off," the guard at his legs said. The walked him out onto the salt flat. The sky above was unimaginably black, with more stars than he'd ever seen in his life – and he'd thought the view in Newcastle was fantastic, so different from the polluted atmosphere on Earth. The air above was shockingly cool, while below he still felt the salt radiating the heat it had collected through the day.

The two guards made it about twenty steps from the jeep when they dropped Shige, their hands coming up to clutch at their throats. Each took a few more steps before collapsing gracelessly down. There were no words, just strangled gasps of closed-off throats, then the scent of bowel and bladder giving way in death.

"No joking!" the driver, still at the jeep, shouted. After a minute, she cursed and her footsteps approached. Shige slipped another microinjector into one hand and the garrote into his other and tried to imagine a universe in which he could be fast enough.

The steps suddenly stopped, but there was no further sound, no breathing, no cursing, no weapon being drawn. Shige counted to one hundred, then cautiously turned his head to look: the guard had stopped, still as a statue, some five meters away. But there was something strange about her indeed, which he could not quite define while she was only a shadow with the headlights of the jeep at her back.

Bemused, Shige moved a hand. No reaction. He dragged himself to his feet, and when there was still no movement, staggered forward rather than trying to run in to attack. He got in close, and saw no movement at all, not even breathing. He stepped around to see her back in the headlights – she'd become entirely red-orange, the color of the sand on this benighted world. Curious, he reached out to touch her...

She collapsed, blowing apart into sand and dust, leaving him ankle deep in a drift. Shige inspected his finger with bemused suspicion. Grains of orange sand had stuck to the tacky blood.

He had no explanation. And even if he had, it wouldn't stop him from bleeding out. Practical considerations were in order first, and the rest could wait until he was no longer at the edge of death. First aid, then see if he could fix the jeep, then... he'd figure out the next step later.

He staggered back to the jeep and dug until he found the medical kit. It was dishearteningly basic, but there was little he could do about that. There was at least a sharp scalpel, and he could get the tube off his pen to let his chest drain. And there were pain meds, and a blessed unit of universal synthetic blood that was past its date by three months, but given the alternative, he'd take it. Shige swallowed all the meds he could safely take, then a few more, picked up the scalpel, and set about giving himself the fuel of nightmares for years to come if he was lucky enough to survive this.

That pure song faded into a silence, with no more shouting, no more gunfire. Seemed fair enough to Hob, since it was easier to sleep without all that shit going on anyway. She felt the weight of her motorcycle vanish off her leg, and that was a relief. Maybe the part where she flew up to heaven or down to hell and told Old Nick to go fuck himself in person would soon follow.

Cool fingers touched her cheek, tilting her face up. She managed to open her eye to find the Bone Collector looking at her, his eyes fit to swallow the world. The sight of him was welcome, and then goddamn infuriating – which gave her enough strength to choke out strangled, pissed-off words: "You son of a bitch, I fuckin' *told*–"

He rested his fingers over her lips and she debated if her last earthly act should be biting him. It was tempting.

"You won," he said.

"What?"

"You won. And I'm not done with you yet." His lips quirked in a smug-ass smile that for just this moment, she could admit to herself that she loved. He leaned in to rest his forehead against hers, and then like that wasn't enough, kissed her.

Hell of a way to… not die. It wasn't a normal kiss, even the fumbling kind she'd expect from herself being years out of practice, let alone from him having no idea what to do. He breathed into her, and it was a cool river, it was fire, it was strength. For a moment, all the pain that had faded out into fatigue flared back up, and she screamed into his mouth. Then he kissed her again, with a ferocity she'd never known him to have, and she felt her guts shift back into place, the bullets get pushed out of her skin by muscles knitting back together, and it was strange and painful and horrifying and beautiful.

When he drew away, only a quick grab at his collar saved her from falling back onto the salt. He laughed, the bastard, and wrapped an arm around her to steady her.

Maybe she should have been thinking about how good that felt, and a part of her did, and thinking about kissing him back in the hopes that a second time wouldn't feel that passing strange. But she remembered seeing her people in bloody heaps, and that was more important than any other thoughts she had. She jerked him closer. "You better be fuckin' plannin' on doin' that trick for everyone else."

"I am," he agreed. "I have."

"...What?"

He nudged her cheek to get her to turn her head. She looked across the now-haphazardly lit camp and its wreckage. New drifts of orange sand sat in the distance, but the question of where the hell any of that had come from was less important than the people still flat out on the salt. And near all of them, the Bone Collector, pale and glowing and ghostly, knelt. She saw a hundred different hims touching faces and chests and stomachs, straightening legs and arms.

"Fuck me," she whispered. "I can't hardly handle one of you."

He laughed. "There is still only one of me, I assure you. But I wanted to see to all of my people who were still alive as soon as I could... in order to keep them in that state."

"*Your* people?" She turned to look back at him. He'd never talked about anyone like that except her, and maybe–

"Mag can be very convincing, when she likes," he said.

"Mag's good at that." She eyed him, glanced at the ghostly replicas, eyed him again. "What happened?"

"I stand at the bottom of the Well now. At the eye of the storm, I suppose. And in so doing, I have become the storm."

She stared at him, and then gave him a firm poke. He felt solid, for all he was a mass of ghosts scattered across the wildcat site. "Say it in plain dummy talk."

He looked slightly pained. "I am the Well now."

She tried to wrap her head around that, and found it too big to swallow all at once. So she focused in on the selfish thing most important to her. "But you're back out of it now?"

"No," he said quietly. "Not like you mean."

"But you're comin' back out."

"I don't think that I can." He took one of her hands, lifted it, and wove their fingers together. She wished she wasn't wearing gloves. "This isn't really me you're touching."

"You lying son of a bitch." She took a careful breath. "So you're goin' away?"

"I don't know." He squeezed her hand. "But I suppose we'll find out. I need to go now. I can only split my attention so many ways, and there's much I need to do."

She opened her mouth to protest, to ask another question, because none of it made a bit of goddamn sense, then gave up and pulled him forward until their lips met again. For one beautiful moment, he was alive and kissing her back, tasting like blood and vanilla. His hand cradled the back of her head, as hers pulled the collar of his shirt open…

And then he went still like she'd seen him do before, going from flesh to stone. Hob leaned back to see him fade from pale to orange pink like sand. Then he burst into a cloud of dust carried away by the wind.

Hob curled up around the sudden emptiness and pain she felt. She hated it; she'd rather be angry, and in a minute she might be. But all she felt now was the absence of someone who she'd never wanted to be important to her. Was he dead? Was he the next best thing?

She should get up and see how many of *her* people he'd saved. She needed to get everyone organized, and figure out how the hell to get them back home. Maybe there were more cargo ospreys that hadn't been destroyed in whatever explosion she'd missed while laid down by the witch fence. But this moment was hers, to feel something as human as pain and sadness and loss.

Then she took a deep breath and cast around until she found another of her scattered cigarettes. Flame leaped easily to her fingers to light it. Her blood felt alive with fire. On the breeze, she heard other voices now, murmurs of confusion, of wonder, people crying with hoarse sobs. Hob stood and looked at the swath of destruction. No greenbellies to be seen, just drifts of sand that had no business being out this far in the middle of the saltpan. But she knew, suddenly, where it had all come from.

There was a godling that lived in the Well now, and he'd turned all the greenbellies to sand. She sucked in a deep lungful of smoke, trying to wrap her brain around the thousand ways the world had changed in an instant, even while she still felt the phantom pressure of his lips against hers. "The fuck do we do now?" she whispered, to herself, maybe to him, to the whole fucking world.

That was all she allowed herself. Because she was Hob Fucking Ravani, and she'd never given up, never stopped. She wasn't about to start now. She sucked in another lungful of smoke and bellowed, "Coyote! Dambala! Get 'em lined up!"

DAWN

CHAPTER FIFTY-FIVE

"Mag?" Omar's voice came low, but urgent.

She raised her head from the stack of documents she'd been going through in Bill Weld's office. It was something to do, something that had gotten her away from the never-ending barrage of questions that had battered her since that one, perfect moment when the world sang. *What happened? What do we do now?*

The latter question, she'd had an answer to, at least. Go to the other towns. Find the survivors. Make sure everyone had water and food. And always, always – organize. The Bone Collector, whatever he was calling himself now, sweeping the green and blue clean off the surface of the planet wasn't a forever solution. There was a world out there that had a lot of interest in them, and there were people on this world that needed to be fed and cared for.

She should say something, she thought. With Clarence gone, people were still looking to her for answers. Even the damn Bone Collector had. "What is it?"

"Osprey been sighted."

A shock of fear hit her, but no, it was impossible. All of the TransRift and Mariposa men were gone. The Bone Collector had promised that. Mag made herself take a deep breath, then another. "It heading this way?"

"Yeah," Omar said. "Dunno why."

Mag stood, smoothing her skirt. "Guess we'll find out."

She followed Omar to broken pieces of Ludlow's wall. Every miner who had survived, made whole by the Bone Collector, arrayed around them, brandishing stolen rifles and their own weapons. Their silence broken only by Brother Rami's murmured prayer to the god in the sky and the new god in the Well, they watched the lights approach in the darkening sky, resolving into a massive cargo osprey... which slowed neatly and lowered itself to the ground.

No one breathed as the ramp slowly came down, not quite in unison.

And then Hob walked down the ramp of the osprey, her black coat whipping in the wind, the spark of a cigarette visible against her mouth even at this distance. Relief took Mag and dropped her to her knees. Of course Hob was alive. She was too damn mean to die.

And behind her, a wave of miners followed.

The crowd broke out in cheers, and then people began to run across the sand, some toward loved ones they spotted, some to search. Mag struggled back up to her feet, her eyes first fixed on Hob and then... behind her. Anabi was dressed in a strange hotchpotch of clothes, her hair in tangled knots, but she was there. Mag ran faster than she ever had in her life.

"Mag–" she heard Hob say, and didn't pause. She threw herself into Anabi's arms, and they took turns trying to squeeze the breath out of each other. Anabi threw her head back to laugh in silent breaths, tears streaming down her cheeks. Mag pressed her hands on the woman's cheeks to bring that mouth down to hers, to kiss the salt of it away. Anabi's hands tangled in her hair, and for that one, blessed moment, the death and tiredness fell away and all was right in the world.

It was the need to breathe that finally got her to step back, just enough to keep her hands around Anabi's waist. But she looked around to find Hob, carefully studying the star-scattered sky like she'd just walked in on someone naked. Mag caught a flash, then, of the pale ghost of a shape behind her, but it was gone when she blinked. Somehow, she doubted that Hob even felt it.

"You said I ain't ever given up," Hob remarked, after a sidelong glance to make sure Mag was put back together.

"Guess you better start believin' what I say."

Mag looked around the massive office, an entire floor of the stupidly tall TransRift tower, with mingled wonder and anger. *How the hell did any one person need this much space, this much luxury?* she asked herself for the fifth time. *How the hell does any one person think they're that much* better?

By the palatial windows, Hob was a dark, stick-thin figure. She kept pushing the buttons on the wall, watching the curtains open and close, open and close. Mag half wanted to scream at her, but she knew it wasn't fair. She wanted to yell at Hob because it was the only way she could get around the anxiety already clutching at her gut. And Hob was playing with the curtains for the same damn reason.

The only reason they were in the sand-filled ghost town that was Newcastle at all was because they'd seen the flimsies dug out of the wrecked manager tents at the wildcat site, and Coyote had helped review them all. He'd pulled out the news about the inspector arriving, and pointed out that the only place to really talk to them was in Newcastle, at the tower. And it was the Bone Collector, a ghost of him in Mag's mirror that she still hadn't brought herself to tell Hob about, that told her just what *he'd* done about it.

The TransRift tower had been full of little drifts of orange-pink sand, sitting in chairs, in the middle of elevators, smeared across hallways. Mag found it eerie, but also couldn't find it in herself to feel bad. They'd lost so many people in Ludlow, in the other towns, before the Bone Collector had stopped everything. Hob had lost well over half of her Wolves – it was easier to name off the living than the dead: Geri with his hair gone white, Coyote, Dambala, Hati, Lykaios, Maheegan, Diablo. Mag thought about the dead ones she'd known the best – Lobo and his supply runs, Freki and the ribbon candy they'd shared as children, Raff and his goofy smile – and felt numb. There were too many dead in such a short time for her to feel anything else. She had to focus on the one personal good Hob had brought her, Anabi whole and alive, or she'd get sucked under with despair – and even then, it felt wrong, to think of good when there was so much mourning to do.

But good was the reason to keep going through all the bad, the hope of it sometimes the only way to keep the heart beating.

"Think I got it workin' right now," Hati said, from under the stupidly massive desk that was the centerpiece of the whole stupidly massive room. "Y'all ready?"

"I am. Hob?"

"Don't fuckin' know why you wanted me here anyhow," Hob muttered, but she stopped messing with the curtains.

"Because you look damn scary," Mag said. There were a lot of other reasons, ones that she was going to try to lead Hob around later. There were too many open questions right now, about how they'd organize themselves, how they'd make sure everyone was safe and had enough to eat. So many things to vote on. But if anyone was going to be able to run the bandit hunting and do it right, train a militia and do it right, it'd be Hob. She was a legend now, along with the surviving Wolves. She might still play the mercenary card, but no one was fooled by that any more.

Hob just needed to realize that about Hob, too.

Mag set those thoughts aside for now and took her spot at the desk. She smoothed down the front of her best dress, which at this point was the one with no blood stains showing on the faded red calico. Hob loomed over her, scowling, hands clutched at the back of the stupid chair. Mag sighed. "Smoke your cigarette if it'll get you to stop fidgeting."

Hob's sigh of relief was almost comical. Once she was more settled with smoke wreathing her head, Mag nodded to Hati. "Go ahead."

He did some more fiddling, then crawled out from under the desk, a manual in one hand. He read a bit more, finger tracing over the lines, and then typed some commands on the recessed keyboard. "Ought to work... but we ain't got that Weatherman here..."

"It'll work," Hob said, flatly. Mag wondered if she could feel it too, the presence of the Bone Collector in the room like an amused ghost, watching them. Probably not. That had never been Hob's kind of witchiness.

A screen rose up from the desk; it had been impossible to see before it lifted up, all smooth and perfect. A logo came on that Mag recognized as TransRift's, with *Ship Frequency Broadcast* under it. Mag took a deep breath and began: "I am calling to Rift Ship *Jentayu*, to speak with Captain Santos and Federal Union Inspector Liu Fei Xing. Please respond."

Hati, hovering just out of what he claimed was range of the video, snuck in a hand to tap a button. "OK. Now they can't see or hear you."

"And?"

He shrugged. "And we wait to see if–" A tone sounded from the screen, and the words changed to, *Incoming Call, Rift Ship* Jentayu *TR-0910, Channel Secure. Receive?* "Um. They responded."

Mag took another deep breath and straightened her spine. "I'm ready."

Hati pecked at another button, and the static TransRift logo changed to show the faces of two women. One of them, her skin brown and dark brown hair cut extremely short, wore a blue uniform that Mag didn't recognize, but figured had to be for the ship pilots. The other wore clothes just as strange to Mag, a type of suit she'd never seen before with no lapels and no tie. She had her long, straight black hair pulled back from her round face, and her expression was severe. She said, "I am Federal Union Inspector Liu. I demand to know by what means and by what right you have conspired to hold my ship hostage in your orbit, and with whom I am speaking." Her frown deepened as she seemed to examine Mag and her plain work dress from the screen. "I will only speak to the governing authority of this planet."

Mag reminded herself that this woman must be frightened; ships weren't supposed to just hang in one place, but that was what the Bone Collector had done with the *Jentayu*. But she still felt annoyed. "My name is Magdala Kushtrim," she said. It felt good to say her name proudly for the first time in months, for herself and for her parents. "I am the duly elected representative of the Tanegawa's World Laborers' Union. Behind me is General Hob Ravani."

And bless Hob, for not choking at her sudden promotion. She just crossed her arms and glared. Hob was always good at that.

"Where is Vice President Meetchim?" the inspector demanded.

"Dead," Mag said flatly. "This planet no longer belongs to TransRift. It belongs to the miners and the farmers and all those between. And if you want to talk to someone, you're gonna have to talk to me."

"If you want to negotiate, you *will* let us land," the inspector said. Still trying to cow her, Mag thought. Maybe being an inspector didn't call for the same level of sly that being a spy did. Shige had been better at this.

"You are in our space. If you come with an offer of peace, we'll hear you and put it to a vote." She held up a handful of orange-pink dust she'd scraped off one of the chairs in the building's echoing, empty lobby. "This here used to be Vice President Meetchim. We done this to her the same way we're holdin' your ship. So you think about that." She let the sand pour through her fingers. She felt the Bone Collector's attention on her like a weight, his amusement and his approval. They'd had a long talk, the two of them, in that timeless moment when the whole universe had changed.

She could do this, Mag thought, as she took in the expressions of the ship captain and the inspector with outward calm. She would do this. She was doing this. They had organized and fought and bled and died – and now it was their turn to set the terms. "Only a fool would come here lookin' for war."

EPILOGUE

He could barely remember his name, he'd had so many. And none of those mattered now. All that mattered was the purpose that drove him. That was what put one foot in front of another as he wandered from salt flat to shifting sand – had he really gone so far? The thirst didn't matter, the pain didn't matter, only duty. Finish the job.

His hand was glued to his side with dried blood, and his tongue had gone to leather with thirst. The eagles weren't even bothering to shadow him any more, like the desert had baked every last bit of water from his body long ago.

He remembered dimly, being in a cool theater. He wondered if, when his death was reported, his mother would walk silently away. Her greatest effort, the sum of her strength and dedication, and he'd still failed. It was unfair. He'd never asked to be made, to have the hopes of a political dynasty placed on him, to have the survival of the limping democracy they called the Federal Union placed on his shoulders.

He couldn't remember his name clearly, but he could remember Kazu. Hating him. Worshiping him like only a younger brother could. Wishing that he could follow.

Never having the will to see that course of action as possible, even as he snuck glances into his file. He'd looked down his nose at Kazu, just like he was supposed to, but in his secret heart he'd been jealous. Kazu was an idiot, a layabout, a troublemaker, shiftless. He didn't have a right to look as happy as he always had in surveillance files. Madness. How did he have anything to live for, when he'd abandoned everything built for him?

And how, the wind seemed to ask, shifting to blow dust into his eyes, *do you have anything to live for when everything you've built has abandoned you?*

It wasn't fair. It wasn't true. It was fair and true. He tumbled down the slip face of a dune and lay face down in the shadow of it.

No. He wouldn't stop because there was still something he could do. Some action he could take. To what end, he no longer knew, his strategies gone hazy and incoherent. Who would he actually serve? Did the people he had met here, whom he'd killed with his manipulation and conscious inaction, deserve to have what was coming to them? What was *deserve* anyway? What had any of this meant?

It would mean, he thought as the sunlight knifed into his scalp and his unprotected neck, what he made it mean. What Magdala Kushtrim and her unwashed miners – they all no doubt smelled better than him now – and that madwoman Hob Ravani made it mean.

And he reached out to pull himself along. His legs no longer had the strength to support him. But he kept going, because there was still work to do.

He fell down another slip face and lay gasping at the bottom, trying to gather his strength. And he heard – did he hear, or was it a hallucination? He ought to have been dead days ago – footsteps approaching. He found the strength to turn his head and see booted feet that left no mark in the sand.

The feet stopped next to him, then shifted as the man they bore crouched down. And a familiar, impossible voice asked, "Thirsty, brother?"

ACKNOWLEDGMENTS

I've written quite a few first books, most of which will never see the light of day. But the book you've just finished is the first *second* book I've ever written. *Hunger Makes the Wolf* took me 12 years and nine drafts to finish; *Blood Binds the Pack* took one month to outline, three months to write, and four drafts. It was a strange, intimidating, and sometimes exhilarating experience. And it wouldn't have been possible without the help of a lot of fantastic people:

DongWon Song, my agent, who gently but implacably cornered me into just writing the damn thing already and did several rounds of proto-editing on my ridiculous, 11,000 word outline.

Corina Stark, my first reader.

Phil Jourdan, who did not destroy my soul this time, but instead made me believe I could actually do the thing.

The rest of the Angry Robot crew: Mike Underwood, Penny Reeve, Nick Tyler, and Marc Gascoigne.

The historians whose research on the labor wars of the first Gilded Age provided inspiration and depth for the world I've built – in which history is repeating itself just like it is today. Their work is acknowledged individually in the bibliography that follows.

The fire for this comes from my brothers and sisters and other siblings still fighting every day for fair pay and the basic dignity owed to them as workers in this new Gilded Age.

Solidarity forever.

BIBLIOGRAPHY

ANDREWS, THOMAS G. *Killing for Coal: America's Deadliest Labor War*. Harvard University Press, 2010.

CLYNE, RICK J. *Coal People: Life in Southern Colorado's Company Towns, 1890-1930*. Colorado Historical Society, 2000.

GREEN, JAMES. *Death in the Haymarket: A Story of Chicago, the First Labor Movements and the Bombing that Divided Gilded Age America*. Anchor, 2007.

JONES, MARY HARRIS. *The Autobiography of Mother Jones*. Dover Publications, 2012.

MARTELLE, SCOTT. *Blood Passion: The Ludlow Massacre and Class War in the American West*. Rutgers University Press, 2008.

PAPANIKOLAS, ZEESE. *Buried Unsung: Louis Tikas and the Ludlow Massacre*. University of Nebraska Press, 1991.